Billion

Book 4

By: Blair Babylon

Xan Valentine, the lead singer for the rock band Killer Valentine, is the guy that *Rolling Stone* calls "sex incarnate." They aren't wrong, but they don't know the half of it. He's the alpha-est male who ever walked onto a stage or into a bedroom and might be crazy, and Georgie is definitely in love with him. Plus, he hired her ex-boyfriend, her first "real" boyfriend, to play in the band, and now she's stuck between them.

So she tried to leave. That's what any sane girl would do.

And just as she feared, the Russian mafia kidnapped her.

She prays that Xan won't try to rescue her because they said they'll kill him. *But she knows he will, even if it costs him everything.*

Make sure you sign up for
Blair's private newsletter!
www.blairbabylon.com/emailbx

PRAISE FOR BLAIR BABYLON

"The book oozed heart and passion from every page, it was as if it was traveling through my fingers to touch my very soul - I'm gobsmacked at how I feel about it! It showed more than I thought I was going to get it gave me *love and passion in absolute bin loads and moreover it was full of desire, hope, longing, honesty and devotion* - not just from the characters but from the author also because her devotion to her craft was clearly evident in this book - she nailed it!!" -- *Books Laid Bare Blog, (Every Breath You Take, Rock Stars in Disguise: Xan)*

"*Every Breath You Take* was an absolutely stunning and creatively passionate exploration of two lost and lonely people finding the missing part of their heart and soul in each other. What a breathtaking journey filled with unwanted hope, unwavering love, and unexpected devotion! This series is continuing with such a brilliant depth of heart and soul that I just can't get enough of. I am definitely looking forward to more of these ground-breaking stories." --*Shadowplay Book Blog, (Every Breath You Take, Rock Stars in Disguise: Xan)*

"The writing is great, as usual, and the characters are so well developed. **Author Blair Babylon has extreme talent here."** -- *Sammy's Book Obsession Blog, (Every Breath You Take, Rock Stars in Disguise: Xan)*

"This book brings together two of the author's series, Billionaires in Disguise and Rock Stars in Disguise. Prior to this book, the two were entirely separate. If you haven't yet read any of the books in these series, then what are you waiting for? **You do not need to read them to understand this book, but reading them will give you a broader understanding of the incredible canvas Blair is using as her background. She has basically created these worlds and characters from scratch, and what a world it is."** ~*Fictional Men's Page for Book Ho's*

"**This was one incredible story.** I can't wait to continue with this series." ~*Books and Beyond Fifty Shades*

"Let me first say WOW… I am seriously addicted to Blair Babylon's books her imagination whether it be Crime, Rockstar or Billionaire. **She creates a world where you are immersed with colourful and diverse characters and situations that you don't want to escape from."** ~*Kat's Book Promotions*

"What a pair! This story had me clutching my chest. **I loved Tryp. His damaged and broken soul tugs at your heart strings.** His need to spiral down into the darkness to escape his past will have you wanting to comfort him and just whisper sweet nothings in his ear. The unlikely friendship was definitely the perfect route for this story. It takes a special kind of person to handle all of Tryp's darkness. Elfie definitely proved herself worthy and I loved her determination and strength even though she has a past of her own that she is desperately trying to run from. **Blair Babylon delivers a truly emotional story that had me on one helluva emotional rollercoaster.** I am definitely looking forward to reading more from this series." *~Jennifer's Book Obsession, (Somebody to Love, Rock Stars in Disguise: Tryp)*

"Just believe me when I say you DON'T want to miss this one." *~Jo's Book Addictions (Somebody to Love, Rock Stars in Disguise: Tryp)*

"This was my first Blair Babylon book and I was on a rollercoaster. **Tryp and Elfie need to read by all, a raw story of friendship and love.** Truly only the strong survive. I want more of these two."*~Romance Bytes (Every Breath You Take, Rock Stars in Disguise: Xan)*

"The chemistry Wulf and Raegan have is amazing and the fact that they are both so stubborn makes their relationship funny at times. The series covers everything from finding out about the good, bad, and ugly of each other to meeting the family. There are raw emotions in these books." *~~Random Musesomy Book Blog*

"Blair Babylon knows what she is doing. **This is some of the best romance I have read, hands down.** It's got a little bit of everything, for everyone....the story was so well written, infused with sex, humor and drama, that **I would gladly read it over and over again."** *~Contagious Reads Blog*

"If I could give 10 stars I would! I adore this book, I have read it two times completely and many times parts of it." *~Katrina's Books Blog*

"AWESOME! When I first started reading this book I thought it was going to be your regular romance book and I thought, what kind of spin could possibly be put on this kind of relationship. Don't get me wrong, I am the first person to admit that I love a good relationship. I think it's hot but I was still waiting for a new refreshing spin on romance novels, and this was it for me. So of course you still had the typical kind of damsel in distress and then that sexy as hell man coming to save her. **Well the twist is something that you wouldn't expect....** Wulf also has a secret, and when I mean secret, it's a big secret. No, it's nothing that you might be thinking, like he is married or he is gay. **I mean huge, I was in complete shock when I found out.** That is one of the things that I loved most about this novel, **everything that I thought was completely wrong and it kept me intrigued the entire time.**" ~*Fictional Book Ho's Blog*

"The writing was great and **I loved the way the author "peeled away" the layers** of them and let us really get to know them gradually. I loved the mystery in the characters backgrounds and personalities. **I loved the suspense and action thrown in the story also!"** ~*Sammy's Book Obsession*

PRAISE FOR *ONCE UPON A TIME* FLICKA #1

5.0 out of 5 stars ~ ***I Blame Blair*** ~ Blair Babylon, you Evil Genius! I want to hate you. But I love your work *sob*. Why cain't I just quit you??? . . . **Great galloping court jesters, am I glad I picked this one up!"** ~ *Once Upon A Time,* Amazon Reviewer

5.0 out of 5 stars ~ "I LOVE this Author's work. I have no idea how she keeps her complex, intricate & intertwined worlds straight throughout each series of books . Thankfully she does and we all reap the staggering benefits in books like this!! **A 10 star read "** ~ *Once Upon A Time,* Amazon Reviewer

5.0 out of 5 stars ~ "I am a Blair Babylon junkie. **I can't get enough of each series and must read them again (and again).** Princess Flicka, our heroine, is strong and capable. Dieter remarks that she would make a fine general mustering the troops and setting detailed plans in place to win a war. She takes command of the preparations for Wulf's wedding down to the smallest detail. Nothing escapes her notice. Her organizational skills are what she does best. The interaction with Dieter leaves me wanting more of them together. **The pace of the Flicka series keeps getting faster and faster as we get to the end of this first book.** My dilemma: to go right on to the next book in the series or reread this first one, pulling out additional clues and enjoying the action." ~ *Once Upon A Time,* Amazon Reviewer

5.0 out of 5 stars ~ **"I can't even begin to tell how much I loved this book.** It was in constant motion, and I learned so much about the aristocracy of this world. I was drawn to Flicka and her cynical, sarcastic attitude. Something about her words and actions told me how broken she still was inside, especially knowing how she'd grown up and what she'd been through as a child. Though this world it entirely out of my league, the characters are human and easy to relate to. **The good guys are not all good. And the bad guys are worse than I expected.** The story pulled at my heartstrings, and I wanted to climb into the book and kick some royal butt myself. We see sides of some of the characters we already know in a new light, through the eyes of two people who know them well. I don't know which direction the author is going to take us next, but the outcome is up for grabs. It was **intense and heartbreaking, sweet and sexy."** ~ *Amazon Reviewer*

REVIEWS OF *ROGUE*, MAXENCE BOOK #1

"Maxence is everything I love in a romance novel - a whipsmart man with an anguishing call to serve that conflicts with his love for Dree. I was spellbound!" - **New York Times bestselling author Julia Kent**

"What a wild and sexy race through Paris! Rogue masterfully combines nail biting suspense with high steam for the ride of your life with Maxence and Dree." ~ **USA Today bestselling author JJ Knight**

"Another masterpiece from Blair Babylon, who I am convinced keeps getting better and better. Max is not at all as I'd imagined him, and really it's no wonder, since he has been forced to repress who he is. The real Max keeps popping up his head, doing real-Max things that the other Max wishes he wouldn't do. He struggles with his inner demons to be a Godly man, but he hasn't quite figured out how to balance the different parts of himself, and as a result, tortures himself. He is a man searching for himself, impeded by too many bad guys who wish him harm. It's hard to focus on self-actualization while trying to simply survive without getting yourself killed." -- E.C., Goodreads Reviewer

"Blair's stories have always been hot but

this one might be the hottest yet." -- Xtreme Delusions Book Blog

"I just couldn't stop reading! This book is addictive!" -- Kat, Goodreads Reviewer

"Rogue is a phenomenal romantic suspense that is sure to delight and entertain as it holds your heart and mind captive. Nothing can prepare you for the roller coaster ride that is Maxence. He will take you unawares and leave you completely breathless and wanting. If nothing else, you will learn why he is so addicting to the women that he meets." -- Words Are The Breath of Life Book Blog

"Good gosh! Author Blair Babylon is a master at building suspense. I have been eagerly awaiting Maxence's story for YEARS. Finally it arrives and I am practically salivating as I tear into the book, excited that I will finally learn the truth about the elusive Maxence. As I am reading, I am finding that Maxence's unveiling is happening at the rate of an excruciatingly slow strips tease. The end of "Rogue" finds me with almost as many questions regarding who Maxence is as the beginning of the book-- but I promise that slooowly he is starting to be unveiled. **One thing that is made abundantly clear is that Maxence lives two polar opposite lives and this results in my finding myself even MORE intrigued by him. Now THIS is what I consider phenomenal writing!"** -- Lil Miss Reads A Lot Book Blog

ONE NIGHT IN MONACO

"Holy Maxence! Max hotness! Max suspense! Max everything! Follow your favorite book boyfriends Casimir and Arthur as they try to figure out WHAT the hell happened to Maxence in Monaco, with all the opulence and lavish lifestyle you'd expect from Blair."

~~ **USA Today bestselling romance author JJKnight**

"Blair!! LOVED it! **A fun, sexy, fast-paced read** that had me on the edge of my seat wanting to know what happened that night!"

~~ Pippa Grant, USA Today Bestselling Author

"What I love about Blair Babylon books is the worlds she creates, and One Night in Monaco is no exception. **Luxury, power, wealth - all of it beyond your dreams - is a backdrop for our very human, very vulnerable, and often extremely alpha characters who show us how uniquely human we all are** -- but Maxence? He's one of a kind. And hot. Whooooo boy."

-- New York Times bestselling author Julia Kent

"Addictively entertaining and full of escapist goodness,this stylish page-turner left me breathless and begging for more!"

~~New York Times bestselling author Annika Martin

PRAISE FOR CONNING THE BILLIONAIRE, MICAH #1

"Micah and Kylie are fire from the beginning!! The attraction is mutual, and the things they get up to had me fanning myself!!! So many pieces to the big con that Micah and Kylie are playing, of course ends up with mob bosses and mafia families, (its Atlantic City after all!!) Add lots of subterfuge and plans that don't go exactly as planned, and this story becomes a very funny, action packed, train wreck of amazing - ness !!! Can you read it as a stand alone?? Probably. But then you wouldn't know all the players, or all of the little," Easter eggs", that are dropped here and there from previous books. And those are AMAZING!!!!" ~ Amazon Reviewer

"WOW! This is a "seat of your pants" wild ride. Throughout this story, I put the book aside several times, shaking my head, wondering "what the …" Con is the name of the game and both Kylie and Micah have mastery, but Micah excels at the game." ~ Amazon Reviewer

ALSO BY BLAIR BABYLON

Secret Billionaires Series

Working Stiff ~~~ *Working Stiff Audiobook*

Hard Work ~~~ *Hard Work Audiobook*

Stiff Drink ~~~ *Stiff Drink Audiobook*

Hot Toddy ~~~ *Hot Toddy Audiobook*

Hard Liquor ~~~ *Hard Liquor Audiobook*

Strong Spirits ~~~ *Strong Spirits Audiobook*

Billionaires in Disguise Series (Wulf and Rae)

A Billionaire in Disguise ~~~ *BID Audiobook*

A Tycoon Undercover ~~~ *ATU Audiobook*

A Prince Incognito ~~~ *API Audiobook*

Billionaire Ever After ~~~ *BEA Audiobook*

"An Extravagant Proposal (Charley)"

Billionaires in Disguise: Theo Series

Falling Hard

Playing Rough

Breaking Rules

Burning Bright

Rock Stars in Disguise Series

What A Girl Wants (Rhiannon)

Somebody to Love (Tryp)

The Rock Star's Secret Baby (Cadell)

Santa, Baby (Peyton)

All I Want for Christmas (Epilogue)

Billionaires in Disguise: Xan Series

"Alwaysland" (Prequel)

Every Breath You Take

Wild Thing

Lay Your Hands On Me

Nothing Else Matters

"Dream On" and "Keep Dreaming" (Epilogues)

"Small Miracles" (Epilogue)

Runaway Princess Series

Once Upon A Time ~~~ OUAT Audiobook

In Shining Armor ~~~ ISA Audiobook

In A Faraway Land ~~~ IAFL Audiobook

At Midnight ~~~ AM Audiobook

Happily Ever After ~~~ HEA Audiobook

Billionaires in Disguise: Maxence Series

One Night in Monaco ~~~ ONIM Audiobook

Rogue ~~~ Rogue Audiobook

Order ~~~ Order Audiobook

Prince ~~~ Prince Audiobook

Royal ~~~ Royal Audiobook

Reign ~~~ Reign Audiobook

Twisted Billionaires

Twisted Billionaire (Book #1)

Tangled Billionaire (Book #2)

Conning the Billionaire (Book #3)

Tempting the Billionaire (Book #4)

Blaze (Twisted Billionaires #5)

Last Chance, Inc. Billionaires

Under Parr (Book #1)

Match Play (Book #2)

Skins Game (Book #3)

Sand Trap (Book #4)

Shark (Book #5)

Dragon's Den Paranormal Romance

Dragons & Magic

Dragons & Mayhem

Dragons & Fire

Third Print Edition: February, 2023

4 GEORGIE
BILLIONAIRES IN DISGUISE

USA TODAY BESTSELLING AUTHOR
BLAIR BABYLON

CONTENTS

Chapter One

VODKA WITH TATIANA BUTORIN

Georgie

The plane's engines reversed and howled, the noise whirling in the cabin and filling Georgie's ears. She lolled forward as the plane braked, the wheels squealing on the runway.

Her stomach roiled, the vodka swirling around in her guts and scalding her throat. She held onto the arms of the seat and swallowed hard as sour sweat popped out of her pores.

The red carpet in the aisle between the seats swam like a snake.

The shell of the plane cut through the air as Georgie swayed in her seat. Trying to claw her way out through the titanium wouldn't work. She might as well be buried in a cave a hundred feet underground.

Across the small table from her, Tatiana Butorin smiled a prim, matronly smile for someone in her early thirties. She fluffed her brown curls and looked out the porthole window at the lines of streetlights rising out of the dark outside. Her beige suit was cut tight to her slim body.

Georgie flopped against the back of the seat, pretending to pass out again. Drool seeped out the corner of her mouth. Tendrils of her brown hair had escaped from her long braid and clung to her cheek and neck. One tickled her eyelid.

She had to look dead drunk. Her own life and the life of some unknown passport inspector depended on it.

Tatiana Butorin and the men from the Russian mafia, a *bratva,* had kidnapped Georgie mere feet away from Xan, who had been standing at the stage door of the arena in Milan.

Georgie hadn't fought them too hard. If she had broken away, it might have delayed their getaway and given Xan enough time to track her down. Tatiana had assured Georgie that she would kill him if he interfered, and Georgie believed every word that Tatiana said.

Xan hadn't been able to reach her before the Russians had wheeled the car into traffic, and Georgie thanked the Father, the Son, the Holy Ghost, Mother Mary, and all the saints that she had had that one last glimpse of Alexandre as he stood on the sidewalk, safe, while the car pulled away.

Alexandre was safe. He would be okay. He hadn't been hurt or killed.

They had driven her to the airport and wrestled her aboard a private plane for the States. Tatiana's Gulfstream jet had flown west from Italy, chasing the sun across the Atlantic Ocean through a long sunset that had lasted for hours and hours. The interior of the jet was upholstered in ecru leather and trimmed in garish gold, and the sun had glared off the brassy finishes with every dip of the wings.

Georgie had stared at Peyton's ring on her right hand, focusing on the diamond, watching the sparkles glitter on the sides of the jet to distract herself from crying.

With the sun finally sinking below the horizon and the jet swan-diving toward the East Coast of the US, one of Tatiana's thugs had forced Georgie to drink shot after shot of vodka, literally holding a handgun pressed to her temple while she threw back the burning liquor. Tatiana had eyed Georgie's slim, runner's body, obviously estimating how much she could handle, and then they'd doubled that.

The jet's wheels screeched against the runway, and the plane slowed like a giant rubber band was drawing it back.

Tatiana may have estimated Georgie's body weight, but she evidently didn't know jack about Southwestern State, the university that Georgie had attended for two and half years. *Playboy Magazine,* Kaplan, *USA Today,* and Dewer's Scotch Whisky had all ranked SSU as the number one party school in the nation for five years running. SSU tailgated longer than the University of Iowa, partied harder than everyone in Syracuse and Cham-bana, and had a more rambunctious night club scene than downtown Philly around the University of Pennsylvania.

Plus, Georgie's job had often entailed watching sports and drinking shots with men who had more money than friends.

And then, for the last three months, Georgie had

been partying with actual rock stars, never photographed without a drink in her mouth.

Her liver must look like a bodybuilder's abs and could probably detoxify rat poison.

But Tatiana didn't know that.

The Gulfstream ground to a slow taxi speed and turned off the runway, heading for the private terminal and a customs official who would check their passports before they deplaned, a person who didn't know that his or her life depended on Georgie not trying to get away from Tatiana and her Russian mafia men.

Georgie let her eyes roll in her head and twitched to make it look like she was indeed wasted.

The inside of the plane wavered as she gazed from under her eyelashes, and her head spun as she let it flop to the side as the plane stopped. The engines wound down like a siren fading away. She was buzzed, sure, and driving would probably be stupid. However, she only had to drive a car as far as the nearest road and crash it into a wall to make the police come.

The Russian flight attendants opened the hatch, and fetid summer air swarmed into the air-conditioned tube of the plane.

Georgie sniffed the humid heat, recognizing the sour stink of New Jersey's swamps and factories. They must be at Liberty Airport again.

A stairway drove itself across the runway toward the plane, throwing cones of headlights through the night.

It was kind of funny how the rich people walked down a stairway and across the steaming tarmac to private planes like it was 1974, while the poor souls who rode steerage strolled down a cooled, carpeted jetway to their plane.

Georgie was beginning to channel her inner spoiled brat. Must be the proximity of Connecticut and the impending visit to her mother.

Footsteps tapped up the stairs, and a bright voice said, "Hello! Welcome to the United States! Passports, please."

Georgie squinted, looking at the person whose life was going to end if she tried to escape. The woman accepted a stack of passports from one of Tatiana Butorin's thugs.

The customs official was portly, and her navy blue uniform fit very snugly across the tummy.

No, the woman was pregnant.

Jesus, Mary and Joseph.

Georgie closed her eyes and waited for the woman to get off the plane.

The woman said, "Welcome to the US, Ms. Butorin, Mr. Utkin, and Mr. Popov. Welcome home, Ms. Bordeaux."

That was Georgie's new name on her passport, Liliana Bordeaux, the name under which she had been supposed to hide in Atlanta and go to college at Emory University, somewhere safe from the Butorins.

A tear warmed her eye.

She probably wouldn't have liked Emory, anyway, not after the riotous college life of Southwestern State. Even Hotlanta couldn't compensate for the staid reputation of the school.

Tatiana Butorin said, "Liliana has gotten drunk on plane. Just stamp passport."

"Okay," the agent said. "And the rest of these are for you guys back there?" Some riffling as she matched photos to the several men standing farther back in the small jet. The blond guy with the cold, blue eyes was back there, somewhere. He had glared at Georgie the whole flight.

The agent said, "Just the usual questions, then. Anything to declare, any fruits or vegetables, any cash in excess of the limit? You know the drill."

Tatiana answered for them all. "Yes, we know drill. No, we have nothing to declare."

Right now, Georgie should get up and run, shove past the agent, and stumble down the stairs.

All Tatiana's men had their guns tucked in the backs of their pants.

Tatiana had assured Georgie that if she tried anything stupid, they would shoot the customs agent first, this bright-voiced, pregnant woman, then aim for Georgie.

The goon standing beside Georgie's seat reached behind his back like he was scratching his back, but he moved his suit jacket aside and bared his gun, nearly touching it.

Georgie lay in the plane seat, her head dangling to the side, pretending to be dead drunk.

Damn it.

Chapter Two

PHIND-A-PHONE

Alex de Valentinois

The small, private jet bumped down on the runway, landing. Each tire screech was a bright flash of turquoise sparks behind Alex's eyes, and the rising roar of the reversing engines pounded his ears and turned his head to the left.

Alex's fingers curled around the arms of the seat, almost cramping as he watched the light-studded night speeding behind them. Outside the long porthole, pinlights lining the runway blurred, peeping like a piping flute in his mind.

The door called to him, and he kept trying to stand up, to leap up and keep running to find Georgie. Alex held onto the arms of the chair as air bucked under the plane's wings.

Paul had commandeered Jonas's laptop with its

tracking software, a necessity when dealing with wasted or drugged-out rock stars, but they had left Jonas at the theater to deal with the chaos of cancelling a concert halfway through the show. They tracked Georgie's phone to Linate Airport, a small airport just a few kilometers from the city center, where the Butorins must have had a plane waiting.

As soon as they had realized where the Butorins were headed and that there was no conceivable way to intercept them, Adrien had spun the car across the highway lanes to drive out of the city. Alex's plane, a Gulfstream G650 that had been following them around Europe, had been flown to the Malpensa Airport, fifty kilometers outside of Milan.

Yes, Alex de Valentinois was an obscenely rich Monégasque nobleman and had a plane tag along behind him while he was moonlighting at being a rock star. That plane was currently speeding about an hour behind the Russians who had kidnapped Georgie.

Seemed like a damned good idea now, didn't it?

The plane taxied on the runway, heading toward the private terminal that glowed from within like a glass cube brimming with sulfurous yellow light.

Alex's phone screen said that it was nine-thirty at night in New Jersey, though it felt more like it was two-thirty in the dark, early morning, like it was in Milan. He had slept little during the flight, no matter how exhausted he was and how hard he had tried to turn off his mind and soul that roiled with color and despair. He had finally changed into jeans and a black tee shirt that he had stashed on the plane because his clothes stank of sweat from the show he had left.

Alex stood in the aisle, crouching a little so he

wouldn't hit his head on the low ceiling. He asked Paul, "Where is she?"

"Yep, looks like she's being driven to Connecticut," he said. The blue light from Jonas's computer glinted on Paul's brown eyebrows and hair. "I can't believe they're doing this. This is a stunt or something. There's no way that her mother has that kind of cash lying around the house. This is a—" He looked up at Alex, stopping short with whatever he had been thinking, "—a statement of some kind."

Alex had been raised around the children of mobsters and courtiers who had parroted what their parents said. He could think of several endings for that sentence—a public execution, a warning to other parents, a way to save face—and all of them wound him up further.

Adrien slept in the seat beside Paul, stretched far backward and snoring.

Alex told Paul, "Nudge him. We'll need everyone functional as soon as customs clears us, especially him."

Paul shook Adrien's biceps. "Hey, Adrien. Almost time to fly."

Adrien rubbed his face with his hand and looked out the porthole. Spotlights poured light over a black helicopter landing on a helipad beside the terminal building. "Seriously, Paul? A Twin Squirrel?"

Paul shrugged. "I took what they had."

Adrien shook his head. "I miss Interpol sometimes."

Alex left them to squabble over whether a Eurocopter Twin Squirrel was an appropriate choice for a rescue mission, but at least they had a helicopter.

Considering that Paul had had twenty minutes on the phone to make all the arrangements before they had sprinted up the stairs at the Malpensa airport, Alex thought that he had done pretty damn well.

He walked up to the front where he had been sitting, going over the songs on his tablet in a desperate attempt to distract himself and to somehow reach out to Georgie by some insane magic through the music. Light flashed as he read the notes, turning to color and scent in his head. He had felt nothing, of course, but he wished that he had been able to communicate that they were coming for her, that she should hold on, and that she shouldn't be frightened. Imagining her crying with fear had made his hands shake, and he couldn't let the anger out, not yet.

Peyton Cabot was asleep in a chair on the aisle, his long legs splayed under the table between the chairs.

A small, jealous part of Alex was quite tempted to sneak out of the plane without waking Peyton up, but they might need an extra person to rescue Georgie. The odds of rescuing Georgie from the Russians were minuscule. Every set of hands might be the difference between success and all of them dying.

Even the hands of her ex-boyfriend who made sad deer-eyes at her every chance he got.

If Peyton hadn't been a fucking brilliant musician, Alex would have thrown him out of the band weeks ago, even over Georgie's argument that he was by far the best keyboardist who had auditioned.

And he was, damn it.

Alex bent his knees and crouched beside Peyton. His British accent roughened to a working-class, East End clip. "'*Ey,* Peyton. We're in New Jersey."

Peyton shook his head, his blond hair falling on his forehead, and blinked his weird green-blue eyes. "Are we there?"

"Yeah," Xan Valentine said. "Time to go."

Chapter Three

THE GATES OF HELL

Georgie

Georgie swung her head from side to side, still drunk, as the car wove through the night-darkened Connecticut countryside. She sat in the back seat on the passenger side. Tatiana Butorin's brown curls bobbed around the headrest in front of her.

Georgie leaned against the locked car door. Vodka-and-acid burps burned her throat. Hard plastic pinched her wrists together behind her back.

If they had used duct tape to tie her up, she could have gotten her hands free. If you get the right angle or a notch, duct tape will rip.

Handcuffs would have been okay. She had learned all kinds of handcuff escape tricks at the Devilhouse.

But, no. Butorin's burly goons had bound Georgie's hands behind her back with thick, black cable ties, damn them. Two of them were looped around her wrists and chained together. Zip ties were impossible to get out of.

She squirmed in the dark back seat, rolling her hands around, trying to stretch the plastic, but zip ties don't stretch. The hard plastic sawed her skin. She tried to fold her strong, slim hands in to wiggle out, but they weren't even close to being small enough to slip free.

A streetlight threw a circle of light over the car in front of them, which was carrying more of Butorin's henchmen. They passed under it, and the pool of light whipped through their car. Another car followed them, somewhere among the black shadows of the huge trees overhanging the road.

This part of Connecticut seemed rural when viewed from the road, but it was an illusion. The enormous estates of the Conyers Farm area were carpeted in emerald lawns and jeweled gardens more manicured than most private golf courses, lest the neighbors talk. The air streaming through the vents smelled like mown grass and clean horse manure, like home.

She almost threw up at that thought, but she swallowed the scalding bitterness back down again.

The car coasted to a stop, and Georgie peeked. When they had shoved her into the car, the guy had clicked the childproof lock on the inside of the car's door, or else Georgie might have made a run for it right then.

Someone's phone chanted directions, and the car turned a corner.

Even though she hadn't been back for years, Georgie knew every stretch of this road. Her family's chauffeur had driven her to her country day school every day around these bends, even after her father had been arrested. At Georgie's insistence, Rizwan had taught her to drive when she was sixteen, starting on these lonely streets. He had hushed her when she had told him that she wanted to know how to drive just in case she needed to drive her own car someday.

She had been planning to run away even then, and now Tatiana Butorin and her *bratva* men had brought Georgie back.

The vodka in her bloodstream was still messing with her. Every time Georgie let her head move, the whole car seemed to jump sideways across the road. Her liver needed to hurry up and metabolize that crap. When they had tried to hustle her out of the plane, Georgie had gone limp, pretending to be passed out, and Tatiana had tsked her tongue at Georgie not being able to hold her liquor.

Georgie's pride had wanted to stand up and march down the stairs in as straight a line as was possible under the circumstances, but she had lain crumpled on the airplane's carpeting, faking it. One of Butorin's henchmen had ended up carrying her down the stairs to the tarmac. Every step jostled her stomach while her head dangled over the ramp's railing. She stared at the dark asphalt far below and had a hard time resisting the urge to cling his neck so she wouldn't fall over the side head-first and die.

She had stayed limp all during the ride to Conyer's Farm, conserving her energy and her strength and hopefully metabolizing the alcohol. It was almost eleven o'clock in Connecticut and almost four in the morning back in Europe, where she had awakened almost a full day ago.

The car slowed, braking. Georgie let her body flop bonelessly in the seat belt.

Beside her, one of Butorin's ghouls shoved her back against the door, probably thinking she was going to drunk-hurl on him.

She considered it. Puking on her future murderer would have been passive-aggressively awesome. Maybe that would be the clue that the CSI guys matched to her dead body, some special pasta found only in Milan squishing in his shoes.

Her sense of humor, normally quite dry, was turning darker now that she was probably going to die slowly and painfully in the next couple hours if she didn't manage to somehow get away.

Soon after one of these guys killed her, she would arrive at the Gates of Hell, if such a thing existed. There was no reason to be optimistic about anything else. She hadn't managed to pay back even ten percent of her father's swindling victims, not the widows, not the children's charities, and not any of her friends. Maybe, after the police found her body, the DAs would discover her savings accounts and mutual funds that she had been saving for law school and distribute that money in some stupid posthumous act of contrition.

The news media would probably talk about how selfish she was, just like her father, hoarding that measly hundred grand when she owed millions to so many people. It wouldn't have been enough for law school, anyway. She would have had to take out loans, too, and then she would have owed more, if she hadn't had that deal with Xan and if she had lived long enough to take advantage of it.

Her chest fluttered, trying to sob.

Georgie sucked in a deep breath, holding it together.

She couldn't lose it now. If a chance came, she knew these fields and these gardens, and she could run. She was even wearing jeans and tennis shoes and could sprint through the hedges and brush. Staying alert and seeing a chance might mean a chance to stay alive.

Greasepaint still smeared her face from the Milan show. Half the mascara had flowed to settle beneath her eyes, and she was sure that she probably looked ghastly. The photos of her dead body would be hideous.

Butorin's men might blow her head off. Then the makeup wouldn't matter.

That was a happy thought.

It was the happiest one she had had lately, anyway.

Georgie sucked in a deep breath and clenched her fists behind her back. Thinking about death was stupid. Thinking about escape might keep her alive.

Her black backpack lay in the front seat at Tatiana Butorin's feet, stuffed with her laptop, clothes, and some sheet music in Xan's handwriting that she hadn't been able to bring herself to leave behind. It was all copies, not originals, so she hadn't been absconding with priceless manuscripts. She had just wanted to have some of the music with her in Atlanta, just in case she had found a piano, just to look at what they had made together.

More importantly, that backpack held her passport and over ten thousand dollars in cash. That might make a huge difference in whether she could continue to elude the Butorins or not.

Just feet away. Just over the seat and between Tatiana Butorin's ankles.

So damn close.

Georgie grimaced, trying not to open her eyes and peer over the seat at that damned backpack.

The car's tires crunched on the asphalt, and it came to a dead stop.

Georgie peeked between her eyelids. Beyond the front windshield of the car, black wrought-iron gates cut swirls out of the star-strewn sky. Dim floodlights blossomed with light far down by the house.

Steel razor-sharp spikes subtly gleamed atop each of the thousands of black steel bars that ran in both directions. Someone would lose all their fingers if they tried to climb it.

Every one of the stakes was buried in the earth, which hid a deep cement foundation. A tank couldn't push that fence down.

Georgie had indeed arrived at the Gates of Hell, her childhood home.

The long fence that ringed the Conyer's Farm estate looked like the Gates of Hell should look: efficient and unscalable. If the Butorins managed to take Georgie inside there, she would have to hide until she could sneak out when the gates opened again.

A motor whined, and the driver's window rolled down. Sultry night air flowed into the car, and the humidity made Georgie's tee shirt cling to her sweaty chest.

The lead car was parked behind them on the road, but their car was directly beside the gate's monitor. Another car pulled up behind them.

A man's voice, made robotic by a speaker on the gate, growled, "State your business."

The driver yelled, "We need to talk to Grace Oelrichs!" His Russian accent flattened his words.

Georgie wanted to cringe at her mother's name, but she kept her breathing deep and even. She even managed to put a little nasal snore in there.

The plastic zip ties chafed her wrists as she tugged, trying to free her arms.

The guard said over the speaker, "The house is closed for the night. Please call for an appointment tomorrow."

"We have Grace Oelrich's daughter, Georgiana. You need to let us in to talk or we start cutting off fingers."

Floodlights slammed on, drenching the car with brilliant, white light.

The Russians blinked and rubbed their eyes.

Georgie squinted, accustomed to the sudden glare of stage lights and fountains of pyrotechnics sprouting from the dark, and watched, waiting for an opportunity.

Static crackled from the speaker. "The police have been called. Threats will not be tolerated."

"Oh, it is not threat," the driver said. "Look at camera."

A yank on the back of Georgie's head jerked her. The brute sitting in the back seat with her had grabbed the long braid on the back of her head and dragged her across the seat until she was lying on his knees. She gasped and tried to stay limp, flailing her arms just a little and not in any sort of aggression. If one of them punched her, he might really knock her out, and then she would be punch-drunk for a while, at least.

Her best shot at escaping might be soon.

Her liver was finally beginning to chew through the vodka. Even when she was being dragged across the seat by her hair with her eyes closed, the car spun less than before. Her skin stank as alcohol crap oozed out of her pores.

The guy bent her neck so her face turned up toward the camera and jabbed a button to roll down the window.

She kept her eyes closed, still playing drunk.

The goon in the front seat said, "We kill her if you do not open gate."

Georgie held her breath. She believed him.

The speaker said, "The police are on their way. Do not attempt to enter the gate."

Tatiana Butorin said something in Russian.

All the doors thumped as they unlocked.

Georgie was still sprawled across the seat, and she worked hard not to tense, not to run. They could all jump out and shoot her faster than she could struggle to her feet, open the door, stumble out, and run away.

This was a false chance to give her hope or make her give away her plan.

Luckily for Georgie, she had neither.

The man in the back seat with her got out of his door, slammed his door, and walked around the trunk of the car.

Georgie scraped her feet against the floor of the car, pretending to struggle while she sat up. Some of the drunken flopping wasn't pretend, damn it.

Her door opened. Hotter air washed into the car.

A hand closed on her arm and yanked her through the door and into the blazing spotlights.

She stumbled for real that time, trying not to fall to the brick pavers and scrape her palms. She grabbed the side edge of the car to steady herself and yanked her hand back as the door slammed right where her fingers had been.

She almost laughed at the ridiculousness of it: these men were about to kill her, but she was still obsessed with protecting her hands and her fingers, her musician's tools and trade.

The man spun Georgie around and she fell to her knees, but she still didn't even try to catch herself with her hands. She dropped and rolled, her hands still tied behind her back, and then struggled back to her knees.

What an idiot.

Her heart pounded in her ears like a gale-force wind was buffeting her.

The driver yelled into the speaker, "We'll shoot her! We'll shoot her right here if you don't open that gate!"

A hot wind whipped her clothes, flapping her tee shirt against her chest. Her long braid lifted and pointed toward the car.

Weird. The rolling hills around Conyer's Farm usually softened the wind unless a real storm was brewing. The full moon was visible even though the spotlights blazed on the car and the Russian man held a gun to her head, so the sky was clear, not stormy.

Her heart pounded harder, fluttering in her ears. Her eardrums hurt with the force of her pulse.

After all those concerts, she would have thought that her eardrums would be too callused to hurt like this.

The sound intensified, beating her ears.

The wind blew harder, almost knocking her over.

Georgie looked up.

A helicopter was landing beside her.

She dropped flat to the ground, scraping her elbows on the sharp edges of the pavers. A pebble under her knee drove a spike of pain into her leg.

When did the Greenwich Police Department get a helicopter? And *why?* One of the most affluent zip codes in the country didn't need a ghetto bird.

She glanced up, expecting black-clad SWAT stormtroopers to pour out of the helicopter, or maybe paunchy Greenwich cops to tumble out of the swinging doors.

Xan Valentine jumped out and sprinted toward her. He wore a black tee shirt and jeans, and his blond hair flew behind him as he sprinted.

Adrien leapt out of the pilot's side and ran toward her, handgun raised.

Holy shit.

The Russian *bratva* guy beside her lifted his gun toward Xan.

Georgie jumped straight up, knocking the Russian's thick arm aside with her shoulder.

A gunshot blasted near her head. Gunpowder flecks burned her face, and sulfur burned in her sinuses. A high pitch wailed in her ears that sounded like she had just finished a three-hour rock concert.

Xan slammed into the guy, pummeling him with closed fists. His face was set in grim determination, not rage.

Another Russian jumped on Xan as the *bratva* men leapt out of the other cars and joined the fight, fists swinging, guns pointing.

Georgie slammed her shoulder into one of the guys on Xan, and he went down on one knee. She leapt upon him, trying to push him down with her weight, and struggled with the cable ties binding her wrists behind her back. He rose underneath her and she grabbed him with her legs, riding him like a horse, except that he smelled like onions and sweat instead of a clean animal.

Flailing bodies leapt into the fight. Punches swung and legs jabbed and blood splattered.

Hands grabbed Georgie, hurting her shoulders, and wrapped her neck.

Her scream choked in her throat.

Cold steel poked her head beside her eye, and the scent of oil wormed around her face.

A long barrel of a handgun stretched away from her temple.

A man yelled beside her head, "Down on knees or I shoot her! I shoot this bitch!"

One of Butorin's goons, the blond guy with the wide, Slavic face, shoved Xan to his knees. Xan looked up at her, his dark eyes cold and angry. The guy grabbed Xan's long hair, yelling, "Put hands behind head!"

Xan raised his hands, still staring at her.

She didn't look away, trying to hold him with her eyes. He should have stayed in Italy and been safe. She wasn't worth it.

Hard metal pressed her temple.

Around her, the sounds of the fight faded away with the Russians yelling for everyone to get down to their knees.

The Russians outnumbered Xan and his guys by at least five people. They should never have gotten out of that helicopter.

The man standing over Xan grabbed one of his hands away from his head and looped one of the cruel, black cable ties over it, binding his wrist. He wrenched both of Xan's hands behind his back, and Georgie heard the hiss of another thick zip tie fastening his hands together.

Bastards.

One of the Russians shouted at the guard's monitor. "Open gate now! Open gate now or we kill them all!"

Georgie closed her eyes. *God, please, no. Not Alexandre.*

"Open gate now!" The Russian's voice was hoarse with shouting.

The man's arm tightened around Georgie's throat and lifted her chin. He yanked her to her feet by her head and neck, and he dragged her, her feet stumbling and sliding on the flat stone, to the camera perched on the side of the gate. The cold gun pressed her head again.

The driver pointed to her and yelled, *"Open gate or he shoot her now!"*

One tear squeezed out from between Georgie's cramping eyelids.

Beside her, the gate creaked and slowly slid aside.

She gasped air, desperate with relief that she wasn't going to die right that instant.

Scuffling and cursing trickled through the night as two Russian men shoved Georgie in a car and clambered in on both sides of her. One still had his gun pressed against her temple.

The other Russian aimed his gun at the person in the front passenger seat, Alexandre. The goon grabbed Alexandre's long hair in his fist, holding it over the back of the seat, and poked his gun at the back of Alexandre's skull.

Tatiana Butorin got in a different car this time.

Georgie's stomach clenched. Tears stung her eyes. *Alexandre shouldn't have come.*

The gun scraped against her temple and hair as the Russian's hand shook. His fist holding her shirt trembled, and she could hear the grate of his teeth sliding across each other.

She wanted to say something to Alex, to chew him out for coming to rescue her or to touch his shoulder to comfort him or herself, but she didn't dare move.

The car lurched through the gate, throwing Georgie back against the seat.

Chapter Four

INSIDE THE GATES

Georgie

Out of the corner of her eye, Georgie watched the headlights of the other two cars race down the dark driveway toward the house. The guy next to Georgie was still shaking from adrenaline, his whole body quivering and ready to jump or shoot her in the head.

Georgie leaned forward to rest her shoulders. The cable ties around her wrists pulled her arms back unnaturally, and her shoulders hurt.

The wings of the house sprawled around the end of the circular driveway with a fountain at its center. When Georgie was a child, on dinner party nights, dozens of cars had driven around the fountain, all shining in the floodlights from the house. The guests had emerged, sparkling with jewelry and rustling with silk, and valets had removed the cars and parked them over by the stables. On the days after party nights, her horses had been skittish from the cars and the commotion, and Georgie had had to be careful during her dressage or jumping lessons that her mount didn't prance out from under her or rear up.

The Russian drove the car up to the front door and parked.

A sliver of light sprayed out of the cracked-open front door. Through the two-story window above the door, an enormous chandelier glowed like a white sun surrounded by star clusters.

The driver muttered, "At least we not have to do that again."

The man holding the gun to Georgie's head shook her shoulder. "Get out with me."

The other Russian held the gun to Alexandre's head and told him, "Wait until I open your door."

The man pulled Georgie with him, sliding across the seat, as he stepped out of the car, leaving Alexandre in there with a gun pointed at his head.

Georgie clenched her hands into fists where they were bound behind her back, wishing that she could somehow swing her arms and knock the guy out and grab his gun to rescue everyone.

Yet more useless hope. Her only real hope was to create a distraction so Alexandre could get away.

The other guy yanked Alexandre from the car, and they all climbed the wide steps to the towering double door.

She glanced back. Tatiana's other goons held Adrien, Paul, and Peyton at gunpoint.

Good God, they had brought *Peyton.*

One of the Russians who held a gun pointed at

Adrien's head was the man with the wide, Slavic face and ice-blue eyes.

Asshole.

Tatiana Butorin took the lead and pushed the doors open herself, surveying the wide and empty foyer, which Georgie had to respect even though she would have gladly ripped Butorin's throat out with her teeth just then.

The huge chandelier above the entryway was just as Georgie remembered it from her childhood. It had been designed by some famous, hard-to-book chandelier designer. Georgie didn't care then and didn't care now who it was. Her mother did, of course, though she had never had to tell anyone who had designed the glorious, fiery structure of crystal and platinum. At that socioeconomic level, people just *knew* and coveted both the lighting fixture and the connections required to obtain it.

The designer had been one of her father's clients, swindled out of millions and this trophy.

Dust dulled the crystal.

Georgie hoped that when Butorin's goons shot her, one of the bullets ricocheted and shattered that motherfucker.

A man's voice echoed from speakers set into the ceiling and walls. "The police are on their way. Video cameras are recording from multiple angles. All members of the Oelrichs family are in safe rooms. Leave, now."

Georgie's heart leapt.

All members of the family? Was Benedict there, too? She hadn't heard that he had been paroled.

Then again, it could just be a ploy.

Yeah, it probably was. She bit her lip.

Tatiana strode to the middle of the foyer. A table in the center supported an enormous bouquet of white and pale blue flowers in a matching Wedgewood vase that towered seven feet in the air, leaching a subtle scent of wildflowers into the air. Two grand staircases curved up and away from the marble floor.

"Grace Oelrichs!" Tatiana called. "We have your daughter! You will come out to negotiate!"

Silence filled the house all the way up to the dark timbers crossing the ceiling four stories above them. Some of the Russians shuffled their feet, guarding their prisoners and watching around them.

Georgie wished that she were surprised.

Maybe the security staff hadn't even told her mother what was happening, just shoved her in the safe room and locked it. That pathetic hope made Georgie's chest tighten.

The Russian holding a gun to her head looked up at the ceiling, scanning, distracted. She risked a glance back.

Adrien and Paul stood with their shoulders down, looking relaxed rather than defeated even with their hands tied behind their backs, probably with yet more fucking zip ties. They were looking away from each other, surveilling the Russians.

Peyton stood with his shoulders hunched, his arms tense. He glanced furtively back and forth, and he noticed Georgie looking at him. The horrified look in his teal-green eyes would have haunted her night-mares, but luckily, she probably wouldn't live long enough to have any more nightmares.

Alexandre stared straight at her. His dark eyes had locked onto her like nothing else mattered, not the Russian beside him who was reaching up to hold a gun to the underside of his jaw, not Tatiana Butorin who was tapping her foot and growing impatient, and not the deafening silence of Georgie's mother not answering. One blond tendril had drifted from behind his shoulder and rested on the gun.

Georgie closed her eyes. She wanted to slump to the floor and let them shoot her, but as long as she stayed upright, there was a slim chance that she might do something that would allow the four men to escape.

Tatiana called out again, "Grace Oelrichs, I know that you can hear me. Your daughter is here. Don't you want to say something to her?"

Silence. Nothing. The shuffling of feet and a sniff from one of the Russians.

Georgie's fingernails drove into her palms, and she opened her eyes. "She's not going to answer you, Ms. Butorin. I'm sorry."

"She can hear me," Tatiana Butorin said, turning to stare at Georgie. Her Russian accent was more pronounced, the sounds harsher in her throat. "I know she can hear me. Safe rooms always have monitors."

"Yeah, probably. But I can't imagine that she'll answer you."

Tatiana walked over to her, dark eyes narrowed with anger. "Why she not answer when we have her daughter?"

"She just won't," Georgie said, shrugging.

Tatiana's lip lifted in a sneer. "What kind of woman not even answer when daughter has a gun to her head?"

A wry laugh escaped Georgie's mouth, and her chest heaved. "I don't know what to say to that."

"Disgusting." Tatiana Butorin lifted her head.

"Grace Oelrichs, you say something now or I start to break Georgiana's fingers."

A zap of horror ran through Georgie at the thought of Tatiana breaking her *fingers.*

Even when she had pretended to trip and fall at Juilliard, Alex's first concern—her hands—had pissed her off at the time, but he was *right.* It was always the hands. A bad break of even a pinky finger could cripple a musician.

She glanced back at Alexandre, who was still staring at her. His whole life, from the time that someone had identified his talent and determined that he would be a prodigy, had been an endless succession of brutal work and draconian limits.

And now it was going to be over. He was so close to breaking out of the life prescribed for him and becoming a musician in his own right and under his own power, and he was probably going to die tonight, all because of her.

Georgie swallowed hard.

But if Tatiana was going to break Georgie's fingers, they would probably cut the cable ties behind her back. Her hands would be free.

She would do anything, *anything,* to create a diversion so that Adrien and Paul and Peyton and Alexandre could get to safety. She prayed to all the saints in Heaven that Adrien and Paul would do their damn jobs this time and get those guys out of there.

Tatiana told a guy behind Georgie, "Cut the ties on her."

One of the goons who had been holding onto Alexandre stepped forward. The *snickt* of a knife flipping out hissed very near Georgie's ear. His hot hands held hers, and the tension of the harsh plastic bands around her wrists broke. Her arms flopped free, and her shoulders jerked forward from the release.

Tatiana Butorin held out her hand, palm up. "Give me your hand."

Butorin couldn't expect Georgie to voluntarily hold out her hand to be broken. No one was that arrogant.

The Russian goon beside her nudged Georgie's head with his gun. The cold steel pressed her temple, a threat.

Georgie lifted her hand, watching her own shaking fingers approach Butorin's outstretched hand.

This couldn't be happening.

A woman's voice rang from speakers all around the room, "I won't come out, Butorin. I don't owe you anything."

Georgie dropped her head forward in momentary relief, even though she knew this wouldn't end well.

Tatiana Butorin spun, looking at the ceiling.

Georgie let her hand fall and braced herself on her knees, breathing hard.

Butorin pointed to a speaker in the ceiling. "You will come out. We will arrange payment or I kill your daughter here."

Georgie's mother said, "I can't control what you do, but I don't owe you anything. The district attorneys said that I don't owe anyone anything."

Tatiana shook her head. "This is not about law, Grace Oelrichs. This is about what is right and fair."

Georgie rolled her eyes from where she was hunched over. That line of logic would never work on her mother.

Her mother's voice hardened. "I won't talk to you anymore. I'm turning off my monitors now. The security system is recording everything you do and everything you say. The police are on their way."

Butorin snorted a laugh and leaned toward Georgie. "She say that like it's a threat or something."

Georgie swallowed sour bile in her throat. Her hands were shaking so much.

Butorin said, "You come out to balcony, Grace Oelrichs, and we negotiate in person, like civilized people."

She waited.

Georgie waited.

They all stood silently until Butorin raised a slim eyebrow. "I said, Grace Oelrichs, that you come out now. You say that you are coming out."

Georgie's heart punched her chest so hard that she could feel it all the way up her neck. She knew her mother wasn't going to answer. When her mother had been angry, she used sharp silence like a weapon. Georgie could practically hear her designer heels clicking on the marble as she walked away.

"Grace Oelrichs?" Tatiana asked the empty air.

Nothing.

Butorin stared at the ceiling. "Grace Oelrichs!"

The Russians and their hostages all breathed, fluttering the air, but everything else was silent.

Georgie's breath came out too much like a sob, and she swallowed hard to calm herself down. Nothing had changed. Nothing was worse. She had known how this would end. Her hands tightened into fists, and Peyton's promise ring cut into her fingers on her right hand.

Tatiana looked back at Georgie, her eyes angry, and she lifted her head to the ceiling again. "Grace Oelrichs! This is done. This is over. I not break her fingers. When I count to three, I shoot your daughter in the head and we call your debt to me paid. Gregor, give me gun."

The man holding Georgie flipped his gun around his hand and offered it to Butorin grip-first.

Tatiana Butorin took the gun and held it with a practiced hand.

She pressed the barrel to the center of Georgie's forehead, just above her eyes.

Shaking began deep in Georgie's chest, a fluttering like her heart was giving out. She refused to close her eyes. She stared straight down the underside of the gun, past Tatiana Butorin's finger on the trigger, into the woman's glare.

Butorin said, *"One."*

Georgie kept staring right at her. If Tatiana was going to shoot her in the head, Georgie was going to stare her down until she did. She wasn't going to close her eyes like a good little victim.

"Two," Tatiana called out.

A crack zipped through the air, a hard snap like a stalking predator popping a twig deep in the woods.

The Russian guy holding Georgie's shirt in his fist flinched, jerking her. He looked around.

Tatiana lifted her gaze away from Georgie and looked around, too. Her aim strayed from Georgie's forehead.

The other Russian guys alerted like something was out of place. They looked around the marble and crystal foyer like deer scenting a mountain lion.

Alexandre hadn't flinched. He hadn't jumped when the rest of them had, and nothing about him moved. His dark eyes watched Georgie.

One side of his mouth rose in the subtlest of smiles.

Chapter Five

BREAK ON THROUGH

Alex de Valentinois

Alex clenched his fists behind his back, screaming inside, but he clamped down on it all. Helplessness assailed him.

He had promised to hold Georgie until she was safe on the other side, and he couldn't. He couldn't touch her. He couldn't *save* her.

Tatiana Butorin pressed a steel handgun to Georgie's forehead. *"One."*

Alex flailed inside, reaching for anything, any resource.

He found a wall of stone and metal.

Behind it, he could feel pain and rage, like turning and discovering a dark lake just beyond your back yard that roiled with black waves.

The pain breached the wall with dim tendrils, reaching for him.

Alex dug his fingers into the wall within his mind and broke through.

A thousand lashes striped his back from his neck to his waist, and white-hot pain engulfed him. He had forgotten. He had survived because he had forgotten the pain.

Alex shattered and became light.

Chapter Six

SMOKE AND MIRRORS

Xan Valentine

Xan swirled and took form.

Xan Valentine had condensed from the smoke rising when Alexandre burned with pain and rage. He was the focused pain—the fire and rage—and he released it during a performance. The audience responded to him destroying himself from the inside. They basked in his heat.

He reflected himself on the smoke, a ghost, and surveyed the foyer of the house.

Tatiana Butorin pressed the revolver to Georgie's forehead.

Georgie glared at her, unbroken.

Bright flames erupted behind Xan, and he turned inward.

The other one strode out of the flames, a burning apparition, rushing toward Xan like a wildfire.

If anyone could save Georgie, the other one could.

Xan opened himself to the burning wind, spreading his arms wide.

Pain assailed him, pain that he had felt deep in his flesh but not understood.

He dissipated into smoke and blew away, becoming the darkness that rose from the fire.

Chapter Seven

YESTERDAY

Alexandre Grimaldi

Y*ears* had led to this moment.

Years of Alexandre's life—ever since he had been given to Domingo Soto, his violin tutor first in Monaco, who then had moved to Rolle, Switzerland to instruct him when he had started kindergarten at Le Rosey boarding school—those years had been striped with pain, pain that he had played through, pain in his hands and back and neck, pain cutting his soul to ribbons while he played and could not stop.

Alexandre could play the violin through anything. His expression was beautiful, he had been told, and his interpretation of the music was that of a mature musician by the time he turned twelve. They marveled that a child could have such a sense of art, of the deep emotions of grief and sadness and suffering that ran through the music.

Soto had said that he would kill Alexandre if he told anyone how he was taught, that Soto would kill his sister and his friends, and the nine-year-old had believed him.

So he had played the violin through the pain.

And thus he was forged in fire and could walk through pain, smiling and playing the violin, and his only cry was his instrument.

Audiences heard only his music.

He had absorbed all the fire, all the pain. Scars from lashes grew thicker on his back for every dropped note, every flat tone, every missed intonation.

Prodigies aren't born; they're made. They are created by an adult with enough drive, enough vision, and enough anger to fold and harden a child with fire.

Years of endured pain had led Alexandre to this moment where he could save Georgie.

His hands were bound behind his back with the sharp cable ties, the backs of his wrists pressed together. The Russians had looped them tightly, and the position kept him from even turning his hands within the plastic cuffs. The thick plastic cut his skin.

He couldn't move his left hand, the hand that pressed the strings on the neck of the violin, to reach his right.

But the zip tie around his right hand—the hand that had held the bow for so many years—was a little looser.

If he twisted his right hand, he could reach the pinkie and ring finger of his left.

Tough plastic sliced into his wrist. Blood dribbled down his thumb.

He had played the violin through pain so many times.

The fingers of his right hand found his other pinkie finger and walked up it to the last knuckle of his left hand.

Tatiana Butorin glanced at the corners of the room, looking for cameras or microphones, and drew in a breath. She yelled to the security cameras, *"Two."*

Alexandre stilled the fire inside him, drawing it inward to a white-hot point.

And broke his hand.

Chapter Eight

CHOOSE

Georgie

The Russians were still looking around the foyer, scanning the windows and the balcony and the closed front door, trying to figure out where the popping sound came from.

Georgie watched Alexandre and his small, secretive smile. Anger was a dark fire in his eyes.

A second crack split the air.

The Russians ducked their heads at the pop.

Georgie watched Alexandre, who had not wavered at the sound. Blond strands of hair hung over his shoulders.

Far back behind Alexandre, Adrien and Paul exchanged a glance and were looking around to see where the noise had come from.

Adrien glanced at Alexandre, looking at his hands. His eyes widened, and his shoulders tensed.

Tatiana's gun drifted farther from Georgie's forehead as she scanned the upper corners of the room.

Alexandre's lips opened—those lips that had kissed her a thousand times—and he mouthed one word, *Run.*

Georgie ducked to the side, wrenched her shoulder away from the Russian holding her, and slammed her palm against Butorin's hand that held the gun.

A shot blasted near the side of her head and scattered blistering gunpowder on her arm.

Georgie spun around, searching for help.

Alexandre had freed his hands. His arm was stretching into a forceful punch at the Russian who had been holding him, who turned toward the fist coming at him. His fist connected. Blood sprayed from the man's face.

Georgie spun and slammed her palm into Tatiana Butorin's elbow, the one holding the gun, and broke Butorin's arm with a hard snap that echoed above the fight. Butorin grunted and kicked at her while she switched the gun to her good hand.

Glimpses of the fight flashed through Georgie's vision as she struggled, trying to grab Butorin's hand to pry the gun away. Adrien's arms swung in front of him, and he crashed both his hands in one big fist into a Russian's face. Paul sprinted toward Alexandre. Peyton whipped a back roundhouse kick at the man holding him, and the guy flew hard at the floor.

And Alexandre.

Alexandre punched with his right fist, ducking and slamming his knuckles into men who came at him. His left arm was tucked to his chest.

Gunshots blasted, and bullets ricocheted. Crystal shards sliced the air like falling knives.

Georgie covered her head, protecting her eyes and face from the rain of glass, and scrambled after Butorin's gun.

Tatiana Butorin jerked the gun away from Georgie and fired into the seething fight.

Georgie clambered over her, chasing the gun, snatching at it as Tatiana tried to aim a shot at Alexandre or Paul.

Butorin punched her good elbow back, smashing the point into Georgie's throat.

Georgie's throat slammed shut. *No air.* She struggled to breathe and tasted hot copper and vomit. *No air.*

Butorin rolled under her as Georgie grabbed her throat, choking, but then grabbed for the gun again. She couldn't reach it. Butorin had moved too far.

Georgie slid off Butorin as the woman aimed. Someone stepped on Georgie's legs, his feet crushing her flesh, and fell.

A gun skittered across the floor.

Georgie went after that one as air trickled into her throat, bubbling the blood in her mouth, but she breathed. Her hand closed on the hot steel as another hand landed on hers. She yanked and rolled, bringing the gun up to aim at the guy.

The Russian skittered backward and stumbled to his feet, running away. Peyton skidded in front of him —his hands still tied behind his back—and kicked up hard, catching the guy under the jaw. The Russian was out cold before his skull thunked the floor.

Georgie flipped over, tracking Tatiana Butorin with the black barrel in front of her.

Beyond Butorin, the man with ice-blue eyes was walking toward her. He grabbed Adrien—*Adrien*

—around the neck as he was fighting his way toward Alexandre.

Adrien grabbed the man's elbow and pulled, trying to get away.

Georgie started to swing the gun toward the Slavic man, running the sights across the crowd.

The man's wide jaw clenched as he jabbed a gun to Adrien's skull and squeezed his hand.

Gunshots blasted off all over the room, crashing over the other.

Adrien's face went slack, and he collapsed.

Georgie gasped to hold in her scream.

The Slavic man dropped Adrien's limp body and started walking toward her, raising the gun as he strode through the glass crashing around him.

Georgie swung the gun back toward Butorin.

Closer to Georgie, Tatiana Butorin raised her gun in her left hand, aiming for Alexandre's back as he caught the fist of another Russian trying to punch him.

No. Not Alexandre. *God, no.*

The blue-eyed man walked at Georgie, his handgun almost brought to bear on her. In another instant, he would shoot her.

Her gun was almost aimed at Tatiana. She could swing it back to the Slavic man and save herself.

Choose.

The gun in Georgie's hand blasted and jumped, tossing her arm upward.

Georgie stared, horrified, at the hot gun in her hand.

Tatiana Butorin fell sideways, holding her side. Her gun clattered on the marble floor. Red soaked her beige suit, and a terrible gurgle bubbled from her throat instead of a scream.

Alexandre threw a punch at another Russian and grabbed his arm.

The Slavic man's blue eyes stared at Georgie down his gun, aimed at her face.

Georgie was swinging her gun around, still shocked that it had fired at Butorin when she had pulled the trigger, but the blue-eyed man's finger was already reddening where he was squeezing to shoot her.

She couldn't bring it up in time and she didn't know how to aim but she jerked the gun at him.

The man stumbled, his blue eyes wide. He staggered and grabbed his back as he fell.

As he fell, Georgie saw past him that Alexandre was aiming a gun at his back.

Alexandre pushed off, running to her. He held the gun in his right hand. His left hand was a clenched fist held to his chest.

Georgie struggled to her feet, slipping on the marble. When she looked down, blood soaked her shoe, and long scrape marks tracked the tile. She jumped away.

Alexandre grabbed her arm and pulled her the rest of the way up.

Paul was holding Adrien around his chest and dragging the man, aiming his gun back at the crowd.

Alexandre grabbed Adrien away from Paul, hauling him over his shoulder. The three of them ran for the front door, Adrien limp in Alexandre's arms, his shoes dangling at Alexandre's waist.

Georgie glanced back.

Peyton fell into step with them as they ran, his hands still bound behind his back.

Paul grabbed the front door and yanked it open. Gunshots chipped plaster off the walls beside them and crashed into the crystal chandelier above, shattering its glassy skeletal remains.

"Get to a car, *now,*" Paul ground out as he ran.

Chapter Nine

GETAWAY

Georgie

They sprinted out the front door into the night and clattered down the stone steps toward the cars. Alexandre held Adrien over his shoulder with one arm. Paul watched around them, swinging his gun to cover anything that moved. Peyton ran with his hands still bound behind his back.

Georgie started to climb in the passenger side of the front car, but Paul pulled her backward. "You drive."

Her liver had finished chewing through the vodka, and adrenaline had burned off any trace of a hangover. She ran around the front of the car and leaped in, relieved to find the keys in the ignition.

Her black backpack was on the passenger side, lying on the floor. *Hallelujah.* She had her cash, her passport, and the few artifacts from her life before.

Alexandre slid Adrien into the back seat and then jumped into the front seat with her. Paul and Peyton climbed in the back. Paul and Alexandre aimed guns out the passenger-side windows as Georgie stomped on the accelerator and peeled out. She slid the car around the fountain and sped down the long driveway, racing for the gate.

The evil-looking front gate was still open, and she floored the pedal. The car jumped out the gate, and she turned it onto the road. "Anyone chasing us?"

"Not yet," Paul said.

Alexandre said, "The helicopter. We can fly out."

"Adrien isn't in any shape to fly us out," Paul said.

"We can't leave the scene of the crime," Georgie said. "We should go to a police station and explain what happened."

Peyton was cranked around, looking out the rear window. "I don't see anyone behind us."

Alexandre turned to look in the back seat. "Is Adrien all right? Did he wake up yet?"

Peyton stared at Georgie through the rearview mirror, his eyes huge.

Georgie blinked tears back and drove hard down the dark lanes. Alexandre had had his back to Adrien when the Slavic guy had shot him in the back of the head. He didn't know. There hadn't been an exit wound, which probably meant that the damage inside was even worse. "Alexandre," she said.

"Did he get kicked in the head or something?" Alexandre peered into the back seat.

"Greenwich Hospital is about fifteen minutes away." Georgie changed lanes to turn left.

Paul said, "Continue to Liberty Airport. I want you off this continent. He wanted you to be safe." He pulled his cell phone out of his pocket and shook his head. "What idiots. They were probably just going to kill us all."

Georgie drove from memory, whipping down the dark lanes until they reached busier streets, where she blended in with the traffic. "It's just a few minutes to the hospital."

"Not the hospital," Paul told her. "Drive for Liberty International Airport. Hello, Ned!" he said into his phone, his voice rising over the growling road noise. "We've had a problem. I need someone to run interference with the local authorities, and we need to leave the country *now.*" Paul slapped the back of the car seat near Georgie's ear, insisting that they go to the airport.

"Okay," she said. "To the airport."

The hot, metallic tang of blood filled the car, and Georgie swallowed hard.

She sped along the dark streets toward Greenwich Hospital. Paul wouldn't know which way the airport was.

"Georgie," Alexandre said. "Adrien needs a doctor."

She glanced at him and barely inclined her head, nodding.

Alexandre looked into the back seat, still holding his left hand against his chest.

Peyton half-turned in the seat, his hands still tied behind his back. "Could someone cut this damn thing?"

Paul leaned over Adrien to Peyton while he talked on the phone. "Ned, we had a self-defense situation. We were taken hostage and fought our way out. There are video and sound feeds, a lot of them, beginning at the front gate. And witnesses who were watching the video. The perps are on Interpol's lists, Russian mafia from the Butorin *bratva.* I'm pretty sure Tatiana Butorin was shot, maybe dead. No, don't thank me yet. I need to get myself and my people on a plane *now.* No stop for interrogation."

Peyton muttered, "Thanks."

Georgie glanced at him through the rearview mirror. He was rubbing his wrists and frowning, leaning away from Adrien's limp form.

Ahead of them on the darkened street, five police cars screamed around a corner and approached them on the other side of the road, sirens wailing, flashing red and blue lights in Georgie's eyes.

Ambulances trailed the cop cars.

Georgie muttered, "Finally."

She spun the steering wheel, cutting off the last ambulance, and braked.

The ambulance's hood dipped as it stopped hard, and the driver started yelling through the windshield at them.

Paul was already leaping out of the car and dragging Adrien with him, waving over his head while he held the cell phone between his cheek and shoulder.

Alexandre jumped out of the car and ran over to help. He grabbed Adrien under his other arm.

Peyton hopped out, waving and yelling, "We need help!"

The driver got the message and jumped down from the cab, running over to help. Other guys ran around from the back with a stretcher. Georgie jammed the car into park and almost fell out of her door.

"What happened?" the driver yelled over the howl of the ambulance's engine.

"We were at the hostage situation!" Paul yelled.

The guy's dark eyes widened and he stepped backward.

"Number fifteen Conyers Farms Road," Georgie yelled to the paramedic. "We *are* the hostages. We got away. There are security video recordings of everything."

The stretcher nudged Georgie, and she staggered out of the way. Paul and Alexandre lifted Adrien's limp body onto the stretcher and arranged his arms and legs. The paramedics strapped him down.

After a startled glance, one paramedic climbed on top of the stretcher and started pumping Adrien's chest—performing chest compressions—while the other two guys wheeled him toward the back of the truck.

Two police cars squealed to a stop beside them, and the officers aimed guns over their cars at Georgie and the men.

Georgie lifted her hands to beside her ears. "We didn't do anything wrong!"

Alexandre trotted beside the stretcher, asking, "Adrien?" His voice held a note of panic.

Beside her, Paul still had his phone wedged against his face and shoulder. "I need you to make those calls right now, Ned. Local authorities have arrived—cars say Greenwich PD on them—and they've got guns aimed at us. One of our party is down, and we were acquiring medical attention. I know, I know, but I couldn't secure the target first."

A police officer was pointing his hollow hole of a gun at Georgie's face and stared through the air at her, his dark eyes as wide-open as hers felt. His black uniform and skin blended in with the night. The red and blue emergency lights gleamed on the sinister steel of his gun.

Georgie raised her open hands higher over her head, and her heartbeat sped to a long scream.

"You're a peach, Ned," Paul said. "I'll send you scans of our passports. I assure you this was entirely self-defense. The video will back me up a hundred percent, and you'll know where to find us if you have any questions."

The police officer's aim and gaze at Georgie's face hadn't wavered. She swallowed the sick lump in her throat.

Paul called to the officers. "I'm going to hang up my phone now."

One of the officers who was shielding herself behind a car door nodded, the shiny brim of her hat dipping in the streetlights.

Blue-gray exhaust from the running cars floated in the breeze, a wrong scent in the air scented green from the lawns of the estates.

Paul let the phone fall into his hand and tucked it back in his pocket, keeping his other hand raised the whole time.

Alexandre was still standing over Adrien's body. *"Adrien?"*

Georgie glanced back, keeping her hands well above her head.

"Adrien!" His accent had turned deeply French, growling in his throat.

"Alexandre," she said, careful to keep her voice calm. She angled herself just enough that she could see him out of the corner of her eye. "You need to step back. You need to get your hands up. The police are here."

"Adrien?" Alexandre asked again, hopelessness rising in his voice.

A paramedic muttered something to him.

Alexandre stumbled back a step and raised his right hand over his head.

His left fist was still pressed to his chest, and his hand looked smaller, somehow. Purple and red mottled the skin.

A radio inside a police car squawked, and one of the officers ducked into the car to respond. She was in there for a few seconds, and then she glanced, startled, through the window at them. She swiveled her chin to talk into her microphone.

Georgie couldn't hear what the officer said over the howl of the police cars' huge engines. The light bars flashed red and blue in her eyes, and she blinked from the glare.

The other police officers all flipped their guns to the sky and backed up.

Georgie dropped her burning arms and clutched her chest.

The officer got out of the car. She yelled, "You guys are free to go, but you need to leave *now.*"

All the saints in Heaven be praised. Georgie hopped two steps and grabbed Alexandre's raised hand—his dark eyes looked terribly blank—and tugged him toward the car. His other hand still pressed his chest. He stumbled along beside her, but she just wanted them all in the car and speeding out of this trap.

Alexandre twisted. "We can't leave Adrien."

"He's going to get the best care," Georgie said. "If they need to, Greenwich Hospital can airlift him to Yale." *If he survived long enough to get to Greenwich Hospital. If he wasn't already dead because he sure looked like he was.*

Georgie gritted her teeth and started to get in the passenger side.

Alexandre shook his head. "Drive, please. I can't."

They all tumbled back in the car—Paul and Peyton in the back—and Georgie pulled back onto the road.

Alexandre still cradled his left hand to his chest.

Georgie swallowed. On the stoplight in the dark, a green arrow glowed, and she turned left to drive toward the interstate. Streetlights led far away into the dark. "What's wrong with your hand?"

"Nothing," he said and looked away from her.

He was still clutching his left hand to his chest. In the intermittent light from the streetlamps, it looked crushed. "Did you hurt your *hand?*"

"You heard Paul. Drive for the airport."

"Alex! You have to go to a hospital! Are you bleeding?"

"No."

A streetlight flashed through the car. Dark lines traced down his forearm. "You're bleeding!"

"There was a cut on my wrist, but it's scabbed over now. It's nothing."

"Yale is close. Their orthopedic department is stellar." She began looking for somewhere to turn the car around.

From the back seat, Paul said, "Georgie, go to the plane. A few hours won't matter. He'll have it looked at in Rome. I want you and him out of the country."

"But his *hand!* His *left* hand!" The fingers that danced down the neck of the violin and pressed the strings.

"We'll have it looked at in Rome," Alexandre said. "It can't get any worse."

"How bad is it?" Georgie asked, keeping her eyes on the dark road that wound through the night.

A moment passed, then another. The car rolled over the road while she waited for him to say something, but he just wasn't answering.

"Is that why you insisted that I drive? Because your hand is too bad even to *drive?*"

Alexandre chuckled once and sniffed. "I can't drive."

"Because your hand is too hurt?" Georgie spun the wheel around a corner and sped down a ramp toward a dark parkway.

"No, I mean that I *can't* drive. I never learned how. I grew up in a boarding school, and then I moved to Manhattan. When I left Juilliard, the band bought a tour bus."

From the back seat, Paul said to her, "You should teach him to drive. You're aggressive."

"You were amazing back there," Peyton added.

"You weren't so bad, yourself, Peys. I had forgotten you took tae kwon do."

"I got my black belt after you left," he said. "You should have trained, too. You were cold in there, Ice Princess, calmly fighting that woman for the gun and then driving the getaway car."

Georgie sped down the parkway, passing trucks and other cars. She held the thick steering wheel tightly so Peyton wouldn't see that her hands were shaking. The Ice Princess didn't *shake.* "When I was learning to drive, I bragged to the guy who taught me that I could drive as well as he could, so he signed me out of high school for a day and made me drive around Boston. No traffic scares me."

"Was that Rizwan?" Peyton asked.

Rizwan had driven Peyton and Georgie on some of their dates before everything had crashed down around her. "Yeah. Rizwan."

"What happened to him?"

"I don't know. He still works for my mother, as far as I know."

"I don't think so. A few months after you left, I stopped seeing him drive your mother around. Some white woman was her chauffeur after that."

When she glanced back in the rearview mirror, Peyton was gazing out his window as if that conversation hadn't been loaded with bombs.

"Oh. Well, I don't know." Georgie drove down the parkway, the diamond on Peyton's promise ring glinting on her right hand as they passed under streetlights.

"Are we going toward the airport this time?" Paul sighed.

"Yeah. Takes a couple hours to get there from here." Georgie startled herself when she heard her New Englander accent, *to get theh from hee-uh.* It was like the bright green smell of Connecticut had made her tongue too lazy to say R's correctly. She would have to get Lizzy to growl in the mirror with her again to re-learn how to say R's right.

Nobody else seemed to have noticed her New Englander speech impediment, as she kind of thought of it nowadays. No wonder Alexandre had gotten away with three different accents for years.

She glanced one more time at Alexandre, who was holding his left hand to his chest with his other hand. A streetlight frosted his face with yellow light. His expression was as calm as ever, but Alexandre was the quiet one, the one whose dark, liquid eyes seemed fathomless when she stared into them.

Georgie drove hard for the airport, slamming the car through the dark parkway that vined through the New England forest, and they all swayed with the accelerations.

If she drove hard enough, maybe the Butorin *bratva* wouldn't catch them.

When they got to Liberty International, she had every intention of hoisting that backpack that lay at Alexandre's feet on her shoulder and walking out of his life forever. Tatiana Butorin was likely dead, and no one else would think to look for Liliana Bordeaux in Atlanta.

Chapter Ten

SOMETHING ELSE

Georgie

Georgie stood in the hot night air of the parking lot, staring at the dartlike Gulfstream jet that stood just beyond the private terminal. The asphalt fumed, giving off the smell of tar. Floodlights lit the silver fuselage of the plane and red, scrolled lettering toward the back that spelled out *Valentinois.*

Peyton stood beside her, surveying the plane. "This is weird."

"What?" she asked, pulling her backpack farther up her shoulders.

"I was born stupidly wealthy, have more money in my trust fund than I could spend in three lifetimes, and graduated from the most prestigious music conservatory in the world. I have been tapped as a classical soloist and, if I ever get a chance to sit in, could be a bona fide rock star. Yet, I feel inadequate."

Georgie laughed at him, keeping her voice low so Alexandre wouldn't hear. "It's good for you, Peys."

"Usually, when someone says that something is good for you, it sucks."

"Yep, that's true." She twisted his ring on her finger, not quite willing to take it off and hand it to him.

She was just about to turn and walk away.

She had Alexandre's sheet music, including a copy of that song that he called "Scrambled Eggs" because the lyrics continued to elude him, but she had nothing else to remind her of this life, just Peyton's ring and Alex's sheet music.

"Come on, let's get on His Grace Xan Valentine's ducal airplane," Peyton said.

"You aren't jealous, are you?" she joked, but she didn't step toward the plane.

"Hell, yeah," Peyton whispered, his head ducking near hers. "Every time he touches you, every time he tells you what to do, and especially every time he climbs up on stage and fucks you with his eyes."

"He does not," she protested.

"He does. Every damn show."

"He doesn't mean it."

Peyton snorted, something that he had never done in high school. "Sure, he doesn't. The Ice Princess wouldn't deign to notice, I guess. Come on, let's get on the plane."

"I'm not going," she said.

"I beg your pardon?" Peyton asked. His voice carried across the parking lot.

Paul, getting some bags out of the back of the car,

stood up to peer at them. Alexandre was stepping out of the front seat, and he turned toward them.

Peyton asked, still too damn loudly, "What do you *mean*, you're not *going?*"

The stale summer breeze carried his voice between the parked cars and to the small terminal.

She glanced back toward the car. Alexandre was already striding toward them, his arm still pressed to his heart.

She said, loud enough for them all to hear her, "I'm leaving now. I'm going to Atlanta, just as planned."

"Now?" Alexandre called across the parking lot as he walked toward her. "After all this?"

She faced him even though she would have rather slipped away. "I appreciate the rescue. I really do. Thank you for saving my life. Anything else I forgot?"

He stopped right in front of her. He held his right hand over his left hand, the damaged one, hiding it because it was pretty much at eye level for Georgie since she was wearing sneakers. Livid bruises crawled down his arm. He asked, "You're still leaving?"

"Nothing has changed." She started walking toward the private terminal, planning to call a cab to get to the main airport's terminals.

"You saw what they'll do if they catch you," he said.

She walked faster, as if that would keep the Russians from finding her. "I'm pretty sure they'll just shoot me next time. They must be done with the drama. My dead body will send a message to anyone else who was thinking about swindling them, anyone with kids, anyway."

"If you go to Atlanta, I won't be there to help you next time."

"If I hide, there won't be a next time."

"While you were with the band, they couldn't get you."

"They snatched me off the sidewalk, right in front of you."

"You left. No one was with you. Paul or someone else will *always* be with you, or others."

"They will *always* be able to get to me."

"So, don't leave *yet,*" he said.

"Why delay this?" she asked, slamming her heels into the asphalt as she marched. "Why make it worse? How will going back to Rome help this at all?"

"Not Rome," Alexandre said. "Montreux. We'll go to Montreux for Wulfram and Rae's religious wedding."

Georgie stopped walking. "You have a concert in Rome tonight."

"I'm cancelling it."

"Why?"

"Flicka called me yesterday," he admitted.

Oh, the machinations. Of course Princess Bossy-pants had read Machiavelli. No surprise, there.

Alexandre continued, "She was insistent that I cancel the concert in Rome to attend her brother's wedding."

"But the concert! Xan, you have to get on that plane and go."

Alexandre's lips parted, and he glanced back at Paul and Peyton, standing between the lined-up cars a few spaces away. "We'll need to cancel the concert anyway."

Georgie snagged her phone out of her pocket. The

screen glowed green numbers, *3:08,* three o'clock in the godforsaken morning, which meant that it was only eight in the morning in Rome. "You can get back in time for it. We've slid into town and onto the stage before. We do it all the time."

They stood in the circle of a harsh streetlight, and the moon glowed behind him. His eyes seemed impossibly dark. "I can't go on right now."

"Your hand?"

He hesitated, watching her, his dark eyes shining in the moonlight, and he nodded.

That didn't look right, but she wasn't sure why.

"Peyton can make the synthesizers play the bass lines," she reminded him. "The ones that I laid down are saved. He knows how to hit the buttons."

"Let's go to Montreux. We can make the wedding. You were going to go to the wedding before you left Europe, anyway. That's not changing your plans."

Oh, sure. It was just like Alex to use her own logic against her.

But he didn't sound like Alex, who had a droll, upper-crust British accent. Alexandre's soft French sibilances still blurred his words.

She made her voice firm. "Afterward, I'm getting on a plane and going to Atlanta. I swear to God that I will."

Alexandre leaned forward like he wanted to touch her, but his hands stayed tucked to his chest. *"D'accord."*

Georgie sighed. "I don't have anything to wear."

"We'll call Flicka. The designers adore her. She can summon clothes with a snap of her fingers."

Georgie smiled. "It's like she's a princess and a fairy godmother, all rolled into one."

"Don't say that around her. She thinks far too much of herself as it is."

Georgie allowed Alexandre to herd her toward the terminal. She got the feeling that he would have led her by the hand, except that both his hands remained clasped in front of himself. He did lower them to his stomach as they walked.

Peyton and Paul met them by the front doors.

"Change of plans," Alexandre said as Paul opened the door for him. "Tell Jacques to change the flight plan. We'll be heading to Montreux."

Paul nodded. *"Geneva Cointrin?"*

"Yes. And we'll need cars waiting for us. And a good tail wind."

"Yes, certainly." Paul's voice turned dry. "I'll just arrange for the winds to be favorable while Jacques rewrites pages of paperwork. And I'll need everyone's passport for a few minutes."

"In my rucksack in the forward cabinets," Alexandre said. He sat down in an overstuffed chair—a luxurious kind that would never be found in commercial terminal's waiting area—and leaned back, closing his eyes.

"Right. Georgie? Peyton?"

Georgie dug through her backpack. The little blue booklet had drifted down to the bottom under her clothes and the sheet music, and she dug through the soft fabric, chasing it to the bottom.

"Left it on the plane," Peyton told Paul.

"I'll have Jacques get it. Where?"

Peyton told him while Georgie handed over her passport. They all wandered a little way from Alexandre, whose breath was already evening out into sleep. It was three in the morning on the East

Coast, which was eight o'clock in the morning in Paris. They had all been awake more than a full day, and the weight of fatigue was grinding them all down.

Paul flipped through Georgie's passport and flicked it against his knuckles. "Shiny," he said. "Hopefully, Ned won't look too closely at it."

"It's real," she said. "I changed my name a few months ago and got a new one for the tour. Yvonne did the paperwork for me."

"Yvonne," Paul sighed. "Shit."

"What's wrong?"

Paul glanced over at Alexandre and ducked his head near Georgie. "Adrien and Yvonne had a *thing*, a long-standing flirtation, even though I'm pretty sure it was unrequited on his part."

"Oh, *no.*"

"I'll call her as soon as I get off the phone with Ned."

"How badly was Adrien hurt?"

Paul glanced at her. "I never found a pulse."

Her eyes burned harder than just the gritty fatigue, and she nodded.

Paul spread her passport on a table and suspended his phone between his long fingers to take a picture of it. "Hold that damn thing flat. Ned needs a clear image."

Georgie pressed the corners down with her fingertips. "Who is 'Ned,' anyway?"

"FBI," Paul said. "I was with Interpol for years. I have contacts in most federal police forces."

"Oh."

"It's good to have friends in high places."

"I guess so."

Paul sighed. His French accent strengthened as he whispered near her shoulder, "How bad is his hand?"

"He won't let me see it."

He nodded. "Adrien and I both signed on so he could continue to perform the violin, and we always assumed that he would get over this lark and go back to serious music. Maybe it's better that Adrien didn't live to see this."

"But Adrien might be okay. If he makes it to Greenwich, they can air-evac him to Yale. Yale can do anything." Georgie's passport flapped closed, and she stood. "And his hand just needs to be set. They'll set it and it'll heal, and it'll be fine, right?"

"Maybe so," he said. "All right. I've got the picture. I need to retrieve the other ones."

He wandered toward the plane. A man wearing a blue suit met him at the door and handed something small to him, probably Alexandre's and Peyton's passports. Paul walked over to a table and spread them open before holding his phone above them again.

Georgie settled herself beside Alexandre in another overstuffed chair. His hands still rested on his stomach, the right one covering the left.

By craning her neck, she could see through his fingers. His left hand was hideously swollen, and the skin was mottled livid red.

Fuck. She should have driven him straight to Yale, even if it had meant that Butorin's henchmen had dragged her away while he was in surgery. The fact that she had been outvoted was immaterial. She had been driving. Paul wouldn't have known that they were heading to Yale until it was too late.

Assuming that they hadn't read the signs that said they were entering New Haven rather than driving toward New Jersey or realized that they were going northeast instead of southwest.

Paul probably would have read the signs or the stars and figured it out in minutes.

She settled back in the chair and dozed for a few minutes, exhaustion overtaking her as soon as her head touched the chair.

Georgie awoke.

A woman's voice was speaking over the intercom system, "Mister Valentinois and company. Your flight has been cleared, and you may board your plane."

She struggled to sit up.

Paul stood in front of her, watching the other people in the terminal.

Peyton slumped in a chair beside her, asleep, his long legs splayed wide.

She jostled his shoulder. "Peys, time to go."

He squinted at her and rolled up, stretching his neck.

On the other side of her, Alexandre still slept.

Shaking either one of his shoulders might hurt his hand. The swollen skin hurt her to look at it. "Alexandre," she whispered and stroked his hair. "Time to wake up. Alexandre?"

He stirred, his face still impassive. Even when he sat up, curling his tall body, he didn't wince. "Let's go."

They walked across the tarmac to the plane. Warm summer air washed over them the whole way, and it felt like the air whirled around them too much because one of them was missing.

Peyton climbed the stairs to the plane behind her. "Bet you'll be glad to put all this traveling behind you," he said. "It'll be nice to stay in one place and have all your stuff where you know where it is. And not live out of a suitcase. I am so tired of these three pairs of pants."

Georgie laughed at him, but Alexandre looked back at them from the door of the plane. He wasn't exactly frowning, but one of his dark eyebrows dipped.

The chubby butler met her at the door. "Good evening, miss. May I?" He held out his hands for her backpack.

All her worldly possessions were in her backpack. Every last one of them. "I've got it. Thanks, anyway."

"As you wish. Can I get you a drink?"

"Oh, hell, yes. What have you got?"

"I'm sure this plane is stocked with just about everything that a rock star might require." His tone flattened with just the slightest bit of sarcasm.

"Scotch?" she asked.

"Shall I select a nice one for you, miss?"

"Sure. Thanks."

She dodged past him and was confronted with the conundrum of where to sit.

Alexandre was seated near a window, halfway back, at one of the table set-ups. He gazed out the porthole, maybe wistfully, she thought.

Sitting anywhere else would invite Peyton to sit next to her.

Georgie made her way halfway back through the plane and tossed her backpack into the chair opposite Alexandre. "Is it okay to sit here?"

"I was saving it for you."

The waiter guy brought her a drink and winked.

The smokey drink warmed her tongue and burned down her throat. "An emergency flight, and you brought your butler?"

"Adrien called him while we were on our way to the airport," Alexandre said.

Of course, *Adrien* had. What a fucking klutz, she was.

"Have you heard anything about Adrien?" Alexandre asked her.

"Nothing official," she said.

"What did Paul tell you?"

Georgie's eyes burned, and she blinked. "He doesn't know anything for sure."

Alexandre nodded. "I thought that might be the case." His voice was unnaturally soft. His face reflected in the plastic window, and his expression was as smooth as moonlight. He wasn't frowning or smiling.

He was so different than when Rade had died, but that had been Xan Valentine, the volatile rock star, not Alexandre. "Are you okay?"

He shrugged. "I'll be all right."

"Does your hand hurt?"

At this, he turned a smooth, slow pivot in the chair toward her. His calm eyes searched her face.

He nodded, just a slight dip of his chin.

Her heart hurt for him. "Oh, Alexandre."

"I'm fine."

"Don't you have a medical kit here or something? At least aspirin?"

He said, "I don't need it. I can sleep through it."

"*Aspirin* isn't going to make you groggy. You can't get addicted to *aspirin.* You should take some. Sir?" she called down the aisle, waving to get the butler-guy's attention.

He bustled back. "Yes, miss? Another drink?"

"Can we get some aspirin?"

The butler's wild eyebrows creased for a moment,

but then he looked over at Alexandre cradling his hand. "Sir?"

"There was a problem," Alexandre told him.

"Oh, no." He lowered himself into the other chair across the table from her. His dark eyes flicked from Alexandre's hand to his face. "Is there anything I can do?"

"I'm fine. *Merci, Guillaume."* Alexandre looked out the window again.

"Just the aspirin," Georgie said. "And preferably real aspirin. It's stronger than the other painkillers. A lot stronger."

The butler sighed. "It's his left hand, isn't it?" he asked Georgie.

Alexandre stared out the window, so Georgie nodded quickly to answer.

A crease of pain appeared between Guillaume's eyes. "I'll get some aspirin."

Guillaume hefted his body out of the chair and walked to the forward galley while the plane rolled back, rocking Georgie in her seat.

"Is there anything I can do?" she asked Alexandre.

He shook his head. "We only have a few hours before we get to Montreux. You should sleep. I have to call Jonas."

He swiveled away from her, still hiding his hand.

Georgie wasn't sure whether to force him to let her see it or not.

The body of the plane vibrated around them as the jet engines wound up.

It was too late, anyway. Their next stop was Montreux, Switzerland.

Alexandre turned back, his phone in his right hand. His left hand was on his other side, the side next to the curved wall of the airplane, and he had let it drop between his leg and the seat and under the table.

It must be really, really bad. Georgie didn't lean to see it, but she worried.

"Jonas," Alexandre said into the phone. His French accent softened the *J* at the beginning to a buzzing *jzhe* sound. He cleared his throat. "Jonas," and that time the *J* was harder, "we need to cancel the concert in Rome tonight."

His accent was more British, upper-crust and cultured—*to cahn-cel the concert*—his teeth barely opening as he spoke, but Georgie could still hear the soft slurs of French in there.

That was weird. His accents never mixed.

He was faking it.

A man's voice squawked from his phone like an angry parrot.

Alexandre replied, "There were many problems, actually. We're heading to Switzerland for tonight. I'm not sure where we'll be after that."

Jonas said something short and barky.

Georgie watched Alexandre's face. His dark eyes stared at the empty seat across the table from him, not even blinking.

"I wouldn't cancel it if I thought I could perform," he said.

More squawking from the phone. Man, Jonas was having a fit.

"I'm not sure about next week," Alexandre said. The phone edged away from his ear a little.

Georgie heard Jonas say, "You picked a shitty time to finally start taking care of yourself. Do you know how hard it is to book that particular recording studio? The only one that you think has 'superior acoustics?'"

"I'll call you when I know more."

Acceleration pressed Georgie to the seat as the plane sped down the runway.

"Must go. The plane is taking off."

"It's a private plane," Jonas said. "You can talk on a cell phone if you want to. You don't have to—"

Alexandre had hung up. He used his thumb to hold a button on the side to power down his phone and dropped it on the table.

Georgie reached over and held his uninjured hand.

His fingers gripped hers. Scabbed abrasions scraped the side of his hand, and the black plastic cable tie was still cinched around his wrist. The round loop of another zip tie dangled on the other side.

He hadn't broken the cable tie to free his hand.

He must have broken something else.

Georgie looked up at him, horrified. *"Oh."*

"Yes?" His query was still preternaturally calm.

So he obviously didn't want her to know how he had saved them. Or he didn't want anyone to know.

"You still have that zip tie on you," she said. "We'll have to get some scissors."

He nodded and leaned his head back against the seat.

The plane tilted off the rumbling ground and into the darkness. Georgie held his right hand as he dozed.

A few minutes later, Guillaume came back with the aspirin and a glass of water.

Alexandre took the aspirin from Guillaume with his right hand, popped them in his mouth, and drank the water to swallow them. "Do you have a few napkins, Guillaume?"

The butler nodded and hurried away. He returned with a small stack.

"Are you bleeding?" she asked.

He shook his head, his long hair fluttering around his jaw and shoulders. "Could I have a moment?"

"Um, sure."

Georgie walked up the aisle to the front of the plane.

Guillaume stood in the forward galley, leaning on the counter with his elbows, his face buried in his hands.

He stood as she stepped in. "Yes, Miss Georgiana?"

Echoes of voices from her childhood—chauffeurs and maids and nannies and instructors—ran through her head. Georgie asked him, "Do you by any chance have some snacks or something? I haven't eaten since before the concert yesterday."

Her stomach growled. It might have been to prove a point, and it might have been in horror at what Alexandre had done to himself. She felt like she might throw up stomach acid and bile.

"Of course," Guillaume said, toweling his hands. "Any preferences? We have a nice chicken Marsala with potatoes and salad, or I can fix you a sandwich of practically any sort."

"The dinner sounds great. I appreciate it."

"I'll bring it right around. Would His Grace like some supper?"

"I'm sorry. I didn't ask."

"He's always hungry. He gets on my plane and starts poking around my galley like he's still a teenager. I'll put it in front of him and see what happens."

Georgie started to return, but Guillaume touched her hand. "I didn't want to ask in front of everyone, but where's Adrien?"

She sucked in her lip.

"Oh," Guillaume said.

"He was taken to a hospital, but it didn't look good. They were doing chest compressions when we left, and we *had* to go."

Guillaume swallowed hard. "Thank you. It's better to know. I'll have your supper in a moment."

The plane vibrated through the floor under Georgie's feet. She meandered back down the slanting aisle of the plane, holding onto the seatbacks as the plane climbed into the air, but she could see that Alexandre was still concentrating and working with the napkins.

Closer, Peyton sat next to the window and was holding a large tumbler of clear liquid. Georgie asked him, "You okay?"

He raised the glass toward her. "Doing my best to get back to being a rock star."

"Looks like you're well on your way." She leaned on the seatback next to her, holding on. Under her elbows, the scrolled *V* monogram wound through the creamy leather.

"You'll probably be glad to be on your own again," Peyton said, his voice laughing with good humor, real humor. "The Ice Princess was always a soloist, right?"

"Thought that Ice Princess thing was just a joke," she said, adjusting her arms on the chair. "Because of the baby squirrel."

"Yes and no," he admitted. "Except for right before a performance in front of an audience, you were always the very definition of *sangfroid.* Some of those competitions were brutal, and you just walked up there in the prelims and played like you didn't give a damn what the judges thought. It was pretty spectacular. You used to play as aggressively as you drive. We used to joke that if you could harness that in front of an audience, the rest of us would be competing for second place our whole lives."

"Surely that's not true." She looked back into the plane.

Alexandre was watching her, one eyebrow lowered. He went back to working on his hand, and his face smoothed.

"Sure, it was true," Peyton said and sipped his drink. "I always respected that about you, and you understood what it means to sacrifice for music and art."

"Well, you have to," she said, watching Alexandre concentrate on tying a napkin with one hand. She turned back to Peyton.

Peyton stared toward the front of the plane, his teal-blue eyes becoming unfocused by unfinished dreams or the large glass of vodka he was holding. "I thought we would end up in a big house with two music rooms, each working on our own music during the day, traveling to our concerts and then returning to be together when we could. It seemed like the perfect life."

"Yeah, it sounds nice." Traveling by herself to play concerts sounded lonely.

"We could still do it."

"I'm going to Atlanta, Peys."

Peyton looked up at her, a secretive smile playing around the corners of his lush mouth. He reached up to the seatback and took her hand, pulling her down to sit beside him.

He whispered to her, his breath brushing her collarbone, "Let's ditch it all. I'll run away to Atlanta with you. You can go to law school, and I'll call the

L.A. Phil. to get my soloist gig back. I'll fly back to Atlanta in the summer and between concerts. We would be together, and you can be a lawyer and do what you think is right."

They could be together for the little time that he had off, when he wasn't traveling or playing in L.A.

She wanted to tell him that it could never happen, that too much time had gone by, that she didn't love him anymore, but she didn't know if that was true. She had missed Peyton so much for all those years, and every time she saw him, that old ache eased.

"You don't have to say anything now," Peyton said. "Think about it. I will go to Atlanta with you. We'll be together, just like it was always supposed to be, just like these years never really happened."

He touched the diamond ring on her right hand.

"Just move it over to your other hand. Later, I'll buy you anything you want, anything to symbolize that I still love you, that I've always loved you."

He wanted her to move it to her *left* hand.

Georgie glanced down the aisle to where Alexandre was bandaging his mangled left hand.

She rolled her long fingers into fists. "I need to think."

"Right," he said. Peyton dropped his head another inch and brushed his lips against her shoulder. Even through her tee shirt, his breath warmed her skin. "We'll talk later."

Georgie stood and fled down the aisle, bouncing between the seats as the plane bobbled in a little turbulence. She had to get back to Alexandre.

Halfway back, Alexandre was leaning back in his seat. He was as calm as ever, but he seemed paler than usual, even his lips.

White napkins wrapped his hand into a mass of fabric. The napkins were all pristine white. No blood was seeping through.

At the very least, it meant that he wasn't going to die of blood loss somewhere over the Atlantic Ocean, far away from any airports near hospitals they could have landed at.

"You okay?" she asked him.

"Fine," he said, a little breathlessly and without opening his eyes.

She slid into the seat beside him and held his other hand.

He didn't open his eyes, but he clutched her fingers. "Did you say yes?"

"To what?"

"Peyton Cabot."

Oh, God, he had heard it even over the roar of the plane's engines and while he had been bandaging his crushed hand. After being a rock star for four years, she was surprised he wasn't completely deaf. "No, I didn't."

"Are you going to?"

She wanted to get mad at him. She wanted to yell at him, asking what was in it for him if she did shack up with Peyton, because *Peyton* understood how important it was to her to be a lawyer and pay back all her father's victims. It wasn't like Alexandre was willing to let her go and be with her when he could, like he was willing to give one iota, because he didn't understand how it could be so important for her to do the honorable thing and make restitution to all those people.

He had dragged his injured hand off the table to lie in his lap, but the white bandages were still visible in the shadow.

And yet, he had come after her, and he had saved her.

So she couldn't be angry with him.

"I don't know what I'm going to do," she said. "It's complex."

"What do you want to do?" he asked her.

Tour.

The word echoing in her mind shocked her.

Tour with you.

She wanted to be in Xan's bed—a different bed every night—and she wanted to blaze in the spotlights and make music with him.

Tour with you and make music and never stop.

It took her breath away, and she couldn't make herself say it.

"You don't know," Alexandre said.

She nodded because she couldn't speak.

"All right," he breathed.

She told him, "Let me see your hand."

"It's fine."

"Let me see it."

Alexandre lifted his hand slowly from the chair seat beside him and laid it on the table. The white napkins wrapped around his hand were tied in loose and uneven knots like a ball of laundry was eating his hand.

She said, "I can tie it a little better."

"It's fine."

"I did Girl Scouts when I was little. Did you use a splint of some sort?"

"I rolled up napkins to support it underneath."

"And padded between your fingers?"

"Yes."

"That's good. You tied these knots with just your other hand?"

"And my teeth."

"So resourceful of you." Yeah, she was babying him a little. "I'll take off just the outer layer and retie it to make sure it's secure."

"Just the outer layer," he confirmed.

"Yeah." Georgie picked out the loose knots and took seven napkins off, leaving the rolled ones he was using as splints and padding and the last one covering his hand.

"Stop there," he said.

"I am. I'll just tie these a little more neatly." Very carefully, slowly, she wrapped two napkins around his hand, securing them with tight knots at the very corners of the napkins. When she was done, the makeshift bandage was a lot smaller and neater. "Is that okay? Do you want another one?"

"This is fine. It supports the hand better."

"Is the aspirin kicking in?"

"It is." He lifted his hand and examined it. "It feels better. Thank you."

"Oh, it's fine. I'm glad it feels better."

He leaned his head back against the seat. "I'm used to taking care of myself."

Georgie tucked a strand of his hair that had come loose from his ponytail behind his ear.

Alexandre reached with his good hand and found her fingers, holding her hand on the table top, and closed his eyes.

He held her hand until his fingers loosened and his breathing evened out in sleep.

Guillaume brought their supper just minutes later

and tilted his head, looking at Alexandre. "If he wakes up, call me, and I'll heat this up for him."

She nibbled some of the steaming chicken Marsala, the wine and butter sauce mixing with the bitter taste on her tongue. Her whole body felt raw on the inside from the vodka and the acid pouring into her stomach while she had been held hostage. Georgie leaned her seat back as they flew across the Atlantic.

The lights dimmed as everyone settled down.

This night, flying over the dark seas to Switzerland, was almost her last night with Alexandre. After the wedding, they might spend one last night together. Perhaps she might sit by his hospital bed if he had surgery the next day.

Yes, she would. She had to make sure that he was all right.

She didn't want to miss a moment of these last few hours, but she was so tired and sore that she drifted away through the night.

Chapter Eleven

MONTREUX

Georgie

Alexandre clattered down the steps from the airplane after Georgie, saying, "We'll call Flicka and have her meet us at the church. The wedding won't start for an hour after we're scheduled to get there. We can change in the back rooms. We'll be fine."

A bruise was developing on his jaw under a day's dark growth of beard.

Georgie skipped down the steps, her tennis shoes tapping each step. Her long braid of unwashed hair fell down her back. She had changed into her only other set of clothes, another pair of jeans and a red tee shirt, but she hadn't had a chance to clean up because the Gulfstream didn't have a shower and a water heater like the Boeing did.

Peyton trotted down the stairs right after them. "I'll see you guys at the hotel."

"Aren't you going?" Georgie asked him. She gripped the sides of her phone and powered it on.

Peyton shrugged. "I don't know Flicka's brother or his wife."

"Oh, yeah. I guess not." She glanced at her phone. *"Fuck.* Alex? *Alex?"*

"Alex?" Peyton laughed. "I guess *you* can call him that."

Alexandre turned as she pattered up to him.

Georgie said, "It's not three o'clock here. It's *four.* We did the math wrong. Rae's wedding is starting in half an hour, and we're an hour away from Montreux."

"And we're not near the autobahn," Alexandre muttered and grabbed her hand with his good one. "And we don't have a helicopter pilot. We'll just have to drive and hope we make good time. Maybe we can slip in at the end. At least we'll get to the reception."

"Shit," Georgie said. In her hand, her phone blurred, and she wiped her eyes with the back of her hand. "I'm sorry. I just screw everything up."

"It's been a rough couple of days." Alexandre wrapped his arm around her and nudged, encouraging her to speed up. "Come on. We'll see what we can do. Paul?"

"Right behind you," Paul said.

Alexandre led Georgie to a waiting sedan and climbed in the back seat with her. She scooted over to sit behind the driver's seat, careful not to touch the makeshift bandage on his hand.

Alexandre asked, "Can you think of any other options, Paul?"

Paul shook his head. "Not without notice, no."

"Then let's go. The Hannovers are Lutheran, right? All Lutheran weddings start at least an hour late."

"Really?" Georgie asked, her voice squeaking at the top with hope.

"I made that up," he admitted. "Let's go, Paul."

Paul swung the car out of the parking spot and sped for the highway.

Georgie bounced off the upholstered side and grabbed the door handle, frantically keeping herself from falling on Alexandre's injured hand that lay on the seat between them. The thought of falling on his crushed bones and flesh and the pain it would cause him nauseated her.

Alexandre had his phone in his other hand and was searching on his browser with his thumb. "They took Adrien to Greenwich Hospital, right?"

Georgie nodded. When she glanced up, Paul's brown eyes were watching Alex through the rearview mirror.

Alexandre tapped the screen. "Hello? I need to check on the status of a patient, Adrien Girard Roche. He was brought there by ambulance early this morning." He paused. "I should be listed as an emergency contact in his wallet, Alexandre Grimaldi de Valentinois." He paused. "Yes, Valentin-*oys.* Can you tell me his condition?"

Georgie watched him, sitting just two feet away on the back seat of the car.

The engine surged as Paul passed a car and broke out of a traffic cluster, the acceleration pressing her back against the seat.

A tiny voice spoke, audible even over the roar of

the engine. The downward cadences sounded like bad news.

Georgie reached over and touched Alexandre's knee.

Alexandre's expression didn't move, not at all, not even the tiny quirks and tics and blinks that make a person look alive instead of like a picture. He had just stopped.

Under Georgie's hand, even his leg was as still as stone.

The car sped through the Swiss city, dodging traffic, but he didn't move, like it all passed through him and around him.

Alexandre finally took a breath. "I see. Thank you for the information."

He lowered the phone to his leg.

Georgie reached over and pressed the red bar across the screen to end the call. "Are you okay?"

"Yes," Alexandre said.

Georgie swayed as Paul zoomed the car around a truck and opened up the throttle on a long stretch of highway.

Paul asked, "Adrien?"

"He didn't make it," Alexandre said, his voice flat.

"I'm sorry," Georgie said, her heart pulling in her chest.

The car swerved under them within the lane, but Paul corrected it.

Alexandre nodded. "Do we need to pull over for a minute, Paul?"

"I'm all right to drive," Paul said. "Should we pull over anyway?"

"We can continue."

"All right."

Alexandre stared out the front window, still as granite, not even blinking. His only movement was a slight turn of his head and dip of his chin to the left. His left hand, still wrapped in the white napkins, didn't move on the seat between them.

Paul swung the car through a thick spot of traffic and gunned the engine again.

"The car feels unbalanced," Alexandre said. "The tire noise is the wrong color. The air tastes wrong."

The monotone in his voice didn't sound like the whine of complaining, not at all.

Georgie was careful not to brush his left hand, and she wrapped her arms around his stiff body.

Warmth touched the top of her head.

When she glanced up, she could see that Alexandre had laid his cheek against her, pressing the violin callus on his jaw to her hair.

Chapter Twelve

THE COLOR OF MOURNING

Alexandre Grimaldi

The color of mourning should have been darkness, a deafening fog that shut down his eyes, but a cutting light stabbed through Alexandre.

The noise of the tires grating on the road spiked in his ears, the car unbalanced by the lack of Adrien weighing it down. Plastic chemicals fumed from the upholstery and trims in the new car, the colors of harsh desert sunlight glaring on alpine snow.

The grinding broken-bone pain in his hand was a constant piercing in his flesh.

A part of his body was missing. He was truncated, the antique wood and varnish that completed him had fallen away, and emptiness ached near his throat.

Colors sliced inside him, stuck like knives in bone.

Softness touched his side.

The last traces of mint wafting through the scent

of a warm woman shaded him, cooling his burning skin.

Alexandre laid his cheek on her soft hair, feeling the softness, the cool touch of her, a dimming of the pain.

In front of him, the road raced through the front windshield as Paul drove them toward Flicka's brother's wedding.

Alexandre wasn't sure how he would be able to stand it, talking to people while Adrien's looming void spiraled around him.

Alex Valentinois, his first mask, could have attended that wedding and said all the right things. Xan Valentine could have charmed everyone.

Alexandre could have walled the pain off from either one of them and let them walk through the world while he mourned.

But they were gone.

Chapter Thirteen

THE WEDDING OF WULF AND RAE

Georgie

The car screeched to a stop in front of the Swiss cathedral. Gothic spires needled the summer sky. Late afternoon sunlight stroked the underside of wispy clouds and made them glow.

Traffic honked and veered around the car. Paul jammed the stick into park. *"Go."*

"You don't have to go in," Georgie told Alexandre, grabbing at the door handle but missing with her first two tries. She flipped her long braid over her shoulder. Wisps of brown hair were escaping each plait so that it looked furry. She should have wet it down and rebraided it in the plane's lavatory. "You can stay here. It'll be okay. I'm just going to slip in the back and sit in the last row."

"I'll go with you. I knew Wulfram a little bit from

school." Alexandre stepped out of his side and ran around the car, catching Georgie's hand in his good one as they bounded up the church steps. The falling sun behind them warmed her back through her red tee shirt and heated her butt through her jeans.

Georgie glanced down at her clothes, wishing fervently that she had at least slipped a sundress in her backpack when she had taken off yesterday, even though Boris had not bought her a casual sundress while she had been touring with Killer Valentine because she never wore such girlie-girl things. She said, "We'd better slip out as soon as we see them kiss."

"Europeans don't kiss," Alexandre told her, holding her hand up as they reached the top. "It will be fine. No one will see us."

The church's golden wood doors loomed over them, stretching up through the towering stones of the cathedral.

"Of course the Hannovers needed an enormous church," Alexandre muttered. "He's related to everyone."

"To you?" Georgie asked.

"Only through Flicka and Pierre's marriage," he said, grasping the long handle in his right hand, testing the carved metal. "The Hannovers are royalty. None of them would have married into Monaco's line of mere princes except for love."

"Wulfram is marrying Rae, and she's a dirt rancher," as Rae had described herself on many occasions.

"Must be love." Alexandre yanked the thick door.

The enormous carved-wood door, which must have weighed hundreds of pounds, had been hung with loaded hinges, set with thick springs.

It smashed open, crashing against the wall. Alexandre stumbled back with it but kept his footing on the stone steps.

Light from the setting sun behind them poured through the door and into the dim church, outshining the hundreds of candles and tiny glowing fairy lights and silhouetting Georgie in her jeans and tee shirt with a long braid knotted down her back.

Her shadow cut the brilliant light and pointed down the blue aisle carpet straight toward the altar at the front. Incense smoke drifted toward her, a sweet smell almost like the dorms at Southwestern State.

The people in the church turned and stared at her.

Georgie was praying that the priest hadn't just asked if anyone knew why the marriage should not take place.

Rumbling and rustling, and all the guests turned in their seats to stare at Georgie.

At the altar, the woman in the white dress—who was definitely Georgie's friend Rae Stone though a bit more voluptuous than when Georgie had last seen her —raised her hand to her brow, right in front of the glittering tiara and long veil she wore in her curling auburn hair.

Rae squinted into the sunlight. *"Georgie?"* she called through the murmuring church.

Georgie waved weakly. So much for slipping in casually.

Up at the front, a tiny blonde stood next to Rae.

Lizzy, their mutual friend and Georgie's dorm roommate until a few months ago when she had run away with Alex and Killer Valentine, wore a slim ivory dress. She started laughing.

Beside Lizzy, the tall, willowy blonde was Flicka, Wulf's sister, also wearing creamy white. Her Royal Highness Bossypants leaned over Lizzy's head and whispered something to Rae. Lizzy looked up at the conspiracy above her.

Rae's head popped up like she had heard the most excellent idea. She shoved her green and white bouquet at Lizzy, who juggled it with her own, and —*dear God, no*—Rae marched down the aisle toward Georgie.

The rustling of ivory silk filled the cathedral as she flounced past the rows upon rows of wedding guests, a bobbing field of men's heads and pastel hats. Rae held handfuls of her skirt, swishing as she walked. Sunlight shined on the delicate shimmer of seed pearls embroidered on the fabric.

Alexandre angled himself in front of Georgie, trying to protect her even from an irate, slightly pregnant bride, but Georgie guided him back.

She braced herself to be slapped. She had ruined Rae's wedding by barging in. She deserved it. Georgie closed her eyes to wait for it.

Georgie's hand lifted, and her arm jerked forward.

"What?" Georgie asked, stumbling after Rae.

"I thought you weren't going to come," Rae said, smiling back at her and holding her hand while she tugged Georgie's arm.

"You would not believe what I went through the last couple days to get to your wedding," Georgie said. Tears burned in her eyes, and the church turned watery in her vision.

"Come on." Rae pulled harder at Georgie's hand.

Georgie set her heels into the carpeting, balking. "What are you doing?"

"I want you to be my bridesmaid."

"I'm wearing jeans!" Georgie said, gesturing to her red tee shirt, messy braid, and barely washed face. "I'll just sit back here."

Georgie started to turn to slide into a pew, but her leg hung in mid-air as Rae pulled her toward the front of the church.

Rae announced to everyone in the whole damn church, "Clothes don't matter. People do."

Georgie stumbled after her. She knew better than to argue with Rae when she went all Westerner like that. Georgie was liable to get threatened with a branding iron or a cast iron frying pan if she didn't get her tarnation up there, or however Rae would say it.

Behind her, the sound of many shoes pattered. Georgie glanced back.

People were shuffling over, letting Alexandre sit in the aisle seat of a pew. He slouched in the bench, his long leg jutting into the aisle. Hanks of his long hair had escaped the elastic that bound his ponytail and hung around his face.

Georgie should have helped him with that.

The man next to him whispered something, and Alexandre replied, "Bar fight."

Rae led Georgie up the long aisle between all the people dressed in what Georgie recognized were designer suits and dresses. As the wedding was a late afternoon affair, attire was more formal than for a morning ceremony. Plus, it was an honest-to-God royal wedding, and that meant that people were wearing elegant, restrained, simply lovely clothes.

Georgie's jeans were Levi's, and faded ones at that. An old stain splotched pink on one of her thighs. Probably red wine.

So fucking sophisticated.

Loyalty to her best friend kept Georgie from escaping and sprinting for the door, but it was a close fight.

Up at the front, on the right side of the priest, Wulfram von Hannover, the groom and Georgie's old friend, stood with three other men in the tallest, blondest line of men that she had ever seen. The symmetry was broken only by one Asian man who was looking at the floor to hide his laughter.

The middle man, closest to Wulfram himself, was the gray-eyed man who had been on the plane after Rae's first wedding, Dieter the Meatier. The Asian guy was still laughing but looking up and wiping his eyes, even though his chuckles were entirely silent. The last man in the line looked eerily familiar, another blue-eyed blonde, and seemed gently amused about everything he was seeing.

Wulfram von Hannover, with his dark blue eyes and hard-cut jaw and cheekbones, stood with his hands folded in front of himself, smiling his usual cold smile and waiting for his bride to finish whatever this was.

"I don't know about this," Georgie said.

"I didn't ask you earlier because Flicka said that Alexandre is a slavedriver and wouldn't let you come. I didn't want to make you feel bad if you couldn't make it."

"I don't want to ruin your pictures."

"Not having you in them would be worse. Flicka has a dress for you for the formal shots. I'm so glad you're here."

Georgie admitted, "I wouldn't have missed it for the world."

"I almost did," Rae said in far too nonchalant a

tone. "You would not believe some of the insanity going on around here. We were almost an hour late starting."

"Is that because they're Lutherans?" Georgie whispered to her.

Rae stopped walking and stared at her. "What?"

"Nothing. Nevermind. Congratulations, Rae."

Georgie hugged her friend, stretching up to reach Rae's shoulders, and Rae hugged her back. "I'm so glad you could make it."

"I'm so glad I'm here."

Rae sniffed Georgie's hair. "You smell like gunpowder."

"I'll tell you all about it later."

"I will hold you to that, missy. Go stand by Flicka."

Flicka was holding out her hand, and Georgie took her fingers as she filed into place between HRH Bossypants and tiny little Lizzy. Flicka's ivory opera glove was such soft silk that threads caught on Georgie's writing callus.

Beside her, Lizzy gave Rae back her bouquet and whispered up at Georgie in her gravelly little voice, "Took you long enough."

Georgie mock-frowned at her. "Killed at least two people to get here. What did you do to prove your love?"

"Got my ass to the church on time."

Flicka shushed them both.

Georgie stood with her hands folded in front of her while the priest began to speak about the sanctity of marriage.

Lizzy glanced back at Georgie, looking her up and down.

Yeah, she was a mess. Damn, fifteen minutes

sooner and she might have been able to change clothes, at least.

Lizzy held her bouquet up to her mouth and used her teeth to rip the ribbon around the stems so she could divide the mass of white jasmine and lily of the valley. She shoved half of the flowers at Georgie. A few delicate stalks drifted to the blue carpeting near Georgie's tennis shoes.

With the flowers drooping over her knuckles, Georgie felt better. The sweet scent of the jasmine filled her nose like summertime in the Southwestern deserts.

She glanced back into the church, hoping for a glimpse of Alexandre.

The ladies were wearing hats, probably all from designer milliners—Georgie almost snorted at remembering her mother's intense relationship with her milliner—and the pastel rounds wove and bobbed.

Georgie raised to her toes just a little to see over them. The waving field of hats parted like a breeze had rippled across them.

Far back in the church, Alexandre was rising from where he sat, and he lowered himself to his knees. His left hand, still swaddled in napkins, was pressed against his chest again. He bowed his head, holding onto the back of the pew in front of him with his one good hand. The darker hair near the crown of his head shaded to blond ends as waves fell around his face.

He bent and rested his forehead on the pew in front of him.

The man next to him, a guy their age whom Georgie vaguely recognized from Flicka's wedding months ago, patted Alexandre on the back and then rested his hand there.

Georgie watched her friend Rae marry Wulfram, but she kept glancing back at Alexandre to make sure he was all right.

Chapter Fourteen

GETTING HITCHED

Rae Stone-von Hannover

In this moment, this tremulous moment, I have everything that I want: my husband before me, holding my hands, all my friends around me (even the one we couldn't find for a while,) and my cousin over on the side of the church, holding up his cell phone to livestream my wedding to my mother (who is hiding in the barn to watch,) and a child growing inside me.

The autism clinic that I used to doodle about in boring lectures will break ground in a few weeks. When I finish college, I will turn the key to the front door and walk in.

I have love, I have good work, and I have my life. I am free and yet I am held and loved.

My most desperate, impossible hopes have become my future.

Chapter Fifteen

VIGILANT

Wulf von Hannover

I hold her hands in this impossible moment, a moment that I never thought I would see, and my heart is full.

Beyond Rae—my Rae, my wife—my sister Flicka is smiling at me. The child that I raised from kindergarten is a young woman and married. She doesn't need me anymore, which means that I did well. I used to pray that I would live until she could take care of herself.

Now, Rae is giving me another chance to be a father. This time, I will watch the child grow from infancy. Every day that I see changes in Rae is a revelation. Every moment is a prayer.

I am vigilant, listening for the click of a hammer or the lens flare from a telescopic sight, but there is nothing, nothing but music and light glowing from the candles and tiny lights and her small hands in mine.

I had been a ghost, but now I am alive.
And, God help me, I feel like I might live.

Chapter Sixteen

RECESSIONAL

Georgie

The priest—or minister or reverend or whatever the Protestant heathens called their clergy—pronounced Rae and Wulfram to be man and wife, which amused Georgie no end because the two of them had been legally married for months. And living together. And Rae was very slightly visibly preggers.

Rae turned, holding her face up to the candlelight and sparkling fairy lights sprinkled into the summer foliage that decked the church.

Wulfram kissed her.

See? They kissed.

Rae had probably told him to just kiss her, dammit. A weddin' wasn't complete without the kissin', or something pithy and earthy like that.

Yeah, that was probably what had happened.

Just a few months ago, Georgie had been sitting

with Rae in their dorm room. Rae had been crying her eyes out because she had thought that she should go back to her cultish family that would eventually excommunicate her again rather than stay with the man she loved and who loved her. Georgie had given her the best advice that she had had, which was to do the right thing, and the right thing was love.

The church and the couple blurred, and Georgie ducked her head to wipe her eyes on her shoulder, darkening her red cotton tee shirt.

Hey, that was one advantage to having no time for even the most rudimentary makeup. No mascara blobs were going to run down her face and tattle that the Ice Princess had been blubbering at a wedding.

Their situation was different than her own, of course. Because Rae had taken a chance on love, she had gotten the man and her dreams of helping autistic kids with that clinic that she had been prattling about for years. Her choice had been between everything and nothing.

Georgie's choice had always been between doing what was right and doing what was selfish and hedonistic and callous.

Wulfram and Rae turned and walked down the aisle together while the string quartet in the choir loft played. Georgie wondered for a moment what Alexandre thought of how the first violinist was playing, but then her throat pinched.

When she looked back, Alexandre was standing, but his bandaged hand was still clutched to his chest. It was going to be a while before his hand healed enough to play the violin again.

Lizzy followed, and Dieter the Meatier met her at the aisle and offered the tiny blonde his arm.

The Asian guy, who was about the same height as Georgie in her tennis shoes, met her at the altar and gallantly offered her his elbow with a small bow. His other arm hung loosely at his side. His huge grin was unperturbed, as if royal weddings were interrupted by scruffy friends every day.

"Thank you," she whispered as they walked past the first few pews.

"I think it's beautiful, that you came running in to be here for her," he said. "I'm Yoshi, friend of the groom."

"I'm Georgie. Rae is my college suitemate and friend. How do you know Wulfram?"

"I took a bullet for Prince Brilliant when we were nine."

Georgie grinned back at him. "Prince Brilliant? We must talk more later."

Behind her, Georgie heard Flicka whisper to the guy walking with her, "You know, Rae calls her cousins, 'Cuz,' like a familial title."

"'Cuz,'" repeated the man, very quietly, almost under his breath. "I like that. We should call each other Cuz." His low voice was very British, as cultured as Alex de Valentinois's when he was in his French Duke mode.

Flicka chuckled. "What will Kate think of that?"

"Kate will take video and play it for her parents, I presume."

"I am going to call you Cuz in front of your grandmother."

"She won't deign to know what it means. I will call you Cuz next summer in Hannover for her birthday, right in front of your father."

"I will tell Harry about it the next time he's wasted, and he will call everyone Cuz."

When Georgie and Yoshi reached Alexandre, halfway back in the church, Alexandre stood and held out his hand, and Yoshi relinquished Georgie's arm.

Alexandre bowed from the waist—awfully courtly for a fucking rock star—and offered her his elbow. She was on his right side, his good arm, so she slid her hand under his arm for the last few yards before they emerged into the sunset outside the church. The jasmine flowers cooled her other hand and dampened her palm.

God, what a ragtag couple they were, beat-up and exhausted and reeking of gunsmoke and adrenaline, but maybe that was, indeed, rock and roll.

Chapter Seventeen

SECURITY DETAILS

Alexandre Grimaldi

Georgie's hand tucked under his arm, and she smiled up at him with that ironic little half-smile that only curved one side of her mouth. He wasn't sure that she knew she did that, but it amused him no end. Despite the trauma to his hand and his soul, he managed a wan smile back.

Now, both sides of her sweet little mouth smiled at him.

Even better.

They walked through the candlelit church arm-in-arm, tattered and stumbling, but they managed it. The muttering and clattering rose in gray sparks around him.

During the ceremony, after he had fallen to his knees in a fruitless attempt to empty the desperate grief in his heart, he had taken dim notice of the wedding. It had been a beautiful ceremony, much more personal than Flicka's wedding.

Wulfram von Hannover was thought to be a recluse due to the childhood incident and his security measures ever since, but this wedding had seemed to Alexandre to be less like a religious rite and more like theater. With the music and the flowers and the vows, it felt like art.

It felt like a celebration of what made them and Alexandre himself human, and that was love.

And now, seeing Georgie holding onto his arm even after all they had been through in the last few days, parts of him began to mend back together, to hold on, to become more human.

It was a healing, this theater of love.

It wasn't just a legal piece of paper. It wasn't just a religious rite. It was art, and art is meant to be shared.

If no one listens, it isn't music.

If no one sees, it isn't theater.

If it doesn't communicate, it isn't art.

And people did see. They had seen Wulfram and Rae, and now they were seeing Alexandre and Georgie as they walked out of the church and into the swelling major chords of the setting sun, something which he hadn't considered.

If he had let Georgie pass with a nod, she probably would have been mollified and his friends would have either not noticed anything that happened that night at the reception or not taken it as significant.

When they reached the church doors and Alexandre glanced back, his own cousin Pierre was walking behind Flicka and her cousin William, who were still trying to crack each other up in public. They both remained as serene as moonlight on still water, properly smiling and nodding at the wedding guests as they strolled out, despite threatening mayhem to each other.

Pierre, the gossip, would tell everyone back home about Alexandre swooping in to retrieve the common girl who had intruded on the Hannover wedding from Yoshi, as if she mattered.

He tightened his arm, drawing Georgie's hand closer to his side, and smiled down at her again.

Let them talk.

They broke out of the dim church into the setting sun. Bright white light flashed in his eyes with the sour tang of sulfur and a flatted flash of a fifth that broke the symphony of the sunlight.

The wedding photographer, working to catch them in all their glory, snapped pictures with a fat-lensed camera. She walked around them to get several angles, including the rip in the sleeve of his black tee shirt where one of Butorin's *bratva* men had grabbed him before Alexandre had punched him. The photographer got a lovely shot of him clutching his wrapped hand to his chest like an invalid before she moved on to photograph Flicka and William coming out the doors.

Alexandre and Georgie meandered off to the side of the wide stone steps.

Paul jogged up to them. "I've contacted Wulfram's security. Georgie will be under their umbrella while I take you to hospital. They're good. I've informed them that she'll need extra precautions and why." He turned to Georgie. "You'll be riding with the Prince and Princess to their hotel after the formal pictures. We managed to get rooms there, too."

No fucking way was Alexandre letting Georgie get

in the back of a car with Pierre Grimaldi, even if Pierre's wife Flicka was sitting right there with them. He knew his older cousin Pierre far too well, the Rat Bastard.

Alexandre asked Paul, "The Prince and Princess of—?"

"Hannover," Paul assured him. "The Prince and Princess of *Hannover."*

Alexandre nodded. As long as it wasn't his own predatory cousin. "Their security is good?"

"They've hired a private firm for extra manpower. They have a small army here. Do you see those guys?" He gestured at the rooftop of the columned town hall across the plaza.

Small figures dressed in black held long sticks pointing at the front of the church.

"You're sure those snipers are his?" Alexandre asked, stepping in front of Georgie. Behind his back, he heard a small, "Hey!"

"He assures me they are." Paul leaned to talk to Georgie around Alexandre. "You're supposed to change clothes for pictures. Friedhelm Vonlanthen will take you from here."

Another man joined them. His sandy brown hair seemed too shaggy for a security guy. "Miss Johnson? We can take you around to the changing rooms."

Georgie said, "I remember you from Paris. You drove Lizzy and me from the airport to the hotel."

The security guy smiled at her, and Alexandre didn't like his overly familiar leer or the way he leaned at her. "I remember it."

Georgie tugged on Alexandre's arm. "You'll be all right?"

"I'll see you at the reception, if not sooner. This shouldn't take long," he lied.

Her hand dropped away from Alexandre's elbow, and she walked around the church with Vonlanthen, her lithe body swaying in the dark shadows.

Alexandre's side felt cold without her, like he was partially blind in that one eye.

Paul said, "The other guests are starting to come out of the church. If you don't want to be swarmed and have to answer a lot of questions, I'd suggest we go to the hospital now. I saw Moririshi Morimoto over on the other side."

Alexandre did not want to explain how injured his hand was to the conductor of the Tokyo Philharmonic, who would doubtless have many, many questions and even more opinions on the matter. "Let's go."

Chapter Eighteen

WEDDING PICTURES

Georgie

As soon as Georgie walked into the church's side door, a swarm of ladies descended upon her, pulling her away from Friedhelm the security guy and into a back room. She caught one last look at his grin as he took out his phone and leaned against the wall to wait.

The women worked like interlocking machines.

One lady grabbed Georgie's braid, finger-combed her hair free, and began brushing out the snarls. Another lady water-boarded her with makeup towelettes to clean her face, patted her skin dry, and started wiping on powder-scented moisturizer and then primer.

When the hair stylist worked around to Georgie's front, the makeup artist ducked and continued working. When the makeup artist rose up to work on

Georgie's eyes, the hairstylist rotated around but kept ratting Georgie's hair without missing a beat. They chattered in what Georgie presumed was French the whole time.

Flicka must have trained them to do this, somehow. Their synchronization was not natural.

They tugged Georgie out of the chair, stripped her tee shirt off without smearing her makeup or nudging her hair, and shoved her jeans down her thighs. Georgie hopped out of her pants, and they handed her pantyhose and began preparing the slim, white dress that hung near the back of the room.

Damn. If she had still been with Killer Valentine, she would have hired these ladies to tour with her. She could have done nine costume changes per show with this kind of efficiency.

Georgie stood with the pantyhose on, and the ladies whisked the dress onto her, buttoned the thousands of little buttons up the back so fast that it felt like a zipper being pulled up, and showed her a row of five pairs of identical shoes, waiting for her to pick her size.

The door opened, and Flicka leaned against the doorjamb, surveying. She smiled.

The ladies redoubled their efforts, showing Georgie the shoes and telling Flicka something in very rapid French.

Lord, Almighty. When Flicka decreed that you would get dressed, you got *dressed.* You had to admire that.

Georgie tried on the middle pair of pumps, too small, and went up one pair from that. They fit perfectly, rather like Cinderella if the handsome prince had had a selection of glass slippers to make damn sure that one of them had fit her.

And if the handsome prince was actually a bossy-pants princess.

Flicka glanced at her phone and said something in French.

The ladies cheered like they had won the lottery.

Georgie suspected they had.

"Come on," Flicka said. "The photographer is waiting for us."

Georgie followed Flicka through the church, trailed by Friedhelm and two more black-suited guys whom he seemed to have picked up.

Georgie posed for all the photos with the wedding party as if she had actually gotten her butt to the church on time and had been dressed appropriately. Indeed, truth be told, the ladies had done such an excellent job with the makeup that Georgie was trying to figure out how to shower before the reception but not mess any of it up.

Yoshi told her that she looked delightful and then pressed her for details about Alexandre. "He was quite a lot younger than we were at school, but I knew him because he was driven to music with Flicka."

Georgie looked at her white high-heeled shoes. "Yeah. I don't know much about that time of his life."

"I heard he's a rock star in the States."

"Something like that." She was so guarded when anyone asked questions about Alexandre, even with Yoshi, who seemed guileless.

"That's wonderful," Yoshi said. "I love happy endings."

After the pictures, Flicka told Georgie, "I have a dress for you for the reception in my suite at the hotel. I have a tuxedo for Alex, too, and his other things."

"You have saved my ass," Georgie told her.

"Nope," Flicka said. "You're still hanging out with Alex de Valentinois, so your butt isn't safe at all. Is he playing that violin around you?"

She must not have seen the napkins splinting Alexandre's hand during the wedding. It would probably be six weeks until the bones knit enough for the cast to come off, maybe two months.

Georgie said, "Not for a while."

Chapter Nineteen

CHANGE OF PLANS

Georgie

Friedhelm told Georgie that she was to ride to the hotel with Rae and Wulfram von Hannover.

At the curb in front of the church, Georgie lifted the hem of her white dress and stumbled back to the far-rear seat of the black SUV with Friedhelm. A line of black-suited men directed Rae and Wulf to the middle seat. Dieter the Meatier rode shotgun and another of the hunky security guys drove.

Georgie settled herself in the back and found the seatbelt. Latching it around herself instantly wrinkled the white silk dress.

In front of Georgie, as soon as Rae sat down, Wulf put his arm around her and drew her close to him, an astonishingly demonstrative move for him. Georgie tried not to gape.

Rae muttered to him, "You're doing it again."

"And now you have to put up with it forever," Wulfram said, nuzzling her hair.

"Come on," Rae said. "Everything's fine."

Wulfram cradled Rae closer to himself, and she squirmed around in the seat to get comfortable.

Georgie watched them, reminded of trips on the tour bus before she had been an official band member and thus officially, contractually, off-limits to Xan Valentine, the lead singer. They had passed the miles with his strong arms around her, talking about music, working on his songs. He had laid his cheek against her hair while they talked.

They had never finished that song, "Scrambled Eggs."

Maybe someday, Killer Valentine would record it, and she would hear whatever words he had finally written, wherever she was.

Their black SUV drove through the slim streets of Montreux and out of town with more black SUVs leading and trailing them. Sunlight sparkled on the lakes and green fields clinging to the mountains outside.

She tightened the seatbelt around her stomach when her phone rang, buzzing in her hand. It was a number that she didn't recognize.

Tatiana Butorin had always called from an unknown number and then threatened Georgie's life and sanity over the cell phone.

Georgie looked at Friedhelm and caught his eye as she thumbed the phone and answered it. "Hello?"

Friedhelm leaned toward her, his brown eyes intent.

A man's voice said in a French accent, "Georgie?" He slurred the G's in her name to *zhuh*-sounds just like Alexandre did. "This is Paul Chevalier. His Grace has been seen by the surgeons."

Friedhelm sat back in his seat. He scanned the road while the SUV pulled into the light traffic.

"Surgeons?" she asked, her heart beating in her throat.

"His Grace will have surgery tomorrow morning in Geneva," Paul said. "He is insisting on attending the wedding reception tonight. They've stabilized his hand for now. However, they want him to rest here until the last possible moment before the reception, and then he will need to return to Geneva tomorrow morning by five o'clock. Could you get the clothes from Her Serene Highness?"

Georgie's hand holding the phone shook. "Yes, of course. I'll ask Flicka for them."

"Is she in the car with you?"

"No. I'm riding with Rae and Wulfram von Hannover."

"Bon."

"But she's staying at the same hotel as we are."

"Oh, yes. Of course. If you could arrive around seven o'clock, it would expedite matters."

"I'll try."

"I will relay all this to Friedhelm. Thank you for your help in this matter."

Georgie said goodbye and hung up.

Friedhelm's phone rang almost immediately, and he glanced at her while he set out the schedule for the evening.

The city of Montreux rolled by as the SUV drove

to the hotel. The town had been built on lush hills overlooking the sparkling blue water of Lake Geneva. The scent of the fresh water filled the car from the vents.

Georgie took a deep breath and tapped the contact for HRH Bossypants to get their clothes.

Chapter Twenty

RING

Georgie

Georgie dodged around the hotel suite's bedroom, digging clean underwear for herself out of her backpack and some for Alexandre out of his emergency overnight bag that he had had stashed on the plane.

She dumped her backpack on the bed, her clothes and the sheet music for "Scrambled Eggs" fluttering over the golden velvet bedspread. She had to get to Flicka's room to get their stuff. She had to get to the hospital to help Alexandre get dressed. No time for a shower. No time to eat. Had to run to get to the car in time. She stuffed their underwear and some socks and hairbrushes and things in her now-empty backpack and sprinted to the door.

When she yanked it open, Peyton stood outside, his fist raised to knock. "Hi."

"Um, hi," she said. "I'm on my way out."

"Can we talk?"

"I really don't have even a minute."

He strode into her suite and looked around at the silk-covered furniture and carved-wood tables, raising his blond eyebrows. "Nice."

"Peys, I have to run. Time is tight."

"Could you shut the door please?" he asked.

She clicked it shut because she didn't want people out there hearing how rude she was about to get. "Peyton, you need to leave, and I need to go *now.*"

He took two steps and had his hands at her waist. "Which hand are you wearing the ring on?"

She glanced at her right hand, and the diamond sparkle there caught the fading sunlight streaming through the curtains.

"Move it over," Peyton said, his fingers playing over her hand. "Move it to your left. Let's go back to how things were, and let's make a new life together."

Alexandre was waiting for her in the hospital. Frantic worry and a desperation to get to him shook her. "Peyton, I can't do this right now."

"We can go anywhere and I'll support you," he said. "If you want to pursue your music, we can do that. I can use my trust fund. You don't have to go to law school if you don't want to, if you just want to play music."

Horror slammed her. She dropped the backpack. "What do you *mean,* no law school?"

"I'll take care of you. We'll hide from the Russians and whoever else is after you because of your father."

"But the people that he swindled. How would I pay them back if I don't go to law school?"

"I was wrong when we were in high school. You don't owe them anything. You don't owe *me* anything. Your mother kept all of that money. Even the Russian mafia knew who to hit up for the money. They didn't takc *you* to the bank. They went to your mother. She's the one who owes all those people what your father stole from them."

"But she won't. And they can't get it from anywhere else."

"Look, it's not like you can *return* the money. They would just be stealing it from you. It would be two wrongs, not a right."

Georgie backed up a step, holding out her hands. "We're talking old people and orphans here. It doesn't matter that the money comes from me instead of him, as long as they get *the money.*"

"You've always wanted to be a musician. Come be a musician with me."

"I'm the *sensible* one," Georgie cried. "I'm the one who does the right thing, who makes a plan to pay back all the people who got swindled by my father, all the families, all the charities who put their money with him. I opened my heart and grabbed my heart strings and flung music out so I could do the *right thing.* I'm going to be a lawyer, and I'm good at it, but I had to give up music to do it. Being a classical musician wouldn't have paid the millions and millions that it will take to make restitution. If I give up law school now, if I follow you, I will be going back on all those promises I made. I'll be just like him, a thief, a criminal, and a coward. I won't do it. I won't do what I want to, what I am dying to. I won't hurt all those people all over again by abandoning them."

With her hands spread-eagle in front of her,

Peyton's ring on her finger caught the light and shined a gleam right in her eyes. She blinked.

"Let's go," he said. "I'll take care of you."

"No," Georgie said, and she grabbed the ring on her finger and wrenched it off. "No. Thank you, Peyton. Thank you for offering. Thank you for everything. But no. I have to go to Atlanta. I have to go to law school. And I have to pay them all back so they'll be okay."

He didn't make a move. "Georgie, no. Keep the ring."

"No," she said, holding out the gold band with the small, antique-cut diamond in it. "No. You should have it back. I owe it to you."

"Georgie—"

She stepped forward, turned up his hand, and closed his fingers over the ring. "It's yours. It was never mine unless we had a promise, and we don't anymore. I have to go. I have to go now to take Xan his clothes, and then I have to go to Atlanta to do the right thing."

"I'm sorry," he said, his teal eyes large on his face. He wasn't used to being turned down for anything. "I'm sorry that we couldn't make it work."

Georgie said, "I have to go."

Chapter Twenty-One

BETTER THAN STUDENT DEATH

Georgie

Georgie pushed open the door to the hospital room, her backpack light on her back. Friedhelm stood behind her, holding two stuffed garment bags above his head with one hand.

The antiseptic smell that pervades all hospitals fouled the air, but the floors were spotless and the nurses were efficient but not harried. Georgie had seen the spectrum of the American health care system, from the toniest boutique doctors as a child in Connecticut, where her parents had paid a ten-grand fee per year to get her into the *right* pediatrician's practice, to Southwestern State's student health clinic, colloquially called "Student Death." The nurse practitioners there had a sense of humor and ready scrips for antidepressants, painkillers, and STD antibiotics.

Paul sat in a chair near the door, holding his head

in his hands. He looked up when she came in and met her at the door to take the garment bags from Friedhelm, but he pushed them both out into the hall. "His Grace is resting."

Georgie asked, "Are you sure that he's going to be able to go tonight? Because it's okay if he can't. I won't go either."

Paul rolled his brown eyes. "His Grace was adamant that he will attend the reception."

Georgie tried to look around him. "Is he all drugged up?"

"His Grace would only accept local anesthetics, but he is resting."

"Why do you do that?" Georgie asked.

"What?"

"'His Grace.' 'Your Grace.' The titles. It's so stilted."

Paul closed the door behind himself. The latch clicked. "His mother insisted on it when he was a teenager. His Grace convinced us to try informality once. We stuttered like idiots for a week before he gave up."

Paul twitched, and he took his phone out of his pants' pocket. "Yes, Your Grace? Yes, they've arrived. Yes, sir." He clicked the phone. "You're to go in, Georgie. We'll wait outside."

Georgie pushed the door open and found Alexandre sitting on the bed, his good arm resting across his bent knees. He was wearing his jeans, but he had on a blue hospital gown instead of a shirt. His hair was escaping his ponytail, blond strands of it glinting in the fading sunlight streaming in the long windows.

His hurt arm rested in his lap behind his knees.

He said, "Sorry about making you the fetch-and-carry girl."

"It's fine. I don't mind." Georgie pulled the drape that cordoned off the door to the private room and scooted onto the foot of his bed, careful not to jostle the mattress too much under her legs.

"Are you going to wear your jeans again?" His weak smile worried her. "It's considered déclassé to not change into yet another designer outfit for the reception. Perhaps your black jeans?"

"I have a dress that Flicka brought for me," she told him. "It's red."

"Too bad you don't have that black dress with the silver chains from their civil wedding. It looked smashing on you."

"And on your floor."

"Indeed." His smile grew a little warmer.

"Are you okay?" she asked.

He didn't even glance at his hand, but his quiet voice was just slightly breathy. "I don't think so."

"Is there anything I can do?"

He shook his head, a slight movement from side to side, but his expression was still so calm.

"Are you sure that you want to go tonight? We don't have to. We can just stay in Geneva tonight, if that would be better. I'd stay with you."

"It wouldn't matter. The surgery is scheduled for tomorrow because the best surgeon in Europe is flying in to do it. Going now wouldn't change anything. A distraction might be welcome."

"Well, then. Let's get this party started," Georgie said, bracing her arms on her knees to stand and get their clothes.

He lifted his wrapped arm from his lap where it

had been hidden behind his legs and the long part of the hospital gown. Elastic bandages wrapped his forearm and hand down to his fingertips where the ends of a foam and silver splint stuck out of the beige cloth. "I don't know how I'll get clothes on over this."

Georgie smiled, cocking her head and looking up from the corner of her eyes like she had been very smart. "I called the concierge at the hotel and got sewing supplies. I have scissors and a needle, and white thread for the shirt and black thread for the jacket. I can sew you into it. If they look closely, it might look like Frankenstein," she admitted. "But if they don't, the tux should cover most of that."

A slow smile grew on his face while she spoke. He said, "That's amazing."

She patted his long, bare foot because it was closest to her. "It's okay, man. I'll just grab those garment bags."

Georgie slid off the end of the bed and got the garment bags from Friedhelm, who looked entirely relaxed leaning against the wall, pleasantly hanging out with Paul, except that his brown eyes tracked everyone who moved in the long hospital hallway. He had a resting sweet face.

When she brought the bags back to Alexandre, he was already standing up and was shrugging off the cotton hospital gown, facing her. The cotton slid down his chest and dropped to the floor.

She hoisted the bags up and hung them on the curtain track that ran near the ceiling.

"Let's get you dressed first," she said. "You'll wrinkle less."

"You can wait outside," he said. "I'll just be a minute. Then we can sew me in."

"Oh, come on. I'll just help you button up the shirt."

He unbuttoned his jeans with his one hand and shoved them down his long legs. "I don't need any help."

"One last night, okay?"

"I beg your pardon?" he asked as he sat on the bed and yanked the denim off his foot with one hand.

"One last night. I'm going to Atlanta tomorrow. Let me help you."

"I keep hearing that, but you never leave."

"Now you're daring me," she said.

He pulled the other leg of his jeans off his foot and threw them behind himself on the pillow. He wore blue boxer-briefs that hugged his slim hips and rode below the ripples of his abs.

Red-gray bruises stained his skin on his ribs and thighs, mostly on his left side.

He said, "I am merely commenting on a trend. One that I like."

"Well, I'm just saying that you should let me help you because this really is our last night," she said, trying not to look at the bleeding under his skin. "Don't push me away, even for a minute, even to just get dressed."

"Then don't go to Atlanta," he said.

She ignored him because she ignored the people on the sidewalks of Southwestern State who hollered that little green men were following her, too. Indulging in fantasies was not something that the Ice Princess did. She said, "Even now. Even just for a few minutes. Just pretend that I'm helping you so I can stay."

He blinked, those lush eyelashes blinking over his dark eyes. "All right."

"So we need to get ready for the reception," she said.

He nodded, some of his blond hair slipping over his shoulder.

"Do you want to shower?" she asked.

He gestured to the splint and bandages on his left hand and shrugged his strong shoulder, pulling up the ripples of muscle along his torso.

Yeah, his splint and bandages shouldn't get soggy.

"I can give you a sponge bath," Georgie said. "Isn't that what you're supposed to do in hospitals?"

One of his dark eyebrows rose, pulling the side of his mouth with it. He looked a little devilish, like Xan.

Come to think of it, she hadn't seen Alexandre let Xan Valentine out of the bag since the concert in Milan, not on the flight around Peyton or any time since.

Plus, Alex de Valentinois and his posh British accent had stayed submerged, even at the wedding with the royal people, which would be exactly the type of place where he would take over.

But this sexy smile, bordering on a smirk, *almost* seemed like Xan, except that Xan would have said something sexy back, maybe even something downright dirty.

But Alexandre wouldn't have.

Georgie smiled, putting a little heat in it. "Lay back."

Alexandre rolled back on the bed, laying his wrapped arm on the sheets. His tall body stretched over the bed, his feet hanging off the end.

Georgie found a little wash tub and a thick washcloth in the bathroom and grabbed all the towels. She wasn't exactly sure how to do this, but she figured that as long as she didn't hurt him or soak the mattress, there really wasn't a wrong way.

When she came back, he was half-sitting up, waiting, his dark eyes intense.

Georgie lifted her chin. "I said, lay back."

He did, slowly, curling down so that his abdominals bulged with each inch he rolled backward.

Georgie gripped the tub more tightly in her arms. That door didn't lock. Granted, there were two strapping men guarding them, but they weren't guarding His Grace from nurses who wanted to check his blood pressure and might get an eyeful if they walked in and ripped back that curtain.

Life was full of chances, wasn't it? You never knew when Russian mafia hitmen were going to grab you off the street, press the cold steel of a gun to your head, and threaten to blow your brains out if your mother didn't pay them off.

Plus, Alexandre had said that a little diversion would be welcome.

What the hell.

Georgie walked toward him, hips swinging, holding the tub in front of herself. "Now relax. This won't hurt a bit."

He chuckled.

That sounded like Alex, the one with the puckish, sexy sense of humor, but again, Alex would have made a joke back to her.

Even beyond that sexy laugh, Alexandre looked out of his dark eyes. He was quieter and more solemn than the others.

Georgie told him, "Lift up so I can slide these towels under you." She pointed to the other side of the bed, toward the blue drape that hung between them and the door. "That way."

He rolled on the bed a little, lifting his side and his shoulder, watching her as he turned away with a mischievous glint in his eyes. Blond strands of his hair dragged across the white pillow case.

Considering how grief-stricken he had been about Adrien—even though it had been the quiet pain of Alexandre rather than Xan's wild grief—a moment of amusement for him was worth all the risk. She could deal with her own feelings later.

Or with the police if they got caught naked.

Georgie folded the towels and stuffed them under his back in case the washcloth dripped. He rolled back. She did the other side the same way so that he had towels ringing him.

She dipped the washcloth into the warm water and wrung it out until it was damp.

His hurt hand lay on the bed right next to her. She asked, "Does it hurt?"

He shook his head. "It's numb. It feels like they cut off my hand."

She trailed her fingers down his biceps. "Where does it get numb?"

"I can feel that."

Her fingers trickled lower, past his elbow and down the thick muscles of his forearm.

"It feels odd," he said. "It tingles."

She scratched the elastic bandages over the bandages on his wrist.

"I can't feel that at all."

"It really doesn't hurt?" she asked.

"I can't feel anything below that."

"Okay." She was still going to be really careful. If

he couldn't feel it, he couldn't tell whether she was damaging his hand even more.

Georgie sponged that arm lightly above his elbow, then ran the washcloth over the thick muscles of his shoulder. A blue, tattooed tendril crept over his shoulder in the crevice between the globe of his shoulder and the hard trapezius muscles leading up to his neck. She stroked the cloth down his neck, and he stretched under her hand and closed his eyes.

Her finger grazed the blue tattoo trickling around his neck toward his collarbone. A hard cord of scar tissue ran under it.

Jesus, Mary, and Joseph.

The tendril weaving around his bicep hid another, thinner line.

His extensive tattoo hid so much. She hadn't really ever explored his body like this, clear-eyed, without the haze of lust.

Georgie ran the washcloth over his strong pectorals. The hardness of the muscles under his skin felt like wiping down the curves of a sportscar. His abdominals were the horizontal grid of the grill.

The bruises spreading under his skin blackened splotches on his ribs and thighs, and she brushed the cloth over those as gently as she could, hoping the doctors had checked him for broken ribs, too.

She walked around the bed and washed his other arm, holding it up. His whole arm bulged with muscle, each cord of flesh braided into others. His forearm muscles were thicker than her biceps. She moved around the sides of the bed and washed his legs, skipping the parts covered by his blue boxer brief underwear.

His erection was a thick rod under the cotton.

Later.

The long sinews of his thighs and calves felt like steel ropes under his skin as she washed his legs and feet. When she slipped the warm cloth over his feet, he sighed, and his whole body sagged into the bed, so she wrapped the warm cloth around his feet and massaged for a moment.

"Wow," he breathed.

Nope, not wow. Not yet.

But soon.

Georgie finished massaging his feet and walked beside the bed. She leaned over to whisper in his ear, "Roll over."

His eyes opened just a slit. "You don't have to."

"I won't ask about anything if you don't want me to."

Alexandre paused, watching her, assessing what she knew. He drew in a quick breath, a prelude to saying something, but he rolled over without a word. It took him a minute to adjust himself so that he could lie flat.

On his back, that aqueous green and teal tattoo flooded his skin, the variations in the color hiding the hideous scars beneath. Georgie had felt them while they had made love, running her fingers over them, and finally realized that the tattoo covered the scars and not that she was somehow feeling the ink in his skin.

She twisted the washcloth, wringing it out, and wiped it over the broad muscles of his back. His trapezius muscles, the triangles of sinew from the sides of his neck to his shoulders, were amazingly thick under her fingers, and she laid the warm cloth across his back to knead his shoulders for a few seconds.

Again, his whole body sank with relief under her hands.

So many scars crossed his back that his skin felt like corduroy badly sewn with jagged seams.

Georgie ran her fingers lightly down his sides, and he smiled as her fingerpads skimmed his ribs. Her fingers found the waistband of his underwear, and she tugged the elastic. "Let's take these off."

Alexandre lifted his body and his knees, essentially planking on his one good arm, and she dragged them off. His ass was as strong as the rest of his back and legs, all smooth muscle.

No wonder she liked watching him shake his butt in his jeans during the concerts. *Damn.*

She washed the hard muscles of his butt and the backs of his legs.

Georgie was enjoying running her hands over him far too much. Far, far too much. It was great when Xan shoved her up against a wall and didn't let her move and barely let her breathe, but her hands were nearly trembling, touching him and enjoying the feel of his skin under her palms. Looking at all his skin was burning memories into her head that would last the whole rest of her life. Every inch of him was delicious.

Speaking of delicious—

She walked up to the top of the bed and whispered near his ear, "Turn back over."

Alexandre raised himself up on his good elbow and looked at her from the corners of his dark eyes. "I seem to be enjoying this sponge bath."

Georgie laid her lips on the side of his jaw, near his ear, a brief, warm kiss. She let her lips trail across his cheekbone while she said, "That's the whole point."

He rolled over on his back.

Georgie rinsed the washcloth again and squeezed the excess water from it.

She started on his hips, laving the warm washcloth over his skin like a broad tongue.

Alexandre wedged his good arm behind his head, propping himself up to watch her. Every time she glanced up, he was watching her face. His dark eyes weren't glazing over with lust, but his intense look suggested that she had his full attention.

Georgie wrapped the washcloth around her hand, and gently stroked his groin, running the washcloth under and over his balls. Such delicate little things in her hand, a light fuzz running over the velvety skin, and she released them to stroke upward.

When she glanced up this time, his lush lips had parted, and his dark eyes blinked slowly.

Oh, yeah. She was getting to him.

She ran the washcloth down his cock. The warm hardness twitched in her hand, and Alexandre's chest rose as he inhaled hard. It was thick in her hand, and long, and the rosy bulb of it peeked out of the washcloth with each stroke.

His groan was quiet, just a low sound in his throat.

Georgie dropped the washcloth lower, barely massaging his balls again, and she leaned forward to take him into her mouth.

As her lips closed over him, Alexandre's breath puffed out. His healthy hand found her shoulder, and he caressed her, rubbing her skin and her neck.

His breath formed the sound, "Ah."

Georgie licked his cock with it still inside her mouth, running her tongue under the bulb of the top and on the soft gathers of skin underneath. She moved lazily, licking and sucking him, as his cock swelled. A faint, male scent lingered on his skin, and she inhaled the earthiness as she moved down.

His fingers tightened on her shoulder.

He whispered, "You have been teasing me for half an hour. I'm not going to last."

She nodded slightly, his cock rubbing her tongue with each bob of her head.

His breathing hitched, and the hard ripples of his abdominals clenched under her hand.

She swirled her tongue around the soft head, feeling him pulse and grow more, and she dived down over him, pumping hard.

His hand clutched her shoulder, his fingertips pressing her skin. He slid his hand up the back of her neck but not into the convoluted updo of her hair, and he pressed while his hips bucked.

A strangled gasp escaped his lips when his cock pulsed on her tongue. His fingers gripped the back of her neck as warmth released into her mouth and she swallowed it down.

He still pulsed in her mouth, his fingers digging into the back of her neck, while she sucked him for another second, until a shiver ran through him. She sat back, wiping his deflating erection with the wet washcloth and then dabbing him with a dry towel.

Yeah, now he would remember her for the rest of his life, too.

He probably would have remembered her, anyway. They had a whole album's worth of songs that they had written together.

Too bad Xan Valentine had admitted, even bragged, that they were just poetry and he didn't believe in love.

But the songs were art, and creating them together

had been wonderful. They would always have the songs.

Alexandre stroked her shoulder. She almost laughed when she felt his hand shake.

He tugged at the shoulder of her tee shirt. "Come here."

"What?"

"Come here," he repeated. His voice broke in his throat and he held out his one good hand. "Empty arms."

Georgie slid into the bed and under his good arm, snuggling up to his side.

He dragged the sheet over himself and her, even though she was wearing jeans. "One of the few drawbacks of blowjobs is that my arms are empty afterward."

"Oh, come on," Georgie said. No guy regretted anything about a blowjob.

"No matter what way I make love to you—"

"And no one could fault you for the *many* ways," she said.

"—I always end up with you in my arms. I may be holding your arms over your head, or I may be biting the back of your neck—"

Tingles alighted on Georgie's wrists and the back of her neck as Alexandre described what he had done to her.

"—but at the end, I have my arms around you, and I can hold you while I feel you tremble."

"I'm not trembling." She might be trembling a little at the thought of his teeth on the back of her neck.

"And that's the other problem with blowjobs." He traced the side of her arm with his fingertips.

Georgie snuggled down closer to him. "I have *never* heard anyone have so many quibbles about getting a BJ."

"I don't get to feel you writhe in my arms when you come."

"I don't *writhe,*" she protested.

He chuckled. "You think you don't?"

"No." The Ice Princess did not *writhe.*

He turned his head to look down at her. "You need a sponge bath, too."

"I'm fine." She actually hadn't had time to take a shower. "I'll just jump in the shower in your little bathroom."

"You wouldn't want to muss your hair or makeup."

Georgie mock-frowned at him. "I thought most guys couldn't tell if women were wearing makeup except for lipstick, and I'll bet that I need to put more of that on."

Alexandre laughed. "I wear stage makeup for over two hundred gigs a year. I can see makeup."

"I can just splash around. I don't want you to hurt that hand any more."

"Oh, no. I insist. Get undressed." He rolled over her, bracing himself with his good arm that had been around her, and stepped out of the bed. He grabbed his underwear off the floor.

"Clean everything is in my backpack or the outside pockets of the garment bags," Georgie called to him.

He poked in her backpack until he snagged some fresh underwear, picked up the bin of water, and walked to the bathroom.

Good Lord, he was actually going to do it.

Essentially, with one hand tied behind his back.

Chapter Twenty-Two

IN FLAGRANTE DELICTO

Georgie

Georgie glanced at the swaying curtain that cordoned off the door to the hallway.

Having some fun with Alexandre hadn't felt too risky, but being the one wearing clothes was a lot less embarrassing if one were caught *in flagrante delicto.*

Ah, Hell. You only live once.

Georgie stripped her tee shirt off, stretching the neckline to keep from ripping her hair apart or wiping her makeup off, and shucked her jeans and underwear. She stretched on the cool sheets of the hospital bed, waiting for Alexandre to come back. He had wrinkled the towels from *writhing,* so she straightened those out.

Alexandre came back just a minute later, his underwear clinging to his hips and thighs, and holding the tub of water against his hip. His hair had been released from the ponytail, and he had combed it out so that it drifted, shining and blond, around his face. A dry washcloth was draped over the bin.

He said, "On your stomach."

Georgie flipped over, pressing her belly to the mattress, and tucked the towels under herself securely. The makeup people had sprayed some sort of a finishing spray on her face, kind of like face hairspray, and none of the cosmetics had rubbed off on anything else so far. She didn't grind her face into the pillow, though.

He sat down on the bed beside her, the mattress leaning toward him as he sat. He might be trim and strong without an ounce of chub on him, but at six-feet-four, the weight of just all that muscle and bones bent the bedding. He set the wash basin on the rolling table and dunked the washcloth in the water, gathering it into a ball with the long, strong fingers of his good hand and squeezing the excess water out.

She had been kind of concerned about how he was going to do that so as not to slop water all over the place or get his bandage wet, but he had that under control, too. Georgie relaxed onto the bed.

The cloth touched her shoulder, and she jumped a little.

"There, there," he murmured to her. "Gentle, gentle."

It sounded like he was soothing a child. "I'm okay."

"Mmm-hmm," he hummed, smoothing the damp cloth over her shoulders and the back of her neck. The cloth warmed the skin on the back of her arms.

"That feels good," she said.

"Bon."

"Are you sure that your hand is okay?"

"I haven't moved it at all." His voice was still hoarse from his last few concerts. Only two days off wasn't going to heal his throat.

He sponged her shoulders and the middle of her back, the warm cloth slipping over her skin. "This is like afterward, when I like to clean you up," he whispered near her ear.

She chuckled. "I noticed."

"You know what I am thinking the whole time?" His breath tickled her shoulder, and warmth from his chest spread over her back.

Oh, yeah. He was probably thinking all sorts of things while he inspected her after the rosy tint of sex had fallen away. She listed some. "'Why is she so weirdly boney, and why doesn't she have boobs?' 'Good God, doesn't the shampoo ever rinse out of all this hair?' 'When is she going to shave those nasty legs?'"

He chuckled low in his throat that time. His lips brushed her shoulder, his breath cold where her skin was still damp. "I am thinking *mine, mine, mine.*"

Georgie opened her eyes and glanced up at him.

"Don't tense." He sat back, sponging her lower back with the warm cloth. A bead of water dripped around her waist.

Arguing about what he had said—those terrifying words, *mine, mine, mine*—would be ridiculous. She was walking away from him the next morning. Her life in Atlanta was waiting for her.

She wasn't *his.*

And he wasn't *hers.*

So that was just fantasizing or wishful thinking or *something.*

Georgie pressed her cheek to the pillow and closed her eyes.

She tried to relax, but her back felt like a snarled, knotted rope.

Alexandre slid the warm cloth down her spine and butt. Her skin had been sticky from running to the car and church, the fear-sweat while they were being held hostage, and even the hot lights of the concert so many hours ago. The warmth and wetness of the cloth were a relief, washing away the salt, the terror of Tatiana Butorin pressing a gun to her head, and the horror of watching Alexandre, Paul, and Peyton nearly die because they had come after her.

Adrien had died because he had come after her.

A heavy cloud pressed on her. Not even Alexandre's strong hands could wash that away.

He moved down the backs of her legs, stroking her thighs, skimming over her calves, washing away the dust and salt of the last few days.

His fingers found her feet, and he massaged the sore soles and bones of her arches and the balls of her feet. The high-heeled pumps that Flicka had chosen for her had been obviously selected for fashion, not for standing behind a bank of keyboards for several hours during a concert. The state of her raw feet made her appreciate Boris and his excellent shoe choices even more.

The wet cloth rubbed over the swell of her hips and her thighs. She adjusted her legs, parting them, as Alexandre washed the insides of her legs.

Just when he was nearing the good part, he stopped.

Georgie twisted, pushing herself up on her arms. "Yeah?"

He rubbed a towel over her back and legs, drying her skin. "Sit up," he said.

"Turn over?" She pulled her legs under her, flipping onto her back so that her spare boobs would be right there on display if anyone walked in. The door hadn't opened, even though she had been listening for a click of the latch the whole time so she might have a chance to grab the sheet.

"No. Sit here." Alexandre stood and patted the towel on the edge of the bed.

Georgie scooted to the edge of the bed. Her legs dangled off the high mattress, nowhere near the ground, even though she had long, runner's legs. Her heel found the bed frame, and she crossed her other leg over her knee.

"No," Alexandre said. He touched her knee with one finger and guided it back to the side, then he nudged her other knee so that her legs were parted. With her legs spread just enough, the folds of her body opened. He said, "Yes. Like that."

Her open legs felt too vulnerable, but she had been fondling his balls. That must have taken some trust on his part.

He rinsed out the washrag and squeezed it in his fist again. Water dripped into the basin.

Georgie watched it, a little breathless while the water slowed.

He maneuvered his bandaged arm behind himself, laying it against the small of his back, and he stepped between her knees and leaned over her. The waistband of his underwear and the smooth skin of his waist touched her knees.

His lips pressed to her shoulder, a soft kiss, and he

wiped the warm washcloth from the back of her ear around to her collarbone.

The warm cloth felt like his mouth was on her neck. She stretched, feeling him. His breath cooled her damp skin.

When she turned her face up to let him wash her neck, he kissed her softly, his lips just sucking on hers for a moment. He broke it off to stroke down the other side of her neck, still leaning over her with his lush lips just an inch from her skin. His hand and the cloth moved on her chest, washing away the sticky sweat.

She hadn't realized how grimy and sticky she was until he had started washing it away.

Alexandre backed up for a moment, and she raised her arms to his shoulders to pull him closer.

Damn him, he was getting to her. Her breath already trembled with a soft, ragged edge.

He rinsed the washcloth, squeezed it again, and ran the cloth up and down one arm, then the other, sponging away gunpowder grit and salty residue. Water dripped from her elbow onto her bare thigh.

When he washed her right arm, he paused at her fingers. "No ring?"

"I gave it back to him," Georgie said as he stared at her hand.

Alexandre nodded and toweled her arms dry, then leaned over to her again, running his lips up the side of her neck.

His hand rubbed the washcloth lower, circling the softness of her breasts, washing around and under them. He spiraled in, gently gathering her flesh into his hand and the cloth, and thumbed the nipple of one, then the other. Her heart sped under the warm cloth and his hand.

"I don't think this is how you're supposed to give a sponge bath," she whispered.

He nipped her shoulder. "That's the whole point," he said, a smile lightening his hoarse voice.

Tricky bastard, using her own words against her.

Georgie let her head fall back, and she leaned back on her hands.

Alexandre moved with her, but his hand dipped lower to the skin over her ribs. He pressed the cloth to her sides. The nubbly washcloth didn't tickle her, luckily. If she would have jumped, her shoulder might have clacked his teeth and bumped his hurt arm, which was still resting behind his back.

His hand dipped lower, washing her stomach while his lips trailed along her neck and shoulder, kissing and nipping her.

Again, just as the washcloth was close to dipping between her legs, he straightened to rinse it out again.

Seriously? Was this going to happen or not?

He bounced his fist as he squeezed out the clean water.

Seriously.

Air fluttered in her chest. She swallowed and licked her lips, trying to calm her breathing.

He turned back, and he kneeled in front of her, resting his hand on the bed beside her leg as he bent.

Georgie reached and held Alexandre's shoulders as he descended, steadying him more. If he slipped, he might reach out to break his fall, and even though the Novocain might block the pain, landing on that hand would damage it.

He settled to the floor, but he was so tall that, even kneeling and with her sitting on a high, medical bed, his shoulders still rose above her knees.

Her naked, spread knees.

She had to open her legs farther when he leaned forward.

Alexandre ran the washcloth down her shins and over her knees beside him, brushing her legs with his broad shoulders.

Then he washed farther up, alternating the insides of her legs, each swipe closer to the tops of her thighs.

He massaged the sore muscles of her legs. She must have strained them a little when she had been grappling with Tatiana Butorin, fighting for the gun. His fingers dug just the right amount through the washcloth, releasing the tension.

His lips touched her knee, his hot breath wavering on her skin.

He washed the sensitive skin on the inside of her thighs, stroking the nubbly cloth over her skin, then higher. His hand moved higher, brushing the outside of her folds, while his tongue and breath danced on her skin near her knee.

She could not decide which to concentrate on, to *feel.* Her attention vacillated between the cloth feathering over her folds, just missing the sensitive parts underneath, and *him,* Alexandre, his lips pressing her skin and moving up, following the teasing path of the cloth.

A whimper lilted in her throat, but she tried to not let even that out. If he kept doing that—the heat of his mouth crawling up the inside of her thigh—she might need to keep herself from screaming, lest everyone on the whole floor hear his name, maybe *all* his names.

The cloth splatted into the wash basin, and Alexandre breathed on the soft skin between her legs. His humid breath sent shivers up her back, weakening

Georgie's arms. She dropped back to her elbows as his lips touched her like a soft kiss.

He started gently, brushing her folds, and then his tongue licked her more deeply, a hot stripe of pleasure.

The velvet roughness of his tongue swiped over her clit. The shock spun up and through her stomach.

Her fingers curled into fists on the sheets.

Alexandre pressed into her, licking and sucking, his tongue against and inside her, while she panted and her belly tightened. The rhythm of his mouth on her clit and her folds intensified, faster and rougher, rocking her back and forth on the bed.

Her fingers cramped around handfuls of bedsheets, and her panting softened into low moans in her throat.

He licked her faster, harder, building the rhythm until she was shaking at the pinnacle of tension, unable to breathe, and he pressed his whole mouth to her and flicked his tongue and sucked until her breath broke in her throat and the orgasm ripped through her body.

Throbbing pounded through her, cresting at the top of her head, and sight and sound fled except for the blossoming pleasure and the sound of her breath and heartbeat for long minutes.

The darkness cleared, and Georgie sucked in a long gasp.

Alexandre ran his lips over her skin, amplifying the last, lingering tremors to soft pulses that faded away. She was just reaching to nudge his shoulder back when he moved away, nuzzling her legs and resting his violin callus on the left side of his chin against her thigh.

"Oh my God," she said and glanced at the curtain, which was still circling the bed. "I wasn't too loud, was I?"

"No one outside could have heard anything," he said, smiling. His long, blond hair trailed over her knee.

When she sat up, the sheets and towels were snarled underneath her like someone had tried to braid them.

Great. She did *writhe.* Just lovely.

Her phone's screen flashed, indicating a text, and the time above the text icon was *7:31.* "Holy cow. We need to get dressed now. We can't enter the reception after Wulf and Rae. *Shit.*"

"Lean back." He rinsed the washcloth one more time and cleaned her up with the cooling water.

Mine, mine, mine.

A different kind of shiver went down Georgie's spine.

She scooted back on the mattress, away from him, and closed her legs, turning away. "We need to get dressed right now and *leave.*"

With his hands and the washcloth away from her, she felt more steadfast in her resolution to leave the next morning. She wasn't *his.* She wasn't anyone's *anything.* No one should ever fucking trust her until she paid back all those people she owed so much to.

Alexandre nodded and pushed back on his feet, standing.

He was right. Her arms felt empty. And lonely.

Georgie wrapped her arms around his waist and pressed her face to his bare stomach. His rippled abs clenched under her cheek, but his arm settled around her. He stroked the back of her shoulder.

"We have to go," she said, her voice muffled by his skin. "We need to get dressed and *leave.* This is over. It was all just stolen time. We have to *go.*"

"Stolen time," he echoed, his voice a whisper. The way he exaggerated the inflection sounded almost like music.

She didn't let go for another minute and neither did he, until she worried that her makeup would rub off on him like someone had painted a clown face on his stomach.

When she loosened her arms, Alexandre muttered, "I'll get my clothes."

"I'll help." She hopped off the bed and fiddled around in her backpack for the fresh set of panties she had stuffed in there. The silky wisp slipped through her fingers, but she caught it and stepped into them, hopping. "Give me a sec."

Alexandre reached into her backpack. A white undershirt dangled from his fingers, and he stretched the sleeve over the bandages of his left hand before he struggled to get it over his head.

She grabbed the hem and tugged it, slipping it down over his shoulders and the blue and green tattoo over the muscles of his back.

He unzipped the garment bag hanging from the curtain track with his good hand and reached in the bag.

Georgie reached into the bag, too, but Alexandre angled his body to block her.

"Come on," she said. "I'm staying so that I can help, right?"

"You don't need to." He tried to lift the hanger with the tux out of the bag, but the hanger was wedged into the track and the bag dragged on it. Every time he shoved the hanger up, the bag caught on the tux and wouldn't let it move.

He stopped fighting the hanger and started

pinching at the shirt's buttons, trying to unbutton them with one hand.

She said, "You're obviously struggling."

"I don't need help," he insisted.

"Come on. I've unbuttoned your shirts more than once."

"This is different."

"Bet you I can do it with my teeth again."

"No one needs to help me. I've always survived it all alone."

Survived it all alone?

Blue and green tendrils of his tattoo crept out of the collar of his white tee shirt, up his neck, and down the backs of his arms, the color covering where he had been whipped as a child.

She pulled her hands back. *"Oh."*

"What?" Alexandre swiveled and stared at her, looking in her eyes to figure out what she meant.

That red flush across his cheekbones and tension in his voice wasn't anger. It looked like anger, and people thought it was, but it wasn't.

The few times that Alex or Xan or Alexandre had gotten really angry was when people had tried to help him or, God forbid, expressed concern that he was harming himself.

Whenever Jonas or the others suggested that they cancel a show to rest his voice, which was still rough in his throat after two days without concerts, he had fought them off, nearly always successfully.

He had auditioned pretty much every keyboard player, first at Juilliard and then at the open auditions, personally. He'd barely allowed Tryp and Cadell to even vet first-round possibilities.

He was running himself into the ground with

promotion. For Killer Valentine's music, he wrote all the lyrics and music unless someone else had already written a song and offered it or unless Cadell tracked him down and insisted on collaborating.

Even when Georgie had worked on the songs with him, he had written everything. She had just played it back to him and talked about music.

He had had doctors and then Yvonne inject steroids directly into his throat because he would endure any pain, any suffering, *in secret.*

Xan Valentine wasn't a workaholic monomaniac. The damage ran far deeper than that.

If anyone *helped* him now, even with shirt buttons because one of his hands was smashed, it meant that someone should have helped him *then.*

When he was a child.

When some horrible excuse for a human being had flayed his back over and over.

But no one had.

If someone *should* have helped him and yet no one had, it would be too much for even Alexandre Grimaldi to bear.

No one had helped him, and he'd had to survive it all, even as a child.

Georgie stroked his silky cheek. He had somehow managed to shave at some point, by himself, without help. "Alexandre."

He turned his chin, almost like he was turning his face away from a blow. His dark eyes, tilted up at the corners, with those long, dark lashes, watched her warily. "What?"

Georgie was the Ice Princess, and she didn't let herself tear up. He wouldn't want that. "Let me help you with the buttons, just this one time, just because it's me."

The wariness in the way his gaze flickered between her eyes and her lips was heartbreaking. He finally said, "All right."

He stepped back, and Georgie made quick work of unbuttoning the glass buttons peeping through the buttonholes on the front of the shirt. She found the small pair of scissors that the hotel concierge had given her and mentally lined the shirt up with Alexandre's arms, figuring out which of the sleeves she should mangle. Chopping up the wrong sleeve would be pretty idiotic. The shirt's cuff flopped open —it hadn't been buttoned—and she clipped a few extra inches of the seam that would run up the inside of his arm. "Okay, let's try to get this over the bandages."

Georgie held the sleeve and guided it over his hand, holding the silky fabric and trying not to even let the material touch him. He didn't flinch at all as she pulled it up his arm.

"Okay," she said. "Let me sew you into it."

Alexandre sat on the bed with his arm flipped up while she whip-stitched the material together.

She held his trousers while he stepped into them and fastened them, tucking his shirt in. His body under her hands nearly vibrated with tension. "Just think of me like Boris," she said.

"Oh, I never think about Boris the way that I think about you."

She laughed quietly. "Okay, then just pretend I'm a servant. You're a duke. You probably have hot and cold running servants in Monaco."

He ran one finger under her jaw and tilted her

head up to look at him. "I never think of you like a servant."

That was quite a reaction. "Um, okay. Time for the jacket."

She tore the seam out of the left arm and held the jacket like a valet to slip it over his shoulders. He shrugged it on, stepping out of her reach to pull it up.

Damn, this was hard for him.

They sat on the bed again while she sewed the sleeve, the black thread puckering the soft wool of the jacket. He held his arm out stiffly like she was drawing blood and stared at the thread, not at her.

"We just have the tie and the pocket square and stuff," Georgie said, stroking his shoulder. "I used to tie my dad's bow ties. He was a klutz, and they always came out lop-sided."

Because Alexandre was so tall, he sat on a bedside melamine chair and Georgie stood between his knees to knot the white tie. He lifted his chin and looked as serene as ever while she tied it, but his good hand resting on his knee was clenched in a fist.

His blond hair straggled over his shoulders, tangled in back where he had been lying on it. Georgie tried smoothing it, but the frayed, golden hairs caught the light.

She grabbed her hairbrush from her garment bag and stood behind him, tugging the covered elastic band out of his hair and brushing it until it was shining and smooth. Boris had really outdone himself. Instead of the blond starting halfway down his hair, like always, his hair shaded smoothly from his dark roots, through rich gold near his ears, to silvery platinum ends. His dark eyes looked all the more dramatic.

"I could do that," he said.

Georgie doubted that, especially tying it back. "I let you brush my hair."

"That's different."

"And hold onto it, and wrap it around your hands."

He shifted in his chair, crossing his legs. "That's very different."

She whispered beside his ear. "Not to me."

He crossed his leg more tightly over the other one, threatening to wrinkle his black tux slacks.

She gathered his hair into her hands—the strands of silk caught on her fingers—and tied it into a ponytail at the nape of his neck.

"There," she said, stroking his shoulders. "You're all done. I'll throw my dress on, and we'll go."

"One more thing," Alexandre said. His voice cracked.

"Yeah?" She tried to sound casual and welcoming, but the Ice Princess really wasn't used to being those things. Maybe it worked.

His voice was low, embarrassed. "Flicka said that she had sent over my Saint Charles set."

Georgie blinked in utter confusion. "What's that?"

"Jewelry," Alexandre said. "Sort of. For men."

"Okay, I'll look."

She found a long, blue velvet jewelry case in another of the pockets. When she opened the top, the tube lights above caught the glitter of diamonds and threw sparks all over the curtain and the bed.

"Wow." She lifted one cross out, which dangled from a red and white-striped ribbon. Diamond-studded petals radiated from behind the cross, and the sparkles whirled around the walls. "Is this a headband to hold your hair back?"

Alexandre smiled a little. "The neckband slides under my tie."

She stood behind him to latch the ribbon and tucked it under his white bow tie. The cross hung below the knot, and the red and white band just peeked out.

Georgie held up the larger cross with diamond-encrusted star, about as big as her palm. "My grandmother had a brooch like this."

He smiled a little more, ducking his head. "The star is worn on the left side."

She held it up to his jacket. "No beauty pageant sash?"

"Not for this one."

"You have others?" She opened the pin.

"Tradition is to wear one's highest honor. This is my highest one."

"So is it like a knighthood or something?"

He raised his eyebrows and smiled. "I am a Knight Grand Cross of the Order of Saint Charles."

"Did you win it for doing something honorable and valiant?" she asked, letting a little good-natured mockery into her voice while she pinned it on his tux jacket. His heart beat against her knuckles while she guided the pin back through the fine wool. "Did you have to kill a dragon?"

"I rescued a fair maiden."

She smiled at him and patted it on his chest. "Yeah, you did."

He chuckled. "Actually, I won it in a poker game from my cousin Pierre, Flicka's husband, when I was eleven and he was eighteen, in school. I cleaned him out. Won his car, all his discretionary funds for the year, *everything.* He offered induction into the order instead, and I was drunk enough to say yes."

"You said you were eleven."

He shrugged. "It was a boarding school. When we went home that summer, our mutual uncle gave me the honor. I wear it mostly to remind Pierre that he sucks at cards."

She grinned.

He cleared his throat. "There's more."

"More?" Georgie looked in the pocket and came up with a smaller case. Inside, a row of medals were pinned to a black ribbon. "Were you in the military?"

"No. Those are other honors. I have to wear the little ones, too. Guillaume pins them on a ribbon for me because I can't remember the order."

Georgie pinned them right through the ribbon to the jacket above the star, where Alexandre was pointing. "Guillaume is a protocol droid."

"Certainly. He runs on scotch whisky."

She smiled up at him, watching him relax more. "I'll just get dressed."

"I'll watch." His smile grew sly as he settled back in the chair.

That sounded a little more like Alex, her favorite hedonist.

She dressed quickly because they had to leave, but she rolled her pantyhose onto her legs suggestively—as suggestively as she could with a control top bungee-cording her thighs together—and wiggled her hips a little more than absolutely necessary as she shimmied into the dark red dress that Flicka had magically procured in under an hour, and in the right size, and with a couture label sewn in the back.

Damn, Flicka had that princess thing *down.*

Flicka had been training for it all her life, though. Georgie probably would have made a halfway decent snobby Connecticut socialite or a classical musician, given the chance.

People could change, she guessed.

Georgie swayed as she zipped the dress up the back, finishing her inverse striptease, and turned around. She growled, "Oh, yeah, baby. Put it on."

Alexandre was watching her from under his thick, dark lashes, a sexy smile playing on his lips. "There's more."

"More than the dress and stuff?"

"There should be jewelry."

"Oh?" Georgie poked in the pockets of her garment bag that Flicka had sent and came up with another case.

Inside, a necklace and earrings set with glittering, deep red stones larger than Georgie's thumbnail and surrounded by smaller, glittering diamonds lay on black velvet. "Are those—"

Alexandre glanced carelessly over at them. "Rubies, yes. And diamonds."

"Wow, Flicka outdid herself."

Alexandre smiled a slow smile, and he even chuckled. "Yes, Flicka outdid herself."

Georgie latched the necklace around her neck, where she could feel the weight of the stones and platinum on her neck, and poked the heavy earrings through her ears. "They're amazing. I *love* rubies. There's just something about the rich, red color to them that floats my boat. You're sure they're real?"

"Quite sure," he said. "They're Burmese rubies, over a century old. Few of that color and clarity are mined these days. The setting is newer, not more than a few years old, and very fashionable, I've been assured. The half-carat diamonds are a recent addition, all of them matched for perfect white color, very fine clarity, and size. There's a matching brooch, too, but it seemed like too much. One of the stones in the brooch is spectacular, no occlusions, fantastic color, and heart-shaped."

Georgie gaped at him. "You really know your pretty rocks."

He shrugged. "It's a royalty-nobility thing. It's as if the stones give off an RFID signal that only we can sense."

"Is it that synesthete thing again? Something about the rocks, like they make music or something?"

He paused, looking at her, maybe evaluating whether she was being kind or cruel. "You've caught me."

Georgie laid her hand on his shoulder. "You don't have to hide it from me."

He leaned forward from where he sat in the chair and touched her arm with his cheekbone. "Sometimes I forget that I don't have to."

She nodded and stepped back, and she spun to show off Flicka's dress. "How do I look?"

His smile turned sultry again. "It's a good thing you've sewn me into this penguin suit. Otherwise, we might have been very late."

She had actually sewn both very loose so that he could take that jacket off if he got too warm or whatever.

Georgie grinned at him and kicked her foot up in back, flirting. "Come on, lover. Take me dancing."

Chapter Twenty-Three

HIS GRACE ALEXANDRE GRIMALDI, DUKE OF VALENTINOIS

Georgie

Georgie and Alexandre stood in an antechamber that led to a hallway where far too many *important* people formed a ragged line, waiting to be presented to the congregated wedding guests below. Everyone in the chamber and hallway clumped into small circles, chatting softly with each other, enjoying one of the few times that they had to discuss events or people privately. Chandeliers above twinkled on the jewelry that absolutely everyone wore, from necklace sets and tiaras on the women to honors for both genders. A geologist would have gone hysterical in there, looking at all the pretty rocks.

People who were chatting craned their necks to look above the others, watching their place in line, lest they be presented out of order. *Mortifying.*

Faint perfumes and colognes slid above the scent of

the enormous rose bouquets on the hall tables lining the walls. The sweet scents smelled like a flower show.

Georgie wobbled in her high-heeled pumps for something to do while she gingerly slid her hand under Alexandre's elbow, careful not to jostle him. "You're sure this doesn't hurt you?"

He tucked his arm in closer, pinning her hand to his ribs. "You're holding my healthy arm."

"Still."

"It's fine."

"And you won't be able to hold onto the railing when we go down the stairs. We should switch sides."

"And cause a scandal?"

"It would be a scandal?" Georgie asked, horrified that something so little would be noticed and remarked on and tittered about. Come to think of it, when Georgie had been sixteen, Mrs. Gelder would have had a cow if someone had switched during the Cotillion entry.

Alexandre said, "I'm kidding, but this way is traditional."

"Are you sure? I don't want to accidentally hurt you."

He shook his head, his blond ponytail swishing down his back. "They said it would be numb for hours."

"That's not an answer."

"It is still completely numb," he assured her.

"Well, okay." Georgie fidgeted with the back hem of her dress. The red gown had a short train that dragged the ground, something that Georgie had been sure went out of style a couple of hundred years ago, but Flicka was the princess and would know better than Georgie, who had been hanging out with normal people for the last few years. "You sure that you don't want to go to Geneva, just in case the surgeon gets an earlier flight to the hospital?"

He inclined his head to look at her. "I'd rather that she had a good night's sleep tonight."

Georgie looked up at him. Even in her heels—and they were quite high—she was eye-level with his shoulder. "It's weird to go to these things," she admitted.

"Because you've been hiding for so long."

"And now everyone knows." Everyone out there could look her up. Everyone, everyone, *everyone.*

"And last time, it didn't go so well," he said.

"No shit, huh?" Georgie shuddered a little at the thought of Flicka yelling *Georgiana Oelrichs!* across the room at Rae's civil wedding. Tatiana Butorin's head must have popped out of the crowd like a damn prairie dog.

Alexandre twisted his arm under hers and held her hand. "I'll be right beside you the entire night."

"I don't want to go out there," she blurted.

"It's your best friend's wedding reception. You literally killed people to get here."

Well, there had been some self-defense and other peoples' lives at stake, too. She said, "For the *wedding.* Not the reception."

A man wearing some kind of a red tuxedo uniform —all he needed was a powdered wig to look like a revolutionary war-era British Redcoat—waved to the couple ahead of Georgie and Alexandre. They stepped through the huge double doors and onto some sort of balcony.

Georgie peeked behind herself. The ragged line of bejeweled, bedecked couples stretched around the room. People were meandering back and forth, chatting because they didn't get to see each other very often.

The other groomsman, William, was far back in the line with his wife, and they were laughing with the people ahead of them, including Yoshi, the groomsman who had walked Georgie back to Alexandre, who didn't seem to have anyone else to stand with.

The British Redcoat beckoned to Georgie and Alexandre. "Your Grace and miss, they're ready for you."

They walked up to the tall set of double-doors, and Georgie clung to Alexandre's elbow. Under his tux, his muscled arm was so thick that it felt she was hanging onto a well-upholstered set of bowling balls.

Alexandre said, "I will stay with you."

"I'm fine. Really. It's nothing." Her legs were shaking so hard that her knees felt weak and she bobbled a little.

Alexandre wrapped his arm around her waist and held her up. The warmth of his arm seeped through the fragile red silk of her dress almost immediately.

"I'm fine," she insisted.

He turned her to face him. His French accent softened his words when he assured her, "I will hold you until we are both safely through to the other side."

She told him, "That sounds ominous sometimes."

"Not meant to be."

"Yeah, sure."

"A little later in the evening, there's someone I want you to meet," he said.

"Oh, Jesus, Lord Almighty. Who's that?"

"It's not a big deal."

"Then why'd you tell me like that?"

"To take your mind off of this."

"Now I'm freaking about two things," she said, grumbling.

"This is just a walk down a staircase."

"A very long walk or very quick fall."

"I won't let you fall."

"Okay," she sighed. "Let's do this thing."

The Redcoat opened the door for them, and Georgie and Alexandre walked out onto a balcony. A long flight of alabaster stairs curved down to the ballroom floor below. Silvery curtains draped the arched windows that overlooked the lake, glittering with stars from the night sky above. The chandeliers above and crystal sconces on the walls and candlelit tables below glowed a subdued gold, as if this ballroom was a bastion of sunlight keeping out the night beyond the windows.

Georgie counted one row of tables and multiplied it, estimating that sixty or more round tables studded the floor below, each seating ten people. Hundreds of guests, dressed in the colors of gemstones and obsidian, milled in streams between the tables, greeting one another. Some headed for the large hors-d'oeuvre and drinks area set up in the adjoining ballroom that would become a dance floor after dinner. A string quartet set up in the corner was playing the finale from Handel's *Water Music.*

A concert grand piano stood next to the string quartet. Georgie wondered if they were going to have piano music later, and she smiled at the thought.

The Redcoat beside her took a card that Alexandre slipped him and announced, "His Grace Alexandre Grimaldi, Duke of Valentinois, and Ms. Georgiana Johnson."

Georgie chucked her chin up, something she had

always done before a piano competition, and held onto Alexandre's arm more securely, unsure if it was for her own strength or in case he fell because his other hand couldn't hold onto the railing.

One foot down each step. One step at a time.

Georgie and His Grace, the Duke of Valentinois, descended the long, curving staircase.

Chapter Twenty-Four

FRIEDERIKE VON HANNOVER AND GEORGIANA JOHNSON

Georgie

Georgie glued a prim smile to her face until they reached the bottom of the marble staircase, one long curve like an arabesque from the second-story balcony to the ballroom floor. Only a few of the people, mostly men, who had been streaming among the tables or munching at the hors-d'oeuvre stations had actually looked up at them when the Redcoat's voice rang out over the chattering and refined squeals of recognition. A few people snapped cell phone pictures of them, their flashes twinkling among the candelabra and glowing chandeliers.

Alexandre led her through the crowd to the food area, where they heaped plates with bits of pastry and shrimp because when you are on the road, you never knew when you were going to get another chance to eat good food, sleep in a decent bed, or use a clean bathroom.

"We should find a seat," she said.

Alexandre looked over the crowd, which was easy for him because he was so tall that he stuck out of the top. "Flicka said that we should sit at the head table."

Georgie winced. "Please tell me you're kidding."

He shook his head and, holding his plate in his good hand, broke a path through the crowd to the long table set up at the front in front of everyone.

"Yep. Name cards," Georgie said, finding theirs down toward one end of the table.

Alexandre picked up the one in front of the chair next to his. He looked at it and winced. "Splendid."

When he turned the card and showed it to her, Georgie read the name *Friederike* on it. She rolled her eyes. "Flicka is sitting next to you? There's no way this could end badly."

They sat down anyway—because their names were on the cards and the cards must be obeyed—and scarfed their shrimp and the other tasty bits. Clarified butter slid on her tongue, and flakey pastry shattered in her mouth. At the tastes, Georgie was careful to moan somewhat less than she had during the sponge bath because she was sitting at the head table, right under the enormous, curtained stage, and hundreds of people were examining her table manners.

She examined them back. The men wore tuxedos or formal-style suits if they were young and too hip for a tux. About half the men wore man-jewelry like Alexandre's Order of St. Charles. All glittered with vibrant gems and were different colors and shapes, and some of the guys wore sashes like beauty queens under their suit jackets.

Heh, beauty queens and royal sashes. Those royal honors were probably where the pageants got the idea of the sash to begin with. After all, they had crowns, too.

About half the women also wore honors—sashes and pins and such—over their rustling or slinky ball gowns, which appeased Georgie a bit. As it was summer, women under thirty-five-ish wore strapless gowns or slim ties, showing off their smooth shoulders in all the chocolatey colors of creamy white, milk, and special dark.

After she had plowed through half her plate, she whispered to Alexandre, "I feel kind of weird sitting up here all alone."

"The others all outrank us. They won't be presented for a while yet."

"Oh, well, if they *outrank* us." Georgie chugged champagne.

Alexandre cleared his throat. "I almost wrote 'Their Graces Alexandre and Georgiana Grimaldi, the Duke and Duchess of Valentinois on the card."

She had seen him standing over the card with a pen in his hand for a long minute before he had written anything.

"Oh, you would *not have!"* She whispered, "Why would you even think of doing such a thing?"

His sly grin and flashing dark eyes were all Alex Valentinois, the ornery and funny nobleman, but his French accent softened his words when he said, "Just to see what you would do."

Georgie scoffed, "I would have sprinted out of there like a gazelle in a red dress being chased by a lion."

"You would have looked beautiful doing it."

"Oh my God. People would have been asking me questions all night."

"You could have just told them yes," he said.

"And what would you have done when I disappeared tomorrow? Everyone would have been all over you." Georgie couldn't have done that to him.

He shrugged. "I would have disappeared back to the tour."

She braced her fists on her hips. "Leaving everyone thinking that we had secretly gotten married and I abandoned you."

He shrugged. "What's the harm?"

An icky-shiver ran down her spine. "People would talk!"

He laughed, a careless, ringing laugh that made the genteel people sitting at the near tables stare. He said, "People will always talk. If they don't know facts, they will say the most destructive, vile things about you that they can think of just so they can talk. I don't believe anything about anyone. I won't believe that you will leave tomorrow morning until you actually do."

"Well, I'm going to stick around for a little while." She ducked her head to whisper near him. "I won't leave until after your surgery. I'll make sure you're okay before I say goodbye."

He nodded. "I still won't believe it until it happens."

Georgie frowned. He should believe it. She was getting on a train or a plane or *something* tomorrow and leaving.

Not that they needed to have a fight about it, not on their last night.

She pulled her face into a smile and patted his hand, his healthy one.

The string quartet began playing another piece.

She asked Alexandre, "Any of the instruments out of tune today?"

He chuckled while he broke a pastry in half. "No. Not today."

The string quartet was in the other ballroom, past the long rows of round tables and the glittering crowd. "This wedding is so big."

"Von Hannover has a lot of relatives, including most of the European noble and royal houses. His several-times-great-grandmother was Queen Victoria, just like almost everyone else in this room."

"Seriously?" Georgie looked for Wulfram, but he wasn't around because he outranked them.

"Absolutely."

"You?" she asked.

"No, not me. Nor Pierre. Even though we have mutual ancestors—"

"Nuh-uh. Flicka married her cousin? I thought you guys stopped doing that due to hemophilia and insanity and stuff."

"Oh, no. Not *cousins.* Almost a thousand years ago, *literally,* a thousand years, we had ancestors in common. The Grimaldis and the Hannovers are descended from the Guelph families of Italy. The Grimaldis became feudal lords after we finally captured the castle in Monaco and, eventually, were barely recognized as sovereign princes. The Hannovers ruled huge tracts of Europe as royal kings, and there is a *difference.* Just ask one of them, especially Flicka's father. One of the Grimaldis' great embarrassments is that we have never before married into the Hannovers. It's like being snubbed by a country club. But now, Pierre has regaled everyone with Flicka's lineage. I'm sure he can recite it all back to Duke Welf the Fourth."

"Guelph and Welf and Wulfram, huh?" Georgie quipped, grinning.

"Not very inventive with the names, are they?"

"I thought Wulfram was a recluse," she said. Well, sort of. Georgie actually knew better. But that was the official story.

Alexandre said, "Not so much a recluse as camera-shy."

"God forbid," Georgie cracked, joking about PR. Oh God, the PR.

"If this weren't Wulfram's own wedding, he probably wouldn't have shown up."

"Yet it looks like a lot of people came. He can't have shirked networking too much."

"He used to travel and visit extensively, so he makes his connections privately. Plus, he's evidently a genius with the stock market and tells people a week before it crashes. Everyone wants to be on his mass text list."

A piece of shrimp lodged in Georgie's throat, and she coughed it back into her mouth and chewed it. "The— *Um.* You mean Wulfram von Hannover?"

Alexandre nodded and manipulated a small tart with his long fingers. "No one would dare refuse his invitation, lest he lose their phone number, and everyone loves the guy who saves their financial asses on every occasion. Plus there's the other thing, and I think every person in this room sighed with relief that he appears happy."

"What's that?" Georgie asked, picking at the fruit on her plate.

Alexandre glanced at the crowd as if checking for

eavesdroppers and then glanced at the line of balconies running along the second story.

His serious look made Georgie look, too.

Men in dark suits, very fit men, stood on the balconies, some leaning over the railing and watching the crowd, some talking to themselves and occasionally touching their ears while they scanned the dark hills and lake outside the windows with odd, bulky binoculars.

Alexandre said, "I'll tell you later."

Oh, she was going to ask him, too.

Except that she was leaving tomorrow morning.

That must be yet another dig that he thought she wouldn't go back to her appointed life tomorrow.

Well, he was wrong.

Georgie nibbled her appetizers and scanned the crowd, looking for anyone she knew. "When are Flicka and Rae going to get here?"

Alexandre looked at the staircase, where the redcoat was announcing a princess of Oranje and her escort. "Not for a while."

"Shouldn't Lizzy and her fiancé be around?" Georgie asked.

"Which one is she?"

"The teeny-tiny blond bridesmaid. She's a *commoner.* They don't outrank anybody, I think." Georgie scanned the crowd, looking for a hole among the people like a motorcycle taking up a parking space in a packed lot.

"They should be here," he agreed.

"I could just go find her," Georgie sighed. The room spread out in front of her, wide and long, and hundreds of people meandered through the tables.

Finding tiny, blond Lizzy in that swarm would be impossible, even if they all quit moving around.

"Or I could tell you all the royals' and nobles' dirty secrets," Alexandre said.

"You know everyone's dirty secrets?"

"I went to school with most of these people. If I wasn't actually there for their most stupid follies, I heard about them within hours."

"If these are your school buddies, then why aren't you out there mingling?" Georgie scooted back her chair.

"I'll mingle later." Alexandre reached over with his good hand to touch her fingers. "Just in case you aren't bluffing and it really is our last night together, I want to spend it with you, not them."

She turned her hand over and held his. "I'm not bluffing. I'm sorry."

"For tonight, let me think you might be. Now," Alexandre said, pointing to a guy around their age who had seated himself at one of the nearby round tables. The guy was stunningly handsome with dark auburn-brown hair and light golden skin, like he was tanned. His long legs stretched under the table. "He was a few years ahead of me in school and a particularly sad case. More money than he could spend in a thousand years, several titles, connections to movie stars and models such that he can get invited anywhere he wants to go and fuck any woman he chooses."

Georgie wouldn't have thrown that guy out of her bed even before she had known about all the money stuff. He looked delicious. His broad shoulders filled out his stylish black formal suit that nipped down to his trim waist. "Let me know when this starts getting sad."

"And yet, he cannot maintain a relationship with a woman for more than a few weeks."

The guy turned slowly like he was searching for something and saw Georgie looking at him. She could see his sparkling green eyes from a dozen feet away. He looked at the wooden floor without smiling and turned back to the man he was talking to.

Georgie said, "I mean, other than he seems to have no charisma, or personality, or something."

"Oh, no. Casimir is a great guy. He'd give you the shirt off his back even if it were his only possession in the world, not that that is going to happen anytime soon."

"What's wrong with him?" Georgie watched him, but his body language seemed perfectly normal.

Alexandre leaned over to her. "Do you notice something about the people in this room?"

"They're all obscenely rich?" she asked him, eyebrows raised. The jewelry in that room would have produced a respectable hoard for a dragon to sprawl over and defend from intrepid, handsome princes, who were also in that room.

"Yes, that, too," Alexandre said. "But I mean that they're all beautiful."

"Humility is not you guys' strong point."

"Their mothers have been chosen for their beauty for generations."

She whispered to him, "Shouldn't you include yourself in the royal-bashing?"

"Excellent point. *Our* mothers, then. Especially mine."

"Not fathers?"

"Except for the last generation, most titles were

patriarchal, so mothers were chosen. The kings did the choosing. Don't blame me. I didn't start the system."

"And the mothers weren't chosen for their brains? Is he—" Georgie tried hard to be polite, "—mentally challenged?"

"Not at all. He holds a law degree from Yale and passed the New York and California bars. He's an entertainment lawyer."

"With looks like that, he could have been a movie star."

"He hasn't always looked like that," Alexandre whispered.

"Oh?" Georgie looked harder.

"He was in a car accident when he was six, and he went through the windshield."

Georgie winced. "The poor baby."

"They could only do minimal reconstructive surgery before he finished growing. All through high school, he had half a nose and bashed-in cheekbones."

"Oh, Lord." Georgie had climbed the monkey bars on American upper-class playgrounds and knew the way that people with differences were treated. She could only imagine what the playgrounds were like when the kids were descended from noblemen who had played backstabbing court politics for generations, when their lives and fortunes hung on the pecking order.

"The girls were evil. They teased him by pretending to like him and laughed behind his back until they finally told him that it was a dare or a bet. They did it over and over, and he was so soft-hearted that he fell for it over and over, until one day, he didn't."

"Oh, my God. Now I want to fuck his hurt away."

Alexandre's fingers tightened around hers.

She rolled her eyes at him. "I'm kidding, I'm leaving for Atlanta tomorrow, and don't be a jealous dick."

His hand relaxed. "And the chap next to him is the earl of somewhere—"

Another gorgeous specimen of the result of breeding beautiful women for pretty babies, Georgie was sure. He had glistening black hair and cheekbones sharper than legendary Arthurian swords. His eyes were pale blue, the color of his silvery-blue tie, and she was quite sure that tie color was not an accident.

Alexandre continued, "I can't remember where his seat is because they all run together in my head—but his younger brother is suing him for the earldom based on the fact that Severn's entire life has been nothing but drunken debauchery, as if *that* ever precluded someone from being an earl. The lawsuit is costing them both a fortune, and they may end up bankrupting the earldom fighting over it."

"Okay," she sighed.

Alexandre shifted in his seat to look at her. "You don't seem enthralled at my sparkling repartee."

"I'm sorry. They're your friends. I'll never see them again after tonight. I can't even tell anyone the gossip because I can't let anyone make the connection to the Georgiana name."

Alexandre turned to her. "So what do you want to talk about?"

"Wolfgang Rihm?" The composer about whom they had drunkenly and gleefully argued when they had first met at Rae's first wedding.

Alexandre ran his thumb over the back of her knuckles and smiled. "Every time we talk about Wolfgang Rihm, we end up sneaking away to fuck in a hotel room."

The one time, yes. "I'll chance it if you will."

"He's overrated, and his compositions are rushed."

Georgie gasped. "You take that back!"

The Redcoat standing on the stairs announced, "Their Serene Highnesses Pierre Grimaldi and Friederike von Hannover, Prince and Princess of Hannover and Cumberland." Flicka gracefully descended the stairs with her new husband, her crystal-encrusted pink dress flowing behind her on the steps. Her blond hair twisted around her head in a sophisticated version of Heidi-braids that secured a glittering tiara.

Georgie elbowed Alexandre, "I thought he was your cousin and some bigwig in Monaco."

"Oh, yes. He's the heir apparent to the throne of Monaco unless his uncle has a child at this late date."

"Then why didn't that guy up there say Monaco?"

"Because she outranks Pierre. He took her title after marriage."

"That's weird, right?"

"Royalty outranks principalities. Pierre is greedy for that title."

"Why?" She could feel that her lip was climbing up her face in disgust.

"No offense—"

"Oh, that's always a great way to start a fight."

"—But I'm not sure an American would understand. It's kind of like buying a new car. Pierre has a shiny, new title that no one else can get."

"Oh. Conspicuous consumption."

"You do get it."

"Just like growing up in Connecticut, except it was

understated luxury cars and art." And your kids getting into the right schools or pediatrician's office or sports.

And being in all the most popular hedge funds.

Georgie watched Flicka and her husband make a beeline for the hors-d'oeuvre buffet, barely stopping to greet people who reached their hands toward her as she passed. Flicka filled a plate fast and bustled for their table, chewing as she trotted. Pierre was still dishing up when Flicka settled like a fluttering dove next to Alexandre and leaned across him to talk to Georgie. "It appears that you received the clothes?"

"Yes. Thank you," Georgie said.

"You look sparkly," Flicka said to Alexandre, tugging on the Order of St. Charles cross dangling below his white tie.

Alexandre laughed and batted her hand away. "You're a respectable married woman, now, yes? You can't flirt with the likes of me. What would people say?"

Flicka stared at Alexandre, her green eyes growing wider. "Why are you talking like that?"

Georgie glanced up. Alexandre's French accent had slurred his syllables, and his melodic rhythm was more noticeable after hearing Flicka's clipped British accent. Georgie must have gotten used to Alexandre being around and hadn't even heard his soft French accent until Flicka had said something.

"Talking like what?" Alexandre asked.

"Like a ten-year-old!" Flicka said.

"I am not." That time, Alexandre's accent sounded a little more polished British to Georgie, or maybe it was just because it was a short sentence.

"Master Hamilton would fail you if you spoke with

that abominable native accent in his class." Flicka nibbled on some crackers with meat on them like a starving squirrel.

"Perhaps you would like to sit beside Georgie," Alexandre said, standing and taking his plate. "I'm sure you two have much to discuss."

Georgie took the hint and scooted over.

Flicka told her, "I haven't eaten all day. After I got your clothes squared away, all Hell broke loose again. I cannot tell you how trying this wedding is." She stuffed her face as elegantly as possible.

"You've done an amazing job. Rae is lucky to have you. Thanks for getting me the dress and loaning me the jewelry, by the way." She touched the heavy necklace of rubies at her throat.

Flicka glanced at Alexandre behind Georgie, and then she smiled. "Of course. Anytime."

Georgie held up her champagne flute to toast. "To a fantastic wedding. You've done a wonderful job."

"Give me that." Flicka snatched the glass out of Georgie's hand and slid the wine down her throat like a frat boy. "For the love of all that is holy, call a bartender."

Georgie signaled one of the waitstaff, and she strolled over, balancing a tray of champagne glasses on her shoulder. The lady offered the tray to Flicka, who grabbed at an array of them, about six.

Flicka swigged the champagne and sighed, "Thank you, miss."

Georgie picked up one of the extras in front of Flicka's plate.

Flicka told the waiter, "And a couple more for my friend, here."

"Can I get you something stronger, ma'am?" the waiter asked, raising her eyebrows.

"Yes, please. Scotch. Rocks. Triple. Thank you."

When the waiter toddled off to get Flicka's drinks, Georgie asked her, "Are you okay?"

"I will be, as soon as I eat something, drink a lot, and pass out. Then I'll be fine."

Georgie rubbed her bare shoulder above the back of the strapless dress. "You did an amazing job. It was beautiful."

She stared into the empty bottom of the champagne glass. "I don't want to talk about it. I really don't."

"Runaway bride?" Georgie was pretty sure it hadn't been a runaway groom. Rae would have roped and hog-tied him, which was one of Rae's favorite phrases for any situation.

Flicka snorted. "That was seriously the *only* catastrophe that *didn't* happen."

"Something else?"

"That is *not* not-talking about it. Seriously. Just help me get drunk. Hey, Alex!" Flicka leaned toward the table to call across Georgie. "You're singing 'Alwaysland' tonight, right?"

"Not on your life. We discussed this," he answered, looking out and over the crowd milling around the tables set with white china and crystal that twinkled in the candlelight.

"He can't," Georgie said to Flicka. "Not tonight. He really can't."

"You're saying that as if you're not playing the piano for him."

Fuck, no. "Flicka! He can't. *We* can't. Come on, we

don't want to make a spectacle of ourselves. The string quartet is doing fine."

"Oh, God. *The string quartet.* I only have them because Wulf likes classical so much. I wanted to book Killer Valentine."

"We're supposed to be playing Rome tonight," Alexandre told Flicka, "and I don't think you could have afforded us."

Flicka cracked up. "Oh, that's hysterical, Alex. 'We couldn't have afforded you.'" She fanned herself. "If we had had any notice, we would have scheduled around you. Rae and Wulf's first official date was one of your concerts, the one in L.A. a couple of months ago, so I thought it would have been neat but *fuck me.*"

"They were engaged that quickly?" Alexandre asked, glancing at Flicka again.

"Yes, he said that he knew it was right almost immediately, and you know that he doesn't do anything without analyzing *everything* to the *n*th degree and with so many regressions that he could make a circle into a straight line."

"How long did they know each other?" Alexandre asked over Georgie. His dark eyes didn't leave Flicka while she spoke.

Georgie shifted and looked at him more closely, but he didn't waver at all. This wasn't just a polite conversation to him. *Odd.* Most guys didn't care about the deets.

Flicka waved her hand and said, "About two months before they had the civil ceremony. It was truly a whirlwind courtship, and then they had the civil wedding *months* ago, the day after *my* wedding—"

"I remember," Alexandre said.

"That's right, and then she—" Flicka glanced at

them, "—was indisposed, and we had to delay the social event."

"She's my best friend," Georgie whispered to Flicka. "I know she's pregnant."

"Oh, good. Yeah, so *that* was quick, too. Pulling together this wedding at the last minute has been impossible, just *impossible.*" Flicka slammed back another glass of champagne and hid a burp behind her silk opera-length gloved hand. "I had two fantastic acts lined up for the original wedding because *you* were *on tour,* but they couldn't change their dates to play this one."

Georgie asked, "Who?"

Flicka named a singer and a band, and Georgie's eyebrows rose. "You're kidding me."

"Nope. We could *afford* them. But all the money in the world can't change committed concert dates." She sighed.

Georgie stroked her hand up and down Flicka's spine. The muscles of her shoulders were bunched into knots.

"So come on," Flicka said. "I *need* someone *good* to play tonight."

"It's been a tough couple of days—" Georgie said.

"I have been through the *wringer* this week, and today has been *impossible*—"

"Do you even know what 'the wringer' means?" Georgie asked her.

"Of course not. Don't be vulgar. I *need* to hear 'Alwaysland' tonight."

"It's a bit melancholy for a newlywed," Alexandre said.

Flicka chugged another glass of champagne and reached for the scotch that the waiter was handing her.

"I love that song, Alex. I really do. You knocked it out of the park with that one."

"These people don't want to hear me sing," he said, gesturing with his healthy hand at the crowd. Georgie noticed that he was keeping the hurt one in his lap. "They're all far too sophisticated for that."

"Screw them," Flicka said. *"I* want to hear it."

"He's really not up to it," Georgie told her.

Flicka argued with Georgie, "His voice isn't as hoarse as it was at the civil wedding, and he sang great there."

"We've had a hellish couple of days—" Georgie started.

"I want to hear you play one more time." Flicka glared at Georgie. "You're walking out of everyone's lives again tomorrow—"

Georgie frantically tried to shush her.

"—and I want to hear 'Alwaysland' like Rachmaninoff before that happens."

Georgie turned to Alexandre. "Did you tell her that?"

He shrugged.

"You *did?"*

"I spoke to her *briefly* while we were figuring out how to get the clothes to the hospital without leaving you and myself unattended."

"Not briefly enough," Georgie muttered. "How much did he tell you? Did he tell you that Tatiana Butorin's mafia guys kidnapped us and held us hostage yesterday?"

Flicka leaned around Georgie and glared. "He always skips the good parts."

Alexandre laid his good hand on Georgie's arm,

keeping his other hand in his lap. "But we got away, and we're fine now."

Flicka looked back to Georgie. "Are you?"

Alexandre's hand squeezed her arm. An empty spot moved around the room where Adrien should have been.

Georgie said, "It was a rough day, but we're fine now."

"You're sure?"

Alexandre's fingers loosened on Georgie's elbow. She nodded and assured Flicka, "I'm sure. We're fine."

"Then you can play at least one song." Flicka drained the glass of scotch and rattled the ice to shake loose any remaining whiskey. "Or two. Maybe three."

Georgie rolled her eyes. "Come *on,* Flicka."

"I'm serious. I called *everyone.* I had Casimir make inquiries with all his clients and their friends and their friends' friends. I practically offered him sexual favors, not that he needs any more of *those.*"

Georgie glanced over at the lawyer with the deep green eyes, but his back was toward them. He was nodding and listening to the embattled earl who was explaining something very important, from the way he was leaning forward and holding his fingers pinched together.

"But no one was available. *No one.* I did my best," Flicka said, swirling the champagne glass and watching the spirals of bubbles rising through it. "I swear to God, I did."

"It was beautiful. You did a great job. It was flawless. Did Wulfram or Rae say something to you?"

"No. Well, they said thank you and that they loved it, but they're too busy making goo-goo eyes at each other to notice anything about their own wedding."

When Flicka said that, Georgie was just sliding some champagne into her mouth. The thought of The Dom making *goo-goo eyes* choked her and shot the bubbly wine up into her nose, where it fizzed and stung. Georgie coughed.

Flicka pounded her on the back and continued, "And I wanted everything to be perfect for them, just perfect, and I tried to get a headliner act for the reception. Everyone was busy on such short notice. Rae wanted to have the wedding as soon as the doctor gave her leave to travel because," Flicka dropped her voice to a whisper, "—she didn't want to get any bigger and not be able to fit in any dresses. I told her that Anne Boleyn was eight months pregnant when she and Henry the Eighth married, and she told me to 'hush my mouth.'"

Georgie chuckled behind her wine glass. Yeah, that was Rae.

"And I just wanted someone *good,* someone *nice,* for their reception, but no one was available. Everyone will titter at him," Flicka's voice choked in her throat, "and they'll talk, and they'll say terrible things because he didn't have a huge act play his reception. I *tried.* I tried so *hard.* But it was just too *soon.*"

Georgie glanced over at Alexandre, who had turned to listen to them again. His dark eyes had become very serious. "They will, won't they?"

"People say terrible things, given half a chance." Flicka's flashing glance at him looked guilty. "You know how it is."

Alexandre looked over the crowd. "Yeah."

Oh, God. Yes, people said terrible things, the poor guy. Georgie reached over and took his good hand.

Georgie put the slightest bit of pressure on Alexandre's fingers, a small squeeze. Blue bruises had developed over his knuckles. The sudden inclination to kiss them away seized her, but they were in public and seated at the most visible table, and it wouldn't help, anyway.

"So you'll do it?" Flicka asked.

Alexandre pressed his lips together and looked at Georgie, his dark eyes wary.

He looked over her to Flicka and nodded.

Wow.

Georgie raised her eyebrows. Was he sure?

He nodded again and closed his eyes.

Oh, Hell. They should do it. Maybe Georgie could just have plastic surgery or something once she got to Atlanta. Not a bad idea, really, after the thousands of cell phone videos that were out there with her face all over them. Maybe she would put it on Alexandre's credit card.

Maybe she would get her boobs done at the same time so that she had some for the first time in her life.

Maybe Xan would sneak into her dorm, like he had at Southwestern State, to see her new boobs.

Georgie turned back to Flicka. "Yeah. We can do it."

Flicka watched her holding Alexandre's hand and asked, "'Alwaysland' and what else?"

"We were agreeing to *one,*" Georgie told her.

"One isn't a performance. *Four* is a performance."

"Four? What happened to two or three?" Maybe Flicka should be the damn lawyer.

"What else?" Flicka pressed.

"How about 'Dragons?'" Georgie asked Alexandre. It was a slower power ballad and mostly written in the middle of Xan's range.

His steady gaze into her eyes felt like a warning.

"Which one is that?" Flicka asked her.

"You wouldn't know it anyway," Alexandre said, "as you never listen to *contemporary* music."

"I made an exception," Flicka sniffed, "because I wanted to see *Georgie* play. I had to see how much you've corrupted her."

Georgie rolled her eyes. She was already pretty well corrupted before she had met Alexandre.

"So which one is it?" Flicka asked.

"'I Would Slay Dragons For You,' one of the slower ones," Georgie said.

"It's written in G?" Flicka asked. "I like that one."

Alexandre nodded, his ponytail swishing behind his shoulders.

"So that's two. What else?"

The wariness in Alexandre's dark eyes was shading toward panic.

Georgie said, "That's it. Seriously. That's all we can do tonight."

"I don't suppose you have your violin with you?" Flicka's voice sounded nonchalant, but her furtive eye-flick at Georgie asked a very different question.

"No," Alexandre and Georgie said, in unison and very near in harmony. Georgie continued, "He left it in Milan. It's not here."

"You could borrow one from the string quartet," Flicka said.

Alexandre frowned. The shift of his weight in the chair looked like an attempt to not recoil in horror.

Georgie said, "Flicka, no."

"Just one of Paganini's *Caprices* or a short selection from something would give everyone something to talk about," Flicka pressed.

"It certainly would," Alexandre said. He settled back in his chair, his hurt hand hidden under the tablecloth.

Georgie leaned in to whisper to Flicka. "Absolutely not. You know *what might happen.*"

Yeah, she played the berserker card, but it worked.

Flicka shrank back. "Okay. Fine," Flicka sighed. "Maybe I can convince some of the other guests to play something. When will you do this?"

"After supper, before dancing?" Georgie ventured.

Flicka smiled, even if it was kind of wan. "At least you don't need me to find you a rehearsal piano this time. You guys must know all those songs by now. I liked the way you play 'Lay Your Ghosts To Rest.' I don't suppose—"

"Damn, Flicka!" Georgie said.

"All right, all right. I need to go rustle up some other talent to fill out the program."

"Rustle up?" Georgie asked her.

Flicka sighed and picked up her other glass of scotch. "Rae's Westernisms are contagious. They're so cute that I can't help but repeat them."

"Bless your heart," Georgie recited.

Flicka rolled her huge, green eyes. "That one, too. Last week, I was meeting with the head of an African wildlife reserve about our donations going forward, and I *blessed his heart.* You should have seen the confused look on his face. He wasn't sure whether to be flattered or to press for more money because I had obviously lost my mind."

Georgie laughed at her.

Flicka lifted her chin. "It's funny now, but I may end up having to move money around because the chimps need their little hearts blessed, too. Excuse me, Elton just came in. Maybe I can impose upon him."

Flicka swept off in a rustle of crystal-encrusted silk and whiskey fumes.

Alexandre stared after her, his expression as serenely neutral as always.

Chapter Twenty-Five

UNTIL YOU'RE SAFELY THROUGH TO THE OTHER SIDE

Georgie

A voice boomed through the ballroom, "Their Royal Highnesses Prince Wulfram Augustus and Princess Reagan, Hereditary Prince and Princess of Hannover."

Georgie looked up from her plate at the staircase, where her best friend Rae and Georgie's old friend Wulfram slowly made their way down to applause and a wash of flickering light from camera flashes. Rae wore a silvery dress, slim through her ribs but tucked and full in just the right places that entirely disguised the slight curve of the beginning of a baby bump.

Maybe royalty really did have magic fairy godmothers.

More likely, Rae's sister-in-law Princess Flicka knew designers that could work miracles.

Georgie stood as everyone else at the crowded head

table did, along with hundreds more chairs scuffing on the carpeting as all the guests stood. Applause rippled through the hall, swelling into a cheer.

Far down the head table, Lizzy had finally found some time to sit down and eat. The tiny little sprite of a girl in a fluttering dress was hauntingly reminiscent of a fairy with her pixie-cut blond hair that had grown a bit and curled around her face. Lizzy's fiancé, Theo Valencia, towered over her and bent to listen to what she said as he munched from a plate that looked like a saucer in his hand. His golden skin made him seem astonishingly healthy next to some of the very pale blondes in the room.

Flicka had returned with her husband Pierre, a spectacularly gorgeous man with dark hair, dark eyes, and a mischievous smile. Every move he made radiated self-confidence and good humor, a man who was used to being the center of the social circle and would one day rule a country with some actual authority, unless his uncle married and had children at this late date (unlikely) or something truly unprecedented happened (less so). Flicka seemed relaxed and hadn't pestered Georgie and Alexandre for more songs, which must have meant that Elton or some other guest had come through.

The last groomsman and his wife were sitting on the other end of the table, past Lizzy and Theo, and chatting amiably with them. They looked familiar—the tall, blond man and his brunette wife—especially when they smiled.

The other two groomsmen, Dieter with the stormy gray eyes and the Asian man with laughing, dark eyes —Yoshi, who must be Japanese, Georgie was pretty sure—sat next to the empty chairs where Rae and

Wulfram were supposed to sit, without another chair placed for a wife or significant other. Dieter talked little, except when he looked at his lap and muttered to himself, sometimes pushing a small earpiece farther into one of his ears. The Japanese guy talked to Lizzy, Theo, and the other two and laughed silently and often. His left arm didn't move, but swung awkwardly by his side. Maybe he really had taken a bullet for Wulfram.

Everyone seemed to be smiling except the large men fencing in the wedding party, all wearing black suits, all not applauding, all watching the crowd with restless eyes. Friedhelm, Paul, and their other security had blended into the paramilitary force occupying the wedding when they arrived at the hotel, though Paul stayed close to Alexandre.

Dieter tapped his earpiece and said something.

Five burly men formed a wedge and broke through the crowd, clearing a path for Wulfram and Rae to take their places at the head table.

Like choreography.

Georgie was impressed and creeped out at the same time.

All the rest of the wedding party was smiling and laughing. Pierre had evidently coaxed Flicka into relaxing or plied her with enough alcohol that she didn't care anymore, and she was hanging on his arm, giggling, while he patted her hand and grinned.

Everyone laughed and giggled and chuckled and joked.

Everyone except Alexandre. He held Georgie's hand with his good hand as gently as he did when they were sleeping. He looked at people who were talking and was pretending to respond, but his dark eyes were a little too blank, and his reactions were a little too late.

Georgie held his hand on the tablecloth or under it and waited. He obviously wasn't angry. Angry Alexandre or Xan or Alex was a smoldering beast that lashed out.

Wulfram and Rae made it to the head table and sat.

Georgie disengaged her fingers from Alexandre's, squeezing his hand just a little as she left, and dodged behind Flicka to hug Rae before she sat down. Even upper-class Georgie wasn't sure of the decorum of hugging the princess bride at a royal wedding, but she knew Rae wouldn't feel properly wedded without the huggin'.

Lizzy was standing right behind Rae and joined in a giggly, happy group hug. They had her properly laughing before she sat down, and Georgie noticed The D—, no, *Wulfram,* smiling that odd smile that touched his dark blue eyes, something that she had never seen before a few months ago.

She would hug him, too, she resolved.

But later. In relative privacy.

As accorded both their dignities.

When Georgie returned to her chair between Flicka and Alexandre, he grabbed her hand again and said, "We need to talk."

Georgie looked at her plate and the forest of champagne flutes longingly. "All right."

Wedding guests began drifting up from the tables.

The black-suited security guys twitched but allowed a few people at a time to pass, all the while patting the odd-shaped bulges under their armpits or tucked in the backs of their waistbands.

Alexandre captured her hand and led her against the stream of traffic out one of the gilded doors to the hotel's main lobby while Rae and Wulfram received congratulations from the rest of the wedding party. Georgie caught Rae's eye as she exited, teetering a little on her heels, but Rae smiled and waved her on.

Paul and Friedhelm followed them outside.

Alexandre looked around and made for a stand of tall potted plants, whirling her in and among the big leaves when they got there. Paul and Friedhelm stood a decent distance away and watched the hallway and doors, not the two of them.

"Again?" Georgie asked and stood with her back to the wall, grinning. "I guess we were talking about Wolfgang Rihm earlier."

Alexandre pressed his lean body to hers, his forearms on the wall on either side of her head.

"Jesus, Alex! Your hand!"

He bowed his head and whispered near her shoulder, "I can't sing."

"What? Of course you can. Your voice sounds pretty good, all things considering. You're just a little growly. You've done full concerts in much worse shape than you are now."

"I'm not Xan," he whispered.

All his denials ran through Georgie's head, about how they were really the same person and Alexandre was always there, but this was the truth. "Well, dredge him up."

"I can't," Alexandre sucked in a breath, "right now."

"Oh. Um. Did you know this when you agreed?"

He didn't answer.

"Oh, crap. Okay, um. Let me think." Georgie

thought, and she thought hard, but little was coming to her. "We have a piano in our suite."

"My hand isn't up to playing a piano."

"Not what I meant. We have maybe an hour. Let's go *practice.* Maybe we can—I don't know—*summon* him or something."

"He's not a ghost or a demon. It's not possession." Alexandre's voice cracked, and not from overuse and abuse.

"It's a metaphor. I don't know what else to call it. Work with me, here."

"All right. The piano."

Alexandre whispered to Paul as they passed, and he and Friedhelm shadowed them as far as the elevator and then passed by, heading back to the reception. Georgie and Alexandre took the elevator to their floor, again not touching or necking in the elevator, lest the camera feed be stolen and turned into a tragic, looping gif tagged #GetARoom or #TonsilHockey.

Georgie had a keycard that Friedhelm had given her on the way up. Inside the suite, her empty backpack lay on the couch. When she peeked through the bedroom door, the sheet music to "Scrambled Eggs" and her few clothes were still littered over the bed.

The baby grand piano was tucked in a corner of the enormous suite. She said, "I can't believe they managed to get a suite for us."

Alexandre stood near the floor-to-ceiling windows, looking out at the night and the dark lake. The moon had risen and drew a dashed line of light on the rippling water. "Flicka said that they rented out the entire hotel."

At the piano, Georgie lifted the fallboard to reveal the keys. "Because they could."

"Of course."

She bent over and ran a C-scale up the piano from one end to the other, making sure that it was in tune. Practicing with an off-tune piano might drive Alexandre batty with weird colors or something. Luckily, it rang like it had been freshly tuned. She said, "Come on over here and sit."

He turned and looked at her for a minute, his good hand tucked in his suit pocket, before he sauntered over and sat on the piano bench. "I can't play it."

Did he hurt his other hand fighting? "Not even with your right hand?"

"My piano is rudimentary at best." He set his right hand on the keys and played a B-flat scale, one of the more difficult ones with odd finger-crosses, but he played it in perfect tempo and with excellent touch. He may have been a 'rudimentary pianist,' but he was an excellent musician.

Georgie stood behind him and leaned down close to his shoulder, her cheek nearly touching his. Warmth from his body touched her skin where the silk dress gaped in front. She whispered, "Warm up."

Alexandre cleared his throat and sang the scale while his fingers crawled up and down the keys. He sounded fine and just like Xan when he sang. There was no disconnect.

Georgie had been pretty sure that would be the case. Alex and Xan hadn't known that they could play the violin until they had touched it, but their hands and body had remembered as soon as they had felt the wood. Singing should be the same.

She hoped.

He said, "Scales in a hotel room are different than performing in front of seven hundred people."

"You made me do it at their first wedding."

"That was different."

"You can do it." She stretched her arms out and around him, pressing herself all along his back. "Sing it softly, here, just to warm up."

Georgie played a few notes of the intro to cue him.

Alexandre began to sing, quietly, nearly whispering, "It was late at night in the thundering darkness, and I couldn't break through it to you."

She pressed the piano keys with her strong fingers as he sang, her arms around him, her body pressed to his back.

After a few moments, he rested his head against her shoulder while he sang.

Every time he took a breath, his body swelled in her arms.

Georgie pressed her cheek to his, kind of like they were dancing, but from behind. Alexandre turned his head up while he sang, changing how he touched her. His violin callus was rough against her cheek, and he sighed between lines as he nudged it against her cheek.

They finished the song, and Georgie let a few notes trail off.

His eyes were still closed.

She said, "Your voice sounds stronger than it has in a long time."

"I feel like I've never sung in public before."

"Do you remember the concerts?"

He nodded. "But they feel far away."

"You've played the violin in front of an audience."

His breath chuffed in an aborted laugh. "Thousands of times."

Those thousands of performances had been before he had turned eighteen, when Alexandre Grimaldi, child prodigy, had dropped out of sight, which meant that he had played hundreds of concerts per year as a child.

Georgie wrapped her arms around his shoulders and pressed her cheek against his. "Look at *me.* Sing to *me.* I'll hold you until you're safely through to the other side."

His hand stole up and rubbed her arm, but he didn't say anything more.

Georgie played the intro to "Dragons," and he sang that, breathing more easily during that song, and then it was time to go downstairs.

Chapter Twenty-Six

ALWAYSLAND

Alexandre Grimaldi

Flicka announced, "Ladies and gentlemen, Xan Valentine."

The lights over the ballroom were dimmed, so Alexandre only saw faint shadows weaving amongst the dark tables. Small spotlights shone down on Alexandre from three stories above as he stood near the concert grand piano, haloing himself and Georgie where she sat at the keyboard.

The ruby jewelry set that his sister had brought from Monaco gleamed against Georgie's tan skin, matching her dress and the color of her lips. Everything about her looked decadent, rich with color and music like luscious dark cherries and the music of cellos.

Georgie played the intro to "Alwaysland," which they had decided to do first since they had sung it together so many times. The words hung in his head, shaded with blue and green as the music swelled in him.

He could see the colors. He could touch the music.

But he couldn't feel Xan Valentine.

The last note of the intro sailed through him, and he joined the music, singing the song he had written years ago in a moment of despair and pain and loss.

It had been one of Killer Valentine's breakout hits, and he would probably sing it several times a week until he retired to Monaco and was guarded by men with guns to keep the fans away.

His customary earring swung from his ear: a large, spherical-cut emerald that had reminded him for years with gentle taps against his neck that he was committed to music, that music was a bitch mistress, that there could be no other love in his life than the violin, the band, and music.

The stone weighed on his earlobe.

His throat vibrated like a violin string as he sang, standing behind the piano relative to the audience, with his broken hand dangling at his side and out of sight.

There was a familiarity to this, standing before a crowd and giving them the music, either from his violin or from his body. The colors streamed through him, emerging from him as sound. He felt like he expanded until he filled the room, his life ringing from the walls and ceiling with his voice.

That was Xan Valentine filling the room, touching everyone, the smoke from Alexandre's fire.

The song ended, and he let his voice fall away as Georgie played the last line while smiling at him.

Could she see it?

The sterling zigzag sounds of the piano faded from his sight, replaced with the clattering static of applause until Georgie tapped the first few notes of "I Will Slay Dragons For You."

Considering the events of the last twenty-four hours, this song resonated with Alexandre. He had slain Russian warlords and fought killers, and he would have slain a dragon for her.

The muted stage lights shone on her skin, shimmering like soprano bells. The soft patter of her fingers on the keys traced his skin, and he wanted to touch her.

The introduction ended, and Alexandre sang,

"I love you like Lancelot loved Gwen,
I'll love you 'til they find the Holy Grail
and I'll love you when,
the stars all fall from the sky and the rivers turn to blood and the monsters wail,
and I would slay dragons for you."

This time, he didn't fill the room. He watched her, a laser-like focus that blew through him and felt like he was binding them with a cord.

He wanted to stand at the piano and sing and watch her forever.

Without thinking, he stretched out his left hand and laid it on the top of the piano, reaching toward her as he sang. His sleeve rode up his wrist. The metal splint clinked on the piano top.

The last line rang through him, and the song unraveled in his hands and he let it go.

With another breath, he was the form and shape of Alexandre, and Georgie was smiling broadly for him.

Some people in the audience, however, the ones sitting up close, were muttering, and he heard their unease right before the explosion of applause from the rest of the wedding guests slammed him.

The smoke within him billowed in the slamming noise, and Alexandre turned to face them.

The cacophony didn't threaten to shake him apart like it always had after a violin concert, the crashing hands turning to color and vibration in his chest. The maelstrom spun in the air, invigorating him.

He held out his hand—his healthy right hand—and led Georgie around the piano for a quick bow before they hurried toward the doors to the hallway outside. The next person whom Flicka had coerced into performing was already walking toward the piano, the spotlights flashing on his jewelry and sequined hat.

Flicka was standing near the front row, unwavering, an amazing feat considering how many drinks he had seen her pound within the last few hours. The odd spotlights reflecting off the wooden floor grayed her pink dress, even reflecting silver lines on her bare shoulders. She watched his left hand as he walked, and when she finally looked into his eyes, her steady gaze was serious and frightened.

She had seen the bandages.

Alexandre and Georgie emerged into the hallway right beside the stand of potted plants, a small forest of broad-leafed plants strategically placed to soften the corner of the hallway. He held her hand and whirled her back within them, stalking in after her.

Georgie laughed as he followed her between the plants. "I didn't think performing would do this to *you*—"

Alexandre shoved her up against the wall, grabbed the back of her neck, and kissed her hard. Her soft lips parted under his, and he slanted his mouth over hers and kissed her more deeply. Her hands slid up around his shoulder, and he pressed his body against her, feeling her slim, sleek body barely separated from his by clothes.

"Upstairs," he ground out as the colors of lust swirled in his head.

"We'll miss Elton's performance." A blue and silver rainstorm soothed his skin as her voice whispered in his ear.

He slid his arm down to her waist, careful to keep his numb left hand back and away from her. "Upstairs. Now."

"Xan?" she asked, her light voice tentative.

"*Non.* Alexandre. Always, *Alexandre.*"

He grabbed Georgie's hand and tugged her, leading her to the elevator. She spun around him, laughing, and he tapped the button for their floor.

As the doors were closing, through the gap between the doors, he saw Flicka bustle out of the ballroom and, seeing them in the elevator, rush to try to stop the doors.

He held his hand behind his back and didn't even try to hold the doors for her.

The doors tapped closed, and the elevator dragged upward to their floor.

His phone vibrated in his pocket, but he didn't answer it.

The music had rung through him as clearly as if he were only an instrument. The applause had intensified it until it was nearly unbearable.

He grabbed Georgie around the waist—"What are you doing? *Alexandre!*"—and kissed her roughly, shoving her slight form up against the wall of the elevator. Her hands held onto his shoulders and she kissed him back, but when he bent and ran his teeth down her neck, she stretched in his hands, scanning the ceiling for security cameras.

He kissed her again. Fuck the cameras.

His phone buzzed again against his thigh. And yet again.

As the elevator doors ground their gears and parted, he stepped back from Georgie. Her tanned cheeks had pinkened, and she was breathing hard and watching him with a haze of lust over her sweet, brown eyes. He checked his phone. Four missed-call icons lined up on the top bar. When he tapped the screen to see them, they originated from four different phone numbers.

One was from Flicka, of course, from right after she had missed the elevator. Another was from his sister, Christine Marie.

Both were expected, as they had seen the bandages on his hand.

The third was from Moririshi Morimoto, the conductor of the Tokyo Philharmonic whom he had spotted at the wedding ceremony.

At the sight of the last, long stream of digits, colors swam in Alexandre's head. The numbers became a shaded spectrum that belonged to Teobaldo Sergio

Boerio, a composer and the conductor of the Filarmonica de La Scala in Milano, who had been hounding him for years. Killer Valentine had almost skipped Milan just in case Boerio had made the connection between Alexandre and Xan Valentine.

And now both conductors had Alexandre's phone number.

Probably from Flicka or other mutual friends in classical music.

Alexandre wanted to pound his head against the wall in frustration. He shouldn't have come to this damn wedding. Von Hannover was a major music philanthropist and attended dozens, if not hundreds, of concerts every year, serious music and contemporary. His first, impromptu wedding had been mostly school chums still left in town from Flicka's wedding the night before, so Alexandre had been relatively safe. None of them would have ratted him out.

This wedding was different. Every orchestra wanted an "in" with von Hannover, and no one associated with any one of them would have dared refuse his wedding invitation. Between von Hannover and all this philanthropic friends, this wedding would be one of the networking events of the season for musicians.

Dozens of major musicians and composers and conductors must be at this wedding, had been skulking all around him and sitting at the tables while he had sung.

Alexandre had been so tired and rattled and had just wanted to keep Georgie for one more day that he had walked into what was, for him, a perfect trap.

And then he had allowed himself to be presented as Alexandre Grimaldi, the name with a dozen connotations. He had hidden behind his and Wulfram's security during the supper, and the conductors hadn't dared approach.

He might have made it out.

But then he had allowed Flicka to introduce him before he sang as Xan Valentine.

And then they had all seen his hand, his left hand, trussed up in bandages.

His phone buzzed again in his hand, another number morphed into the colors associated with another conductor, this time from the Moscow Symphony.

Alexandre gripped his phone on the side and powered it down. It buzzed again as it died.

He would deal with them later. The power of the music was still crashing through him. He slammed the suite's door behind him and used his good hand to lead Georgie toward the bedroom.

"Alex!" she protested, but she didn't pull away.

He shouldered the door open and whirled her toward the bed, his body resonating with the music and roar of the crowd. A pile of laundry was heaped up on the other side of the bed, and sheet music spread over the bed fluttered from opening the door.

She stumbled, and he wrapped his good arm around her, holding her up. As soon as she molded her body against him, the vibration amped up and became thunder in his mind.

Georgie's eyes widened, looking at him. *"Xan?"*

"Non," he said. "Not Xan. *Alexandre.* Say it."

She smiled, and her words almost sounded like sliding, soft French as she said, "Alexandre."

Her voice was moonlight-touched blue rain on his skin, but his name was an explosion of darkness and fire.

He kissed her again, his mouth and tongue stroking hers. He grabbed her body through the thin silk of her dress, his hands gripping her spare flesh underneath.

"It'll wrinkle," she murmured against his lips. "We have to go back at some point."

He couldn't imagine anything beyond holding her in his arms and making love to her.

The thin strap of her dress slipped down her arm, and that seemed like an excellent idea. He nipped the side of her neck just below the ruby necklace and chewed down her shoulder. She was squirming against him, almost as hot as he was, and her hand slid down to his ass.

When she pulled his hips against hers, Alexandre thought he was going to lose his mind.

He reached behind her and yanked the short zipper down. The dark red silk slithered down her, a whisper over the pounding of his heartbeat in his ears.

"Just let me hang it up," she whispered.

Alexandre's fingers found the waist of her pantyhose and dragged the side down, catching her panties on the way. She helped him, grabbing the other side near his broken hand and pushing the wispy stuff down her legs. He bent to get them off of her, tasting the warmth of her breast and stomach as he pulled them off, exposing the smooth expanse of her tanned legs and stomach and the lighter skin on her ass and tits.

He *loved* tan lines, loved to run his fingers and tongue over them and follow where they went as he saw the secret parts of her that even the sun didn't get to touch. He licked the shaded line below the smooth spiral of her navel.

A moan slipped from her, and her fingers found the back of his neck under his hair.

Alexandre dropped one knee to the floor and wrapped his good arm around her bare waist, holding her against his mouth as he explored the satiny skin over her stomach and mouthed up to her slim breasts.

Georgie groaned, her low rumble rattling through him. Her breast swelled as he flattened his tongue, laving around the peak, inhaling her faint perfume and natural scent. She kept saying that she was too slim and that she should get implants, but the interplay of her muscles under her skin and the scant softness of her fascinated him. She was supple and strong in his arms, ready for anything he could think of.

And he could think of a *lot.*

His tuxedo jacket shifted on his shoulders as her fingers slipped it backward. The lining slipped down his right arm and he lifted his hand out of the sleeve, but the jacket bogged down on his left.

He was sewn into it. *"Shit."*

"I left enough room. I can help," Georgie whispered. She turned in his arms and worked at the cuff of his jacket. "Tell me if this hurts."

And risk her not taking it off of him? Not a chance.

But his hand was still numb deep inside and covered with dead skin under the thick splint and bandages, and it didn't hurt.

The coat fell to the floor, and Georgie began unbuttoning his shirt.

He grabbed his shirt collar with his good hand, his fist tightening on the fragile fabric.

"Don't rip out the seam," Georgie said. "Give me a sec. We have to go back down there at some point."

Yeah, maybe.

Or he might take hours with her, which seemed far more attractive just then. He wasn't avoiding the conductors or the questions. He just wanted Georgie in his arms and in his bed, and he refused to think that it might be for the last time. He would change her mind. He could convince her. He would *win* her like he had won millions of fans and he would *keep* her.

He had given up everything else for her.

Her fingers danced down the line of buttons between his pecs leading down to his navel, and she pushed and tugged and worked that shirt off of him, too. He pulled at his undershirt, and she guided it off of him, her fingers grazing the skin over his abdominals.

He caressed her shoulders as she unhooked the waistband on his pants and helped him push all the cloth down his thighs and over his feet, hopping out of his shoes. His socks came with the pants, and he could finally touch her.

With his left arm held out to the side for balance, Alexandre slipped his arm under her shoulders and lifted her, sliding the silk of her body up his taut skin and hard dick.

Her hands slipped up his chest.

God, he wished he could lift her in his arms, but his left hand wouldn't allow him to do that, either. If he started to drop her, his fingers couldn't catch her.

He ducked his head to kiss her, tasting wine and warmth on her tongue, and turned her toward the bed.

Georgie wiggled away, sliding out from between him and the bed, and turned him around. "My hair," she whispered. "Stupid hair. If I go down there with a rat's nest—"

He kissed her again. He got it. He'd had long hair for a couple years and had been accused of having freshly fucked bedhead more than once. It was probably worse for women.

Alexandre sat on the bed and scooted back, dragging her with him so that she lay on top of him. He kept his left arm spread-eagle on the bed, but let her kiss him, her slight weight pressing on his torso and rubbing on his dick. Lust swirled fast in him again.

When Georgie came up for air, she giggled one breathless laugh. "Now I know you're not Xan."

"Je m'appelle Alexandre," he said because all his mind was feeling her soft skin on his body and the music of it deafened him and he couldn't quite remember how to speak English, *"toujours."*

She dipped her head and pressed her lips to his neck, and her breath on his skin tightened his muscles. He stretched to feel it, but he stroked her body above him, feeling her skin in his palm and fingers, running his hand down her ribs and the strong flesh of her ass. Her breathing on his neck quickened.

Alexandre shifted her to rest on his left side, appreciating her quick look to make sure that she was nowhere near his outstretched hand, and he rolled her back to feel her breasts. He could swipe his hand around them for days, feeling the softness of her, but she pushed her chest toward him. He thumbed and then stroked the nipple while her hot breath feathered his neck.

The fingers of his right hand slipped downward.

This was one thing that he regretted about shattering his left hand. He had discovered during his teen years that playing a tremolo on a woman's clit could drive her wild, bringing her to orgasm usually within seconds. He thought that his first two fingers might be intact, but he had long suspected that his right hand might have untapped potential, too.

He had held the violin bow with his right hand, his fingers rounded over it. His fingers were the fulcrum and power, drawing sound from the instrument. They controlled the tempo, rhythm, and pressure of the bow.

His fingers slid down, and he found her center was already wet for him. He rolled his fingers in her slickness, spreading it on her skin, and she arched against him. When his fingers slipped easily on her, he drew his fingers over her clit and down the sensitive center, drifting in a largo tempo that made her wait a few heartbeats for each caress.

She squirmed against his side, and he rolled toward her to reach her more easily, his hand slowly moving with her, not letting her have any more even though she was trying to grind herself against him. Her little whimpers beside his neck rippled over his skin as he held himself back. Her perfume on her neck was a drifting pastel fog of cool honey.

He increased his tempo to andante, a "walking" tempo. The arch of her back rewarded him, but her gasp against his neck drove him wild.

"Alexandre—" she whispered, his name whipping like wind over his flesh.

He angled his fingers, just stroking the side of her nub, then the other. She twisted her hips, trying to make him rub her hard and let her come, but he held her on the verge until her fingers dug into his shoulder and her breath was sobbing, "Please, please," against his shoulder.

His right hand was talented, too. Good to know.

He rolled onto his back and grabbed her waist with his good arm, dragging her over him. Her eyes were closed and she was biting her lip, as she maneuvered and settled onto him.

Her warmth and wetness slid over him, taking him inside her, and Alexandre's back bowed hard, lifting her slight weight. Her soft moans and whimpers fell in teal and white feathers, and her body rocked above him, sliding down his shaft. He pressed her lower back with his hand, keeping her clit down and pressed against his body. Her teeth pressed into her lip, and he watched each slide down on him ripple up her body.

The air around them was too still, too quiet with their bodies roiling in the center.

Alexandre whispered, *"Je t'aime,"* and felt his words echo between the walls.

Georgie barely opened her eyes, which were glazed and teary with passion. "I love you," she whispered back. *"Je t'aime,* and I love you."

He gasped, "I love you," and the air flowed like waves with their lovemaking.

She rode him faster, each push back onto him a burst of color behind his eyes. Her heat wrapped his dick with every stroke, rubbing the head and skin of him, and he pushed upward with his hips to stroke into her harder.

Tension pushed on him as his balls tightened. *Slow down.*

Georgie whipped her head back and cried out, slamming down on him. Her whole body shuddered and pulsed under his hand and around his dick, and it shoved him over the edge.

Color and sound rushed through him, a freight train of sensation, and Alexandre plunged into the deep void of oblivion where thought and feeling and color and music stopped.

The darkness whispered silence through him.

His body spurted his seed deep inside her.

He held her hips down on him with his one good hand, music and light singing along his nerves, until it faded away.

Alexandre drew in that first, cold breath that felt like being jolted alive. Georgie was holding herself up on her shaking arms above his chest, staring blankly at his pecs. Tendrils of her brown hair had escaped her updo and straggled down her long neck.

God, he loved it when she *writhed,* her whole body giving up her carefully crafted control.

"Okay?" he asked.

She nodded. "Man, we're going to have to talk about Wolfgang Rihm more often," she looked up at him, *"Alexandre."*

"Oui," he said.

Chapter Twenty-Seven

SOFIYA BUTORIN

Georgie

Georgie's legs were still shaking under her dark red dress. She clutched Alexandre's arm, and they walked back into the wedding reception.

Yes, she had helped him get dressed and button his shirt again. He had argued much less but had still fallen quiet, not sulking, but his shoulders tensed as if he were enduring it until she was finished dressing him.

Alexandre didn't pause at the doorway to the reception to gain his bearings. He strode across the floor while Georgie trotted beside him, dodging tuxedos and evening gowns between the tables as they made their way to the head table.

Paul stood behind Rae and Wulf and the rest of them at the head table, Georgie was relieved to see. He tracked their progress across the floor until they reached the protective circle of the black-suited men.

"Welcome back," Paul said to Alexandre, standing just off to the side of the table.

"How many of them have been looking for me?" Alexandre asked him.

Paul glanced at him from the sides of his eyes. "All of them."

Alexandre sat and shoved his hand under the table.

Georgie sat beside him, next to Flicka.

Flicka leaned over, resting her slim arm on the table. She blinked her huge, green eyes sleepily, or drunkenly, and asked Georgie, "Did you two ever eat?"

She must have noticed that Alexandre and Georgie had been absent for a while, before and after the performance. Georgie admitted, "We didn't get a chance."

"I'll call a waiter over. Atlantic salmon, bison, or pheasant?"

"Don't you royal people eat any normal animals? I'll have a slice of cheetah topped with a bald eagle egg."

"I ate thirty different meals here to decide on the menu," Flicka said, glowering. "These are spectacular."

Georgie flinched. Flicka had worked damn hard on this wedding. "Okay, um, the salmon sounds lovely. Alexandre?"

He watched the crowd, his dark eyes restless. "Whatever you're having."

While Flicka signaled a waiter over, a woman swayed out of the crowd, walking toward the head table.

Georgie barely glanced at her, sure that this svelte, tall women in heels and black evening gown was another beauty-bred princess of somewhere or duchess of somewhere else, probably ready to fangirl all over Xan Valentine, the rock star. Not that Georgie had ever been the jealous type, but this was so old that she didn't even notice Xan being polite and doing public relations duties. It was just part of the gig. Xan sang the songs, he strummed the bass, and he grinned and looked thrilled to meet the groupies, night after night after night.

The woman stopped in front of Georgie and braced her arms on the table.

Georgie glanced up, startled. The girl-groupies generally ignored her. Sometimes their dates did a little passive-aggressive flirting, which Georgie took with good humor.

The woman leaned down, her blond, curled hair falling from behind her shoulders. She smiled with straight, even teeth, and her smile seemed to be concealing more teeth, sharper teeth.

Alexandre looked up and lifted his good hand, signaling.

Paul strolled toward Georgie to stand at her back.

The woman said, "You killed Tatiana yesterday."

The accent within her silky voice was flat and Russian.

Vapor wafted through Georgie's head, and she couldn't form a coherent thought. "I don't know what you're talking about."

"I am Sofiya Butorin—"

A hot wave slapped Georgie in the face, and she scooted her chair back from the table.

"—and Tatiana was my sister. She is dead, shot in the back."

Tatiana was dead, and Georgie was a murderer and didn't regret shooting her for even a second.

Tatiana had been aiming at Alexandre, and Georgie had chosen to save him.

She swallowed hard. "I'm so sorry."

Alexandre was already standing beside her, and Paul had stepped up on her other side. Flicka glanced over from where she was discreetly twiddling her fingers at a waiter.

Sofiya's smile broadened but didn't touch her blue eyes. "You think you have escaped, Georgiana Oelrichs, but you do not understand. A *bratva* is not a snake where you can cut off head. *Solntsevskaya Bratva* is a family, and there is always a new *Pakhan.* I will come after you now."

Alexandre leaned, resting his good hand on the table. "Sofiya, we need to talk."

"We cannot. She has killed my sister, shot her down in cold blood, and six of our men, too. No school connection is worth more than that."

"It wasn't like that," Paul said.

"You are who?" Sofiya asked him, glaring at him.

"Interpol," Paul said.

Sofiya straightened. "We talk later."

"Wait," Alexandre said. "Let's talk now."

"I don't talk in front of him." She jutted her chin at Paul.

"That's understandable. Just hear me out."

Georgie glanced up at him. His French accent was still prominent, soft and sexy slurring, but his rhythm seemed a little crisper, a little more British.

Alexandre said, "I'm sorry about your sister. The situation got very far out of hand." He laid his bandaged left hand on the table. "Very far out of hand."

Sofiya's sharp glance up at him spoke volumes. "She broke *your* hand?"

"I broke it to escape. They were holding guns to all our heads. It was very uncivilized."

Sofiya frowned. "*Your* head? She threatened *you?*"

Alexandre nodded, his eyes solemn.

Paul said, "Tatiana was aiming at Alexandre when Georgie shot her. She was going to shoot him, even though Georgie was right there."

"That's not possible," Sofiya said.

"She was going to shoot him *first,*" Paul repeated.

Sofiya insisted, "That is not *bratva* business. *You* owe us the money," she said to Georgie. "He does not."

"I'll pay you," Georgie said. "I want to pay *everyone* back. I'm going to."

Beside Georgie, Flicka turned and was listening, leaning forward, staring up at Sofiya.

Flicka said, "I can pay you what she owes, now, here, and then she can reimburse me."

No fucking way was someone else going to pay Georgie's debts. "No."

"That is not right," Sofiya said. "It sets a bad example to have someone else pay debt."

"I agree," Georgie said to Sofiya. "*I* owe you that money."

"Yes," Sofiya agreed, rolling her eyes with relief that someone finally understood.

"I have some money saved," Georgie said. "And I can get more."

"It is important that we have all eight million US dollars now," Sofiya said. "Examples are very important right now."

Right now, while Sofiya was taking over the *bratva,*

when she needed several shows of strength to gain the loyalty of the other members.

"I don't have any way to get that much," Georgie told her. "I understand why *you* would want it, but I just can't. There's no *way.*"

Alexandre leaned in. "Yes, examples and public image are *very* important right now. Just between us, Sofiya, I always thought that Tatiana was too hot-headed to run your family business."

Sofiya dropped one light eyebrow at Alexandre. Her tone was dry. "What of it?"

"I thought you could do a good job, though," he said. "Better than Sergey could."

She snorted one dismissive chuckle, obviously aware that she was being flattered by a guy who was used to his flirting working on pretty much anyone. "Yes, thank you. This does not help us with problem."

Alexandre's gaze at Sofiya sharpened. "How are you differentiating yourself from Tatiana and Sergey?"

"I beg pardon?"

"Tatiana had headed the *bratva* since Dima died, right?"

"Yes." Sofiya's head tilted, and she looked at Alexandre with more interest.

He said, "But she never consolidated it."

"She did good job," Sofiya said. "No one is perfect."

"But she left a lot of things hanging," Alexandre said. "Georgie's debt was a PR problem. It undermined Tatiana's authority. She couldn't even get your money back from a young woman with no protection."

"It pissed her off," Sofiya said. "She rant about Georgiana Oelrichs a lot lately."

"She got emotional about it," Alexandre said. "She

went after Georgie with violence, meaning to kill her, even though it should have been business."

"It should have been business," Sofiya agreed.

"And Sergey is a year younger than I am, so he's three years younger than you are, right?"

"Yes."

"So he's twenty-four, which is old enough to make a power grab."

Sofiya's eyes narrowed. "Yes. He is."

"You have a public relations problem. You need an image for people to follow. They need a persona that they understand and can be loyal to. An image, or a mask, if you will.

Sofiya watched him. "Go on."

"Let's conduct *business.* Georgie wants to pay you back. She has committed to pay everyone back. Let's discuss how she will pay *you* back the eight million dollars that her father stole from you."

Georgie sat back. At least Alexandre had the terminology right. It pissed her off when people used polite euphemisms for her father's crimes.

Alexandre continued, "And she will pay *you* quickly and with a profit for you and your business, something that Tatiana wasn't able to accomplish in seven years."

Georgie nodded, trying to back him up.

Sofiya leaned back and crossed her arms. "I am interested."

Alexandre said, "Georgie will earn royalties from the Killer Valentine songs that she co-wrote. Considering how well the last album has done, we can forecast that her songwriting royalties from this album should earn at least two million dollars per year for the first decade or so."

That was new information for Georgie. Two

million dollars a year? For listening to his music and playing it back to him? It was too much. He shouldn't have done it.

Alexandre said, "We can assign the royalties directly to you for *five* years. It's a bit of a risk, but Michael Jackson took a risk when he bought the Beatles' catalog, too, and it paid off for him."

Sofiya nodded. "Two million per year for five years. That would be good business."

"We can have the lawyers draw up the official assignment," Alexandre said, "but business is always conducted with a handshake."

He held out his right hand, palm slightly up, and waited.

Georgie couldn't even breathe.

Sofiya placed her hand in his delicately, her slim fingers slipping into his palm.

Alexandre covered their hands with his left hand, the broken one, bound in bandages, splinted underneath, and he held it there.

Even Georgie could read Alexandre's subtext there. Resting his broken hand on hers was a reminder of what Tatiana had taken from him. The *Solntsevskaya Bratva* owed him, and this was how he was calling in the debt, by releasing Georgie from hers.

Her whole body was shaking in her chair.

Sofiya kept her hand in Alexandre's until he lifted his bandaged one off. "Our lawyers will talk," she said. She turned to Georgie. "I am glad that we are able to do business and end this matter."

"So am I," Georgie said. "Thank you for understanding."

Sofiya nodded and walked away into the crowd, her hips swinging in her slim black dress.

Georgie let her hands fall to her lap, trying very hard not to make a scene and clutch her chest where her heart was vibrating.

Alexandre sat down in his seat.

"Thank you." She grabbed his elbow, the good one. *"Thank you."*

His bandaged hand found where her fingers gripped his arm. The gauze was soft, but the steel splints under it were unforgiving. He whispered, "Anything for you."

She rested her forehead on his shoulder, exhausted. "Thank you."

Alexandre laid his cheek against her hair. "Anything."

Chapter Twenty-Eight

THE MAESTRO

Georgie

After a truly magnificent piece of salmon and assorted delectable side dishes—because Flicka had indeed chosen the entrées well—and several glasses of wine, Alexandre held out his good hand to Georgie and asked if she would like to dance, and she said yes.

Actually, she just wanted his arms around her, but surely that was too much PDA for a royal wedding. Dancing, however, was socially acceptable.

The string quartet played Tchaikovsky's "Waltz from Sleeping Beauty," and Alexandre led her through the milling crowd to the dance floor, now that the hors-d'oeuvre stations had been cleared away. Paul and Friedhelm stuck with them through the crowd and then stood a few feet away on the edge of the dance floor at parade rest, looking for all the world like two burly security guys who would kill you if reached into your coat in a suspicious manner.

Georgie was really glad that they were there.

Alexandre spun her into his arms, wrapped his good arm around her waist, and held up his bandaged hand at shoulder-height, suspended in the air where everyone could see it.

Georgie looked around them. "Alexandre, your hand."

"It's still numb," he said. "You can't hurt it."

"But everyone will see." She held her left hand up in the other direction and said brightly, "I could lead. No one will notice if you just *quit holding it up there in the lights.*"

He chuckled. "Have you ever known me to not lead?"

She pressed on his biceps, round under his tuxedo jacket, trying to lower his arm. "Everyone will see."

"Everyone already knows. Evidently, some people took pictures, including close-ups, while we were performing and posted them on social media and in certain classical music forums. Everyone knows who I am, who I was, and that there are very suspicious and distressing bandages on my left hand."

"Oh my God. I'm so sorry."

He shrugged. "I have been flirting with disaster for years."

"Hey, I love that song."

"Indeed. Today, it finally caught up with me. Everyone knows. So let's dance."

She held her hand up near his, and Alexandre nudged her hand with his bandaged fingers. He said, "Take my hand."

"I don't want to hurt you," she said.

"I will be fine. Don't squeeze."

Georgie curved her fingers and barely touched the gauze, watching his dark eyes the whole time.

He didn't wince, of course. He hadn't twitched when he had broken them.

They waited and began on the beat, carefully waltzing. Georgie held her arm up, and Alexandre led with pressure on her waist and by turning his shoulder under her other hand. Within a few measures, their bodies fell into the rhythm, and they danced.

They waltzed for half a song, grinning and laughing as they compensated for not being able to use their clasped hands to signal each other. The music swirled and they danced. It wasn't as enthralling as performing, but it was darn close. They even managed a few spins with Georgie's hand just brushing his bandages before he tucked her under his healthy arm again.

A hand clapped on Alexandre's shoulder and yanked, spinning him.

Alexandre's healthy arm turned in the air and he shoved Georgie behind himself.

An older man stood there, his wizened face twisted in anger. Even though he only came up to Alexandre's shoulder and even though they were in the middle of a crowded dance floor, he yelled up into Alexandre's face, "What have you done to your *hand?*"

"Maestro, I don't have time to talk to you." Alexandre turned back toward Georgie, but his dark eyes slid to the side.

Oh, great. *Maestro.* The old man was a conductor, evidently one of the conductors who wanted to eat Alexandre Grimaldi, the prodigy violinist, like fugu.

She was just peeking around Alexandre's arm to

see if the guy was leaving, when the old man grabbed Alexandre's shoulder again and wheeled him around. "Alexandre, what did you do?" He grabbed Alexandre's bandaged hand and raised it to his eye-level. "Your *hand?* What did you *do?*"

The crowd turned toward them, tuxedo jackets and white ties and smooth, bare shoulders all swiveling, pointing their glittering jewels and colored sashes at her.

Alexandre jerked his hand out of the man's grip. "Leave me alone."

The man sprayed spittle as he shouted, "You don't have the *right* to break your hand! You don't have the *right* to run away and hide and take your gift from the world!"

Alexandre pushed Georgie behind him again.

She stepped to the side and around him, encroaching on the guy.

Paul pushed through the crowd, trying to reach them, but he was on the far edge of the dance floor. He caught Georgie's eye. Panic registered on his face, and his jaw was clenched.

The man grabbed Alexandre's lapel in his bony fist and shouted in his face, "You don't have the right!"

Alexandre stared down at him, cold anger in his eyes. "Let go."

This was what Alexandre had been hiding from his whole life, and no wonder.

"Hey!" Georgie yelled, stepping forward. "Take your hands off of him!"

"Stay out of this," the old man snarled at her.

The crowd around them pulled back like a retreating wave sliding off the beach.

"I will not." Georgie slapped the man's hand that was holding onto Alexandre's jacket.

He opened his hand, shock widening his leathery eyes.

Georgie planted one fist on her hip and stuck her finger in his face. "You leave him alone. How he lives his life is none of your business."

Alexandre was watching her, and his right hand had curled into a bruised fist.

Stillness swept through the crowd like a shockwave as everyone stopped dancing and turned to stare.

"It *is* my business," the man said, looking down his knobby nose at her. "*Music* is my business. *Music* belongs to humanity and the ages, not to one man."

"It's *his* life and *his* music," Georgie told him. "Have you listened to his music?"

The man's worm-like upper lip twitched. "I only listen to *serious* music."

Paul reached Alexandre and stood beside him, one hand resting on Alexandre's elbow. The string quartet trailed off, the last violin note a squeal.

Georgie told the old man, "*You* get out of here, and *you* stay away from him. *You* don't have the right to tell him how to live his life."

"Georgie—" Alexandre said.

The silence reached the corners of the ballroom.

"No, let me finish. You should *all* hear," she said, turning around and looking at all the faces staring right at her. "Every single one of you who sent out a picture of him and snickered that his hand was broken. Every one of you who think that you know how he should live his life." She couldn't tell them what he had endured as a child. That was his, and private.

She whirled back to face the conductor. "*He's*

touched more people's hearts than you ever will," she told him. *"He's* changed their lives. *He* lifts people up when they're down, and *he* makes music that helps them go on."

The old man's face was reddening, and his mouth twisted.

Georgie went on, "Tens of thousands of people show up to listen to *his* concerts. Millions of people download *his* songs because they need to listen to him again and again."

The conductor sneered, "Popularity is not a measure of quality."

"Yes, it *is,"* she said. "They listen to his music because they *feel* something when he sings. *Millions* of people listen to him. His words and his music and his voice *change* people's lives. They *need* him. They need his *songs,* and they need him to tell them that they're going to be *okay.* Art is *communication,* and if no one is listening, it's not *art."*

"People listen to my music," the conductor stated, his tone growing petulant.

"A few," Georgie conceded. "Not millions, and it's not *your* music. When you're in an arena with him and forty thousand people are pouring their hearts out and singing his songs back to him because he was there when they needed him, it's magic. It's *art.* His music does belong to humanity and the ages, but it's not the violin. It's his *songs."*

He sneered, "An audience of shrilling women, screaming when he flips his hair around."

Georgie rolled her eyes. "So if *women* like his music, it must be somehow flawed. You only count *male* listeners as *real,* don't you? If women listen to or read something, it's not *serious* art, and it's inherently less valuable. Like when a male singer covers songs that a woman wrote and recorded first, and somehow *that* validates them, and *then* they're art. Or if a band's or artist's fanbase is over fifty percent female, then they're not worthy of awards or the hall of fame. Total bullshit. Utter, total bullshit."

"He was a genius violinist," the conductor insisted.

"No. He's a genius *musician.* He's a composer. He used to play the violin."

The conductor turned to Alexandre. "Are you going to let this *woman* speak for you like this?" He gestured, and the back of his open hand slashed perilously near Georgie's face.

"Don't touch her," Alexandre said.

"Or you'll what?" the conductor asked. "Have her yell at me some more?"

The conductor slapped his hand through the air again.

Georgie flinched back and raised her arm to block the blow, but it never came.

A slap, and Alexandre held the guy's wrist in his tightening fist. His dark eyes narrowed, and his teeth ground together when he said, "I told you not to touch her."

The conductor jerked his arm away. "You could have been a great musician, Alexandre. You had such *early* promise. You had a gift, and you squandered it."

Georgie said, "No, he didn't. He did exactly what he needed to do, and he touched millions of people's lives with his music. And that's what music is supposed to do."

The conductor flounced off, stalking through the silent crowd that recoiled in front of him.

Beside Alexandre, Paul's shoulders slumped. "Your Grace," he said quietly. "What do you want to do?"

Alexandre looked around and gathered Georgie under his healthy arm. "Get us out of here."

Paul and Friedhelm, who had been standing behind him, spread their arms and pushed the crowd back, creating a channel to lead Alexandre and Georgie forward.

The security men rushed Alexandre and Georgie out to the hallway and to the elevators. Alexandre kept his arm around her, holding her close to his side.

Chapter Twenty-Nine

CHRISTINE MARIE GRIMALDI

Georgie

They reached the elevator, and Paul herded them in. Friedhelm didn't actually have a gun drawn, but he stayed outside the doors until they were sliding shut and then backed in.

Alexandre leaned against the back of the elevator and rested his head against the wall, his eyes closed, his good arm still around her.

Friedhelm said to Paul, "That wasn't so bad."

Paul smiled with one side of his mouth, somewhere between sarcasm and grimness. "No, it wasn't."

Georgie said, "Crap. Paul, can I have my phone, please?"

He handed it to her, still warm from the pocket inside the breast of his coat.

She tapped icons and texted Rae, *I AM SO SORRY*

THAT I RUINED YOUR WEDDING OMG I AM SO SORRY!

She held the phone to her side, waiting for Rae to tell her that she was officially unfriended in real life, and leaned her head against Alexandre's shoulder.

He was holding his phone in front of him, resting his arm on her shoulders, and it chimed as it powered up.

"You've had your phone off this whole time?" she asked.

He nodded.

Georgie was just about to ask why when she noticed that the missed call icon had a thirty-six above it. "Is everything all right?"

He nodded. "I've been dodging calls from conductors."

"Oh, Jesus."

He shrugged. "I should have known this would happen."

Georgie wrapped her arms around his waist.

His phone rang, right there in his hand, right where she could read it. The caller ID read *Tamar Ben Haim.*

Alexandre sighed and answered it. "Hello, Maestro."

Oh, my God. *Tamar Ben Haim,* the pianist and conductor that Georgie had met walking around Juilliard. Georgie had been a card-carrying Haimite since she was about nine, ever since the first time her father had taken her to see Ben Haim play at Carnegie Hall.

And now Tamar Ben Haim was going to lay into Alexandre for breaking his hand and depriving the world of his violin.

Georgie wanted to grab the phone and fangirl hard because that was *Tamar Ben Haim* on the phone and simultaneously berate the woman for being such an asshole.

"I broke it pretty badly, Tamar," Alexandre said. "We'll know more after they do the surgery tomorrow."

He didn't sound upset. Georgie didn't need to grab the phone yet. She wrapped her arms more securely around his waist.

"The X-rays were concerning, but the doctor is very good." He listened. "Every day. For hours."

The woman's voice wafting from his phone rose, distressed.

He said, "I'm sorry, too, but I never had the time to go back to classical and perform concerts, and I probably never would have. It probably never would have happened, anyway." He smiled, but his smile had an unruly tilt. "I could bring Killer Valentine, and we could do a crossover concert like Metallica or Radiohead."

The woman's voice squawked.

Alexandre's smile bent up in the middle at her reaction to his provocation.

His accent was sliding toward high British but was still shaded with French. "No, I can't promise you that. Even if the surgeon is able to repair it—"

"When," Georgie muttered, stroking his side.

"—tens of thousands of people don't show up to hear me play the violin. No one has ever written to me to tell me that the violin helped them survive a dark night. Art is communication. I'm not going back to the violin."

More squawking, but to Georgie, it sounded like pleading.

"I promise that I will do the physical therapy, but it's not for the violin. I'm done, Tamar. That part of my life is over. I'm committed to this music, not classical. I have everything I need to forge a different life now."

He shifted his weight, pressing his side closer to Georgie. She squeezed her arms around his trim waist, holding him more tightly.

"When I get back to New York, yes. I'll see you then." He tapped the phone.

Georgie stroked his side. "I'm sorry."

"One down," Alexandre said, staring at his phone, "thirty-five to go."

"You don't have to justify yourself," Georgie told him, "and you certainly don't have to do it tonight. Tomorrow, you'll know more, right? Maybe you shouldn't talk to them before you know what's going to happen, anyway."

He nodded, still staring at his phone. "I have one more phone call that I have to make, though."

The elevator doors slid apart to reveal a young woman around Georgie's age marching from the door of their suite toward the elevator, her dark eyes flashing with anger and her dark auburn hair curling over her shoulders. Her blue ball gown swished around her ankles as she strode, and a diamond star that looked just like Alexandre's Order of St. Charles was pinned to the left side of the matching bolero jacket she wore.

She called out, "Alexandre!"

Alexandre actually turned a shade paler. "I was just going to call you, I swear to God."

Georgie stepped in front of Alexandre as the young woman stomped over the carpeting as she reached the elevator.

The woman yelled, "I swear to God!" Her British accent rounded her vowels like a Shakespearean actor's.

Paul pushed the button that held the doors open. Georgie stabbed at the doors-close button to escape, but it was too late now.

"I had the phone in my hand," Alexandre started, and he nudged Georgie aside with his good hand.

Paul moved away and leaned against the wall of the elevator. Friedhelm started to intervene, his hand outreached. Paul snagged his jacket and, with a pointed look, pulled him back.

The woman walked into the elevator, yelling, "You could have *told* me. You could have *texted.* You could have *called.* You could have slapped a *note* on one of my social media pages. You could have walked across the damn floor and whispered it in my ear. 'By the way, some conductors might call you to ask why my hand looks like a mummy.' *Twenty* of them in the last hour!"

She punched him in his right shoulder, hard.

"Ow," Alexandre said and rubbed his shoulder.

Ow?

Georgie turned.

Ow?

This from the man who hadn't flinched when he had broken his own hand or when he had tied a splint on it himself? Georgie tried not to gape, but she could feel her eyebrows sliding together.

Alexandre caught a glimpse of her. "Georgie, may I present my elegant and sophisticated sister, Lady Christine Marie Grimaldi."

Alex's British accent and his dry sarcasm were back online.

The woman turned and extended her hand, smiling. She was taller than Georgie by a few inches. "So lovely to *finally* meet you. I've heard so much about you. Your playing is exquisite. And just call me Christine."

"Oh, um, thank you," Georgie said. "Lovely to meet you, too."

Christine turned back to Alexandre and slugged him in the shoulder again. "Asshole."

"Ow!" More emphatic that time.

Georgie rolled her eyes that time at what was obviously a sibling game.

Christine said, "I've been fielding all the calls that you've been ducking, and I don't know what to tell any of them. Is your phone off?"

It buzzed in his hand, right on cue. "It's on now."

"You explain it to them. What did you do to it, anyway?" She turned her head to look at the bandages and splint on his hand.

"Nothing. I rubbed some dirt in it. It'll be fine."

Her voice softened. "Seriously, are you all right?"

"I'll be fine."

"And how about your hand?"

He didn't answer.

Georgie reached over and held his healthy hand. He gripped her fingers.

Christine asked, "How bad is it?"

"They're not sure," he said. "We'll know more after the surgery tomorrow morning."

"Surgery. Right. You should have *called* me. You should have at least come over to me at the wedding and mentioned it."

"I was planning on introducing the two of you a little later."

Christine looked up at him. "When, later?"

"Later tonight, but we had to leave."

"Yeah. I saw. When is the surgery?"

"Tomorrow morning, nine o'clock. Geneva."

"I'll be there."

He nodded.

Christine shook her head sadly. "What am I going to do with you, Xandre?"

He shrugged. "I'll be all right."

"I have to go back down there," Christine said. "People will talk."

"They always do."

Christine nodded. "Maybe I can quell some of it." She turned to Georgie. "Lovely to meet you. Will I see you tomorrow morning?"

Georgie nodded. "I'll be at the hospital."

"I wish it were under better circumstances, but at least I will see you there." She stepped aside. "All right. All of you, out. I have to go lie about him to people at the reception."

They skirted her, walking off the elevator.

As the doors started to close, she called out, "What should I tell people about how it happened?"

Alexandre turned back. "We were kidnapped by the Russian mafia, and I broke it to get out of handcuffs before we fought our way out and escaped."

Christine rolled her large, dark eyes like only an aggrieved sibling can. *"Fine.* I'll make something up."

The elevator doors tapped shut.

Georgie's phone buzzed in her hand.

The text from Rae read, *You didn't ruin it. Everything back to normal. Not the weirdest thing that has happened today by far, and you should have seen the last funeral that I went to. That was SO MUCH WORSE.*

Chapter Thirty

THREE CALLS

Alexandre Grimaldi

Alexandre waited until Georgie went to sleep in their bedroom in the suite, which didn't take long because it was after midnight in Montreux and sometime the next afternoon in the States. She had only slept a little, sitting up in the airplane the night before.

His hand throbbed. The novocaine had been wearing off for the last hour or so. Soon, the shattered bones inside would grind against each other with every heartbeat. The splint had helped, the improvised one on the plane and then the proper one at the hospital.

He slid out of the bed and stood in the dark, his boxers and tee shirt light on his body, a whisper of fabric that felt like a flute.

Before they had lain down to sleep, Georgie had packed her backpack, rolling up her clothes and some sheet music from where they had been strewn on the floor and bed, joking all the while about what a luxury it was not to fall into bed and barely be awake enough to shove the shoes off her feet.

She looked so sweet, sleeping on her back, one arm above her head and the other straight out to the side like a fencer, her long, brown hair splayed over the pillow and drifting toward the side of the bed.

He picked up his phone and her backpack as he sneaked out of the bedroom and closed the door quietly, twisting the knob in his one good hand to silently latch it.

The living room of the suite had comfortable beige furniture, and he sat and picked through her backpack, looking for the sheet music he had seen on the bed and that she had stuffed back inside.

The few pages of paper were rolled tightly and packed in a corner, and the papers fell open in his hand. He pressed it to his knee before it fell to the floor.

The music was a computer printout of "Scrambled Eggs," and it was an early version of the song Alexandre had struggled in vain to find words for. The coda was still written in F-major, here. They had changed it to F-minor months ago. This hard copy had his writing all over it, in ink from a blue, ballpoint pen, annotating the changes that they had discussed.

If she were going to steal it, the computer file would have been enough and preferable, because this showed in the footer that the file had been printed from his tablet and his handwriting was all over it, not hers. If she were saving it to prove that she had contributed and deserved to share the profits, she would have thrown it away by now because he had had her sign the copyright registration documents weeks ago. She knew that she was on the copyright and would receive songwriting royalties.

It must be a keepsake.

Alexandre smiled to himself. Of course, Georgie would take *music* as a keepsake.

He got up and poked around in the garment bags where she had rehung their clothes and put away the jewelry. A black velvet case hid in one of the pockets. With his one good hand, he managed to pry open the stiff hinges of the case and found his great-grandmother's Burmese rubies, the ones that Christine had had reset for a wedding a few years ago. The brooch was still in Monaco, and he had plans for the very large ruby set into that.

He set the necklace, earrings, and ring in the center of the sheet music, managed to roll it up by walking his fingers around the paper as he did it, and inserted the sheet music back in the corner of her backpack.

Now *that* was a memento.

Just in case.

He smiled, even though the suite was silent and still from the front door to the living room to the grand piano standing by windows overlooking the lake.

He picked up his phone.

Three calls.

First call: Jonas.

This call would probably be the most contentious.

He dialed and heard the click. "Hello, we need to reschedule the Roma concert."

"No shit," Jonas muttered. "Do you know what time it is? No, Rhi. Nothing's wrong. It's just Xan, being a fucking insomniac. Go back to sleep."

Thumping as he walked. "Seriously? You want to talk *now?* I've been leaving messages for *hours.*"

"Is everything all right with the tour?" Alexandre asked,

"Yeah, everything's dandy. *We've had an offer.*"

Alexandre was too exhausted to make sense of it. "An offer of what?"

"Upsilon Records offered Killer Valentine a distribution deal."

Alexandre fell backward on the couch. "No shit."

"We've got a meeting next Thursday in New York to hash out the contract."

Alexandre's head swam, and he planted his feet firmly on the floor to keep from floating away. "We may not take the first offer. Let's keep looking."

"Oh, we will, but Upsilon is prestigious. We should carefully consider their offer, whatever it is."

"We may need to reschedule that meeting next week. Maybe the week after."

"Why? For the love of God, why the fuck would you postpone a meeting with people who *want* to sign you?"

Alexandre's hand spiked a sharp pain that fluttered silver behind his eyes. "I'm having surgery tomorrow."

"What? Your face? Your *throat?* Are you going to *die?"*

Interesting order, there. Alexandre said, "I broke my hand."

"Jesus. Which one?"

"The left one."

"Are you going to be able to play the violin?"

Jonas had been the only one on the tour who had known about Alexandre's "fallback career."

Alexandre glanced at the closed bedroom door.

"It's utterly shattered inside. There's no chance for me to play again in any capacity, probably not even the bass guitar. I haven't told anyone here yet."

"Do you need me to come up there?"

"I have Georgie and other people here. I'll be all right."

"Okay. *Jesus.* If you need anything, let me know."

"Just the Roma concert rescheduled for this week, on Friday."

"I don't know how I'm going to find a venue in Rome that's big enough for *this Friday.* That's impossible. It's *insane.* You can still record in New Jersey this week, though. Right?"

"About that—"

"No way. Not the recording studio with the 'superior acoustics' that I almost had to blow some guy to book."

"We'll record after the Roma concert."

"They're booked," Jonas said. "There's no way to get that studio."

"You can offer them however much money it takes."

"You can't bankrupt Killer Valentine to book a particular recording studio."

"I have other money. We'll dip into that."

"You *do?*"

Jonas didn't know about Alexandre Grimaldi, the child prodigy, the Duke of Valentinois and Monégasque nobleman. He only knew about Xan Valentine, who had played the violin at Juilliard. "Yes. Enough to bribe us into a recording studio."

"Fine. I'll get it. You're nuts."

"You've always known that."

"Yeah. I'm going back to bed. And Xan—"

"Yes?" He had almost asked *Oui?* He would need to watch that when he was tired.

"Take care of yourself. Don't kick the bucket or anything."

Considering the last few days, he lied, "Me? Never going to happen. I'm young and immortal."

They hung up, and Alexandre peeked in at Georgie, who hadn't moved. She was breathing deeply, almost snoring, and he had an inclination to video her for blackmail purposes but refrained.

He sat back on the couch and thumbed through his phone.

Second call: his jeweler.

The best call, the one that made him smile.

This time, he called through a video chat already scheduled by email. *"Bonjour, Juste."*

Juste was a short, slight man, as slender as the filigree he was famous for. *"Bonjour."*

As they dropped into French, Alexandre relaxed. If Georgie heard, she wouldn't understand, and his nerves were already quivering like the quick gold that underscored music from a plucked violin string.

Juste asked, "The earring is doing well for you?"

He touched the huge, almost spherical emerald dangling from his ear. "It's done very well. I'm going to have it made into a necklace for my sister, I think."

"It would look lovely on Lady Christine Marie."

"But the ring that we discussed."

"I have some drawings for you."

Alexandre's screen blanked, and diagrams of rings took the place of the Frenchman. He leaned in to study them. "The upper left is good."

"Your taste has evolved, Monsieur. Your guidance streamlined this process immensely."

Yes, since last time he had had an engagement ring made, disastrously, when he had sworn to never make another. He tapped the emerald in his earring again. "The stones will be delivered by courier from Monaco tomorrow. I think you'll like the ruby. It's from a set that my great-grandmother got in Burma. The brooch is so large that it's unwearable, so we'll break that up."

"Excellent. I will prioritize this ahead of all other projects. I will see you in Monaco on Tuesday for any final adjustments, and it will be delivered on Thursday."

"Merci, Juste."

Just in time.

They hung up, and Alexandre's thumb hung over the screen of his phone.

Third Call: Guillaume.

Alexandre wanted a drink, a strong one, but he wasn't supposed to eat or drink anything after midnight due to the surgery the next morning.

Still, the whiskey bottle over on the minibar looked tempting, and rock stars were supposed to drink every hour, on the hour.

He thumbed his phone and listened to it ring.

A man's gravelly voice asked, *"Oui, Monsieur?"*

"Guillaume," Alexandre said. "We need to arrange a funeral."

"Oh, no. Adrien?"

"Yes."

"At home, sir?"

"We'll need to ask his next of kin. He never told me where he wanted to be."

"I think you were his only legal or blood relative, Your Grace. His parents passed away some time ago. I think you must make this decision."

Alexandre stared at the ceiling, his eyes burning, and he rubbed his face where a day's growth of beard itched.

"Your Grace?"

Alexandre drew a breath through the knot in his throat. "I think cremation, then, and a ceremony on the beach in Monaco." The same as he had specified for himself, someday. "And a Mass. He would have wanted a Mass."

"I think that's appropriate, Your Grace, and very well thought out. I'll make the arrangements."

"I'm here in Switzerland for another day. We could do it Wednesday."

"Yes, Your Grace. My condolences."

"And mine to you as well. He was a good friend to all of us."

"Yes, Your Grace."

They said their goodbyes, and Alexandre hung up.

His chest hurt inside, and he turned off the lights and crawled under the covers with Georgie. Her warmth and the mint of her shampoo and the light feminine scent of her floated all around him like pale pink veils in the air.

The fingers of his right hand slipped into hers without waking her up, and he held her hand, concentrating on the comfort there instead of on the shattered bones slashing the muscles and tendons in his left hand.

He forced himself to fall asleep for a few hours to escape the pain.

Chapter Thirty-One

DRUGS AS GOOD AS ABSINTHE

Georgie

Georgie waited with Christine in a private waiting room that looked like a Parisian hotel suite decked with country French yellow silk and blue fringe, but that astringent hospital smell lingered in the air and furniture. Paul was there, too, but he sat over in a corner, talking on his phone about arrangements for something in Monaco and reading a newspaper.

The two women talked for four hours, watching the clock, first about Alexandre and then about themselves.

Christine was two years younger than Georgie, just twenty-one.

When Christine handed Georgie a cup of coffee —*blessed coffee steaming with caffeine goodness*—from the refreshment table along one wall, she held it out in her left hand. Georgie took the cup and brushed Christine's hard, rough fingertips.

When she looked up at the underside of Christine's jaw, the left side had a dull, thickened spot, a violin hickey.

Georgie asked, "Do you play the violin, too?"

"Oh, yeah," Christine said. "I'm third chair with the Monte-Carlo Philharmonic Orchestra, probably due to nepotism."

"Violin runs in the family?"

Christine shrugged. "Sort of. Not really. I'm not a prodigy by any leap of the imagination. I went to a conservatory in Paris, but I've never been at the head of my class or anything. I'm just different."

"Of course you're different," Georgie said. "Everybody's different. I wasn't a prodigy, either, and I didn't compete or perform after I was sixteen. It must be hard to be a prodigy."

"Yeah, I'll say. Before you ask, I don't remember anything."

God, no. Ice slithered down Georgie's back. "I wasn't going to ask."

"It's okay. Everyone wants to know. I walked into the lesson with Maestro Soto, and then I woke up with all of Alexandre's clothes wrapped around me, lying in the snow. Our violin tutor was dead in the house, and there was blood all over me and Alexandre. Between then, it's just blank."

Georgie sucked in a swallow of the black, bitter coffee. "I didn't want to pry."

Christine spoke brightly, but she was staring out the window over the buildings of Geneva glowing in the morning sunlight. "And he won't talk about it, either.

If you find out anything from him, you'll tell me, right?"

"He hasn't told me anything."

"If he does, let me know. Then I can tell people what happened and they'll stop hinting around and prying every chance they get." She shook her head. "Sorry. Issues."

Georgie said, "Yeah. I understand issues."

"Oh, good."

Georgie's phone buzzed in her pocket, and the screen showed an auburn-haired woman with brown eyes and gorgeous cheekbones. "Hang on a sec. It's Rae. I'd better apologize for screwing up her wedding yesterday some more."

"No problem," Christine said, pressing her thumb to her own phone to unlock it.

Georgie answered, "Hi, Rae? Look, I am so sorry about last night—"

Rae's alto voice—and it was interesting that now Georgie picked out that her low tones were *alto*—said, "It's fine. It's nothing. Have you seen Flicka?"

"Not since last night."

"Or heard from her?" Rae's voice rose half an octave, and Georgie could hear other people speaking in the background. Wulfram's deep baritone voice spoke quickly.

"No. I haven't." Georgie caught Christine's eye. "You haven't heard from Flicka von Hannover, have you?"

Christine shook her head quickly. "No. Is she okay?"

Georgie repeated into the phone, "Is she okay?"

"We don't know," Rae said. "We can't find her. If

you get an email or a text or *anything* from her, call one of us right away, okay?"

"Is she all right?" Tremors ran through Georgie, echoes of being kidnapped less than two days before.

"We don't know. We're looking at surveillance footage. Wulf is calling out everything short of the Foreign Legion. She's not answering anything and her phone isn't active. I've got to go. I've got more calls to make. *Call me* if you hear anything."

"I will."

Rae asked quickly, "Is everything all right with you guys after last night?"

"Yeah. Alexandre is having surgery on his hand this morning, but he's fine. And we're fine. Let me know if you find her, okay?"

"I will. Bye." A click, and Rae's phone disconnected.

Christine asked, "What's going on?"

Georgie updated her with the complete lack of knowledge of Flicka's whereabouts. "So if you hear from her, call them."

Christine nodded.

They talked for a while longer until an orderly came to get them. "Mr. Grimaldi is back in his room. He's still sedated, but the surgeon wants to talk to you about him."

Christine and Georgie followed her through the hallways of the hospital, back to Alexandre's room. Paul was talking on the phone again and waved them on.

The surgeon was sitting in a chair, typing on a computer installed on a swinging shelf. Alexandre was sitting up against pillows, his bed raised like a recliner and his hand wrapped in a splint and bandages. His blond hair was tied back in a messy ponytail.

His radiant smile was almost creepy. *"Bonjour!"*

Christine asked the surgeon, "Is he okay?"

The surgeon looked up from her typing, a twinkle in her dark eyes. "English, yes?"

"Yes, please," Georgie confirmed.

"You are?" the surgeon asked.

Christine said, "Christine Grimaldi, his sister."

"Georgie Johnson, a friend."

"Oh, *you're* Georgie," the surgeon said, grinning.

What the hell was that?

The surgeon continued, speaking with a slight Hindi lilt, "He's having an idiosyncratic but not uncommon reaction to the sedative. He's been an absolute delight to operate on. He sang to us the whole time."

A sparkle lit in Christine's dark eyes. "Tell me you got video."

"No," the surgeon said, still smiling. "That's considered unethical. I usually don't do such extensive work under a local and sedation, but he refused general anesthesia because we would have had to intubate him."

Georgie understood. "Oh, because it might damage his throat."

"Yes, he didn't want to take a chance of bruising his vocal cords or abrading them, which is understandable. I've had patients sob the whole time under sedation. We generally knock them out for their own good, out of kindness to them and us. Some people sleep. Some people can't stop talking. I like to think that, when people have good reactions, that it's their true personality coming through. If they don't, they've had a bad couple of days. But Mr. Grimaldi sang to us the whole time, even encouraging the nurses to sing with him. I have never had a surgery like that. If I hadn't been concentrating so hard, I would have been laughing the whole time."

"He can sing pretty well," Georgie told her, watching Alexandre. She could not take her eyes off his huge, beaming smile.

"Well, of course," the surgeon said. "I desperately wish I could tell my friends that I have been serenaded by Xan Valentine, but privilege prevents me from telling anyone. My heart is breaking. Maybe he will give me permission to tell people privately, but it is still best not to speak of it." She sighed, hard.

Alexandre said, *"Allo, Zhor-zhie.* I see you've met my sister. Be careful. She bites." His French accent was very pronounced, his cadences and consonants soft and sweet.

Christine laughed. "I do *not."*

He said, "I have a scar on my ankle from when she was three, and she latched on like a terrier and would not let go." He started pawing at the bedsheets with his good hand, trying to show her his foot.

"It's okay," Georgie told him. "I believe you. You can show me later."

Alexandre leaned back on the pillow, grinning.

"Anyway," the surgeon said, slapping her knees and hoisting herself to standing. "The sedative should wear off soon, and then he'll be back to normal. We shot his hand up with long-acting local anesthetics. It should be numb for at least twenty-four hours, and then he will have a scrip for pain medication. Aftercare is the usual. Keep the wounds clean and dry until they're properly closed. He can return to normal activities for anything other than that hand tomorrow. Don't jostle it around too much for a few days, perhaps no running or anything that would shock it." She mimed pumping her arms back and forth.

She continued, "That hand will need to remain splinted for a few weeks, at least, even though I used bone glue, fillers, and pins. We'll get him a card for airport security in case he sets off the metal detectors, but the pins are small. He should start physical therapy in about a month or so, maybe two, depending on how well it heals, to attempt to restore some mobility."

"*Some* mobility?" Georgie asked. She and Christine glanced at each other. Christine tucked her left hand close to her jeans.

"Sounds like he didn't tell you," the surgeon said and looked down at her feet. "Yes, *some* mobility. The bones in his pinky and ring finger were shattered, even splintered, and there were breaks far down through the metacarpophalangeal joints. For those two fingers, his hand was like a glove filled with pebbles."

The room spun around Georgie, and she grabbed the footboard of Alexandre's bed. "He's a violinist."

"I know," the surgeon said, her smile gone. She patted Alexandre's other hand, and he grinned up at her. "And it's probably a good thing he was singing and so chipper, because otherwise, I might have wept the whole surgery. I talked to him yesterday after I saw his films. There was really no hope for even normal mobility. I had prayed that the X-rays were making it look worse than it was, but his hand was broken deeply, right through the joints. It wasn't recoverable. I took hours more than I would have for anyone else, trying to fix him."

"Oh, my God," Georgie said, staring at him.

Alexandre smiled at her. Something was wrong with his face, and she realized that he had taken the green crystal earring out of his ear, probably for the surgery. His other hand was bare, too. No rings, not even his death's head ring that he always wore on his right hand.

Christine stepped up beside Georgie and muttered, "That violin is his baby. It's everything to him."

"Are you sure?" Georgie asked the doctor.

"We can pray for a miracle, but the damage was severe. It would take divine intervention, and I've never seen that happen. There really is no scenario where he could play the violin at any level of expertise again." She rubbed his shoulder, and Alexandre beamed up at her. "I saw him play when he was younger, the Tchaikovsky concerto. This breaks my heart."

Georgie walked over and touched his left shoulder, far above the bandages.

Alexandre leaned and laid his cheek against her hand.

The surgeon said, "If he needs counseling, you should make sure he gets it. This could be very hard for him. I've had other patients who have lost major parts of their lives due to injury, and it can go badly."

"He has the band. He has his new music," Georgie said, whistling in the dark.

The doctor said, "He will doubtlessly go through a period of natural mourning. You have to make sure that it doesn't become dangerous to him."

Georgie rested her hand on his broad shoulder. "Christine?"

"I can take some time off," she said, standing at the footboard. She rested her hand on his foot.

Alexandre yanked his foot away. *"Ne me chatouille pas."*

Christine said to Georgie, "Oh, now I *want* to tickle him."

Georgie said to the surgeon, "He doesn't look very upset right now."

"Nope, he doesn't. He probably won't remember anything about our conversation, either. You'll have to explain the post-op instructions to him. He has my phone number in case you need a professional to explain the ramifications to him, but he understood them quite well yesterday. The desk will give you a hard copy of what to do for aftercare."

The surgeon said goodbye to Alexandre, maybe quite fondly, and Paul came in holding his phone. His eyes were bloodshot.

He looked at Christine and Georgie and said, "So it's bad."

Georgie nodded.

Paul looked at his phone. "I thought so."

Christine held out her arm to Paul. "Come on. I'll fill you in. Let's get something to eat. I'm starving."

They went out into the hallway, and Georgie was alone with Alexandre.

He smiled up at her again, softer this time, and held out his good hand. "Come here."

"Christine and Paul will come back in just a minute."

"Come here," he repeated, holding out his arm.

Georgie walked around to the other side of the bed and, at his continued insistence and waving, shucked her shoes and climbed into bed with him and under his arm. The faintest trace of his green grass and amber cologne floated from under the sheets, but mostly he smelled like astringent antiseptic.

She touched his throat above the blue hospital gown. "You look naked without your green earring and your rings and chains and stuff."

He grinned, his innocent smile lacking any of his usual darkness. "Pull back the sheet, and you'll see me naked."

"You're raunchy when you're stoned."

He grinned more. "Pull back the sheet, and you'll see how—"

She was laughing at him. "I get it! I get it."

He bobbled his head back and forth. "Have I been drinking absinthe again?"

"No," she laughed and snuggled her cheek against his round shoulder.

"Because it feels like it."

"No, you're just still hopped up from the surgery."

"Okay. Are you sure it wasn't absinthe?"

He sounded more like they had given him a hypnotic or a hallucinogenic rather than a sedative. "I'm really sure, Xan."

"I'm not Xan. Xan's gone," he said, a blithe lightness in his voice.

"You're Xan Valentine." She must have said that fifty damn times.

"No, Xan was a mask. Alex was a mask. I had to burn them up."

Georgie pushed herself to sitting. "What?"

"I had to burn them up. We burned up. We are the song of fire and smoke and light, and they are gone."

Whoa.

Georgie turned, kneeling on the bed beside him, and held his face between her palms. The smooth skin on his cheekbones and jaw warmed her hands. "Alexandre."

He smiled. *"Oui. C'est moi."*

"Xan."

"Xan's gone," Alexandre said, his French accent evident even in two words.

"Xan," she repeated, looking into his dark eyes. *"Xan Valentine."*

In her hands, Alexandre shook his head and smiled.

"Alex de Valentinois," she said, beginning to panic.

Alexandre shook his head again. "The pain was too much for them. The pain of breaking my hand, and the pain of losing it, of having to leave it behind."

"Losing your hand?" The Novocain probably made it feel like it was gone.

"Losing the violin," he told her, explaining as if it were obvious. "It has always been the violin. The pain of playing it. The pain of not playing it. It has always been the violin."

Under her hand, his violin callus on the left side of his jaw, just a small patch of roughened skin, rubbed her palm. It was going to go away. This part of his skin was going to wither and smooth and peel away until it was gone. "Where did Alex and Xan go?"

"They were thin shells, and they were brittle. They cracked. They shattered. They burned up. Gone."

She touched his face, trying to make them come back. "How can they be gone?"

"I think a better question is why they ever existed to begin with."

"You're awfully philosophical for someone who's stoned out of his gourd."

He shrugged, still grinning like a madman.

"So you're just," she thought about how to phrase this, "you?"

He nodded, his smile calming to something more serene, and lifted his hand to her face. "I don't want to hide anymore. I don't want to miss a moment with you."

"They're really gone?" Alex and Xan, the other two layers of Alexandre, whom she loved?

She loved? Georgie was the Ice Princess. This was ridiculous. She shouldn't even be talking to him like this. She was going to leave in a few hours, so she should be alerting other people about this problem, people who were going to stay with him.

Alexandre moved his head and touched his lips to hers, a slow kiss. He said, his breath whispering over her lips, "They're a part of me, now. They're the smoke and the light of my flame." He smiled a slow grin, pulling back, and let his head fall against the pillow. "I have not been this stoned in years."

A curl of his blond hair had fallen out of his ponytail and was lying against his cheekbone, and she tucked it behind his ear. She asked, "Can you still see music? Or smell it? Or whatever?"

He closed his eyes, still smiling. "When you speak, your voice feels like cool blue and silver rain on my skin."

Okay, so that was intact. He hadn't lost that.

What had he lost?

Alexandre opened his eyes and asked, "Where's Adrien?"

A thousand responses clattered through her head, each more cruel than the last. The sedative had probably made him too loopy to remember.

"He'll be here soon," she said, blinking to hold back tears.

Alexandre nodded. "He's my rock. *Mon rocher.*"

"Yeah, he is." Georgie slid down to cuddle under his arm again.

"He's kind of my father," Alexandre said.

"What?" Georgie pushed herself up again. "Wait. He can't be. He's like ten years older than you are. Right? He can't be over thirty-five."

"He's thirty-eight," Alexandre said.

Must have stayed out of the sun. Still, that was only thirteen years' difference. "Tell me that you're not being literal."

"He was my legal guardian for three years, from the time I was fifteen until I turned eighteen. It was easier that way, with traveling for concerts and any problems that might have emerged. He was the only person who gave a damn about me when I wasn't playing the violin. All the managers and conductors just wanted me to play the violin, and beyond that, I was a burden."

"My God, Alexandre. I can't imagine growing up like that." Georgie laid her arm over his chest and hung on. Man, she was going to miss the feel of his strong body in her arms. "Your parents just signed you away?"

Alexandre shrugged. "My mother was a legal guardian. My biological father had already died."

"So young," Georgie said.

"He was sixty-five."

She did the math. "He was around fifty when you were born?"

"He didn't marry until he had to pop out an heir. He was filthy rich, looked good for his age, and cavorted with actresses and models. Even afterward, he and my mother lived mostly separate lives. It was a very old-fashioned arrangement. I didn't really know him."

He was talking like all his filters were gone, like all the damage and pain didn't trouble him any more.

Her fingers stretched up and reached inside his collar, following one thin cord of scar tissue that lay along the side of his neck.

There was one more thing that she could ask him, something that everyone wanted to know, even Christine.

But she shouldn't. She should not take advantage of him right now, when he was so vulnerable.

"You know, we probably shouldn't be talking about stuff right now. You're hopped up on sodium pentothol or something. I don't think you're competent."

Because she was a lawyer, or would be again, starting in just a few hours.

If he started telling her things again, maybe she could shake her keys in front of him to distract him like a baby. *Look! Shiny!*

"I wish Adrien were here," he sighed.

"Yeah," Georgie said. "I wish he were here, too."

His arm cradled her closer to him. "I don't want you to leave."

The last time he had admitted such a thing, he had sounded like it had been ripped out of him.

Now, the words were ripping out of her. "I have to go."

"I'm going to Monaco for a few days. Come with me. You can lay in the sun, and we can go dancing. I won't work. I won't perform or anything."

"That sounds lovely." She couldn't go.

"Adrien's funeral will be Wednesday, probably Wednesday, in Monaco."

The sedative or whatever must be wearing off. "Oh."

"There are only going to be a few people there, mostly my retinue. He didn't have any other family. It bothers me that there won't be hundreds of people there. It'll be just a few of us: Paul, Guillaume, Christine, our other people, and myself. There should be more."

Georgie snuggled in closer, but she didn't say anything.

"Just for a few days. I don't want to let you go yet."

She should go back to being the Ice Princess, alone and needing no one in her icy castle.

Yes, she had been happier these last few years with Rae and Lizzy to talk to, to confide in, and to giggle and cry with. Touring with Killer Valentine had been amazing, with Alexandre in her bed every night, and Elfie and Rhiannon for girlfriends, and laughing her butt off with Boris, and of course the *music.*

Somehow, performing had become exuberant for Georgie, and she loved the heat of the lights and the blast of screams from the audience and watching Xan control the wall of sound and the fountains of sparks and fire.

And now, she had to leave everything behind, *again.*

She *should* leave it all behind.

She *should.*

"Just a week," she said. "I can stay for just one more week. Then I have to go."

He kissed her forehead. "Just one more week."

"Are you going to ask me to stay for another week after that?"

"Of course."

"I can't. You're breaking my heart. I can't."

"Just one more week then," Alexandre said, yawning. "Just give me one more week." He laid his head back on the pillow. *"Je t'aime, Georgie."*

With his strong French accent, Georgie only recognized her name because he had said it before.

She whispered, "I love you, too."

He fell asleep for a little while, his arm tightly around her.

When they came to discharge him, his dark eyes were confused at first, but the calm, dark serenity that she associated with Alexandre floated back like a wall of silence between him and the rest of the world.

Even her.

While the administrative ladies were asking Alexandre questions and giving him instructions, Georgie listened to *him,* trying to pick out the nuances of Alex's English accent that was like a Royal Shakespearean Company actor or of Xan's working-class British brogue.

His French accent never wavered, not even a little. She hadn't really heard either of his British accents for days.

Georgie wished that she had had a chance to say goodbye to Xan and Alex, but on that night when Xan had been drinking absinthe and she had called them out, she had had a moment with each of them, she had let herself tell them that she loved them, and that was what she would have said anyway.

Chapter Thirty-Two

THERE IS NO GOD

Georgie

After Alexandre was released from the hospital that afternoon, Paul drove Georgie and him straight to the airport and the Gulfstream jet. The Boeing had been sent to Milan to ferry the rest of the band either to New Jersey to record the new album or to Rome if that concert were rescheduled.

No matter what, Georgie wasn't going to play on that album, but her songs would be on it, or at least her minor contributions to songs that Alex had written.

Or Xan had written.

Or maybe Alexandre. She didn't know which one, really.

Paul caught Georgie's eye in the rearview mirror several times during the drive, his brown eyes narrowed.

They settled into the wide seats while Guillaume

bustled around, plying Alexandre with every tidbit that they had on board because he shouldn't drink alcohol yet.

Guillaume made sashimi, phenomenally tender and fresh sashimi, because Alexandre mentioned that he felt like he needed protein.

They were flying out of Switzerland on no notice, and Guillaume conjured up phenomenal sashimi. Georgie wondered if there was a fish tank in the belly of the airplane as she slurped the cool fish, almost buttery in taste, served on ice and greens.

Alexandre held her hand for most of the short flight, but he dozed off somewhere over France. His fingers loosened.

Paul was right beside Georgie, tapping her shoulder and bobbing his head toward the back of the plane. She followed him, and he bent his head and whispered, "Is it true? Is Christine right?"

"About his hand?" she clarified.

"Yes, about his hand!" Paul glanced up the long tube of the plane to see if his whisper had awakened Alexandre, but his blond head, just visible over the seatbacks, was tilted and leaning on the porthole window.

Georgie didn't know any way to sugarcoat it. "With physical therapy, he'll probably regain some range of motion. He won't ever play the violin again, not like he did. I don't think he'll even be able to manage the bass guitar."

Paul leaned against the cabinets back there and covered his face with his hands. Brown bruises stained his knuckles, too. *"Mon Dieu."*

"I'm sorry—" she started.

"It is better that Adrien didn't live to see this."

Georgie stepped backward, and her horror must have shown on her face. No. No, it wasn't better at all.

Paul whispered, "We were with him so that he could keep playing and performing. It's the reason we left our jobs at Interpol and our families and our homes. We believed in him, and then we hoped that he would go back to serious music someday."

Georgie felt tears heating her eyes and started getting pissed. She choked out, "My God, Paul."

"Non. If this is what happens to him, if this is how it ends, if he never plays the violin again, there is no God." Paul rubbed his face and dropped his fists to his legs. "I am sorry, miss. I am distraught. I need to make sure that security is in place for His Grace. The last thing we need is some pompous conductor harassing him right now."

Georgie watched him walk away, and then she went back to Alexandre. His healthy hand was right where she had left it, fingers limp and open. She slipped her hand in his. His fingers twitched, but then he held her hand and adjusted his position against the wall before he was silent and still again.

Chapter Thirty-Three

MONACO

Georgie

They flew through the afternoon and landed in Nice, France, just beyond the borders of Monaco, and then they took a helicopter to a heliport built high on the cliffs above the Mediterranean Sea.

When they stepped off the helicopter into the bright afternoon sun, Georgie took Alexandre's good hand to steady herself as she hopped down, holding back strands of her hair that were whipping in the helicopter's prop wash and the warm sea breeze. The air smelled like sun-dappled water and salt, and she breathed deeply after so many weeks of airplanes, cars, theaters, and hotels.

Alexandre straightened and surveyed the long docks of the helipad that jutted through the air far above the azure water. He blinked more slowly when he was Alexandre, Georgie had noticed, and now he did it all the time, his dark eyes and long lashes looking sleepy as he scanned the area, except that she could see the bright intelligence in his eyes.

Christine jumped down beside Georgie and asked him, "It's good to be home?"

He nodded. "Everywhere else, the sun doesn't feel right." He reached out and took Georgie's hand. "The cars are here."

Georgie followed them to the parade of black sedans that waited at the end of the heliport's cantilevered landing pads.

Georgie rode with Alexandre in the back of one town car, while Christine rode with Paul in the next.

They drove through the brilliant sunshine past a cream and ivory castle that was set back from the narrow, village-like street by a wide tiled area where white delivery vans were parked.

"Was that—" Georgie asked.

"My uncle's house," Alexandre said, his dry tone mocking himself.

She stared out the window at the high walls and crenellations on top. The muscular structure didn't look anything like Sleeping Beauty's castle with its delicate spires. "It looks like a fortress, with those towers and walls."

"It's eight hundred years old, unlike the European castles where the monarchs built new palaces when the ashtrays were full in the old ones. We don't have the land to do that. Land here is sold by the square inch, the most expensive in the world, more expensive than Tokyo, London, Hong Kong, or Singapore. We redecorate and rebuild when we can, but the Prince's Palace is the actual fortress that defended the seaport down below."

On the other side of the road, over a short safety wall, a sheer cliff dropped to high-rises and the sparkling sapphire sea far below. White yachts lined up in the berths. Georgie recoiled from the window a little. The sheer cliff made her dizzy.

"We built a facade around it recently to make it look more like the European palaces, but it's still a fortress underneath. We came to power in 1297—"

"You know the year, huh?" Georgie teased him.

"Like you know 1776—when François Grimaldi, my ancestor and a feudal lord, disguised himself as a monk and sneaked in. He murdered a guard and opened the gates for his men, and so we took the fortress, and thus we came to power. The Prince's Palace is the seat of power in Monaco."

"Sure, in the Middle Ages, but the *building* isn't why you guys are the ruling family now." This was one of the weirdest conversations she had ever had, talking to a guy about whether he or his second-degree relatives actually held the divine right of kings to rule a kingdom—actually, a principality, but that was just vocabulary—or whether that outdated concept of a mutant magic superpower was produced by the stones in a building. "Now, it's lineage, or treaties, or something."

"Supposedly, it's in the treaties with France, but we are superstitious about the building."

Yes, *superstitious,* that was the word Georgie had been looking for.

"In the 1780s, we tried to redecorate it and tore down some of the fortifications to make it elegant, and the French overran the fortress and stripped it of our art and treasure. The Grimaldis were exiled and out of power for a few decades. Yes, it's a fortress, and it will remain a fortress. There is a swimming pool in the back, now."

"As long as the fortress has a *swimming pool,*" she said.

"I'll show it to you Wednesday."

"We're going to the *castle?*"

"There will be a Mass said for Adrien at the Palatine Chapel, inside the palace. It was easier to arrange it here on short notice."

"I'm so sorry," she said, yet again.

Alexandre nodded, and then he went solemn and quiet again, so Georgie held his hand as they threaded through the narrow streets of the old city of Monaco-Ville.

The houses rose around the car like a medieval village, which it absolutely was, except that the houses of Monaco-Ville, the old village of Monaco, had been rebuilt during the Belle Epoque. Gorgeous ceramic whorls framed paintings and mosaics embedded in the terra cotta and dusty pink walls. Curlicue wrought iron fenced the balconies. Graceful houses stood shoulder-to-shoulder along the narrow streets, and tiled pedestrian walkways vined between the blocks.

A small bandstand, built of intricate wrought iron like a spiderweb with Parisian aspirations, stood in a small park. The emerald lawn was more manicured than most golf course fairways.

Alexandre leaned over and pointed it out. "I gave my first violin concert there when I was six."

"Did you really?" She took a closer look at the fairy hut.

"I played Paganini's Caprice Number Twenty-Four. Three hundred people packed into this park."

Must have been packed as tightly as general admission at a Killer Valentine concert. "That's a tough piece for a kid."

He shrugged. "I suppose."

"My first recital was when I was eight, at a local college. I played a simplified version of the 'Prince of Denmark's March.' It was eight bars long."

He chuckled. "Maestro Soto would have been mortified to allow such a simple piece to be played in public."

Georgie wanted to jump on that, *Maestro Soto,* but she settled back against the seat, holding his hand. "I'll bet it was beautiful."

"It was." He leaned against the seat. "I wish I could play it for you."

She stroked his cheek as the car carefully navigated another narrow street. "I'm glad that I got to hear you play, but I'd rather hear you sing. I'd rather hear your music."

Alexandre watched her eyes, assessing something. He said, "I'm glad you did, too. I still wish I could play it."

"You do?"

"I wish I could play at Adrien's Mass or his ceremony on the beach."

Oh, man. "He heard you while he was alive. That's more important." She wrapped her arms around him. "I miss him."

His strong arms tightened around her waist and her back. "I miss him, too."

The car turned, and the nose dipped sharply downward as they drove into a garage under a house that stretched three stories high. The smooth plaster walls glowed warm amber as the car slid downward. Georgie caught a glimpse of a few dwarf citrus trees beside the driveway before darkness enclosed the car. Tube lights turned on above them, striping the black cars with blue lines.

Only Christine and Paul's car and one other had turned in behind them before the door ground shut. "Where are the rest of the cars going?"

"We have three parking spaces under the house. People who need to be here will be dropped off out front, and the cars will go back to the garage in France until we need them."

"France? Won't that take forever to get them back here?"

Alexandre chuckled. "They are fifteen minutes away. The entire country of Monaco is eight-tenths of a square mile in area, and it's two and a half miles long. I can jog from one border of Monaco to the other in twenty minutes, the long way. We walk most places, and the subway system is excellent. It's one of the safest places in the world."

They climbed a spiral staircase from the garage to the house, their feet clanking on wrought iron more ornate than the front gates at Georgie's childhood estate in Connecticut. The door opened up to a small kitchen, larger than apartment-sized but smaller than most McMansions in the States, but every item was the highest high-end everything. Even Georgie didn't recognize some of the brands, but the brilliant shine and materials made her estimate thousands of dollars. Many, many thousands.

Guillaume was already standing at the counter, speaking rapid French on his cell phone. He covered the phone and told them. "Deliveries will start in an hour with essentials. We have been gone too long. I called them this morning to start stocking the kitchen, but nothing has arrived yet. I can make coffee, and I have pastries from Geneva."

"Thank you," Alexandre said and led her through the kitchen. "We'll have them outside."

"You have a yard?" Georgie asked.

"Not exactly."

On the other side of the door was the living room, or the entertaining room, or the sitting-down-with-royalty room. The furniture appeared new when you looked at it because the paint and finishes on the wood were pristine, unmarred, and the bright silk was fresh and unfaded, but Georgie knew that she was seeing the effects of restoration, not of newness. The craftsmanship of the carved legs on the tufted couches and chairs and the rococo frames holding oil portraits on the walls was too perfect to be modern. This furniture was hundreds of years old, probably most of it Louis the Fourteenth.

The windows opened to lush greenery on one side and the sea on the other.

"Come on," Alexandre said. "Let's sit outside. The breeze is nice today."

French doors—of course they were *French* doors—led to a balcony.

The house had been built high atop the rocky headland and looked over the port and marina far below. The row of adjoining houses clung to the side of a cliff, chiseled into the natural terrain, utilizing every square inch of precious Monégasque real estate. The main balconies of Alexandre's house—three of them, one for each floor, overlooked a canyon that was filled with rustling trees and lush shrubs and grass. The cool breeze funneling through the valley plucked Georgie's shirt and waved strands of her hair. A perfect little white church nestled in the bottom of the crevice, about ten stories below where they stood.

The lowest balcony wrapped around the side of the house and overlooked the sea. The Mediterranean sparkled blue and black in the late afternoon sunlight, dotted with yachts dancing in the waves.

So this was how *real* old money lived. Not American somewhat-old money like Georgie's family, the Oelrichs, who had made their money in the Nevada silver mines, and not even American old-old money like Peyton Cabot's family whose fortunes stemmed from the American Revolution, could produce this kind of subtle display that meant generations upon generations of millennia of wealth.

European old money was just *different.*

"Wow," she said.

"You like it?" Alexandre asked.

"I have never seen anything like this," Georgie said. "Trying not to be crass, but I cannot imagine how much this would cost."

"I suppose everything has a price that someone could put on it," Alexandre mused, "but these houses never come up for sale. They're inherited. Selling one would be beyond gauche. It would be insane. You would never get it back. My cousins all live up here."

The wind rustled through the canyon below them. The city noises—honking and traffic and construction equipment—floated on the breeze, but it was far away. "I can't believe how quiet it is."

Alexandre sat on one of the chaise lounges and swung his feet up. "Welcome to *Le Rocher,* the Rock of Monaco. It's the quietest part of the city. No one would be so uncultured as to make a racket. Other than restoration and rebuilding," he waved his hand up the canyon, where one of the houses was covered in a spiderweb of scaffolding, "it is *quiet* up here."

Georgie held onto the railing as she leaned over.

Alexandre said, "The sunrise is over the sea."

"Wow."

"I'm glad you like the house," he said. "I like coming home because I can switch out clothes while I'm here. I'm down to three tee shirts after the pasta incident in Milan."

Georgie nodded. "Yeah, that part of touring is rough. Boris has fifteen stage and PR outfits for me, and yet I have nothing to wear."

"We can go shopping while we're here. I'm told that there is wonderful shopping."

She didn't have to worry about the Russian mafia anymore. She could walk in the sunshine and shop for clothes. "That sounds great."

"I can fly Boris in if you want him to shop with you."

"He doesn't know about all this Duke and Monégasque and violin stuff, does he?"

Alexandre held up his phone. The screen was lit with a wiggling dot, so it was ringing, and text icons lined up across the top bar. "Everyone knows everything now. I've silenced my phone because it is constantly ringing and chiming with texts. I will have to make a statement and email a lot of people, but not yet."

"Yeah, you probably want to make sure all that sodium pentothol or whatever it was is out of your system before you give any interviews. You were pretty loopy."

He watched her, and he set his phone, screen-down, on the table beside him. "I don't remember what was said, afterward."

"The doctor said that you wouldn't. I've got all the post-op instructions written down."

"Georgie."

"Hmmm?" She leaned against the railing but then thought better of it. The house was probably hundreds of years old. The screws holding the stucco and iron railing might be centuries old, too.

He asked her, "What did I say?"

She sat beside him on the chaise lounge. "A couple things."

Guillaume arrived with coffee and buttery Swiss cookies for them, laying a china plate on the table beside Alexandre and fussing at nonexistent dust before he went back into the house.

Georgie waited until Guillaume had closed the French doors. She said, "You said a few things. When I realized that you really shouldn't be talking, I tried to distract you, and then you fell asleep for a while anyway."

"And before that?" He watched her closely, his dark eyes analyzing. The wind blew blond strands of his hair behind him.

"You said a few things," she admitted.

"So what was it? Was I a jackass to the nurses during the surgery? Damn it."

She laughed. "Oh, no. *Worse.* You were so impossibly sweet that you charmed everyone."

His eyes widened in mock horror. "Good God, no. Rock stars aren't *sweet.*"

"Well, you were. You *sang* to the nurses during the whole surgery. You were *adorable.*"

"Fuck me. That's why all the nurses were crowding

around me to say goodbye. I thought I merely gave them all a million dollars or something, but they think I'm," he shuddered, *"cute."*

"Yep. We better pray the press doesn't get ahold of that. You'll be the laughingstock of *Rolling Stone.* 'Sex Incarnate or Blond Cuddle Kitten?'"

He chuckled. "As long as I didn't make an ass out of myself. Acting like an entitled idiot would have been worse."

"That was all that happened in front of other people, as far as I know."

His dark eyes flicked up and stared at her over the rim of his coffee cup. "In front of other people?"

"You said a little more to me."

He set down the coffee. "Like what?"

"That your sister bit you on the ankle when she was three and you still have the scar."

He picked up the coffee again and sipped it. "She was like a rabid ferret at that age. She terrorized the nannies."

Georgie downed a gulp of her steaming coffee, wishing that it was liquid courage instead of java. The lump of lava stuck in her throat before she managed to swallow it down. "You said that Adrien had been your legal guardian for a few years when you were a teenager."

"It was expedient while I was traveling and performing." He sipped the coffee.

Georgie laid her hand on his knee. "I'm so sorry."

"Anything else?" Alexandre asked, setting his coffee down. He seemed unconcerned, like the worst must be over.

"You said that Alex and Xan are gone, that you're just you, now."

He went very still, watching his coffee cup. "Oh."

"I tried to call them out like I did a couple nights ago when you had been drinking absinthe."

His easy nod looked like he remembered that night.

"That was before I figured out that you shouldn't be talking, that you weren't competent."

His nod slowed, and he bit his lip.

"They didn't answer."

"No," he said. "They won't."

"Can you feel them anymore?"

"No. They're gone."

"You said that you had to burn them up in order to break your hand."

He hesitated before he nodded, and he still stared at that cup of coffee on the teak table, not looking at her.

"We don't have to talk about this if you don't want to."

He was reaching across himself with his healthy hand, toying with the cup, and he rotated the cup between his long fingers. "It was the only way to do it. They couldn't take the pain of breaking my hand or the pain of letting go of the violin."

"I heard you break your bones. I didn't know what it was. You didn't even flinch."

"They couldn't take it," he repeated.

"So, are they just part of you now? When you were negotiating with Sofiya Butorin, you sounded just like Alex."

One of his dark eyebrows pressed down. "I did?"

"You didn't have that British accent, but you sounded like you do when you're in Alex mode. You were amazing. You could have been a diplomat."

"I like being a rock star better."

"Do you?"

His eyebrows twitched together. "Did I say anything else?"

"Nothing about your violin tutor, if that's what you're worried about."

He leaned his head back against the cushions. "You know about that?"

"Some people have said things. I didn't believe any of what they said because I could tell that they were wrong or else making up the most vile and terrible things. You want to know how I knew they were lying?"

"How?" he asked, sipping the coffee.

Georgie stared straight at him. "Their lips were moving."

After one beat while he translated it into French or something in his head and watched her over the coffee cup, he laughed and shook his head. "All right. 'Their lips were moving.' All right. So you didn't believe them?"

"I don't listen to rumors."

"And you weren't afraid to be around the crazed, murdering violinist? I might have beat you to death in your sleep."

"I shot and killed someone yesterday." Georgie shrugged. "Shit happens."

He set his coffee cup down. "Shit happens?"

"I've never felt afraid around you. You don't set off my warning bells. I've got halfway decent sensors for all kinds of stuff. I've got fantastic gaydar. Lizzy was involved with a guy, a terrible guy. The minute I met him, I knew he was creepy. He set off all kinds of sirens in my head. Now, it turned out that I knew him when I was a teenager and he was terrible then, too, but even before I remembered that, Mannix made my skin crawl. You don't. I've never been afraid of you."

"Everyone was afraid of Alexandre Grimaldi. It's why I went by Xan Valentine when I moved to go to Juilliard."

"Yeah, well, if everyone jumped off a cliff—"

He leaned forward and took her hand in his, studying her blunt nails, kept short so they wouldn't catch or clack on the piano keys. He asked, "Do you want to know what happened?"

She wasn't sure. "It's okay if you don't want to."

He rubbed his thumb over her knuckles. "I'll tell you. I should probably tell someone."

"I thought you talked to therapists or something." She remembered that he had talked about therapists.

He nodded. "When I was a teenager. In between concerts. Which wasn't as often as I would have liked. I traveled from Switzerland to play concerts every week, plus I took lessons in Paris, after that. I was only at school a few days a week, and then I had to do a week's worth of lessons in three days."

She held his hand more tightly, the warm Mediterranean breeze lifting the strands of her hair that had escaped her braid. "God, Alexandre. No one should grow up that way."

"Do you want to know? Because I'll tell you everything that happened. I remember it all, every moment."

The French door clicked and opened behind them, and Christine walked out, barefoot and with a beach towel wrapped under her armpits. "You don't mind if I sunbathe, right?"

Alexandre set down Georgie's hand and leaned

back. "The other two balconies are entirely unoccupied."

"And I would be bored out of my mind," Christine said, walking past them toward the part of the balcony that oversaw the sea, where the sunlight still shone directly on the plaster. "What are we talking about?"

"Nothing important," Georgie said.

Christine asked, "Do you want to borrow a swimsuit, Georgie? Or you can just strip down to your underwear." She whipped off the towel and laid it on the ground.

Oh, she wasn't wearing a top. How very European.

And Christine had lovely boobies, soft and round, entirely unlike Georgie's barely-there flat boobs.

Everybody had better boobs than Georgie. Like Hell, she was going to take off her top *now.*

Christine laid down on her back.

And they were perky.

Georgie considered hating her later. She couldn't work up the energy just then, in the warm Mediterranean sunlight, her thigh pressed against Alexandre's leg.

Alexandre picked up his phone and scrolled through something, entirely unconcerned that his sister was sunbathing topless in front of him.

He was so very European sometimes, too.

"You could do with some sun, too, Xandre. You're pale," Christine said.

"I'm fine, thanks," he said. "Georgie, we could talk inside."

"Oh, come on. I'm bored," Christine said. "Don't run away."

Christine flipped over on her stomach, baring her back to the bright sunshine.

Three long scars crossed her smooth back, just three.

One trailed up and over her shoulder.

From where Georgie was sitting, ten feet away, she knew exactly how those raised, terrible cords would feel under her fingers.

She turned to Alexandre, who was watching Christine. "I don't think you have to tell me anything."

His dark eyes flicked back to her. "There's more."

Christine started talking about people at Rae and Wulf's wedding, but Alexandre's eyes didn't move from Georgie's.

Christine was lying on her stomach and facing the other way, so Georgie leaned in and kissed him. His soft lips opened under hers, and his fingers reached into her hair and around the back of her head.

After a minute, she backed off, but he held her close to him, resting his forehead against hers. He whispered, *"Je t'aime."*

"I love you, too," she whispered.

It was getting easier to say it every time, and it was getting easier to pretend that she wasn't going to leave.

He whispered, "I'll tell you tonight, when we're alone."

Chapter Thirty-Four

MASS TEXT

Georgie

After dark, Alexandre, Christine, Paul, Georgie, and few other security men walked to a small cafe a few blocks away for supper. They sat outside at one of the last tables, tucked away from anyone passing on the narrow pedestrian mall. A cool breeze carried the scents of Italian cooking from the restaurant, and Georgie's stomach growled.

Paul actually ate with them at their table, something Georgie had never seen the security guy do. Alexandre didn't remark on it, just made sure that Paul took the chair facing outward so he could watch the street from his seat.

She must have been staring because Paul shrugged and said, "*Le Rocher* is one of the safest places in the world."

During the last course, her phone buzzed. Her

battery was low from her checking it so often, hoping for something about Flicka. She swiped the screen to see the text.

The phone number and contact info was from HRH Bossypants.

I have to disappear, Flicka's text read.

Georgie leaned in to show the rest of them. "It's from Flicka."

Christine peered to look at the phone. "Is she all right?"

Alexandre asked, "If she wants us to sing at another wedding, tell her no."

Christine looked up, horrified. "He was still in surgery."

Georgie told him, "She's missing. Rae and Wulf can't find her."

Alexandre set down the fork he had been holding with his right hand. *"Fuck. Wulfram* can't find her?"

They all leaned over the phone.

Flicka had texted, *I'm going away for a while to think. I can't deal with everything. I just want to walk the Earth and think. I'll be in touch when I can. It might be a few months. Fiddlesticks.*

"Fiddlesticks?" Christine grabbed her head. "She swears like a cartoon princess. What the Hell is wrong with her?"

"I have to call Rae." Georgie tapped her phone, and it rang. When Rae picked up, Georgie said, "Rae, I got a text."

"We all did," Rae said, talking fast. "We're trying to figure out what it means and track her phone. I'll call you if I find out anything."

Click.

"Okay," Georgie said.

"Can you call Flicka back?" Christine asked. "Or text her back?"

Georgie scrambled to text, but her fingers turned clumsy as she swiped the words into her phone and she had to keep deleting and trying again. *Are you okay? Where the ducking bell are you?*

They waited, watching the phone.

It took two minutes for the message to be returned as undeliverable.

Georgie sat back. "Shit. I can't believe that she'd do this. Wulfram must be *frantic.* And she shouldn't do this to Rae right now."

Alexandre sipped his sparkling water. "Yes, it must be terrible when someone you love drops off the face of the Earth with no warning and no way to know if they're all right."

She shot him a dirty look. "Smartass."

Christine and Paul leaned over and started talking to each other about the pasta.

At least they knew when to butt out. That was a great quality in a person.

Alexandre scooted his chair and took Georgie's hand in his healthy one. He had kept his wrapped hand in his lap the whole time at supper.

He kept his voice low, which was audible in the quiet of the old village. "I've been dreading it ever since you first told me that you were going to disappear. You know that you don't have to go to Atlanta anymore, right? You can go back to the Southwest and pick up your old life. I'll help you change your name back."

A shudder ran through Georgie. "What if Sofiya Butorin changes her mind?"

"She won't. She's very smart. What she has now is worth far more than your dead body."

"I don't know." The possibility of going *home* shocked her. *Home*, to Rae, to Lizzy, to her other friends, to her job, to the dorm where she left all her stuff, to her bank accounts and her classes in a few weeks, and to her car, which in the Southwest equates with freedom and independence.

And to her secret piano practice hours in the music building before dawn, to her pre-law classes, and her self-ordained destiny of being a lawyer and paying her debts.

Her heart fell a little in her chest.

Alexandre rubbed his thumb over her knuckles. A light callus on the side of his thumb was from plucking the steel strings of the guitar. He said, "You don't have to go back."

"Well, I have to go somewhere," she said. "I'd rather go back to Southwestern State where my friends are than Atlanta."

"You could stay with the band."

Christine and Paul stood and strolled down the tiled pedestrian mall, pointing at something that neither of them was really looking at.

"But I can't," Georgie said. "I have to pay the other people back, and I have to be a lawyer to do that."

"Being a musician paid off the first debt on your list."

The Butorins. "But it's not going to continue to work like that."

"You should check your bank account. Killer Valentine does very well."

"It's too risky," she insisted.

"So you're going to do something you hate—"

"I don't hate the law. It's intellectually challenging."

"Finance law is intellectually challenging?"

"Maybe less so than litigation, but it's not about me."

"I think it is about you." His soft tone wasn't angry or cruel. If anything, the lilt at the end suggested sadness.

"No, it's about my father. He fucked these people over, hard. He knew he was swindling people. He turned lots of people away. He turned Peyton's old money away twice before I intervened and he took their cash. Why didn't he turn away the little old ladies and men who were giving him all their retirement savings? Why didn't he turn away the cancer charities and the Holocaust survivors' charities?"

Alexandre bit his lower lip for a moment, obviously wrestling with himself, and he said, "I can pay all these people back. In a week, this will all be gone. You can take your time to pay me."

"I can't just have somebody else pay them back and then owe him the money. It's about *me* paying them back. It's about *retribution.*"

"It's penance," Alexandre said.

Georgie held his one hand more tightly because *now* he *got* it. "Yeah, it is."

"And if you don't suffer, then it's not penance."

"That's not what I mean. Everyone always said that I was just like my father."

"He had long hair to his waist and looked sexy in a short skirt?"

"I actually do look like him. My mother is blonde and blue-eyed. But also because he loved music. He used to drag her to concerts until I was old enough to go, and then he took me. And he worked hard, or everyone thought that he did. He worked at the office every day from five in the morning until four in the afternoon. Everyone said that I had his work ethic. I was the apple that didn't fall far from the tree. Everyone expected great things from me. People gave me their cards to get to him."

Alexandre sighed, "Oh."

"Yeah. I'm *just like him.* If I run off to become a musician instead of doing the right thing, I really will be *just like him.* He ran away. He swindled everyone, and then when they found out, he killed himself. He was out on bail, and he shot himself through the mouth. It wasn't guilt. It wasn't fear of not having money. It was one last fuck-you at all those people so they couldn't get their money back, he wouldn't have future wages or inheritances garnished, and they wouldn't even have the satisfaction of seeing him in prison."

"I'm sorry," he said.

"He wrote two suicide notes. We gave the police the one that said that he couldn't live with what he had done. The email to my mother was an insane, paranoid rant about how he was being persecuted and was going to kill himself because all his victims deserved what they got and he wasn't going to rot in jail for their greed. *I don't want to be like him.*"

"You're nothing like that. You do everything the right way, with hard practice and harder work, and you can make just as much money with Killer Valentine, but faster." He sounded just like Alex, the bright light of intelligence shining behind his eyes and logically arguing the facts like a lawyer, yet his accent was still sweetly French.

"*Maybe* I can," she said, "but not forever and it's not a steady income. What if the next album flops?"

Alexandre touched his wrapped hand to his chest. "I should spin around three times and spit or something."

"I have to do what's *right* because no one else did," Georgie insisted.

He nodded, his blond hair bobbing past his shoulders. "All right. I won't argue."

"I thought you were the one person who understood."

"I do understand. I just don't agree that it's the best course." He tapped her phone. "I'm going to get one of those texts from you, soon, and there's nothing I can do about it."

"We have these few nights."

He nodded. "I shouldn't ruin what little time we have."

Georgie reached up and tucked his hair behind his ear. "These last few days mean everything to me. It's like the last few days of sunlight before I go underground for the rest of my life."

He rested his cheek on her hand. His violin callus was thick against her palm. "Me, too."

Chapter Thirty-Five

THINKING CAN BE DANGEROUS

Georgie

They walked home after supper through the cool night air. Houses towered over the narrow, winding street. On the paved roads for cars, the sidewalks were only wide enough for one person, so they stuck to the pedestrian malls that wound between the blocks of houses. Beams of light from the back windows of the houses broke the night. Somewhere, someone was roasting meat, and the savory smell made Georgie's mouth water even though she had just eaten.

Alexandre wrapped his arm around her waist the whole way and told her who lived in all the houses.

When they reached his house, they juggled into a single-file line to go in the front door and into the parlor or whatever the Louis Quatorze room should be called.

Alexandre looked at his phone. "I think I'm going to turn in."

Christine laughed. "It's only ten-thirty!"

He shrugged. "It's been a rough couple of days, and I had surgery this morning."

"Georgie will stay up with me and explore the wine cellar. Won't you, Georgie?"

She tightened her fingers on Alexandre's hand. "Yeah, it's been a rough couple of days. I think I'm going to crash, too."

Alexandre raised his eyebrows at Christine and led Georgie up two flights of stairs to the top floor.

Georgie asked him, "This isn't going to scandalize her, is it?"

"What?" he asked, climbing the stairs.

"Us sleeping in the same room together?"

Alexandre stopped climbing for a moment to lean on his knees and laugh quietly. "No. She'll be fine."

The third floor had a landing with a television and some couches—modern and expensive—and a hallway led to a door. "My bedroom," Alexandre explained.

"Where's your sister's room?" Georgie sat on the couch.

"Second floor. There are several bedrooms on the second floor."

"Your mother's?" Georgie asked.

"My mother hasn't been back to Monaco for years. I think I was two, the last time she was here. She lives in Paris."

"I thought you grew up here before you went to boarding school."

"I did. My parents wanted to preserve my claim to the throne in case anything happened to Pierre and

Maxence, God forbid." He actually shuddered. "The Monégasque have an aversion to foreigners inheriting the throne after a German duke would have inherited during World War II, had anything happened to Prince Louis II. My father insisted that Christine and I were raised here until we went to Le Rosey."

"So you lived here with your father?"

"Hmm? No. He lived in New York, mostly."

"Oh. Okay." At least Georgie's parents had made some effort to be around when she was a kid. "Is that what you would want to do when you have kids? Just let the nannies raise them and then ship them off to boarding school when they're five?"

"I'm traveling all the time for the band. Other than a few years at Juilliard when I stopped performing, I have traveled and performed almost constantly since I was ten. I can't imagine that I'll have another chance at a relationship."

"So you're not planning on having kids?" she asked. Not that it was any of her business. Not that she should even be asking.

"I don't think I'll get the chance to have children." He spun to face her, his dark eyes wide. *"Why?"*

Georgie shrugged. "I was just curious. It seems like an odd way to grow up."

He walked back and held her shoulder with his right hand, studying her eyes. His hand drifted down her arm, stroking her. "Is there any other reason why you're asking?"

"My parents were at least around when I was growing up. It must have been really different for you."

"You're sure there was no other reason?" he asked, his hand traveling up her arm and cradling her jaw. He tucked a lock of hair behind her ear and smoothed his hand over her head. "Just, anything? You could tell me anything."

The intensity in his eyes was odd, like there was something that he was waltzing around that she was not understanding.

Then she got it.

Her open hands flew up, pushing away that thought. *"Whoa!* Oh, *no.* No, I'm not. I'm on the pill. I take it *very* consistently. My pack was in my backpack when I ran, so I haven't missed any, even with being kidnapped and the wedding and stuff." She thought back. Nope, everything was on schedule. She even had ten more days until the next one. *"No,* no chance. I wouldn't do that to you."

"Oh." He smiled a little, just a little, and he blinked. "I guess that's for the best, then."

"Yeah. I mean, we couldn't."

"No, of course not."

"We shouldn't even think about such things. It tempts the universe."

"Surely, we could *think* about such things, like a child." His eyes seemed larger, although he was still smiling, a little, like he was joking, a little. "Surely it can't be wrong to *think."*

"Thinking can be dangerous." *Why had he even brought it up?* "Even if we thought about it, you can't just stop taking the pill and then *try."* *Why was she still talking?* "You've got to wait until the next cycle. Because, hormones. Or something."

He frowned. "Is that how it works?"

"Oh, yeah. Totally." *She should totally shut up.* "And in a month, I'll be back at school. And, you know, that would be crazy." She laughed, a note of hysteria creeping in. "Me, in school. You, on tour. That would be crazy."

She was fucking babbling.

He stroked his thumb over her cheekbone. "Were you planning on having children?"

She hadn't thought about it. If she had forgotten to take the Pill the last few months, their child would probably have had brown eyes, maybe large and dark like Alexandre's, maybe with those lush dark eyelashes. Maybe their child would look just like him with those amazing cheekbones and jawline, some day.

Why was she lonely for someone who had never existed?

She said, "I don't know how having a family would fit in with what I have to do."

He nodded. "We're both destined to be alone, aren't we?"

Georgie didn't know what to say to that, so she shrugged. The gesture probably looked more hopeless than she had meant it to.

Alexandre dropped his hand down to hold her fingers. "Then we only have a few more days, and I don't want to waste a moment of it."

"I wish I could stay," she sighed.

"Stay through the weekend."

"I don't know. Classes start the week after."

"I'll have the Gulfstream fly you back on Sunday. It's faster. I'll make sure you get back if you want to go."

"I was planning to go back Friday morning."

He stepped closer to her, almost touching her. "The Rome concert has been rescheduled for Friday night. We could play one last concert together."

She had thought that Milan would be her last

concert, ever. A reprieve for just one more concert was more than she could have hoped for.

She really should go back. She had to buy books and stuff. "I don't know."

He bent, almost kissing her, and whispered near her lips. "I could sing 'Alwaysland' to you one more time."

That would be amazing. "All right."

Alexandre smiled, and his slow smile looked like he really meant it, while he watched her eyes. He closed his eyes, and his lips brushed hers.

He kissed her slowly, like he was savoring what time they had left. Georgie moved toward him and molded herself to his tall body, bending backward.

His left arm wrapped around her waist, pressing her to him.

"Your hand," she whispered against his lips.

"Still numb. I'll be careful." He nibbled down the side of her neck, bowing her farther backward.

Georgie held onto his shoulders, trying to take the weight off of his arm, but his mouth and breath on her skin grew in her mind, pushing out thought except for clinging to him while his mouth drifted lower to her collarbones.

He kissed her mouth again and led her, turning her and guiding her with his hands as surely as if they were dancing, to the bedroom door, which he kicked open. He whispered, "I wish I could carry you to the bed right now."

She muttered, "I just want to get in there."

Alexandre spun her and pressed her back against his body with his arm, holding her hair aside to kiss and nip the back of her neck. Georgie whimpered and ran her hands up the sides of his neck and into his long hair. He held her against himself as they walked backward to the bed, and he pulled her into his lap as he sat.

Georgie turned on his legs, trying to straddle him to push him down so that she could be on top—to save his arm and because she liked it—but he was already turning, bending her back, and crawling on top of her.

He kissed her forever, holding her down by her hair as he dipped to lip under her jaw or down her neck, and then returning to her mouth to run his tongue along hers and slant his lips to kiss her more. She was panting, her breath ragged in her chest from his hot mouth on hers and his body moving above her. With every kiss, he touched her more deeply, his body heavier on her, until he rolled off her to pull her clothes away with his good hand. She fumbled with his clothes, her eyes too wide and her heart beating too hard, and finally got them off of him before he was on her again, his warm body slow and gentle and buried deeply in hers.

She was already tightening. She pushed her hips against him, trying to goad him into being rough with her, but he held her in his arms, kissing her still, murmuring to her to hold him, to be with him.

Georgie could feel what he meant but did not say, *and not to leave him.*

She wrapped her arms around his neck as her body vibrated at a pitch as insistent as a tuning fork. The quiver ran through her, not quite spilling over into the throbbing she craved. She whimpered, calling to him, urging him. Still, he was so gentle, brushing her body with his. He amplified the waves within her, pushing them higher, until he broke off their kiss and whispered near her ear, "*Je t'aime,*" and he thrust into her and shook her world apart with his words echoing through her.

She held onto him as the waves took her someplace beyond light and sound but not his words. *Je t'aime* echoed through her, his voice and his body deep in her.

The light bloomed around her, and she opened her eyes and gasped, "I love you, too."

Chapter Thirty-Six

PILLS

Georgie

After she grabbed a quick shower, Georgie stood in the bathroom and stared at the round package of pills for a long time, wishing about what might have been, before she pushed a pink pill through the foil and dry-swallowed it.

It went down just fine, just like always and all according to her plan.

It was useless to wish for things that could never be. She had a plan. She had to stick to her plan.

She tucked the case back in the side of her makeup bag.

Chapter Thirty-Seven

DON'T TELL ME

Georgie

Georgie was almost asleep, just beginning to drift in the darkness and the soft bed and Alexandre's body wrapped around her, when he said, "I'm trying to convince you not to go."

"I know." It was breaking her heart.

His voice was a little more hoarse than it had been earlier, probably with sleep. "But if you were to stay, you should know it all. You shouldn't make that decision without knowing the truth about what happened."

Her fingers stole up behind her shoulder to his hard, round shoulder, where scars trickled over his skin. In the dark, the scars felt like chains, cords, and strings embedded under his skin. "You don't have to tell me."

"Just in case. You should know all of it."

"I'm greedy. I don't want anything between us to

change. The truth is that I want these last few days with you just as we are now. If it's something worse than I think, then it was a long time ago. Ten years. When you were only fifteen."

"You should know what I am." His voice broke.

"Even if you did, that was a long time ago," she repeated into the dark, trying to convince herself. "That wasn't you. You're someone different now." She turned her head to look at him. The moonlight streaming in the open window glinted off his blond hair and the slash of his cheekbones. "Aren't you?"

"No," he said. The moonlight didn't seem to touch his dark eyes. "I'm not. I'm not different at all."

"Don't tell me," she said, finding his lips and kissing him. "People have been trying to drag it out of you all this time and guessing and gossiping about it. I don't want to know. Obviously, he hurt your sister. That's enough. It was already enough. I know you, and I want these last few days to be perfect," she kissed him again, "just like you. Perfect."

"Georgie—"

"No. Just go to sleep. Let your body heal. The truth is that I love you, and I don't need to know what happened a long time ago."

Chapter Thirty-Eight

CRAZY IS NOT A DIAGNOSIS

Georgie

Some buzzing rings, a click, and the phone call was connected.

Rae's voice asked quickly, "Georgie? Did you hear from Flicka?"

Georgie sighed and plugged her other ear. Even though she had sneaked away into a corner, the convention center hummed and buzzed with people talking, laughing, and haggling. "I guess that answers what I was going to ask you. Did you track her phone?"

A sigh whooshed through the phone. "She turned it off as soon as she sent the text, and when we got to where she sent it from, she was gone. She either hasn't turned it back on or she ditched it. Evidently, the last time she went walkabout, that's how Wulf tracked her, and she learned to turn it off."

"You haven't had any," Georgie didn't even want to say it, "ransom things?"

"No. None. Nothing. No contact."

"Are you doing okay?"

"If you mean, am I laying on my left side and watching television until I'm so bored that I pass out? Sure, I'm *fine.*"

"How about your projects?"

"Yeah, I'm working on those."

"How's the schizophrenic one going?" Georgie asked.

"Not schizophrenia. Schizophrenia is different than Dissociative Identity Disorder. Schizophrenia is when you hear voices and have hallucinations and can't tell what's real. Schizophrenics stumble around talking to themselves when they're off their meds. It's a physiological brain disorder with a strong genetic or epigenetic component. It's kind of the opposite of autism in a lot of ways. Dissociative Identity Disorder is psychological and more like PTSD."

"Yeah," Georgie said. *"But how's it going?"*

"Almost done. I should have a copy to you soon. How come?" Rae yawned through the phone.

"Nothing. Just asking. Idle curiosity. You know that I'm idly curious about everything." Georgie's voice dropped. "But, say, if traumatic events caused a person to fracture into multiple personalities, could another traumatic event glue them back together?"

"I cannot imagine that the American Psychiatric Association would approve *that* as an ethical treatment."

"Well, let's say that it happened in the wild."

"I don't know. It would depend on the person. Dissociative identity disorder is so diverse. If someone comes in with 'classic' symptoms, they're faking it. Considering what causes it—"

Fucking awful child abuse. An instant of homicidal rage passed through Georgie, but the guy was already dead.

"—I would say that someone would need years of therapy, at least cognitive behavioral therapy, to get to a point where they could begin to put the pieces back together."

Alexandre had said that he had done that, mostly.

"I don't know," Rae waffled, "but some sort of symbolic event might make the person decide to integrate, and something traumatic might cause a change in their neurochemistry such that it might happen. It would have to be something awful, though."

"Let's say that it was."

"Something like being held hostage by the Russian mafia and breaking your hand so badly that you have to give up an instrument that you studied your whole life to play?"

Guess who else had seen the gossip pages? "Something like that."

"Does he have dissociative identity disorder?"

"It's a good model to describe some of his coping strategies."

"Now *that's* as good a definition of dissociative identity disorder as I've ever heard."

"But he says that they're gone now."

"Did you pressure him to make them go away?"

"I don't think so. I'm pretty sure that I didn't."

"He's the one who would know. Would he have any reason to misrepresent the situation?"

That was a nice way or putting it. "He was on

sodium pentothol or something. He was higher than the Space Station. I don't think he could have lied."

"Then I would watch for empirical evidence."

Like accents disappearing.

Rae continued, "But I would believe him unless you see evidence to the contrary."

"Thanks, Rae."

"Damn, I would have loved to talk to him before he cured himself."

"Yeah, well, I'll let you know. Maybe you can write a paper on how he cured himself."

Rae laughed. "That would be cool."

Georgie bit her lip, not wanting to even ask this. "So, does that mean he's crazy?"

Another sigh whooshed through the phone. "'Crazy' is not a psychiatric diagnosis recognized by the DSM-Five, and it's a good thing because we're all a little crazy. I'm a flippin' basket case half the time. Why are you worried if he's crazy now?"

"I just am."

"Because now it's become important?"

"Yeah," Georgie sighed. She wedged her finger harder in her other ear.

"Because now you're—" Rae's voice trailed off in a question.

Georgie made a sound in her throat, trying to make non-committal sounds to get out of talking about it.

Rae's voice lowered, "Come on, Ice Princess. Say it."

"You're going to make a lovely shrink someday," Georgie grumbled.

"Yeah, either a psychologist or a psychiatrist.

There's really only one reason that it would be so damn important to you if he's crazy or not."

Georgie grumbled something that wasn't really words.

"Go ahead and own it," Rae told her. "You're—"

The crowd around the corner muttered, and a laugh propagated through them.

"—I'm in love with him," Georgie admitted, "and he wants me to stay with Killer Valentine and be a *musician* instead of going back to college to finish my degree and go to law school."

"I loved it when you performed at our weddings, and I watched some Killer Valentine concerts on the internet," Rae said. "You're amazing on stage. I don't think I've ever seen you grin and laugh like that when you're talking about contract law. And the way Alexandre sings to you, it's obvious that he's in love with you, too."

"Do you think so?" Okay, Georgie might be needy. And the Ice Princess didn't make snap decisions. And she might be needy.

"It is possible that he might be a truly fantastic actor, but everything about his body language and facial expressions looks like he means it. He focuses all that on you, and it's amazing to see. I don't think he's faking it. Do you like being a musician?"

"Of course. I've been practicing all my life for this. I just never thought I would get the chance."

"Is he paying you like a contract musician? Work-for-hire?"

How did Rae know about stuff like that? "No. He signed me on as a full band member and is copy-righting songs with my name on them. The songwriting royalties will be more than I could make as a lawyer, at least before I became a partner."

"Do you like touring?"

"Well, yeah."

"Man, I don't how you do it, the hotels, the flights, sleeping in a different place every night, living out of a suitcase. I'd *hate* it."

"It's not so bad. We don't have a lot of time to sightsee, but the PR can be fun, doing interviews and appearances and meeting the DJs at the radio stations or at least talking to them on the phone. And Alexandre is always there, and we're always talking about music and art and performing and stuff. And the other people in the band are great. I mean, Cadell is a sweetie once you can get him to talk to you, and hanging around Tryp and Elfie is like watching a comedy show. Those guys are hysterical. The techs are great if you treat them right, even though they pretend to not like the musos. It's more like a traveling family."

"What do you like best about being in the band?"

The words almost stuck in Georgie's throat. "The shows. Performing."

Wow. If her professors at Tanglewood had heard her say that, they would have all died a collective death, clutching their shocked hearts.

Rae said, "*So,* the way I see it is: you can come back to school and proceed with your soul-crushing plan of being a lawyer and paying off all your father's investors over your whole life, or you can be a musician like you've wanted to be, perform your music and your art like you love to do, and stay with the man you love and still pay them back, and probably sooner. And if the rock star thing does fall through, you can still go back to Plan A."

Well, fuck. When she put it like that. "You should be the damn lawyer instead of a psychologist."

"And you should let yourself be happy."

"Way to hammer the point there, Rae-Rae. How did you know about my dad's little swindling problem?"

"Honey, I've been hanging out with Flicka for months. That girl knows *everything* about *everyone.*"

"Just fantastic."

"I still love you."

Tears stung Georgie's eyes. "I'm sorry that I didn't tell you. I just didn't want anyone to know."

"Don't be sorry. I get it. And don't be sorry about *this* in ten years."

Georgie said her good-byes and went to join Alexandre and the entourage among the swarms of billionaires desperate to drop exorbitant amounts of cash on pretty rocks.

Gems glittered in long cases that were packed into the glassed-in cubicles of the jewelry show like a swap meet for billionaires.

Alexandre said, "Georgie, I would like you to meet an old friend, Juste." He gestured to a man standing behind a long jeweler's case, arranged with a few filigreed rings and necklace sets displayed on black velvet. "Juste, this is Georgiana, a friend."

At least Alexandre wasn't making good on his threat to introduce her as his wife.

Georgie shook the man's hand. The man standing behind the jeweler's case, wearing a nice suit and a glittering tie-tack, was shorter than Georgie and thin, and his hands were so light that they were almost spidery.

"Enchanté," the man said, examining Georgie's hand as he spoke. "You wear a size seven ring, yes?"

"That's really good," she laughed. "Yeah, I'm a seven."

"You have strong pianist's fingers," Juste said. "Not all blunt like a violinist's." Disapproval soured his voice.

Alexandre rolled his eyes. "Nice to see you again, Juste. I'll be in touch."

They walked into the crowd milling around the booths inside the glass pyramid that looked like the entrance to the Louvre museum in Paris.

"So, do they have a jewelry show every weekend?" Georgie asked.

Alexandre shrugged. "Sometimes it's cars. Sometimes it's antiques. Sometimes it's designer clothes or art. There are always many things for very rich people to do and see here: concerts, performances, gambling of course, and sports. We have the Monaco Formula One Grand Prix every May and a soccer stadium. Monaco is a tourist trap for billionaires."

Chapter Thirty-Nine

SWIMMING AND DRIVING

Georgie

"Seriously," Georgie told Alexandre as she rested her hand on the warm roof of a sedan in a dark parking lot, "everyone should know how to swim and how to drive, just in case you need to save yourself or someone else. Get in the car."

He frowned at the car. "You don't want me behind the wheel. If someone turns on the radio, I'll start dodging all the flashes of light."

"So we won't turn on the radio," she said.

Alexandre glowered at the car. "Shouldn't we hire a professional tutor?"

"In America, friends teach friends how to drive."

"No wonder the accident rate in the US is so high."

"Get in the car."

"This is France, not the US," Alexandre pointed out.

They had had to drive far to France at two in the morning to find a large, empty parking lot. Parking lots in Monaco were underground, cramped, and full, none of which were conducive to a person's first time behind the wheel.

Streetlights projected cones of light through the dark night. Paul and another of the security guys, Ulysse, were sitting on the curb of the parking lot, talking and scrolling on their phones, far enough away that they could jump if the car barreled toward them.

Georgie said, "Get in the car, chicken."

He ,opened the driver's side door with his good hand. His left hand was still wrapped in bandages and splints. "As you wish."

Georgie grinned over the top of the car at him. *"The Princess Bride?"*

He laughed. "Maybe."

"I love that movie."

"I haven't seen it in years. We should watch it together."

"Quit stalling. Get in the car." She ducked and got in the passenger side.

Inside the car, Georgie fastened her seatbelt and waited while he moved the seat all the way back. He still looked like a giraffe climbing into a Volkswagen, even though the car was one of the largest Mercedes sedans.

Georgie told him, "Hold the wheel at the top for now. When your other hand is okay, you should hold it at two and ten."

"I beg your pardon?"

"Like a clock. At the places where the two and ten

are on a clock." She mimed the position. "Then you press the button. In some cars, you have to insert the key into the steering column and turn it."

He poked the button, frowning, and the engine thrummed under her legs.

He said, "I cannot see how any good is going to come of this."

"What if I'd gotten some glass from that damn chandelier in my eyes when we were running away from the Butorins? Paul had to have his hands free to shoot at them if he had needed to. It might have made the difference."

"I don't plan to ever have to run away from Russian mafia again. Sofiya signed the papers transferring the proceeds from the copyrights this afternoon. When you countersign at the lawyer's office tomorrow, it's over. You can live out in the open. You can even change your name back to Oelrichs, if you want to."

"I'm sure there are other criminals out there that my father took money from. I shouldn't advertise who I am."

"Probably for the best."

"Now put your foot on the brake—it's the one on the left, no, your right foot moves back and forth between them—and hold the button on the side of the gearshift to shift the car into drive. There you go."

"So it will move now?"

"Yes. Gently lift your foot off the brake. Just get the feel of coasting and braking."

The car inched forward and slammed to a stop.

He frowned. "Sorry."

"Everybody does that the first time," Georgie said, rubbing her chest where the seatbelt had grabbed her.

"Why don't you try easing off and pressing down a few times?"

They lurched around the parking lot. Georgie caught a glimpse of Paul and Ulysse pointing and laughing at the car.

The second time around the parking lot was a lot smoother.

She said, "Okay, now try giving it a little gas. It's the other one down there. Yep, that's it."

"*Teenagers* do this?" he asked.

"All of us, give or take a few."

"I'm surprised any of you survive."

"You'll get the hang of it soon. It takes everybody a few minutes to figure out."

The third circuit of the parking lot was at an easy fifteen miles an hour, and he eased the sedan to a stop at the end.

"See?" Georgie exclaimed. "Ten minutes, and you've got it."

"It wasn't terrible," Alexandre allowed. "Let's try it again."

The next few trips around the parking lot were smooth rides, and Georgie leaned back, satisfied that she wasn't going to have to vault over the cup holder thing in the middle and grab the wheel.

On their fifth tour of the parking lot, Paul and Ulysse had gone back to looking at their phones, their long legs stretched out.

Alexandre turned the corners smoothly, learning fast. Not surprising, really, when Georgie thought about it. He had been training his fine motor skills his whole life.

"So, about the time I murdered my violin tutor," Alexandre started.

"Let's teach you about turn signals, and maybe you should go the other way around the parking lot," Georgie gestured out the window, "because turning left is important, too."

He turned the car carefully, drove down the middle of the parking lot, and started circling the parking lot counter-clockwise at about twenty miles an hour, too fast for Georgie to jump out and roll without getting a serious case of road rash.

He said, "We need to discuss it."

"We don't. We really don't. I don't want to discuss it. Learning to drive and confessing to murder are mutually exclusive activities."

"It's not a confession. You just need to know what happened."

"The little stick on the left side is your turn signal. Press down to signal that you're going to turn left."

The car clicked as he turned. A circle of yellow light ran through the dark car. "You need to know."

"I don't. It was a long, long time ago. Ten years."

"I did it. I murdered him. I knew what I was doing, and I did it anyway."

"Please don't say any more."

"And I nearly killed someone else a year later."

"Just drive."

"And I almost did it again when those two men tried to drag you off at Madison Square Garden. I wanted to."

Georgie sucked in a deep breath, watching the dark parking lot roll by. Obviously, they were going to discuss this. *Fine.* "The guy, your violin teacher, he hurt Christine, didn't he? Like he hurt you."

Moonlight shone silver over the dash of the car, and the instrument panel glowed blue on Alexandre's face. "He had whipped her. I walked into his house for my lesson, and she was huddled on the floor, sobbing, her blouse ripped open down the back. Her back was bleeding in three stripes. He had whipped her for missing notes, once. The next two were for crying when he did it and for dropping the bow. He insisted that you must be able to play through the pain, to keep your concentration through absolutely anything. After the first time, I never dropped the bow."

Georgie breathed through her nose to keep herself from crying or throwing up at the grotesque things that his violin teacher had done.

Alexandre said, "He was going to do it all to her, too."

She gripped the handle on the door. "He was a terrible man. He shouldn't have done it, to her or to you or to anyone."

"He had threatened Christine all those years. He had said that if I told anyone what was happening or if I did badly at a performance, he would whip her or he would kill her."

She reached over and touched his knee while he turned the corner again. "So you protected her all that time."

His calm tone was the same as if they had been discussing where they should go to eat lunch after having declared that he was not particularly hungry. "And he did it anyway. And he was going to keep doing it. He had that rage in his eyes when he was standing over her, holding it. His whole body was shaking as he shouted at her to get off the floor, to play the fucking song. He was screaming that she had to play through the pain, that she couldn't drop the bow no matter what he did to her."

"That's insane," she said, watching the parking lot slowly revolve around them.

"She was eleven," he said and drove smoothly, slowly. "I hit him. And I kept hitting him. I wasn't out of my mind or berserk, and it wasn't Alex or Xan. It was always me, and I could have stopped. I could have stopped when he was on the floor, and I could have stopped when he was unconscious. I kept hitting him until I was sure that he was dead. There was a lot of blood, all over me, all over the carpet. Christine was terrified of me until I calmed her down."

"It must have traumatized her so much that she couldn't remember it," Georgie mused.

"Yes. I tried to do what I could for her. I got her out of the house. We waited for two hours in the snow for the car to come back, to pick us up to go back to school."

"So you wrapped her in your clothes."

"I hadn't kept her safe from him. At least I could keep her warm."

"You might have frozen to death."

"I thought I would go to jail for the rest of my life. I hated myself for what I had done, but I couldn't think of anything less that would have kept him away from her."

"You might have gotten frostbite. You might have lost your toes, or your fingers."

He was still driving slowly around the parking lot, turning the car precisely at the corners. "I laid down in the snow."

"Oh, Alexandre." She shouldn't take his one hand off the wheel, so she rubbed his shoulder. "Oh, no. Not you."

"The chauffeur found me. He threw Christine in

the car first, then me. Flicka probably saved my life. She wrapped her coat around me and kept trying to warm up my hands, tucking them under her armpits and under her legs, and hugged me until we got to the hospital. She surely saved my hands."

"Okay, so you told me," Georgie said. "And everything's still okay. Nothing has changed."

"There's more."

Georgie bit her lower lip. "I don't want there to be more."

"The other conductor, Maestro Agnarsson."

"You don't have to tell me this."

"For years, Maestro Soto had told the conductors with whom I had worked that the way to get a good performance out of me, no matter how hard I tried, was to threaten Christine. They all knew it. They all did it. They said that it lent a certain fire to my performances. She was there, too, that day. Agnarsson grabbed her arm."

"Oh, God. You grew up like that?"

"Adrien and Paul pulled me off of him. I fought them to get away to beat him until he died, too."

"I don't have any sympathy for him if he grabbed a little girl with the intention of hurting her," Georgie said.

"I did get away from them and hit him again. I damn near killed him."

"*He* should be in jail. You haven't told me anything that makes me think worse of you. You protected your little sister and then you protected me. It was always to protect someone else. Why don't you just tell people that?"

"Because right now, they're afraid of me, and they

should be afraid of me. If they are, no one will threaten Christine. Or you."

"Because of those guys at Madison Square Garden."

"It was doubtlessly one of the reasons that Sofiya Butorin negotiated with us, because I am a raging psychopath who might kill someone at any moment."

"But you're not."

"Everyone thinks I am."

Flicka had bought into that nonsense. "I know that you're not. Protecting someone is different than killing someone just to do it."

"The first time, they didn't put me in jail because they could see the effects of the abuse."

The scars on his back. "Someone should have noticed it a hell of a lot sooner."

"I hid it."

"God, Alexandre. I want to make that guy alive so I can kill him all over again."

"They also didn't put me in jail because I had to perform at concerts, because I was a genius and a prodigy, and the world couldn't lose me, because of the violin. If I had stopped playing, it might have been different."

"Essentially, they forced you to keep playing it."

"The second time, the conductor declined to press charges. Same with the Butorins. I was lucky."

"The conductor didn't press charges because he threatened to abuse your sister, a *child.* The Butorins were mafia. That's not luck. That's because they were the guilty ones. Not you. It's not like you're running around punching random people. You can't let misplaced guilt and other people's gossip and evil thoughts screw up your whole life."

"Yes," Alexandre said, carefully turning the corner.

"Yes, what?" Georgie glanced over at him.

"When you are not the guilty one, you can't let misplaced guilt and other people's gossip and evil thoughts screw up your whole life."

Georgie braced herself on the dashboard, suddenly dizzy. "What are you talking about?"

He said, quietly, "You did not swindle anyone. You did not take their money. You did not misappropriate it. You did not steal it. Yet, you are acting like you're the guilty one."

Holy crap. Had Alex turned that around on her? Wait, not Alex. *Alexandre.* But he was Alex in everything except his accent and how he blinked slowly, sleepily, like he was just rolling out of her bed. That was *Alexandre.*

But the way that he was turning her arguments around on her was all Alex.

She shook her head. "That's different."

"If I'm a different person now, ten years later, then so are you. You didn't swindle those people on purpose. You believed your father's hype, just like all of your father's other investors. How much have you paid back so far?"

"I don't know. Around eighty thousand dollars." Eighty-two thousand, seven hundred thirty-three dollars-worth of less guilt.

"If I'm a different person, then so are you. You may feel the need to pay back those people, and that's admirable, but you need to stop letting your father's crimes dictate your life. If I shouldn't feel guilty for murdering one man and nearly doing it again and again—"

"Saving your sister from abuse in two instances and my life in the later ones."

"—then you should not feel guilty." He looked away from the front windshield and toward her, his dark eyes intent on her. "If motivation matters, then your attempt at martyrdom is misguided."

She nudged his chin to face the front. "We won't be martyred at all if you keep your eyes on the road."

"Let me pay them all back, all your father's investors whom you think should get their money back. They'll get the money *now*, and you can pay me back in small, sane installments and live your life however you choose."

"It's not just the money," she admitted.

"It is just money. It was a long time ago. That wasn't you. You're someone different now. Aren't you?"

She recognized her own words from last night. "You have a pretty good memory for that."

"It made an impression. Let me do it. Let's give all of them the money *now* when they need it, not thirty years from now. Surely getting them the money *now* is more important than from whom it comes."

Georgie toyed with the door handle. "That's convincing."

He drove around the perimeter again, navigating the corners well. "Say yes."

She should do it by the sweat of her own brow. She should work her hands to the bones to pay back the money.

Letting him do this was the wrong, wrong, *wrong* thing.

Except for the fact that her father's victims had

been waiting for years already. They would get the money *now,* not when she finally earned it, someday.

And that was a greater good. Some of the older people had already died.

"Yes. And thank you. And you don't have to. If you want to change your mind, just tell me."

He coasted to a stop, shifted the sedan into park, and reached over to hold her hand. "I won't change my mind. It's the right thing to do, on both our parts."

"We have to have lawyers. We have to sign papers or something."

He smiled. "As you wish."

She smiled back at him. "Let's watch that movie soon, okay?"

"D'accord. Mon Dieu, can I quit driving now?"

Chapter Forty

SOMETHING DIFFERENT

Georgie

Wednesday morning, Georgie slipped on a black dress that Christine had loaned her, which was a little roomy and long on her. She had cinched it with a belt and stuffed her purse with tissues, even though the Ice Princess didn't cry and she certainly wouldn't make a scene when she had known Adrien the least out of anyone who would be there today.

She had already helped Alexandre dress in a black suit and combed his hair back into a ponytail. He had visited the orthopedic hospital in Monaco that morning and had the bulky bandages exchanged for smaller ones, but he wouldn't be able to button anything for a while.

She said, "You haven't put your green crystal earring back in since the surgery."

He looked over at her, a slow smile curving his mouth. “You think it was just a crystal?”

“Yeah, like Swarovski?” She poked small studs through her ears.

“It wasn’t crystal.”

She turned to face him. “That monster is not a real emerald.”

A smile tugged at one side of his mouth. “Yeah.”

“I can’t believe you’ve been walking around with that thing hanging off your ear. It was bigger than a quarter. The hospital didn’t lose it, did they?”

“My sister had it in her purse. She gave it back to me that afternoon.”

“Do you need some help putting it back in? It’s no big deal. It’s just an earring. It doesn’t mean anything.”

Alexandre stood and adjusted his suit coat. “I gave it to Juste to make into a necklace for my sister. She has always liked that stone. I’ve decided that I want something different now.”

Chapter Forty-One

PALATINE CHAPEL

Alexandre Grimaldi

Adrien's Mass was held at the small Palatine Chapel, which was within the walls of the Prince's Palace of Monaco. The group of them walked through the palace entry rooms to a paved courtyard within the palace and straight past the horseshoe staircase toward the chapel.

Georgie walked by Alexandre's side as if she belonged in the palace, holding his elbow. Her touch comforted him.

Alexandre had thought that Pierre would have gotten married on those steps in Monaco like most of the heirs did, but Flicka had insisted on the wedding taking place in Paris. Since she outranked him socially, she had won, but it hadn't been a very long argument from what Alexandre had heard. Back then, a year ago, Pierre had been so infatuated with her that he would have given up the throne for her if she had asked.

Luckily for Maxence and Alexandre, she hadn't asked him to.

As an ostensible joke, Alexandre had sent Pierre and his younger brother Maxence the gift of vitamin pills every Christmas.

Very large bottles of vitamin pills.

The largest bottles of vitamin pills he could find.

For their continuing, very good health.

The last few years, he and Adrien had hunted up enormous bottles at American warehouse stores. This year, he had planned to wrap 55-gallon steel drums for them, full of the most expensive multivitamin pills that money could buy.

It wasn't really a joke. If something ever happened to Pierre and Maxence and the throne had fallen in Alexandre's lap, he would have abdicated immediately and earned the unending ire of his younger sister.

Christine would have sent royal assassins after him for making her the sovereign and reigning Princess of Monaco.

Alexandre smiled one last time before they went into the chapel for Adrien's Mass.

Inside, wooden benches radiated from the central aisle, and a crucifix dominated the small church.

Alexandre walked to the front pew, genuflected, and sat, even though his entire body raged and mourned for Adrien.

Luckily, Alexandre could endure any pain in silence, without flinching, and continue on brilliantly.

That was how he survived Adrien's Mass.

He endured the pain.

Chapter Forty-Two

THE WAVES

Georgie

The white sands stretched far and away on both sides of Georgie and the rest of the small group as they stood on the windswept private beach. Georgie could see sunbathers far in the distance, down on the public section, but they were alone on this stretch. The Mediterranean rippled in the distance and churned on the shore, its restless waters rolling up close to their toes and then dodging away.

Georgie stepped into the foam, and the warm water cooled her feet.

They had all left their shoes in a pile at the beach's entrance and walked barefoot to the water's edge.

Alexandre still wore the black suit and tie. He had refused to take any of the pain pills that the hospital had given him, just shrugging and saying that he didn't need them, even though surely the local anesthetic should have worn off yesterday.

He held a silver urn under his right arm like a football.

Georgie stepped back, and Christine unscrewed the lid for him. Everyone walked out until the waves were lapping at their knees, and Alexandre and Christine lowered the urn into the water together, letting the waves take the fine, gray ash out to sea.

Alexandre and Christine dumped water out of the urn several times, making sure that it was all gone.

Christine held the urn by the rim, and Alexandre put one arm around her for a few minutes, his arm resting on the shrug she wore around her shoulders.

He reached back with his other arm, the sun glaring off the white bandages.

Georgie walked out into the waves and huddled under his left arm, careful not to brush the bandages around his fingers. She wrapped her arm around his waist above Christine's.

Alexandre laid his left cheek against her hair, and the three of them stood that way for long minutes. The warm waves soaked the hem of Georgie's dress as the tides rolled around them, pulling on their legs and burying their feet in the soft sand.

They ate a cold supper that night, all of them quiet with their own thoughts. Later, in the dark, Alexandre wrapped his whole body around Georgie and pressed his cheek to her hair. His breathing didn't deepen into sleep for a long, long time.

Chapter Forty-Three

SCRAMBLED EGGS

Georgie

When Georgie woke up the next morning, Thursday, she was alone in the wide bed.

Alexandre's bedroom was decorated in what she thought of as new antiques, very elaborate yet not gaudy. Curls and pillars had been carved into the dark hardwoods. She might have joked that you could actually see the chisel marks where real humans had carved it, but those artisans wouldn't have left a chisel mark. The perfect finishes shone like glass. The walls were finished in the colors of warm honey and sand. It looked like an Italian faux plaster finish, except that the walls were real plaster and she would have bet that there was nothing faux in this whole house.

She padded out to the living room area. Alexandre was leaning back with one muscular arm lying on the back of the couch, his cell phone pressed to his ear, speaking what Georgie thought was Italian. He said the word "Roma" and "Killer Valentine."

The Rome concert was scheduled for tomorrow night. He must already be doing PR.

And so the grind began again.

She waved at him and went back in to brush her teeth.

When she came back out, Alexandre had hung up and was absently tapping keys on a piano keyboard that was resting on a stand beside him.

"Whoa! What's that?" she asked, walking around it.

He shrugged. "I thought you might want to practice before we go on tomorrow night."

This keyboard was even nicer than the one she had been toting around North America and Europe, a full eighty-eight keys, and when she pressed her fingers to them, the feel was excellent. "You bought this for me to practice for one concert?"

He shrugged. "I'll have it sent wherever you end up. At least you won't have to traipse through the dark to the music building before dawn. You can plug your headphones in and play anytime you want to."

This piano was extravagant. "You don't have to do this."

"I want you to have it. I would be miserable if I thought that you didn't have a piano. Do you remember that song that we wrote, the one that drives me out of my mind, by any chance?"

Did he know that she had lifted a set of the sheet music for it? She wasn't planning on anything nefarious with it. It was just a souvenir. "The one you never found words for, 'Scrambled Eggs?'"

"Yes, that one. I think that it would make a good instrumental piece to throw in somewhere in the middle of the second set. I have it on my tablet, so I printed it out this morning." He held out a couple of crisp pages of music. "I made a few changes to the final draft."

So he must not know that she'd swiped it. The song was intellectual property and probably still uncopyrighted, so it might have looked bad if he had found it, even though her intentions were to hide it in her bottom dresser drawer in her dorm room to stare at when she was alone. "Cool."

He said, "Let's work that up for tomorrow night."

"Right," she said, grinning at him. "I'll have this unfinished song whipped into performance shape by tomorrow afternoon for the sound check."

"Excellent." He was frowning at his phone and scrolling. "I think we'll add it in between 'Nine Levels of Tortured Souls' and 'Rock Like Rome Is Falling.'"

Horror. "Oh, my God. You're serious."

He looked up, dark eyes wide. "Yes, I'm serious."

"For *tomorrow?*"

"Certainly."

"Why?"

Alexandre stared at his phone. "I had hoped to play it as a duet for piano and violin, but it looks like that won't happen. So I'd at least like to hear you perform it once, just to hear it, just to see the colors."

Oh, man. She sat beside him on the couch. "Okay. I'll have it ready."

He looped his arm around her and pulled her to his side. "I can't believe this is our last performance."

She leaned against him. "I don't want it to be, either."

"Then stay. Don't be a damn lawyer."

"It's the best way to make the money back."

"Fuck the money."

"If you talk like that, I won't sign the papers."

"Fine." He sighed. "I'll settle for that. Let's work on 'Scrambled Eggs.'"

Georgie wedged headphones over her ears and noodled, sight-reading and reacquainting herself with the music, and had a working version within a few minutes. She added a strong back-beat that would keep the crowd on their feet while no one was singing to them, making a mental note to run through the song with Tryp, the drummer, before the sound check tomorrow afternoon. He'd have even better ideas.

Xan was lying on the couch, holding his phone in the crook of his elbow and answering emails while he hummed along with her.

No, *Alexandre* was lying on the couch, Georgie corrected herself.

Xan would have been sprawled on the couch, his long legs straddled, taking up all the space in the room with his very presence.

Alexandre had his bare feet crossed at his ankles, and as he scrolled through his phone, his movements were more elegant, more like a violinist's minute adjustments of a bow across the strings.

He was different, but the same.

It had seemed that Alex was around, even if there wasn't the jarring disconnect to his distinct British accent and mannerisms. While they were driving, when he had cornered her with her own words, that was Alex de Valentinois, the diplomat who could discuss and negotiate in any situation. At thc wedding, Alex had negotiated with Sofiya Butorin.

But, even when he had been singing at Rae's wedding, he hadn't quite been Xan.

Even afterward, hyped up on the crowd's energy, his eyes had still been a little hooded, his demeanor a little more reserved, a little less adamant about taking control in bed and utterly possessing her. Xan never let Georgie be on top in any sense of that word.

Xan Valentine might be gone.

Maybe forever.

Georgie swallowed hard, hoping she was wrong, but she didn't think she was.

And they had a concert tomorrow night.

This might go very badly.

Alexandre might have been able to sing two songs while standing behind the piano in the controlled, formal atmosphere of Rae's wedding, but standing centerstage and rockin an arena filled to the brim with twelve thousand screaming fans was different.

Georgie swallowed down her trepidation. "You ready to hear this?"

"Sure." He swung his legs around and sat up on the couch.

She unplugged her headphones and played through the piece.

Alexandre's phone chimed twelve times during the song.

She finished and asked, "Have you put out a press release yet?"

"No," he said. "I'm not sure what to tell them."

"You know that if you don't control the narrative, they'll just make up vile shit, right?"

He shrugged. "I was going to address it from the stage tomorrow."

Xan Valentine wouldn't have let the media control

the message for this long. He would have been out there, on the phone twenty-four and seven, crafting the message to fit within Killer Valentine's image.

Alexandre gestured to her piano. "That's interesting, that take on it. How about more like 'Alwaysland?'"

Georgie felt her eyebrows gather between her eyes. "Like Rachmaninoff? Romantic like that?"

"Yeah, like that."

"And you want to put it between 'Nine Levels of Tortured Souls' and 'Rock Like Rome Is Falling?' The audience will get whiplash."

"We'll put it somewhere else, then. Let's hear it more like 'Alwaysland.'"

Georgie stared at the keyboard and recalibrated her brain. *Okay, Romantic. Okay, like Rachmaninoff.*

She reached for the keyboard and played it. Her hands swayed across the keys, pulling the rich music from the instrument.

When she looked up, Alexandre was smiling at her. "Yes," he said. "That's it. That's it exactly."

Chapter Forty-Four

UPSILON RECORDS

Georgie

Georgie and Alexandre walked into a hotel conference room to meet with the lawyers and look at the first draft of Killer Valentine's contract with Upsilon Records. The long, dark wood table blocked out the center of the room, and people lined the table on both sides, leaning and bobbing in leather executive chairs. The furniture was so lavish that everyone in the room was resting their butt like a CEO.

None of the lawyers from the record company or that Jonas had hired for them had a law office in the exorbitant real estate market of Monaco—*shockers, right?*—so they had rented a conference room for the meeting. When they had rescheduled the conference from New York, the lawyers had jumped at the offer of a vacation in the playground of the princes and billionaires.

The conference room looked like it had been rented at Versailles. Gold veins shot through the mirrors on the walls that reflected each other and the people inside, dizzying Georgie. Silver chafing dishes full of a hot lunch stood on a banquet table against one wall, emanating the brown scents of roasted beef and potatoes. Two of the lawyers had plates by their legal pads, both with a small smear in the center like each of them had eaten one small thing.

Nine people sat on the opposite side of the table from Jonas, opposing counsel. The lawyers and executives for the record company wore designer suits.

All of Georgie's mock trial suits were still hanging in her dorm closet, so she had worn her jeans and red tee shirt again. At least it was clean. She wasn't sure how the outfit had gotten clean, but it had been folded in one of Alexandre's drawers. She suspected a subtle maid service, considering how all the glass sparkled and the whole house smelled like lemon polish.

Alexandre had had one of his costume coats flown in from Rome, where everyone else was staying and waiting for the concert the next day, so he was wearing a velvet frock coat, jeans, and a crisp, ironed white shirt.

Again, Georgie had seen no one who might have ironed. She also suspected house elves.

When he had put the coat on, Georgie had seen the hesitation in his eyes and the stiff way he had put it on, not at all the easy flip that Xan Valentine used to don the costume. He shrugged, saying, "They expect Xan Valentine to show up, expounding about absinthe and poetry. I suppose I should wear the coat."

The Rome concert tomorrow might be a problem.

Jonas sat on their side of the table, thank goodness. He had two suited-up lawyers with him.

The record company's lawyers pushed a contract across the table. The tall lawyer grasped the sheaf with both hands, wrapping her big hands around the thick stack that looked like the manuscript for *War and Peace*. A dozen tiny thumb drives skittered on top of the paper.

Jonas announced, "We'll take a look at it, Dannie and Darla, but I'm sure everything is just how we negotiated. It's the standard contract at the customary rates."

Georgie was chewing on a pen. "But Killer Valentine isn't a *standard* act. Most bands that you guys 'discover' are playing at small clubs. KV is selling out large arenas, internationally."

Jonas shushed her.

Georgie dropped the pen away from her lips. Had he really *shushed* her?

Jonas said, "We're grateful for this opportunity, and we take this offer seriously. We'll get back to you tomorrow to arrange a signing on Saturday."

Alexandre frowned at Jonas and leaned back in his chair. "I thought this was an initial meeting."

"Tomorrow?" Georgie dropped the pen, which clattered to the table. "No way. I want a friend of mine to look over this contract. There is no way that we can get back to anybody *tomorrow.*"

Jonas laughed. "Georgie is Killer Valentine's keyboard player and fancies herself a lawyer."

Alexandre leaned forward, his dark eyebrows slanting down. *"Jonas.* What the fuck is wrong with you?"

"You're not a lawyer, either, Jonas." Georgie glared at the two attorneys sitting beside Jonas, who seemed to be doing their best impressions of blow-up sex dolls strapped to the chairs.

Fuck this.

She swiveled toward the other lawyers. "I'm not an attorney, but I'm pre-law and I've been doing an internship with Professor Lawrence Chen at Southwestern State."

The four lawyers on the other side of the table raised their eyebrows. One woman said, "I read Chen's paper in Georgetown's Ethics Journal last month. It was well done."

"Thanks," Georgie said. "I did the research on the litigation financing section."

"That was a good section," the lawyer allowed, leaning on her hands. Her manicure was dark gray. "Are you going to have Lawrence Chen read this contract?"

"Yep," Georgie said. "He's a great guy. I'll bet he'll jump at the chance to read something so *interesting.*"

All the lawyers on the other side of the table shifted in their seats, and their chairs squeaked under the strain.

To Georgie, it was as if every one of them had a red flag waving over their heads. She could smell the bullshit in the air.

She told Alexandre and Jonas, "We will wait until we hear what Professor Chen has to say about this contract. I'm sending it to a friend of mine's fiancé, too. He's a prosecuting attorney for the state and *huge* on ethics. I'll bet that he'll have something to say about it, too."

Georgie grabbed a fistful of USB drives and stalked out.

She heard Jonas start to talk fast behind her, but when she looked back, Alexandre was half a stride behind her, his frock coat flying behind him like a black cape and the thick paper stack of the contract clutched in his one healthy hand.

Chapter Forty-Five

CONTRACT

Georgie

In the car, as they inched along the streets in the Monte Carlo district of Monaco, Georgie flipped through the contract. The car bobbed forward and braked almost immediately in the packed traffic. "This contract is so dense. There's so much in here. I have to email this to Professor Chen as soon as we get back to the hotel."

Outside the car's windows, bushes trimmed into globes and cones ambled backward as they passed. Afternoon sun spilled inside the car.

Alexandre pulled the frock coat off and shoved it behind him on the seat.

She found paragraphs about the band's responsibilities during promotion, and they didn't sound anything like what Xan had been doing. "They're going to set up interviews with the heads of record stores, and they want KV to do private performances for record store executives."

"What's a record store?" Alexandre asked.

"It's like Tower Records in London, where people go and buy CDs," Georgie explained and then realized that he was smirking at her. "Oh, you're being a dickweed. Fine." She glared at the contract. "What good will that do?"

"It's called 'shmoozing,' right? It's to negotiate better placement within the record stores. Bins. Merch. And such things."

She stared at him. "How many albums are bought at record stores these days?"

He shrugged. "I haven't been to one in years, but I never know how much to generalize my experience."

Which was a nice way of saying, *What do the little people do?*

"Most people direct-download or buy online," she said. "Maybe it's just old school verbiage that they haven't taken out for some reason. Let me see what else is in here." She paged through, reading random paragraphs. "What are recoupable expenses?" she asked.

"It details recoupable expenses?" Alexandre asked, leaning over. "Well, we won't have any. We'll pay for everything up front, just like we always have."

Georgie read the terms and the fucking interest rate. *"Holy shit!* Do you know what they want to do to you?"

He shrugged. "I know how recoupable expenses work."

"They will *loan* you the money for the tour and hotels and booking the arenas and traveling for PR and anything you buy on the tour, from the tour bus to instruments if I need a new keyboard or Mitch needs a new soundboard to the fruit and crackers and bottled water that we set out for snacks during the show, *and then they want to charge you twenty-eight percent interest on that!*"

"That's standard, from what I hear. We'll just continue the way we have been, though."

"But that's not *all!* They want to charge *you* for this bullshit PR that they want you to do, like traveling to it and cabs and hotels, the PR that *they* think is important, and they want you to pay for a theater and for you to set up to play for those record store execs. *And* for the huge buffet lunches that the executives will eat. *And* for the booze. *And* swag! They want little *gift bags* to hand out to CEOs that make millions per year like they're six-year-olds at a birthday party, and they want to take it out of *your earnings!*"

"I've heard that those kinds of events are common. Most bands do them."

"*At twenty-eight percent.* That's *usury.* That would be fucking *illegal* if a bank did it. You'd be better off applying for a buttload of credit cards and financing the tour on Mastercard and Amex!"

"But we won't use their money," Alexandre said. "It doesn't apply to us."

"It applies to some people. *Most* people. Most *musicians.*" She scanned the contract and shook it until it rattled. Paul looked through the rearview mirror at her. "With this page alone, there's a damn good chance that after you sell several million records, go platinum, and tour your ass off for a year, *you* will owe *them* money."

"But we won't—" Alexandre began.

"Jesus, I'll bet that those guys flying here to

Monaco and their hotel rooms and that conference room and everything they ate and didn't eat from that huge buffet are all 'recoupable.' If you sign this contract, you're paying for all of that."

"We won't use their money," Alexandre insisted, craning his head to look at the contract.

Georgie grumbled, "I'll bet they gave themselves a per diem gambling allowance. That *you* will eventually pay for. *With interest.*"

"Except that we won't."

Georgie rooted around in her purse and came up with a red pen. "Well, you *will,* because you aren't going to pay their bill right now and hand them five hundred bucks to blow at the baccarat tables. You won't even *know* until you see it subtracted from your gross, and it won't be a line item. It'll just be a huge number, especially after being bloated for two years at *twenty-eight percent interest.* That they will *keep.* Because they aren't borrowing from a bank, just from their own coffers. Plus, it doesn't matter. That sort of thievery is the *spirit* of the contract. That's the sort of thing that'll be *all the way through* this piece-of-shit contract."

Alexandre said, "We can edit the contract and negotiate terms and conditions, but this is a big opportunity for KV. It's not just me that we're talking about. The rest of the band will benefit from the wider distribution."

"You'll gain listeners, but you will be paying for each additional listener. This isn't good business. This isn't going to bring you new fans, just *listeners.*"

"Getting to the next level is impossible without a record company."

"Who says that?"

"Well, conventional wisdom. Industry knowledge."

"So, the record companies say that. You will still be paying for absolutely everything, but they'll be collecting fees and interest from you to do it." She slashed the recoupable expenses paragraph with red ink, speeding from righteous outrage toward a temper tantrum. *"Fuck* them. Fuck them *and* this contract."

"We've been indie until now, and Upsilon is a prestigious label. The validation is important. I can reach so many more people with my music. The CDs will be in Walmart and record stores. It's the big break we've always wanted."

Georgie glanced up from the contract, her red pen poised over the paper. "You're not going to sign this piece of shit, are you?"

He lifted his hands, almost helplessly. "It's a big step to sign with a label."

"This contract is the worst contract I've ever seen in my life. The *very worst."*

"How many contracts have you seen?" he asked.

"Plenty," Georgie said. "Professor Chen's specialty is ethics and contract law. One of the contracts that I saw was a BDSM slave contract, where a woman gave up everything short of her inalienable constitutional rights to some guy so he would cane her. This one is *worse."*

He frowned and leaned back in his seat. "Jonas said that this is a standard contract."

She demanded, "Are you out of money? You don't have to pay off my dad's investors. Seriously, save yourself and KV first."

Alexandre laughed. "I'm not out of money. Good Lord. Even if Killer Valentine were operating at a loss, which it isn't, I don't come close to burning through rents, interest, and dividends from my estates and holdings."

She stabbed the contract with her red pen. "That is the only reason that I can think of that you would sign such an exploitive contract as this."

"Money is not the reason," he assured her, still chuckling.

Georgie muttered. "Lawrence will shit bricks when he sees it. We can write a paper for a law review on this. We'll compare and contrast it with Lizzy's slave contract, and I'll bet this one will come out looking *worse.*"

"It can't be that bad. Maybe that's not how it's actually put into action."

Georgie found *another* egregious, ass-busting paragraph. "Jesus, Mary, and Joseph, Xan. They would own your *name.* They have the right of all refusal on your next *five* albums, and any future contract with them will include *all* these terms. If you sign this, you can't ever renegotiate the contract. They will own all the music you write, and if you refuse to write music, they can buy music from someone else, hire a lead singer and a band, and release it under your name and Killer Valentine's name, and you can't release music under your own name *or at all.* This is the kind of contract that made Prince write the word *slave* on his cheek and change his name to an unpronounceable symbol. This is why Kesha didn't record for years, because she was stuck in a contract with a producer who she said raped her and contractually couldn't work with anyone else. Why the fuck would Jonas negotiate terms like this, *ever?*"

"Maybe he didn't know what it meant."

"He's supposed to be your manager! He's supposed

to have your best interests! He's supposed to know how the music industry works! He's supposed to have your *back!*"

Alexandre's eyebrows lowered again, bordering on a scowl. "Jonas gets a bonus from KV and a fee from the record company if we sign."

"Oh, so he's a walking, breathing conflict of interest. Lovely." Georgie wanted to stomp on something.

"And he wants to work with Rhiannon next. He's convinced that she's the next big thing, the next breakout star that he can make famous. And she's good. Her voice is interesting and should do well. But yes, he has a conflict of interest."

Georgie slashed another paragraph with bleeding red ink. The pen scratched so hard that she tore the paper. "If you want to do a deal with them, you need to call in hardcore IP attorneys," intellectual property lawyers, "big-ass ones who will hammer this monster until it's dead. For the love of God and all the saints, Alexandre, don't sign this. It's literally a contract with the Devil. They would own your art and your name. They might as well own your soul."

"No other record company has made us an offer," Alexandre said.

"Maybe it's because they assume that you'll cost too much. You should put together a proposal to sell exactly and only what rights you want to and shop *that* around."

Alexandre shrugged. "No one does that."

Her hand flopped helplessly on the paper. "This is insane."

"This may be the best that Jonas could negotiate." He waved to dispel her worries with his gauze-wrapped hand.

Afternoon sunlight caught the white gauze wrapping Alexandre's hand, broken because he had come to save her from the fucking Butorins. He must have known that breaking his hand—*his left hand!*—meant that he wouldn't be able to play the violin anymore. He had known that he was giving it up, that he was throwing away all those hours and years of abuse and practice and dedication and hard, hard work. And he had loved the violin. He had been abused for all those years for it and yet he still loved it. Every time he laid that damn violin callus on his chin against her hair, he thought that she didn't know that he was trying to comfort himself without that violin, but she *did* know.

It wasn't fair that he had had to break his hand.

It wasn't fair that the violin had been taken away from him.

And it wasn't fair that these corporate assholes were trying to steal Killer Valentine from him, the only music he had left.

Her eyes burned. "Please don't sign it. They're going to own everything you've worked for, everything you've built. You've poured your heart and your soul into Killer Valentine. Please, *please,* don't."

A hot stripe burned down her cheek.

"Georgie!" Alexandre's dark eyes widened in horror, and he reached for her with his good arm. "Don't cry. It's not worth crying over."

It was worth crying over. It was worth *everything.*

"I'll stay," she told him. "I'll bribe Professor Chen, and we'll research what an ethical contract would look like and then write one. And I'll stay. I'll tour with you. I'll be your keyboard player until Christmas or next summer or whatever it takes, and we'll shop a proposal around to the other labels. Please don't sign this. Please, *please* don't."

Alexandre pushed the contract off her knees to the floorboards of the car. It splashed over the carpeting, the pages fluttering and flipping. He wrapped both arms around her shoulders and held her to his chest. The faint green grass and spice scent of his cologne lingered in his clothes, and she buried her face in his warm shirt.

"Please don't sign it," she sobbed. "Please don't burn it all down."

"I didn't know you cared about the band that much," he murmured, stroking her hair.

"The band and you, and all you've built. Please don't burn it down."

Chapter Forty-Six

RECOUPABLE EXPENSES

Alexandre Grimaldi

Alexandre calmed Georgie and left her at his house before he went back to the Hotel de Paris Monte-Carlo to find Jonas. Palm trees grew from the manicured grass in the center of the driveway, the wasted square footage shocking in its extravagance. Paul drove around the lawn area to the porte cochère of the palatial hotel, and Alexandre stepped out under the roofed area that was shaded from the needling sunlight.

He bounded into the hotel, talking on his cell phone. "Where are you? All right. I'll see you there."

Jonas met him at the elevator, and they rode up to the penthouse high above the swimming pool and lawns. Inside the penthouse, the record company executives and lawyers were sprawled on the couches. Plates with tails of shrimp and smears of foie gras and caviar streaks littered the furniture. Alexandre almost slid on a champagne cork on the floor as he walked in.

The record company execs and lawyers all yelled, *"Xan!"* as he walked in, like he was in a damn bar.

One of the women walked over and shook Alexandre's hand, a firm shake. With her golden blond bob and brown eyes, she looked about forty, except that her cheekbones and jaw were pronounced in a way that could only mean the extensive use of cosmetic injectables. He revised her age up twenty years.

She asked, "Can we talk about your future with Upsilon Records now?"

"The contract has some problems," Alexandre started.

"Fuck the contract," she said. "That's for the lawyers to figure out. I'm Aspen, Upsilon's veep for A and R. Let's talk about your next album and tour."

"We're not quite done with this tour, Aspen," Alexandre said.

"Yeah, but Jonas here says that you have demos for all your songs and recording time booked in New Jersey next week. So you're all ready to go."

She took Alexandre by the right hand and led him over to Jonas, where she looped her arms around their waists. "Your next record is going to be great, and we're all going to make beautiful music together."

Good God. Exactly *what* had Jonas promised her for signing Killer Valentine?

Alexandre looked at Jonas over her head.

Jonas's pale green eyes were hazy, probably drunk from some of the champagne magnums that littered the floor, but he still raised his eyebrows and stepped back from Aspen's embrace.

Alexandre did the same, shaking off her arm.

"Oh, come on, boys. Don't be like that. Have some champagne." She poured the dregs of a bottle of Dom Pérignon in a glass. Even though Jonas seemed halfway to wasted, Aspen didn't even look tipsy. "I like your demos, and we'll probably be able to use a few of them on your album. We've got some great singles lined up for you, though."

Alexandre frowned at her. "I beg your pardon?"

"Singles," she said. "You'll love them. For your professional debut, it's vital to have blowout singles. I've got two that I've been hoarding, and I'll let you have both of them. They're that good. And we'll get you three or four more."

"We write our own music," Alexandre said.

Jonas rolled his eyes and flopped on a couch. "Not anymore."

A guy was sitting on the couch, holding a plate and dunking a chunk of lobster in a cup of melted butter.

Aspen slapped the guy's arm, spraying melted butter on the couch and his pants. "He writes his own music. Did you hear that, Kuwat? He writes his own songs."

The guy set down the plate and brushed at the butter on his clothes. "We won't risk millions on *your* songs," Kuwat said. "We'll go with songwriters with proven credentials who can crank out hit after hit after hit. All the best songwriters are Norwegian, middle-aged, and bald. Henning and Dag are Upsilon's pet Norwegians. You'll get several of their good ones. We're committed to your music."

Alexandre frowned at them. "It sounds like you're committed to Henning and Dag's music."

"Oh, don't worry," Aspen told him, saluting him with her champagne flute. "You'll get a songwriting credit. 'Change a word, get a third.' Am I right, Kuwat?"

The guy cracked up, his green-streaked hair flopping. "Yeah, man. Henning and Dag are fucking geniuses. Seriously, if you look at Rolling Stone this week, they wrote eight of the twenty songs on their bestseller list. Don't even try to write your own hits. These guys are golden. You don't have a background in melodic math, comping, and track-and-hook structure. You don't want your career record to start with a dud."

"I don't think Cadell will play something that we didn't work on together," Alexandre said.

Aspen started laughing so hard that her champagne flute tilted until she had to juggle it to keep it from spilling, and Kuwat had to set his lobster on the coffee table to wipe his eyes.

Aspen finally explained, "Your band musicians won't actually *play* on the record, Xan. Good God. Musicians are just for touring. *All* the instruments on *all* the hits these days are synthesized."

"Wait," Alexandre said, looking over at Jonas, who was still watching him. "I thought you understood that Cadell's guitar is an integral part of the Killer Valentine sound."

"Oh, his guitar will be on there," Kuwat said. "We can replicate his licks in the studio. It'll sound just like him."

Alexandre didn't let his trepidation show. "I don't think it will be the same."

"Of course it will. We'll synth him and all the other musicians. Then we'll record you singing the song twenty or thirty times, and the engineer and producer will stitch the song together, syllable by syllable, until it's an idealized version of that song. It'll have a new hook every seven seconds, and the rapid shifts in melody and sound effects will claw their way into the listeners' electronically disabled, millisecond attention spans and be sonically addictive. People will stream it like they're mainlining crack."

There was a bottle of Pappy Van Winkle whiskey sitting on the coffee table. Alexandre picked it up by the neck and threw back a gulp. The burning whiskey didn't even begin to dull the slicing pain in his hand or the cramp in his heart.

Kuwat continued, "And if your producer thinks that slick production values aren't right for the sound he's trying for on your album, we can manufacture some lo-fi fuzz to grunge it up, if he thinks you should retain some alternative sound."

"You don't have to sign that contract, Xan," Aspen said, staring straight at him. She wrote something on a cocktail napkin and handed it to him. "Here. Sign this, and this will be our contract."

In her backward-slanting handwriting, she had written, *Xan Valentine and Killer Valentine are now part of Upsilon Records.*

He had heard about tricks like this. If he signed this fucking cocktail napkin, it was the same as signing that piece-of-shit contract.

From the other couch, Jonas was watching him and sipping a glass of champagne.

Alexandre balled up the napkin and stuck it in his pocket. Georgie should be here with him.

Georgie and a phalanx of rabid lawyers.

"You guys have a good time," Alexandre said, looking around at the recoupable champagne, lobster, caviar, and penthouse. "We'll get back to you soon."

He stepped outside and found the elevator.

On the way down, he called Jonas.

"Hey, Xan!" Jonas said. "You forgot to sign the napkin."

"Jonas, there is no way in fucking hell that I am signing that contract or any contract like it. Upsilon Records can go fuck themselves."

"We have worked for *years* to get you a contract. It's what you said you wanted *years* ago."

"Not this contract. Not these terms. And not with Upsilon Records."

"Those are the standard terms, and every record company is going to want a hitmaker to write your singles. That's how this business works. I thought you understood how the business works," Jonas said.

"That's not how Killer Valentine works."

"Well, that's how you're going to have to work if you want to make it in this business."

Alexandre ground his teeth. "We have already made it in this business, and you're fired."

Chapter Forty-Seven

CLUB LIBERTIN

Georgie

Paul drove Georgie and Alexandre to a small nightclub down near the Monte Carlo casinos.

Everything was petite and wee in Monaco, especially after living among the expansive parking lots, acre-sized suburban subdivisions, and wide store aisles in the Southwest. Georgie and Alexandre got out of the car at the front doors to the club.

Georgie lifted her chin and took Alexandre's arm, readying herself for the barrage of camera flashes, but they just blended in with the few other people walking into the nightclub.

No paparazzi.

No groupies taking over-the-shoulder selfies.

No one even remarked that Xan Valentine the rock star was walking in the front doors.

"I thought we were doing PR tonight," she said.

"Tomorrow. Tonight's our last night here, most likely. I thought we could have supper and enjoy ourselves, maybe some dancing."

She grabbed his hand. "I'd love that."

Alexandre was in full Xan PR regalia with a tight black tee shirt stretched over his muscular chest and his blond hair flowing around his shoulders like a rock star.

Georgie was wearing a chiffon and silk dress that just skimmed her slight curves. Boris had sent over a few things for Georgie with Xan's frock coat that he had worn to the contract meeting. A note tucked inside had read, *Tell Duke Xan that he MUST introduce me to Prince Harry. PLEASE!*

She must have been looking around for the camera flashes as they walked into the white lobby because Alexandre bent and whispered to her, "One of the many benefits of living in Monaco is that this is the playground of billionaires, celebrities, and royalty, and the police are strict about privacy. Paparazzi are arrested, and everyone else is used to seeing people of every social stratum. You can walk to the corner market and buy fruit unmolested—"

As they had done just that morning.

"—or have a nice dinner without reserving a private room. This is the perfect retreat."

"No wonder you like living here," she said.

"Now that all this is out," he glared at his phone, which had a four-digit number hanging on the text message icon, "I was thinking about bringing the rest of the band here for a few days' vacation after we record the next album, before we release and begin the new tour."

"That would be great," she said. "They would love that."

They walked with the crowd, unjostled and undisturbed, into a large room. A dance floor was set up on the ground level, and two tiers of balconies ringed the dance floor.

Alexandre said, "I reserved a table for supper."

Georgie grinned at him. "I could eat."

They climbed the wrought iron spiral staircase set in a corner to the second balcony, where a bouncer scanned a bar code displayed on Alexandre's phone and called a hostess to seat them at a table.

While Alexandre settled at a corner table, Georgie paused at the railing to take a look at the first floor below. People danced, and the crowd undulated and flowed around five small, empty stages set up on the floor.

"What did you say the name of this place was?" she asked him.

He chuckled. "Club Libertin." His French accent slurred the consonants.

"Libertine?" she asked. "Like a hedonist?"

His smile tilted up at one corner and he looked at her from under his dark eyelashes, all of which she associated with him thinking dirty, wonderful thoughts. "Yes. Exactly like that."

The dance floor below, stages set up within the field of waving arms and bobbing heads in the dim light, the balconies with supper tables ringing the dance floor, even the white lobby, all of that clicked into place.

She glanced up at Alexandre. "What are those stages for?"

He cleared his throat. "It's Thursday, so there isn't

a show tonight. On Saturdays, this place becomes *quite* decadent."

Wait. Really? "And are there *specialized* rooms in the other wing?"

"Why, yes, now that you mention it." His cunning smile grew, and he didn't look surprised at all. He had probably reserved a *specialized* room when he had reserved a table for supper.

Georgie cracked up. "This place looks *just* like The Devilhouse."

He shrugged. "The rooms in the back are very like The Devilhouse. I thought I recognized the similarities when you took me there."

"This whole nightclub area is *just* like it. *Freakishly* like it. Who owns this place?"

"It's been in the same family, the Malans, for sixty years, which is young in Monégasque terms."

So, that wasn't it, but damn, it was *really* similar.

The food and the wine were excellent, as was expected at a place called Club Libertin. She bet everything here was top-quality, immoral, and fattening.

Maybe she could take a jog on the beach tomorrow to run it off.

Maybe she could do it without a platoon of security men swarming around her.

Wow. She couldn't imagine anything better.

Well, she *could.* Some of those things involved some of the very specialized rooms that Alexandre said were in the back hallways.

She smiled at him over the rim of her wine glass, and he smiled back. That sly grin of Alexandre's looked almost malicious.

Awesome.

After supper, he led her down to the dance floor, and they danced in the scrum of wiggling bodies as if they were just normal people. As it became obvious that they weren't going to be swarmed by crazed fans, Georgie relaxed and danced, and then she looked around her.

There was a *reason* they weren't being swarmed. They weren't the most famous people on the floor, not by far, and no one was messing with those guys, either.

A tall actor, known for his Academy Awards and recent high-profile role as a predatory trader on Wall Street, was dancing with six young women who were fawning over him. On their other side, rock royalty surrounded Georgie and Alexandre, from the one-named singer-songwriter dancing with his wife, to a young hip-hop artist dancing with a gorgeous actress, to the lead singer of one of rock's oldest bands, who was dancing with a woman and yet another rock star, the one whose eyes—one blue and one brown—were always startling at first.

She shouted over the thumping music near Alexandre's ear, "I can't believe who else is here!"

He grabbed her around the waist and pulled her close to him, dancing with his strong body pressed against her stomach and thighs. "Typical Thursday night in Monaco."

She laughed, and they danced until they were breathless and sweating from the beat of the music and the press of their flesh against each other. He kept his gauze-wrapped hand tucked tightly to his chest, and no one asked about it or bumped him that she saw.

After a while, he pulled her away from the dance floor and led her to a double door that led to a hallway, and Georgie nearly rolled her eyes. The corridor was done in dark wood and chandeliers, identical to the public hallways in The Devilhouse.

She asked Alexandre, "Do you know, by any chance, if Flicka's brother came here a lot, *a whole lot,* maybe when he was a teenager or in college or something?"

"Wulfram?" Alexandre mused. "He and Pierre are seven years older than I am. I really don't know him."

"Pierre? Flicka's husband?"

"Yes, my cousin, Pierre. Wulfram and Pierre were roommates in the dormitories for years, until Wulfram got a house off-campus when Flicka came to school. I think I was eight or nine, then. It was the usual story: the younger sister falls in love with the older brother's friend, the older brother threatens to murder the friend if he so much as looks at her, and then the sister gets her husband."

Georgie laughed. "God forbid Her Royal Highness Bossypants not get her way."

"Yeah." He glanced back, his dark eyes worried. "Have you heard from her?"

She shook her head. "I've been checking in with Rae, and they haven't heard anything, good or bad."

"I'm sure Wulfram has called out the militias of three countries to find her, whether she wants to be found or not."

"Do you think she might have just taken off?"

Alexandre stopped in the middle of a hallway and looked up at the ceiling for a second, musing. "Wulfram always had a lot of security on her, *always.* She chafed under it. The chauffeur that dropped us off at music lessons was one of his men, and another was always riding shotgun. I rode with her because Pierre asked him to take me to my violin lessons while she went to the university for her piano lessons. Even back then, she was always hopping out and running ahead of her minders. She ditched them a few times, and she kept talking about wanting to 'walk the Earth.' I don't think anyone knows what Flicka might do, given motivation."

Flicka's text had said that she wanted to do exactly that. "Walk the Earth?" Georgie asked. "Did I show you her text?"

"Yeah, and that phrase jumped out at me, but I wasn't sure what to make of it." He pulled a key out of his pocket and unlocked a heavily carved, thick door.

Just like Play Room Two's door.

Jesus, it was like The Devilhouse was a bigger, newer replica of this place.

Inside, the room was *just like* Play Room Two, a Spanish Inquisition-style dungeon, one of the standard BDSM rooms with the standard equipment, including whips.

Georgie paused for a moment before she said anything because she really wasn't sure how far down the rabbit hole all of Alexandre's counseling had gone. A person who had actually been whipped with real whips as a child might have a very serious reaction to even seeing the equipment, a violent PTSD flashback.

But in the Southwest, she had dragged Alexandre into The Devilhouse and shoved him into a room full of whips and floggers, and he hadn't so much as flinched. Obviously, he was at least all right with seeing them, and considering how familiar he had been with that suspension apparatus, he might have undergone some unorthodox desensitization therapy, so to speak.

It might explain even more about how he had been so very functional all these years.

She turned to him. "So what's the plan?"

His slow smile told her everything. "Get undressed."

"What, you're not going to cut this one off of me?" She held out the skirt to her gauzy dress.

Alexandre grabbed her around the waist with his one good arm and pressed her against the length of his body, bending her backward. His growl vibrated the skin on her throat. "I would cut it off of you, but this time, we don't have anything for you to change into."

"Oh, so rigorously pragmatic," she teased him.

He chuckled, his breath brushing her skin and blowing wisps of her hair backward. "You're laughing now."

She wondered just how comfortable Alexandre had gotten with whips. "Why, am I going to be crying, later?"

"You'll scream so loudly that the dancers down below will hear my name."

A tingle ran down her spine. "I'll hold you to that."

Alexandre used his left arm behind her back to steady her, and he reached down and grabbed her ass with his good hand. His palm and fingers gripped her flesh, tight even over the gauze of her dress.

Georgie lifted her head and kissed him hard on his mouth, leaning against his strong arm across her back. His lips were soft at first, as gentle as Alexandre always was, but his mouth firmed across hers, and he took a few steps with her in his arms to press her against the wall beside the dungeon door. He pinned her hands above her head and started his assault on her by biting her wrists, stretched so far above her head, and then chewing down her arm. His warm breath heated the inside of her arm, nipping at the crook of her elbow.

Georgie's knees weakened, and she slid down the wall an inch. Alexandre shoved his body against hers, pushing her back up, as he bent his neck to keep scraping his teeth over her arm.

His wavy hair hung down the side of his neck. The silken strands slid down her arm first, then the humid warmth of his mouth and the sparks of almost-pain from his teeth.

God, who had known that the inside of her arm was *that* sensitive?

Her throat trembled, and she heard herself moan.

It was quite conceivable that she might end up screaming his name so loudly that the crowd below would hear her over the thumping music.

Alexandre's mouth reached her shoulder. He let her hands go, but she was too limp from passion already to try to grab him or anything. Her arms tumbled to his broad shoulders, and she curled them around his neck, partly to hold herself up and partly to press his mouth against her neck. His lips were barely touching her, whispering across her skin.

Georgie sucked in a shuddering breath, ready for whatever, except that she wasn't ready for him to reach up to where she had twisted her hair into a loose knot on the back of her head and drag her head aside. She couldn't repress a whimper, and a chuckle rumbled in his chest.

Damn, but his aggression didn't feel like Alexandre. Alexandre made love to her until she was sobbing his name from the waves of passion and emotion that wracked her. Now, his hands and his teeth felt more like calm, deliberate Alex who could hold his own response in check and tease the hell out of her until she was, *well,* screaming his name.

She resolved to try to figure out who was behind his eyes tonight, but the feel of his mouth on her neck and his body in her arms degraded that thought to a fuzzy uncertainty.

"Alexandre," she murmured, her voice husky in her throat.

"Oui," he said, his teeth raking her shoulder and trailing down toward her chest, "like that, only louder."

Okay, that answered *that* question, at least for now.

"I want all of you," he said, his accent still softly French.

"You always say that," she said, her eyes closing as trembles ran up her skin.

"Every time," he said, holding her arms above her head and staring into her eyes, "Every time that you're in my arms and in my bed, there's a caveat. There's a reason why you really aren't all mine. You say that it's only for tonight or for a few weeks. It's a stolen moment. It's just a moment for us."

She had said almost exactly that at The Devilhouse when she had been going to leave the next day to run and escape from Tatiana Butorin and he had been going back to rejoin Killer Valentine's tour. He had built a song around it that they had recorded a demo of a few weeks ago.

He whispered against her shoulder, "Are you really going to stay?"

"Wha-*at?*" Her head was spinning, slightly from the wine, mostly from the green-grass and sunshine scent of his cologne in his clothes and the slight musk of warm man under it.

He ran his lips over the curl of her ear. "You said

in the car that you would stay if I didn't sign the contract with Upsilon."

"Did you sign it?" Georgie asked, her voice breathless and her head spinning.

"Non," he said.

"Are you going to?"

"Non. Never."

"Then I'll stay. I said I would stay."

"Only six months?" he asked. "Only until Christmas?"

Her head was boozy with lust for him. It was unfair to ask her this right now, but she couldn't summon any anger, not with his mouth running down the muscles on the side of her neck.

"At least until Christmas," she whispered.

"I want a year," he said, "or more. Much more."

"I shouldn't." Her body hummed with the nearness of his.

"You were drowning for lack of music in your life, but you couldn't let yourself go until I forced you to do what you so desperately wanted to. You've always had the option to run away, and you've always been ready to run. No one could ever touch you. You pride yourself on being the Ice Princess in your frozen castle. You couldn't open yourself and allow yourself to be vulnerable."

"That's not it," she whispered.

His hand reached under her dress and her ass and clutched her skin.

He said, "It can be terrifying to have an experience that you want so much, that is so intense, that you lose yourself, and that experience is music *and me.* You have to trust me to take you through the place that terrifies you, to keep you safe, and to hold you until you emerge on the other side. I don't want six months. Let me have all of you."

"What do you want?" she whispered, dreading the answer.

"You," he said. "You on the stage with me for at least a year. You in my bed every night. You beside me in every meeting, telling me whether to sign or not. I can't bear to lose you—"

Too.

The word hung unspoken in the air.

The man who had cut himself to pieces and built walls around his soul had broken down all those walls for her, and he had lost so much to do it. She could tell herself that she owed it to him, but he was right. His warm body, pressed against her, thawed her, warmed her through to her very bones, and the music filled her every night that they played.

She was dreading going back to college and leaving him and the music behind, so much so that she had allowed him to persuade her, rather easily, every time a deadline approached: to go with him on tour in the first place, to stay when she should have run, and to stay again and again.

She wanted to be with him so very much.

Georgie whispered, "I'll stay."

Alexandre stepped backward. Georgie stumbled after him, trying not to trip with her high heels on the rough tile on the floor. He whirled her around and led her, still stumbling with passion-blindness, farther into the room.

Georgie knew the theoretical uses for most of the pieces of equipment, from the A-shaped frames where a sub was bent over with her buttocks in the air to shining steel spreader bars and stockades and benches embellished with wrought-iron curlicues and vines.

The room might be small but, like everything in Monaco, everything in there was top-notch quality.

They passed by all that, though, and Alexandre stopped in front of a giant X that stood away from the wall.

He spun—his long hair flying—and grabbed her, kissing her again.

Georgie melted against him, drawn to his body, and he pressed her against himself with his good arm.

His hand stole to her back, and he unzipped her dress and pushed all her clothes to the floor.

He whispered, "Keep the shoes on."

Okay, she would keep the toe-pinchers on for him.

"Safe words?" he whispered.

"Same ones," she said and swallowed because her voice was cracking. "Largo and I quit."

"Bon." He spun her and plastered her back against the X, which was a St. Andrew's cross, if she remembered right. Loops of soft cords were laid out on a table, and he lashed her arms and legs to the cross with just his one good hand and his teeth.

She watched him, breathing hard, waiting.

When he was done, he kissed her again, his mouth hard on hers. He raked his mouth over her skin until her throat and breasts were as raw and sensitive as her arm, and he breathed near her ear, whispering, "Do you trust me?"

She nodded because her voice was tight in her throat.

"Tell me," he said, nipping behind her ear.

Georgie sucked in a breath and whispered, "I trust you."

Alexandre stepped back and yanked a lever.

The wooden frame under Georgie's back lifted her. She squeaked as her legs rose and her head dropped back.

Alexandre stripped off his tee shirt, baring his smooth chest and rippled abdominals, and dropped to his knees between her legs. His muscular tongue flicked the insides of her legs and higher, slipping inside her folds and driving her higher with each swipe and whirl.

Georgie balled her hands into fists, stretched high above her, and let her head fall back. The base of her skull wedged in the valley of the crossbeams as he tongued her. *Damn,* Alex was *fantastic* at that. Every rough scrub of his tongue across her clit and inside her drove her higher, sucking and trilling his tongue with just enough pressure to whip her into a frenzy. She pulled against the ropes, but Alex had secured them tightly.

Alex?

Not Alex. *Alexandre.*

Yet, when he licked her just like *that*—his tongue deep inside her and grinding up—*that was Alex.*

Her gasp bordered on a scream.

Alexandre stood and, as she glanced down her body, ripped open his jeans and thrust inside her.

Her back bowed off the wood, and he slammed his cock inside her and shoved his body against her clit. Georgie's fingernails dug into her palms, the pain in her hands holding back her burgeoning orgasm.

He grabbed her, palming her thigh, and his hips bucked hard into her. His long hair swayed as he bowed and pulled back. A few more thrusts, and not even the pain in her hands could hold her back. Pulsing began in her stomach, spreading up her spine.

His rhythm stuttered and changed, and he dug deep inside her. The pressure and friction on her clit shoved her over the edge, and her orgasm blasted through her, throbbing and rushing through her body as she flailed against the ropes.

The hurricane around Georgie faded, and Alexandre was stretched across her, his cheek pressed to her chest. His long hair spilled over her, the blond strands like golden spider silk on her tanned skin.

"Alex," she whispered.

"Oui, mais Alexandre," he said, stroking her skin with his cheek, *"et je t'aime, Georgie."*

Chapter Forty-Eight

MOON OVER THE MEDITERRANEAN

Alexandre Grimaldi

Alexandre stood out on the balcony, toying with a cold cigarette. The moon glimmered a bright stripe like a piping piccolo on the waves in the Mediterranean Sea past the beaches and boats, and the breeze lifted his hair around his face. The coolness of the breeze felt like a pale violet light shining on his face and sang like a far-off trumpet in his mind.

The sun should be rising soon, but his nerves jangled. Even holding onto Georgie hadn't been enough to help him sleep, and he hadn't wanted to wake her by shifting around, trying to get comfortable and relieve the pain slicing his hand. It was healing, slowly, but it had a long way to go.

He tapped the cigarette on the edge of the balcony, wishing that a glowing cherry had fallen off the end into the lush canyon below, but the end was dark and unlit. The tobacco inside was beginning to decompose after a few years, turning dusty in his mouth and like orange-blue on the back of his tongue.

A woman's voice asked from the doors, "You up?"

Her voice had sweet orange and amber tones, like honey. "Obviously."

Christine padded out to the balcony and leaned on the railing with her arms. "You aren't smoking again, are you?"

"No. Just looking at the sea."

"The last thing your throat needs—"

"Yes, Christine."

"It hurts me to hear you when you're so hoarse—"

It probably did. She could see the colors, too.

"—but at least you're better now."

"Indeed," he said. "The concert tomorrow should be quite an affair."

"Oh?"

"Quite." He pulled a small, black box from his pocket and handed it to her.

She opened it. "Is this what I think it is?"

"If you think it's an engagement ring." Alexandre held the ring up to the moonlight. The center ruby shone blood red where the faint light hit it, and it was cut into a glittering heart. Platinum and gold tendrils snaked around it, coiling like filigree, and musical notes and hearts were carved into the gleaming metal. The colors sang a chord in his mind.

It was Georgie's own, personal Killer Valentine.

"At the *concert?*" Christine asked.

He raised his eyebrows at her and smiled.

"You, private, shy Xandre? *You're* going to propose in front of ten thousand people?"

He smirked. "Twelve thousand, four hundred. We sold it out."

"Wow. You're pretty sure that she'll say yes?"

He grasped the ring more tightly. "Not at all."

She handed the box back to him, and he stuck the ring in it and the box in his pocket.

Christine said, "Holy crap. You are really flying without a net these days."

He nodded. She didn't know how true that was. Everything about the concert tomorrow was like his nerves were hooked up to a car battery. He wrapped his arm around his little sister, and they looked at the sea.

"How much have you told her about what happened?" she asked.

He didn't need to ask what she was talking about. "Everything about me."

"Does she know that I remember?"

"No."

Christine leaned against him. "I don't like people asking questions."

"I know, and there's a small possibility that it might cause legal problems. There's no statute of limitations on murder, and someone could revisit it if they got a bug up their ass that you were a witness to everything, and then they would ask questions, like how you got bruises on your knuckles, too."

"Yeah."

He adjusted his arm around her. "You were eleven. You shouldn't have had to answer questions then, and you shouldn't have to now. It's just better if everyone thinks you were lying on the floor, too traumatized to move."

"I should have taken some of the blame."

"There was no blame, and I did most of it, anyway. I made sure that he would never stand up again."

He stroked her hair. The soft strands felt just like when she had been a small child, sobbing in his arms, when he had carried her outside and wrapped her in his coat and then his clothes.

He said, "I have something for you, too."

He gave her a longer, wider box, holding a necklace with a large, almost spherical emerald dangling from a cluster of diamonds and platinum.

She opened it. "This is the one from—, *um,* from your earring."

"Yes, and from the engagement ring that I had made for Natasha." He had met Natasha, a cellist, while they had both attended Juilliard, and he had proposed the same night that she had broken off their relationship, which had been the last time he had performed on the violin. "I thought you might like it. I don't need it anymore."

"It's lovely. Thank you, Xandre." She hugged him, careful to reach around his wounded hand.

He wrapped one arm around her, and they watched the moonlight for a few more minutes until he shoved the slightly mashed cigarette back in his last pack and went inside.

Chapter Forty-Nine

HEAVEN

Georgie

The next morning, Georgie went for a run, just her and her track shoes and her phone in an armband sprouting headphones. With Xan Valentine's voice singing in her ears, she ran from one end of Monaco to the other and back, then up and around the high, rocky headland that Alexandre had called *Le Rocher.*

By the time she got back to Alexandre's house, she was sweaty and exhausted. "You didn't tell me that Monaco had so many *hills.*"

He laughed, having just gotten back from his own run. Paul had gone with him because Paul had needed a run, too. "Did you like it?"

She didn't want to flop her sweaty body on the priceless antique furniture, so she leaned against a wall and stretched her calves."I *loved* it. I haven't been for a good long run, alone, outside, for *months,* since before Tatiana Butorin found me at college. This is *Heaven.* I wish I could live here forever."

He smiled. "The helicopter for Nice leaves in an hour, and then we'll take the Gulfstream to Roma for the concert."

Chapter Fifty

SOUND CHECK

Alexandre Grimaldi

Alexandre walked through the stage door with Georgie, and the afternoon Roman sun blared in with discordant notes and burnt scents until the door clicked shut.

The relative gloom of the arena after the brightness made him blink as Paul shuttled them down the corridor to the floor. They both carried backpacks. Alexandre's bag wasn't as stuffed as Georgie's, but it hung heavily on his shoulder.

They walked through the last set of double doors, and the vast arena unfurled to the horizon, seats rising to the rafters. The air was still, now, but he could already imagine music filling it to the brim.

Alien energy was sparked in his veins.

Georgie walked beside him, and she picked up the pace, walking toward the stage. A smile was already starting around her mouth. She was eager to get to the stage, and a glow filled him. Every time he saw that in her, it thrilled him. She wasn't frightened of her own art anymore.

Down at the end of the wide arena, the rest of the band was already standing on the raised stage: Cadell, Peyton, and Tryp, all of them standing with their arms crossed over their chests and scowling.

Alexandre had been dodging their texts for days.

"Hey!" Tryp called down. "Did you fucking forget to tell us something, Your Royal Asswipe?"

Yes, that was what most of their texts had said.

The overhead working lights shone down on the three men, deepening their eye sockets and turning their faces into skulls. The odd light expanded them sideways, like they should have been standing farther right than they were.

Georgie stepped in front of Alexandre.

He touched her shoulder. "I've got this."

She moved aside, and he walked around the rows and rows and rows of folding chairs set up on the cement floor and toward the stage. Georgie's footsteps followed him.

Alexandre bounded up the aisles, vaulted over the railing, and leapt up onto the edge of the stage, doing exactly what the set-up was designed to prevent fans from doing. His backpack thudded against this spine, sending a shock through his bones to his sliced-open hand.

He had changed the dressing on his hand that morning with Georgie's help. Letting her minister to him was getting easier, a little. Letting her see the twin black seams puckering his skin at his wrist, through his palm, and running down his fingertips on his last two fingers was tougher, but she hadn't remarked on it. She just gently helped him clean his hand with alcohol wipes and wrapped the gauze around his hand and the splint. He had stayed in the bathroom for a few minutes afterward, holding himself together.

Tryp walked across the stage toward him, his boot heels thudding red spikes on the hollow wood. His pace was in two-eight time, perfectly on beat. He demanded, "Why the fuck did you fire Jonas? And why didn't you tell us about the deal with Upsilon?"

Cadell stood behind him, shaking his head. His long, black hair swished around his shoulders. "That's whack, man. Whack."

Alexandre slung his backpack off his shoulder and hung it from the straps over his left forearm, avoiding the white gauze around his hand.

Georgie clattered up the metal steps over on the end of the stage.

Technicians encroached from the wings of the stage and leaned on the catwalk railings far above, a silent army in black all around them.

A tiny shadow separated itself from the crowd of black-clothed technicians who had gathered under the half-constructed risers. Elfie, the pyrotechnics technician with firebug tendencies, slipped over and stood behind Tryp. He had married the roadie a few months before in Las Vegas, shocking the hell out of Alexandre. If the band fell apart, he would consider that the first shot across their bow, the first time that the band had begun to splinter.

Tryp's voice rose. "We have been working so damn hard to get a record deal. We've been working our *asses* off. Jonas said that you had a temper tantrum about artistic control and scorched the Earth. He said that

Upsilon won't even talk to us now, and he's done with us. Rhiannon said that she's doing this one show, but then we have to find ourselves a new backup singer. What the *fuck*, Xan?"

Alexandre unzipped his backpack and upended it. A huge sheaf of paper splashed to the stage floor at their feet, a purple flash of sound. Elfie peeked at the pile from around Tryp's back.

Georgie's running shoes joined the circle around the pile of paper.

"*This* is the fucking contract," Alexandre said. "They wanted us to be a fucking manufactured boy band. They wanted to shove us in one end of the K-Pop Music Machine and extrude us out the other end as a pablum pop music product. They wanted to assign us songs written by hitmakers who churn out hundreds of songs a year that all sound alike. They wanted me to sing the songs over and over, then weave them together into one perfect, soulless take, and you guys weren't going to play on the albums at all. Everything was going to be synthesized, even Cadell's guitar solos."

Cadell frowned. "They can't synthesize my licks."

Alexandre said, "They assured me that they can."

"Well, they could try, but it wouldn't sound like me," he mumbled, his voice turning clear like a pane of glass between them.

"I agree. There's no way that a synthesizer could replicate your music, Cadell. No fucking way. You wouldn't believe the clauses that are in this contract. Georgie explained them to me." He shuffled through the pages on the ground, finding paragraphs marked with Georgie's red slashes. He shook it at them. "This one would mean that they own the name Killer Valentine and Xan Valentine. If we don't do what they want, they can hire other musicians and release anything they want under our names."

The three guys staggered back a step like the piece of paper in Alexandre's hand had launched a fireball straight up and singed their eyelashes. Tryp almost stepped on Elfie, but she dodged his feet.

Peyton raised his blond eyebrows at Georgie, and she nodded at him. She said, "He's right. They could have done that."

Alexandre said, "And they could keep us from releasing anything under KV's name or any other name."

They all swiveled their heads like they were turning away from bloody roadkill.

Beside his shoulder, Georgie said, "Yup."

"And it goes on from there." He stood and kicked the paper pile, his boot scattering the paper. "The record company would take at least seventy-five percent of the gross. It might be more like eighty or ninety percent, depending on how many recoupable expenses they rack up while we're touring. We would need to sell five to ten times as many albums as we are now to break even."

Tryp's nose wrinkled. "Our albums are going platinum, now. How much more room do we have?"

Cadell said, "I don't think *anybody* sells anywhere near ten times what we're selling. I don't think the fucking *Stones* sell *ten times* what we sell."

"And touring would become a risk, although it would also become our primary income source. Right now, we pay for everything up front and in advance. If we sign with Upsilon, they could tack on fucking recoupable expenses as often as they like, for anything they like, for executives flying out to see our show or for swag kits for radio stations that we don't even know about, and then they would want us to pay them back plus interest, which would end up being at least double their cost. We would get a bill at the end of each tour for stuff that they did, and the more they do, the far more that it costs us."

"So they wouldn't just be making money from our albums," Peyton said, his arms tightly crossed over his chest, his metallic green voice becoming angrier and shinier, "they would be making money off of us."

"Ouais," Alexandre said. "I mean, *yes.* That's it."

They all stood in silence for a minute, looking at the contract littering the floor at their feet.

Tryp finally said, "Well, *fuck.*"

Cadell shook his head. "That's not how I thought it would be."

Peyton ran a hand through his hair. "I don't think they do it that way in classical music."

Georgie told Peyton, "You should have a lawyer look at any contract. I think every company throws at least some of this crap in, like the recoupable expenses. At least you don't have to worry about songwriting credits, though, if you stick to classical."

"I just can't believe this bullshit," Tryp said. "I thought that a contract was the big time. I thought that's when we could stop worrying about all this shit and the record company would take care of us so we could be musicians."

"Maybe a long time ago," Alexandre said. "They're not artists who communicate with fans. They are corporations that advertise and sell this particular product to demographics. They don't care about what happens after the person buys it, if they like it or not, if they become a listener or a fan or a lifetime member of the Valentine Victims. They sold the product. They're done. Then they look at our career track record and decide whether we get to put out another album."

"Georgie?" Peyton asked, his eyebrows up again.

"Yep, that's how it is," she said.

"Fuck me," Peyton muttered.

Cadell flipped his guitar pick into the air like a quarter and caught it. "So what the hell should we do?"

Alexandre shrugged. "We're in a better position financially than most bands."

Tryp snorted. "Evidently."

Elfie elbowed Tryp in the ribs, and he flinched.

Alexandre let it go. "I think we should hire an office staff and start negotiating with the big box stores ourselves. Let's scale up and see how far that takes us before we talk to the corporations again. Hell, in five years, maybe we'll buy Upsilon and their distribution platform."

Peyton scratched his chin. "I know people who went to Wharton and Harvard for their MBAs. If you want a top-notch management team, I can call people."

Alexandre nodded. "When we gather in New Jersey to record next week, we'll make decisions on how to proceed."

They went quiet for a few minutes, absorbing this. The stage lights above them flicked on, chiming notes in Alexandre's head.

A nervous energy infiltrated the guys in the band, and they started shuffling their feet. Even Elfie looked up and scanned the other technicians, sitting with their feet dangling over the sides of the catwalks and peering down at them from where they were hanging over the railings.

Cadell coughed, but no one turned to leave.

Alexandre watched them, wondering which one of them would start asking the other questions. His money was on Tryp.

Peyton scratched his cheek, where he was growing in a slight, blond beard, and he examined the skeletal lighting fixtures hung above the stage that intermittently glowed.

"So how's your hand?" Tryp asked Alexandre, jutting his chin at him.

Yep, he could count on Tryp.

Alexandre shrugged and held up the bulbous gauze wrapped around his palm and fingers. "It's been better."

"You going to be able to play the bass?"

Alexandre shook his head. "Probably not ever again."

Tryp poked his thumb at Peyton. "Then we're stuck with this asshole?"

Peyton shoved him, and Tryp stumbled a few steps, laughing.

Cadell asked, "So what's the line-up for tonight?"

Alexandre gathered Georgie under his arm and smiled down at her. "Georgie has decided to stay on the keyboards for the next year."

She smiled up at him with a flirty little tilt to her eyes.

A wild thread shot through him to kiss her on her forehead, so he did. She laughed and pushed at him a little, but not enough to get away from him.

Peyton shot an alert look at her, and Alexandre

tightened his grip on her shoulders. He also caught her eyeroll directed at himself.

Alexandre said, "Peyton, your work on those demos was exceptional, and I liked your performance in Milan. If you would like to join us as a bassist, we can sign that year-long contract."

Peyton nodded. "I signed up for keyboards, but I really wanted to know the music business better. I'm sure as hell getting an education."

"So you'll stay on?" Alexandre pressed.

"Yeah. I'll stay on for a year, and then we'll make some decisions."

"Excellent." Alexandre tucked slender little Georgie more securely under his arm. He wouldn't have to worry about anything between them after tonight, anyway.

Tryp pointed at him and asked, "So is that how you really talk? All frou-frou like that?"

Trust Tryp to poke the elephant in the room. Alexandre nodded. "I grew up speaking mostly French and sometimes a dialect of Italian. I didn't begin learning English until I was six."

"Are you going to sing like that tonight?" Tryp asked.

He wasn't sure he could sing at all tonight. "I'm not sure yet."

"Better figure that out soon."

Yes, indeed.

Cadell asked, "Were you going to tell us about the violin?"

The other guys shuffled their feet like they wanted to walk away.

Alexandre said, "Not if I didn't have to."

Cadell nodded. "Yeah. No wonder you were so fucking sympathetic about stuff."

Alexandre shrugged.

Tryp asked, "So did you kill that guy or what?"

Peyton pretended to swing a back roundhouse kick at Tryp, but Elfie shoved Tryp so hard that he fell over. He rolled onto his back, laughing.

"Dude!" Elfie yelled, standing over him.

"Hey," Alexandre said. "Don't break his leg. He needs that one to play the bass drum tonight."

From the floor, Tryp said, "Yeah, only an idiot breaks a limb right before a major concert."

Peyton stepped back, laughing, too. Cadell mimed like he was going to kick Tryp in the ribs but just scuffed the floor with his boot.

Tryp yelled from the floor, "Did you?"

Cadell threw up his hands, and Peyton groaned, "What the fuck, Tryppy?"

Elfie yelled, "Jesus, give them a couple days, Tryfon. Jesus *Christ.*"

Alexandre looked down at Tryp and pulled his hair out of his eyes. "Fuck, yeah, I killed him."

"See? I told you," Tryp said, springing to his feet and ducking Peyton's next half-hearted attempt at kicking him in the head. Elfie actually did punch him in the gut, but Tryp had a rock-solid core and was used to his wife's stage punches. "Every rock star has murdered at least one person. It's in the job description. Hey, we gonna get wasted tonight so you can tell us what happened when the Russian mafia kidnapped Georgie?"

Alexandre smiled and rubbed Georgie's arm, pulling her against his side.

Her arms wrapped snugly around his waist.

Georgie said, "After the runner, you bring the whiskey, and we'll tell you all about it."

"Fuck that," Tryp said, talking to Alexandre. "You're the one with a vineyard and a castle in France. You're buying the fucking whiskey."

Chapter Fifty-One

SOME DECISIONS

Georgie

Georgie leaned her head on Alexandre's shoulder, letting him wrap his arm around her.

He said, "Georgie has decided to stay on the keyboards for the next year," and he kissed her on the forehead.

It was an absolutely silly move on his part, so ridiculously affectionate and Alexandre-like, without a trace of Xan Valentine.

That might be a problem.

Peyton's sharp look grabbed her attention just as she was shoving at Alexandre, who must have also seen it because he tightened his grip around her shoulders. She wanted to whisper to him to not be a jealous dick, but whatever.

Alexandre said, "Peyton, your work on those

demos was exceptional, and I liked your performance in Milan. If you would like to join us as a bassist, we can sign that year-long contract."

His hand tightened on her upper arm.

Peyton was still watching her, and his wide eyes were a challenge. She shifted, uncomfortable.

He said, "I signed up for keyboards, but I really wanted to know the music business better. I'm sure as hell getting an education."

"So you'll stay on?" Alexandre asked him.

Peyton was still looking straight at Georgie, his sea-green eyes serious. "Yeah. I'll stay on for a year, and then we'll make some decisions."

Some decisions, huh?

Georgie sighed. She and Peyton needed to have a talk. This kind of thing couldn't go on for a whole year.

Chapter Fifty-Two

SET LIST

Georgie

Georgie stood backstage in a concrete tunnel. The corridor connected the dressing rooms to the fenced-off run that led to the stage. Outside the tunnel, the arena was still silent except for the roadies tweaking the last few details before the performance. Elfie was tightening screws on small canisters, securing them to the stage. She wore purple gloves, which Georgie had never seen her do before. She usually packed the flammable chemical packs without wearing gloves.

Georgie looked back to the paper in her hand.

The set list was weird.

Georgie turned it over, deciphering Alexandre's ornate cursive handwriting.

"Scrambled Eggs" wasn't in the middle of the second set, like Alexandre had said it would be. It was the last song on the encore list, even after "Alwaysland."

She turned and walked back along the tunnel.

His dressing room was the first one closest to the stage. Dozens of clear bulbs burned with fiery filaments around the long mirror above the makeup counter, toasting dust in the air to acrid smoke.

She held the paper out toward him and said, "'Alwaysland' is always the last song. People expect it to be the last song. It will freak them out."

"This is a one-time thing," he said while Boris ratted his hair just slightly at the crown of his head before he tied it into a ponytail.

"Putting an instrumental as the last song is weird. You can't even play your guitar, which means that *I'm* doing the last encore as an instrumental. Nobody comes to these concerts to see me, honey. Tell him, Boris."

"I don't know anything about set lists," Boris said, smoothing a flyaway strand. He shifted his bulk around to Alexandre's other side.

"I wrote some lyrics for 'Scrambled Eggs,'" Alexandre said. "I want to try them tonight when the crowd is quiet."

"What's it called?"

"It's a surprise."

"The audience is not going to quiet down if you debut a song. This is *Italy.* They'll storm the barricades and swarm the stage. Tell him, Boris."

"I don't know anything about audiences," Boris said, studiously combing Alexandre's hair.

Alexandre said, "They settle down with 'Alwaysland.' I want to see if we can use the new song instead of 'Alwaysland' as the last encore on the next tour."

"This is the last concert. You shouldn't just throw something out there. Tell him, Boris."

"I don't know anything—"

"You are no help!"

Alexandre said, "Humor me, Georgie. If it doesn't work, I'll carry you offstage and sweep you into the limo."

She frowned at his gauze-wrapped arm. He wasn't fit to carry a kitten, let alone Georgie. "I don't think this is a good idea."

"Trust me," he said.

Chapter Fifty-Three

XAN VALENTINE

Georgie

Georgie stood in the tunnel off the wings of the stage, leaning against the cold concrete wall and waiting for Boris to finish up Alexandre's makeup and hair. Beyond the dark hole where she stood, the long tubes of the house lights still glowed over the audience, a mass of humanity that eddied in the seats and flowed through the aisles like restless water.

She smiled at them from the privacy of the tunnel. They were all out there, so innocent, so anxious, waiting for Killer Valentine to turn their world upside down. Should only be a few more minutes before Xan became their sun and their sky.

If Xan Valentine showed up.

The tiny dressing rooms were just steps from the stage, so they hadn't bothered to set up the privacy tents. Since the arena didn't have full backstage facilities, they had one last runner to end the tour. The European leg of the tour had been mostly runners. Georgie was looking forward to their next North American tour, where the arenas had better backstage facilities and a minority of the shows were ended by the frantic sprint to the cars to get out of the parking lot ahead of the fans.

Alexandre hadn't come out of his dressing room yet. Usually, he was itching to start the show by now, fidgeting in the wings, flinching forward as the lights dimmed, eager to run around the back of the set and climb into position on the top riser to scream the first sustained note of "I Choose Love, I Choose Life."

Georgie turned toward the backstage area.

Black-clad technicians marched through the hallway, their black athletic shoes silent on the floor, talking into their headsets and gesturing to people who weren't there. One snagged a sandwich from the long buffet table and crammed half of it in his mouth while he walked.

She pushed off the wall and went to find Alexandre.

His dressing room was the obvious place, and she knocked and shoved the door open.

Alexandre was alone in the small dressing room, leaning on the makeup counter. He was staring into the lightbulb-ringed mirror, his dark eyes intense. His lavaliere was already taped to his jaw, and his in-ear monitors hung on their wires over his shoulders. The blazing lightbulbs reflected so brightly on the white cotton of his shirt that he looked like he was radiating light.

She asked, "You ready?"

His dark eyes flicked as he glanced to where she was standing in the doorway. He watched her through the mirror.

"Come on, man," she said. "One minute to house-to-half."

He shook his head, a minute motion, and he blinked slowly. Really slowly.

Oh, shit.

She closed the door behind her and leaned on it. "Alexandre?"

He nodded, again just a bounce of his chin. His gestures were subtle, controlled, and entirely Alexandre Grimaldi, the scarred violin prodigy who felt things too deeply and yet didn't show any of his pain.

They were supposed to take the stage in six minutes, and he wasn't Xan Valentine, not in the slightest.

"Can you sing?"

His dismissive nod meant that yes, he could physically sing.

Georgie walked over and touched his shoulder. "Can you feel Xan at all?"

He shook his head. A diamond stud in his earlobe caught the light and threw spangles over the mirror and costume rack behind them.

She touched the earring. "Is that new?"

He nodded.

Georgie looked down at him. The difference in him was disturbing. He looked like Xan Valentine, thin layers of stage makeup exaggerating his eyes and cheekbones and sharpening his already-square jaw, but his reserved expression wouldn't play onstage at a rock concert. She could imagine Alexandre standing on a stage with his violin, his precise movements drawing perfect tones from the instrument as he manipulated the bow and studied the strings, glancing at the other musicians only to coordinate the music.

But Alexandre was not a rock star.

And they needed a rock star.

Georgie shoved his shoulder, toppling him back into the makeup chair. She lifted her skirt and sat astride his lap, straddling his strong thighs with her bare legs. He was so tall that the only way for her to tower over him was by sitting on his lap and leaning over him. Good thing that Boris dressed her in voluminous skirts that blew in the fans set up on edge of the stage.

Alexandre's dark eyes widened, and he leaned his head back, startled.

She grabbed both sides of his jaw and kissed him hard.

His lips didn't move for an instant, and her heart sank that he might be paralyzed inside. He drew in a breath, and his hand found her hip, holding on while she kissed him.

His lips opened under hers, and she kissed him more deeply, pressing him back in the chair and holding him down with her body.

He pushed back, lifting his head and trying to nudge her backward.

Good.

She moved her hands and pressed his strong shoulders against the chair harder, holding him down. Her fingers barely reached around the thick muscles of his shoulders, and he moved like he wanted to stand up. He was a hell of a lot stronger than she was, and if he'd wanted to, he could have stood up and shoved her up against the wall.

Which was exactly what Georgie was hoping for.

She slanted her mouth across his and invaded his warm mouth with her tongue, swirling and stroking his until his fingers tightened on her hips.

She squeezed his shoulders, letting her nails bite him through his crisp shirt.

He bent forward, his abdominals bulging under her stomach and rising up from the back of the chair no matter how hard she laid on him to press him back. His arms wrapped around her back, and his fingers climbed into her hair.

Almost.

She broke off the kiss and looked into his eyes. Lust glazed his dark eyes, yes, but something sharper lurked underneath.

Georgie said, "It can be terrifying to have an experience that you want so much, that is so intense, that you lose yourself. You have to trust me to take you through the dark place and hold you until we emerge on the other side."

She kissed him hard, biting at his lips, and his fist tightened in her hair. He yanked her head back and wrapped his teeth around her throat.

She ground her hips down on him, and he made a noise in his throat. "Come on, Xan. *Feel me.* Let yourself go."

His other arm, the hurt one, was tight against her back. When he leaned forward and stood, she wrapped her legs around his waist and held on. The waistband of his jeans was sharp on the insides of her thighs.

Alexandre took three steps and slammed her against the door, his body tight against hers, and he kissed her hard.

Oh, God. She was melting into him, *submitting.* She had to stay strong to coax Xan out.

His body shoved against hers, holding her and pinning her, and every time she lifted her head and kissed him, he kissed her harder. He held her hair and scraped his teeth down her neck to her shoulder, and she could barely get any air because she was breathing so fast. A whimper trickled out of her throat, and energy seized his body, his muscles becoming coiled steel as he strained against her.

His good hand stole to the zipper running down her side.

A knock rattled her spine like someone had tapped on her back. *"Oh!"*

From the other side of the door, a man called, "One minute to showtime, Mr. Valentine."

Alexandre lifted his head away from her neck, his dark eyes blazing. *"Afterward.* I will have you afterward."

"Or I'll have you," she managed to say. Her chest was tight while she panted.

His mouth crashed down on hers, leaving no doubt about who would be having whom after the show. He ground his lips and his body against her until she grabbed him by the neck and pushed back at him, desperate.

When he pulled away this time, a diabolical smile was forming at the corners of his swollen lips, and wildness blazed in his eyes.

"Xan?" she gasped, pulling the strap of her dress back up to her shoulder.

"Non," he murmured, *"Alexandre. Toujours, Alexandre."*

He grabbed her hand and spun her around, slinging his blue frock coat over his other arm and pulling her away from the door. They sprinted for the stage. The tunnel opened into the dark arena, and camera flashes glittered out of the dark as they ran between the railings and behind the silky curtain that fluttered with the breath of twelve thousand people.

Georgie swung up in her keyboard array, stuffed her monitors in her ears, and positioned her hands on the keyboard just as Tryp clacked his drumsticks together to establish the beat.

The risers rattled as Alexandre scaled the steel poles up the back, one-handed.

Through her monitors, Mitch's voice said, "Get ready. And we're at three, two, one—"

Tryp slammed his sticks on the skins, and Georgie struck the chord that blared through the speakers positioned all around the stage.

The curtain released from the rod far above the stage and fell like a waterfall.

Bright white spotlights picked out a lone figure on the very top riser, their candlepower so intense that they washed him out into a gleaming angel. He held a prop microphone to his mouth, and his blond hair and long coat flew in the wind from the blowing fans set under him.

His back bowed hard as he blasted the opening note like the scream of heartbreak.

Georgie smiled and brought her hands down on the keyboard.

Call him whatever you want, but Xan Valentine was back.

Chapter Fifty-Four

ROMA

Georgie

The stage lights bore down on Georgie as she stood dancing inside her keyboard array. People seethed along the floor and two balconies that wrapped the stage. Georgie estimated the crowd at about twelve thousand from the depth and height of the balconies and the expanse of the floor, not to mention the blast of sound between songs. She brought her fingers back down on the piano keys, warmed by the stage lights glaring down from the lighting arrays far above.

Despite the concert being rescheduled to an even larger venue than they had originally booked, the *Pala-Lottomatica* Arena had sold out, thank God. The last thing they needed was a strike on their career track record, a non-sellout at their last stop. *Yuck.*

Upstage of Georgie and past Tryp on the top riser,

Rhiannon bopped and sang her heart out on the backup vocals. As always, she wasn't quite upstaging Xan, but if someone looked up there, she wasn't phoning it in. You would have never known it was her last performance with Killer Valentine.

Downstage, Xan sang "Rock Like Rome Is Falling," crouching and singing to the raving audience below his feet. They clawed at the stage, their mouths open as they screamed.

Not, Xan. *Alexandre.*

Probably.

He straightened and sang to the balconies, his gauze-wrapped hand punching the air. The nosebleed seats went wild, becoming a field of undulating arms.

If anything, because his voice had had a week off, Xan was in fine form tonight. His tenor was clear and open as he sang the high notes.

Georgie punched the keys on her keyboards while the guys and Rhiannon sang backup.

Big finish.

The song finished with a run of arpeggios for Georgie. Tryp rolled around the drum set, his strikes dead on the beat as always.

Fireworks fountained into the air between Georgie and the audience, a blast of heat far beyond the burning stage lights beating down from the light battens. Surviving the Southwestern desert was decent training for being a rock star.

The pyrotechnic effects died away, leaving a light scattering of ash around them on the wooden stage.

Georgie found her water bottle tucked under her keyboards and took a swig of the water, the coolness sliding into her mouth. She glanced at the set list taped above her keyboards to the edge of Tryp's riser.

The next song on the set list was "Break."

"Hey, Mitch," she said into the mic taped to her jaw. Her mic wasn't patched into the speakers because Georgie did not sing. *Ever.* "What're we supposed to do for the break?"

"Xan just said that he wanted his lavaliere and his hand mic on and nothing else," Mitch, the technician in the sound booth, said through her earbuds. "Said it should be a couple minutes, tops."

Georgie leaned back against her keyboard array and watched Alexandre in the spotlight. The lights on the rest of the stage and all the other musicians grayed out and dimmed. Tryp spun his drumsticks around his fingers, and Cadell unslung his guitar from around his shoulders and twisted his arm around.

Alexandre was holding the prop mic at his side.

Georgie could see the tension crawling over his skin by the stiff way he stood, entirely unlike Xan Valentine's loose-limbed, careless grace while on stage. She kept her hands on the keyboard, ready to slam her hands down and start the next song. She stayed standing in case she needed to run over to him and get him off the stage.

Alexandre spoke to the crowd in the whole theater in Italian for a few sentences, and then he switched to English. "There have been some odd rumors going around about me, lately. Have you heard some of them?"

The crowd cheered, but he pressed his palms down, signaling for quiet. Georgie tensed.

He said, "Go ahead and take your phones out. This is an exclusive scoop. You'll get to ask me questions before the media do, if I do hold a media op at all." He looked at the front row. "Who has a question?"

The entire floor waved their hands like wildflowers in a hurricane.

Xan crouched and held the business end of his hand mic down to someone.

A preppie guy asked, "Boxers or briefs?"

Xan laughed, his head thrown back and his blond hair streaming down his back. "Those close-cut boxer things that go to here." He rubbed the side of his thigh. "Anyone else?" He pointed the mic into the front row.

A woman asked, "Are you dating anyone?"

"Yes," Xan said, and the arena erupted in low cheers and soprano boos. He waved a hand back toward Georgie. "My keyboard player, Georgiana Johnson."

Georgie had her water bottle stuck in her face when the lights came up on her. She choked, nearly spitting water, and waved to the cheering crowd with water burning her sinuses. *So fucking sophisticated.* Water dripped out her left nostril, and she rubbed it away.

Xan stuck the mic into the audience again.

A woman's alto voice asked, "Were you really a violinist as a kid, and is that why you play the guitar and the bass so well?"

Here it came. Georgie braced to either rescue him from the pounding of the questions or just start playing to pre-empt them. God, they were going to want to know everything: being a child prodigy, murdering his tutor, beating the shit out of the other conductor, where he had gone for those intervening years, and more.

This couldn't be good for him. Maybe she should intervene right now.

Georgie moved her foot to climb down off her riser.

"Yes, I was." Alexandre held up his wrapped hand. "But Cadell, our lead guitarist, has always been far and away better than I am on the guitar, and Peyton Cabot is our new bass player. He's excellent."

The lights rose on the other side of the stage, and Peyton waved. Cadell had his arm wrapped around his own head, stretching, so he nodded to the audience.

Another woman's voice shouted from the side, *"How'd you hurt your hand!"*

"The question is, how did I hurt my hand?" Xan repeated. "I rescued Georgie after she was kidnapped by the Russian mafia and had to fight my way out."

The audience cracked up, and laughter rang to the rafters.

Someone near the stage yelled, *"Fine! Don't tell us!"*

Xan shrugged, raising both his hands in an exaggerated motion of helplessness. He pushed the microphone into the crowd again.

A woman's gravelly voice asked, "When will your next album be out?"

"Late fall," Xan said. "Before Christmas, definitely."

"Will it be all new songs or a greatest hits?"

"All new. We don't have enough for a greatest hits compilation yet." Xan's voice was a little softer, like he was confused.

The next question into the microphone was, "How often do you work out?"

"Every day that I can in the hotel gyms, which is most days. I only miss a couple of days a month."

"What do you do to work out?"

"Mostly circuit training with high-intensity intervals. Next?"

"Take off your shirt!"

"No, thank you. Next?"

"When are you going to stop talking and sing your next song?"

"Soon. Next?"

"The lyrics for 'Nine Levels of Tortured Souls' are really about a woman, right?"

"Right. About a failed relationship. You?" He pointed a few rows back.

"Who is 'Alwaysland' about?"

"A former girlfriend. Next?"

"What kind of conditioner do you use on your hair?"

"The guy who does my costumes supplies me with something. I don't know what it's called. It's in white bottles with blue writing."

"Is your hair naturally curly? Do you blow it out?"

"It's got a bit of a wave, and it curls if it's cut above my shoulders. Next?"

"Is it naturally blond?"

"No. My costume manager, again, decided that we should try it, and I liked it. Next?" Each time he asked for the next question, his voice rose another note with more confusion.

"Will you sing at my wedding next month?"

"Sorry, *mon amie.* We'll probably be recording in North America by then. Next?"

"When are you going to come to Austria again?"

"We'll try on our next European tour. Next?"

"Will you give a concert in Terni next time?"

"We'll have to see how the tour works out. All right, thank you for your questions, and let's go on!"

When he turned back, Georgie could see bafflement in his dark eyes. He clapped his hands above his head and called out "One-two-three-*four!*"

Georgie slapped her hands on the keyboard for the intro to "Break the Bank Tonight," a loud, hard-drumming party anthem that they seldom played.

At intermission, while Alexandre sat in his dressing room with Yvonne applying the eel-like electrostimulation device to his throat to ease inflammation, he said to Georgie, "I can't believe that they didn't care. I've been crafting responses to questions about murder all week."

Georgie shrugged. "It was a long time ago, and it's not an album that they can buy."

Alexandre shrugged. "Do you think I should even do a press conference?"

She shook her head. "We'll put together a press release and an email thanking everyone for their concern, and yes, your birth name was Alexandre Grimaldi and you used to play the violin, and no, you won't be playing any instrument anymore. And that will end it."

Alexandre blinked a slow, deliberate blink. "And that will end it. If I had known that breaking my hand would end it, I would have bashed it to smithereens with a hammer years ago."

Georgie scooted her chair around and snuggled under his arm. "No, you wouldn't have."

He pressed his violin callus to her hair. "You're right. I wouldn't have."

Chapter Fifty-Five

I BELIEVE IN LOVE

Georgie

Thankfully, after Alexandre's little outburst about Georgie being his *girlfriend,* Xan stayed downstage while he sang "Alwaysland." That all-too-personal announcement would have caused too much speculation and way too many catcalls if Alexandre had climbed up on her riser and, as Peyton had said, fucked her with his eyes.

He did not fuck her with his eyes. That was stupid.

She let herself enjoy the way her hands moved over the keys and listening to Xan singing through her in-ear monitors. This was their last show for a while and, if "Scrambled Eggs" was well-received, they might not close concerts with "Alwaysland" anymore. This might be the last time they played it together.

Xan started singing more softly near the end, and Georgie toned down her playing to match him.

He ended with the microphone near his heart amid the applause.

When the clapping and whistles petered out, Alexandre said, "We usually close with 'Alwaysland,' but tonight, we want to debut another song for you."

Shockingly, the audience went nuts. Georgie rolled her eyes.

She flicked a couple switches on her instrument panel to create a romantic, lilting sound for "Scrambled Eggs." It seemed weird that Alexandre had been speaking English for the whole concert because he usually spoke at least what he could of whatever language the local populace spoke, and he spoke a lot of languages, including Italian. He had been speaking it yesterday morning for that radio interview. But, whatevs. She settled her hands on the keys.

Alexandre said, "It's called, 'I Believe In Love.'"

Georgie's breath caught in her throat, and she glanced over at him, but he didn't look back at her.

That was a little too personal. She wasn't sure if the lyrics were going to be ironic because she had teased him that he didn't believe in love or if he had just callously used it as a hook for a song. An edge of anger crept into her veins.

She played the intro for "Scrambled Eggs," letting it get a little wistful, just in case he hadn't appropriated it and used it like a dishrag.

On the other side of the stage, Cadell walked out of the gloom and sat on a barstool. He held his acoustic guitar and set it up on his leg like a classical guitarist.

That was weird. Georgie hadn't known that Alexandre had given Cadell the sheet music for "Scrambled Eggs."

Okay.

Cadell's quiet plucking faded into Georgie's monitors in her ears. He played a nice counterpoint melody, so she kept playing the primary tune.

On what was supposed to be the first line, Alexandre started to sing.

His voice was still clear despite having sung the whole concert, and Georgie could hear every word through her earbuds.

He sang about the darkness where he had been trapped, the sunless desert of his disbelief where he had walked alone, and how he had prayed for the sun and found only cold, bitter rain and enemies who broke him into a thousand pieces.

He sang that he had believed in nothing, loved nothing, and been nothing.

Tears burned her eyes.

Oh, crap. It was more personal than she had believed that he would dare write. She felt flayed open in front of the crowd.

Now, oh God, *now,* Alexandre turned and walked toward the side of the stage to climb up on her riser.

When Georgie looked past Cadell, the rest of the band had gathered at the edge of the other side of the stage: Tryp, Peyton, even Rhiannon and Elfie.

The pyro effects were over with, so Elfie was probably waiting to strike the set and pack away her equipment for the long trip back to the States. The others should have already done their runner and been driven at breakneck speeds back to their hotel.

Alexandre climbed the steps to her riser and sang behind her, whispering imagery about how he had been shattered to shards on the cold sand, but with her, he could build himself again.

Georgie played the melody, insisting to herself that she could play through anything.

Her fingers shook, but she pressed them to the keys.

Alexandre stood behind her, stroking her arms, and he gently slipped his arms around her so that he was singing softly in her ear, "But now I," he let his voice rise through delicate notes for almost an octave and then drift back down, "believe in love, because I believe in you."

His French accent softened his words, though he still sang from his throat and chest like Xan Valentine always had. His body was flushed from the performance, and his strong chest warmed her back even through his shirt and the chiffon of her dress.

In the small break between verses, he pressed his left cheek to hers, and his thick violin callus touched her temple.

He kept singing to her, holding her in his arms.

The next verse was about how the sunlight had warmed his heart and mended his soul, how he had gathered himself and begun to build, because every part of him wanted to be with her.

That was what he actually said in one line: "Every part of me wants to be with you."

A hot drip slid down Georgie's face and splashed on her arm, but she didn't turn around. She could play through anything, *everything,* even her own heart breaking for him.

He sang that haunting refrain again, "And now I believe in love because I believe in you."

She had teased him too many times about being the heartless rock star who couldn't love. She hadn't known how broken he was. She hadn't known how gentle she should have been with him.

He backed up, and Georgie prayed that she would have a minute to compose herself. There was another verse coming up and then that devastating refrain again. It was a good thing that she had the music memorized already because the whole stage looked like it was underwater. The risers surged and receded like they were riding on ocean waves. Another hot drip fell down her face, and her vision cleared for a moment before water flowed over the stage again.

Murmuring started in the audience behind Georgie's back.

It grew into a chatter and a squall, and then a wave of sound swept through the audience and over the stage in a cheering roar so loud that Georgie looked up at Cadell to see what the hell was going on.

Camera flashes whited out the stage, casting a long shadow behind Xan's abandoned microphone stand that flickered in all directions like a swinging needle. The strobes of the cameras glared on Cadell, freezing him as he played chords up the neck of his guitar, and he kept stealing glances at Georgie.

Beyond Cadell, in the darkness over on the other wings of the stage, most of the rest of the band were grinning and laughing and sticking their monitors in their ears. Tryp was a wiggly puppy with excitement. They all seemed thrilled except for Peyton, whose wide, sea-blue eyes looked like he had been punched in the gut.

Georgie kept playing the bridge. She was a professional. She would play through anything, but her hands were starting to shake from the constant flare of flashes and the swelling barrage of screams.

The front row was waving their arms, trying to attract Georgie's attention. When she looked, they pointed toward the wings of the stage behind her.

In Georgie's ears, Mitch's voice said, "I think you should turn around and see this."

Georgie sneaked a quick glance behind herself like she was checking her car's blind spot before changing lanes in heavy traffic.

Alexandre was still on the riser with her, but his blond head was *lower*.

Good God, he wasn't *really*—

Georgie's fingers stopped working. She couldn't make them hit the keys. Her hands crumbled and fell apart.

Cadell's guitar music continued in her ears, audible even over the crowd screaming and boiling just beyond the lights and the security staff working like hell to keep them off the stage. Cadell took the melody line.

Georgie turned, holding onto the keyboards for balance.

Her palm hit a couple of keys and blared noise in her ears. She lifted her hand.

Alexandre was behind her, bent on one knee.

The crowd roared like a stampeding swarm of elephants and surged, but the bouncers shoved them back off the stage.

Alexandre watched her with his dark, deep eyes, glittering in the lights. He said, "Only you can hear me. They can't."

His voice didn't have that weird doubled sound like it did when it was also blasting over the speakers.

He had both hands folded on his bent knee, his good hand covering the gauze-wrapped one, and he said, "I'm not asking what you think you *should* do. I'm not asking if it's wise or prudent or sensible or the best course for the world or how we will work it out. Nothing else matters, except whether you *want* to. I'm asking you if you *want* to marry me, if you *want* to be with me, if you *want* me to protect you, if you *want* to live with me and through our music, for the rest of our lives. Do you *want* to marry me?"

Her throat snapped closed, and she couldn't breathe, so Georgie nodded.

She nodded so hard that Alexandre and the whole world bobbed up and down and drowned in the water in her eyes.

He reached into his pocket and pulled something out, something small and black and a box.

The world was still bobbing up and down and she couldn't focus on him, but the crowd's screaming rose, slamming the walls and the ceiling of the arena.

Alexandre was fumbling with the box, his wrapped hand tapping on it, and he held it out to her. She pried open the lid, and something inside was as blood red as her rushing pulse.

He plucked out the ring and held it out. Gold threaded around the ruby, and Georgie could see hearts and musical notes in the setting. He whispered in her ears, "It's the song. The notes are the first line of the chorus from 'I Believe In Love.'"

The box fell from her fingers, and she held her hand out to meet his in the glare of the stage lights and twelve thousand blinding camera flashes.

The ring was on her finger. The light glared red and gold on her hand. She was in his arms.

Her throat cracked open.

"Yes," Georgie whispered, and her voice echoed through the arena and over the screaming crowd.

For just her ears, Alexandre whispered, *"Je t'aime. Je t'adore. Je t'aime."*

Because French was the language of his heart, and she heard it in hers.

Chapter Fifty-Six

RUNNER

Georgie

Alexandre didn't actually carry Georgie off the stage and away from the frantic fans that bubbled over the edge of the stage at them, but he did sweep her under his arm and hurry her to the cars. The tunnel was short, and she scooted into the back seat of a town car waiting at the loading dock.

Georgie moved quickly to get out of Alexandre's way. He dove hard into the back of the car. She sat up and tugged her skirt out from under him as he slammed the door.

Paul was driving, and he peeled out, fishtailing the car to get out of the back lot before the parking lot became gridlock. He glanced into the mirror. "Unless you'd like to drive, Your Grace?"

Alexandre laughed. "Carry on. She said yes."

"Hey!" Georgie slapped his arm. "Who didn't know?"

Alexandre grinned. "Just you."

Paul's eyes crinkled in the rearview mirror. "Then congratulations to you both. To the airport?"

"Of course," Alexandre said.

"Aren't we going to the hotel with the rest of them?"

"No, we're going home."

"Home?" Her heart trembled at the word. She didn't have a home. Home was where your family lived. Home was where the police came and took away your family or where you ran away from.

Alexandre said, "We will so seldom be anywhere near home, we might as well spend our last night there before we decamp to New Jersey tomorrow. Besides, if you don't show my sister your ring, she might implode into a small pile of hysterical glitter."

It would be nice to see Christine one more time before they left. And Alexandre had a really great bed in his bedroom. She had melted into the softness the last few nights. And it had a beautiful view, and the little market on the corner where they got fruit for breakfast was really good.

Maybe she could get a croissant from that little patisserie down the block that smelled so heavenly at six o'clock every morning. Maybe she could run from one end of Monaco to the other before their plane took off tomorrow. Maybe she could even walk down to the beach for a quick swim.

Maybe she could sleep in Alexandre's arms and lie there all morning and never do any of those other things.

Maybe Monaco could be home.

Chapter Fifty-Seven

ONE NIGHT IN MONACO

Georgie

When Georgie and Alexandre walked in the kitchen door from the garage, Christine pounced on them, her dark eyes huge, and she looked back and forth between them without uttering a word.

She was wearing flannel pajamas, thank goodness.

Alexandre laughed at her. "She said yes."

"Oh my God oh my God!" Christine launched herself at them both, grabbing Georgie around the neck and Alexandre around the chest and shoving them both back against the wall.

Georgie started laughing with her.

Christine yammered, "And now we can be sisters and I've always wanted a sister because he's just a big stick in the mud and I can throw you a bachelorette party. No one over here does bachelorette parties. It's more just like a typical Saturday night. But you need a bachelorette party."

Christine started bouncing, jostling Georgie and thumping her under the chin.

Georgie patted her back. "There, there. We'll have a bachelorette party."

"And the wedding! When? Where? Which church?"

Georgie hadn't thought about it at all. Would Alexandre be obligated to have a huge wedding because he was an actual duke in line for the throne here? Would there be heads of state? *Would the world's royalty come like she had seen at Rae's wedding?*

"And the reception?" Christine crowed. "And where? Here? Paris? The United States? Connecticut or the Southwest? *How soon?* Is Flicka going to be involved? Because she'll take over and you'll never get a say in anything and you don't want that. You'll want to know *everything* that's going on."

Georgie kind of didn't want to know everything. Georgie kind of wanted to run away right then.

Christine went on, "Who's going to do your dress? Your reception dress? Your hair? Your makeup? The decorations? The food and the cake and the hors-d'oeuvres and the dessert!"

Air rushed into Georgie's lungs and stomach and she couldn't seem to stop sucking and blowing the air. Every time Christine said something else, the air in the room thinned and she gasped harder.

Alexandre set Christine back and away from them. "Enough." He poked around under the kitchen sink and came up with handfuls of string that he threw back.

Georgie couldn't catch her breath no matter how

hard she sucked at the air and her chest shook with breathing. She grabbed her sternum, and the room darkened.

Alexandre shoved a paper bag up to her face and said, "Breathe into this."

Georgie sucked all the air out of it, and the brown paper collapsed in her hand and then puffed out with her exhale.

Oh. Paper bag. Hyperventilating. Okay.

Georgie breathed into the crackling bag until the kitchen stopped spinning around them.

Christine watched her with wide eyes. "I'm so sorry. I didn't mean to. I just got excited."

"I'm fine," Georgie said, her voice echoing in the bag stuck to her face. "I just hadn't thought about it."

She should have thought about it. Wulf and Rae's gigantic wedding had been last week. She had spent her childhood at enormous society weddings at the country club. That was how things were *done.*

"It doesn't have to be a parade like Wulfram and Rae," Alexandre said. "We can be married privately. Or we can do something like they did, a small ceremony soon and a larger one later."

"Or just a small one?" Georgie asked.

"If you wanted," Alexandre said. "But some people should be there. If people don't see, it isn't art. I have a few people I have to invite, or they might send royal assassins after me."

Christine slugged him in his good arm. Georgie had seen her aim for the right one and so had not jumped up to grab her.

Not that she would have been able to remain standing afterward.

Georgie said, still talking into the bag, "We could

pull a Jon Bon Jovi and go to Las Vegas and get married at a cheesy wedding chapel and not do any of that stuff."

She was joking, of course.

Probably.

Really not at all. That sounded like an excellent idea.

Christine covered her mouth with her hand, horrified.

"Why go all the way to Vegas?" Alexandre asked.

"Because you can get a marriage license in Vegas and get married in a few hours with absolutely no fuss. You know I'm kidding, right?" She totally wasn't.

Alexandre crouched down, his arms braced on his knees. "We can do that here. We could be married tomorrow if you wanted."

"But you don't want to," Georgie said.

He took her hand in his one good one. "I can't think of anything I would like more. I'll call my uncle, and I'll have the Gulfstream go back to Roma for the rest of the band in the morning."

"I have to call some people," Georgie said.

"It's two in the morning," Alexandre said. "Let's call people after sunrise."

"Okay," Georgie said and lowered the bag. "We might change our minds in the morning, anyway."

He touched her cheek. "I won't."

Georgie wasn't sure what to reply to that because there was a damn good chance that, when she wasn't hyperventilating and exhausted, she might change her mind, so she laid her cheek in his hand and smiled at him.

"Come on," Alexandre said. "Let's go upstairs."

"Already?" Christine asked.

Alexandre pulled Georgie to her feet and wrapped his good arm around her.

"You have to tell me all about it!" Christine called after them. "How long did it take you to convince her? An hour? Two? Were there threats or blackmail involved?"

"Search for it online," he shot back. "There were twelve thousand phones there."

A sound like a cross between a squeak and a scream followed them as Alexandre led Georgie up the stairs.

He whispered, "Are you all right?"

She nodded. "Just a little panic thing. I'm fine now." Her hands had almost stopped shaking.

They walked through the television room that Alexandre had upstairs. "Good," he said and opened the door to his bedroom. "Are you tired?"

"Not particularly." Georgie walked into his bedroom, intending to beat him to the shower. Between the lights and the dancing around and the nerves, she was always a sweaty, salty mess after a concert, and they hadn't had time to shower before the plane ride or the helicopter commute. "I'm still kind of keyed up from the show."

The door slammed behind her.

"Me, too," Alexandre said.

In those two words, Georgie heard a working-class British accent.

He grabbed her arm. He spun her to face him and then stepped around her to shove her back up against the wall.

The dark fire in his eyes was all Xan Valentine.

Oh, God, no. Not when Alexandre had worked so hard to put himself back together by whatever alchemy and then written that song, *that gorgeous song,* that was a vindication and a release of all his pain.

Had he broken apart again to perform?

She would rather have had him whole and healthy as Alexandre. She would have given up the fragment of him called Xan Valentine, even if he had never performed again, even if Killer Valentine died, for him to be okay.

But maybe he had chosen it. He had given up the violin to save her from the Butorins. He shouldn't have to give up Killer Valentine, too.

Even if he wasn't quite sane.

But, God, she hoped he was.

His mouth crashed down on hers, and his good hand grappled with her wrists and pushed them up over her head.

When he backed off to let her breathe, she asked, terrified for him, "Xan?"

"Non," he whispered. *"Alexandre."*

But his teeth raked down her neck, and his body flattened hers against the wall just like Xan.

The energy of the show wound up in Georgie again. She had thought that the airplane flight had cooled her off, but the minute Xan's rough hands grabbed her wrists and then her ass as he dragged her leg up and around his waist, her body hungered for him.

She should take a shower she should brush her teeth she should take the engagement ring off so he didn't mash it flat but his hands and his mouth and his hot breath on her skin spun her around. She slid her palms up his rounded chest to his shoulders and up into his hair while he kissed her, and he pulled her dress aside to run his lips over her shoulder.

He leaned his left forearm against the wall, keeping his hand well above her head, and kneaded her ass with his right.

He was grabbing her like Xan did. He was shoving his body against hers like Xan did.

His hand dipped lower, cupping the top of her thigh, and he trailed his fingers over her underwear, stroking the folds of her pussy and farther back, deftly stroking her sensitive skin.

Whoa.

Yeah, that was Xan all right.

His hand flipped, and he grabbed her hip, spinning her around again to face the wall. He gathered her hair with his good hand. The complicated updo that Boris had concocted had melted with time and the heat of the stage lamps. His mouth found the back of her neck.

His lush lips caressed the tight cords on the back of her neck, and his warm breath feathered over her skin just before she felt the first nip of his teeth.

Georgie reached behind herself, sliding her hands over his trim hips and feeling for him, but he grabbed both her hands—somehow while still keeping his injured hand against the wall above her—and leaned into her. The hard rod of his erection pressed against the small of her back as he bent to chew down her back, dragging the straining fabric aside with his chin.

Her palms were flat against the smooth plaster, which was cool against the front of her body while Xan's body drove waves of heat from behind her. When he moved, his skin clung to her sticky back. Her own sweat was beginning to turn sour. Xan's natural musk blended with the new green grass of his cologne, and breathing him in turned her on even more.

But her own sweat was distressing. She managed to gasp, "I need a shower."

He growled against her skin, the vibration traveling down her spine, and her throat constricted as she whimpered.

"Really," she whispered. "I don't want to be like this."

He dropped her wrists and wrapped one arm around her waist, pulling her back against himself. "Come on."

His low voice bordered on angry, and he dragged her by the hand to the bathroom. He twisted the water taps and let them run while he stripped the clothes from her body, each handful of fabric almost tearing as he pulled the dress away. The zipper caught in the middle, and he broke it apart to get it off of her. He caught his thumb in the side of her underwear—and you bet that she was wearing boyshorts because a fan had been blowing her chiffon skirt on the stage all night—and she hopped fast as he flipped them off of her.

He peeled his white dress shirt and undershirt over his head without bothering to undo the buttons and pried his jeans off his hips. Georgie pushed down the other side, and he crowded her into the shower, pushing her with his chest and grabbing her to him. They danced into the warm water, flowing from a showerhead set very high on the wall, probably seven feet up there.

Alexandre held his wrapped arm out of the spray, but he herded her into the water and washed her quickly, almost desperately, because he kept yanking her to his slippery, soapy body and crushing her against the marble wall of the shower to kiss her. Soap bubbles formed streams around his pecs and trickled like river rapids down the stacks of his abdominal muscles.

After a few seconds, he asked, "Good enough?"

"Yeah," she gasped, running her hands over the smooth globes of his shoulders and down his front, pretending to wash him but just feeling his slick skin and hard flesh.

"Good." He shoved the glass shower door open and wheeled her out, following close behind, and his arms snaked around her, holding her tightly against himself as he moved her toward the bed. A towel whirled around them both, rubbing away most of the water, and he threw it aside. He kissed her hard, his tongue diving deeply into her mouth and swirling around hers, then he spun her around and bit her shoulder to walk a few steps, then another whirl to kiss her again. Dizziness circled her as she was kissing him and then her ass was pressed against him and he was holding her breast in his palm, stroking the peak between his fingers, and then her belly and boobs were tight against his hard flesh again and he grabbed her ass while he kissed her again. He dropped to his knees to mouth her breasts, restraining her around the waist with his right arm. Each suck on her nips pulled her forward, bending her, until he staggered to his feet and pushed her toward the bed again.

Somehow, after they meandered across the floor forever, he held her in his arms, and the bed bumped the backs of her thighs.

When she bobbled forward from the impact, Alexandre chewed down her throat, then spun her around one more time to face the white sheets and soft mattress.

His hand on her back pushed her between her shoulder blades, and she pitched forward onto the bed, catching herself on her hands, and he stroked his hand from the back of her neck, down her spine, and over her right buttcheek.

When Georgie started to climb onto the bed, he shoved his strong thigh between her legs and pushed her knees farther apart. His fingers swirled in her center, spreading her cream until his hand slipped easily with every motion. He pressed his hand against her from behind, his long fingers stretching down to her clit, his palm rubbing her center, and the heel of his hand firmly pressed against her asshole.

Oh, wow.

His hand moved slowly, each fraction of an inch an exquisite forever that sent shivers through her skin.

Georgie arched her back, gasping, as his hand found every sensitive part of her. At first, when he had touched her asshole, she had tensed, but the sensations connected to the waves of pleasure coming from the rest of her. He leaned into her, his thigh pressing on his hand, not hard, but a firmness over her whole pussy.

Each stroke of his body sent a wave up her all the way to her head, and she pushed back against him.

Her whole core softened, and she opened to him.

Usually, her body tightened, but this erotic massage felt more like she was going to dissolve. Her breath blossomed in her body.

He nudged her forward, and Georgie crawled a step forward. The bed bent as he climbed up behind her.

His hand slipped up from her clit, dipped inside her a few times to rub that stripe of sensation inside her, and he pulled back.

Georgie glanced back over her shoulder. Alexandre was angling himself, ready to guide himself into her. She turned back, bracing herself on her arms.

He touched her with the tip of his cock, pressing himself into her center, just dipping himself inside. She leaned back, trying to take him in, but he toyed with her, giving her what she wanted but pulling back as she tried to take more of him.

She was panting, grasping the bedspread with her fists, as he slid inside her and popped out.

Her body was so open, so ready for him. Why didn't he just ram himself in?

His next stroke was deeper, longer, and she opened all her muscles to him. Her body was so relaxed from that intimate massage, soft and tender, even more sensitive.

He slid inside her, all the way up to his hips, filling her with himself.

He slid one knee between her legs and pressed on the small of her back with his right hand, pushing her hips down. Her swollen clit contacted the rough skin on his thigh, and he pulled her backward with his one hand on her hip. Her clit rubbed over the curled hair and hard muscle there, a delicious slide over him.

Her body opened more to him, and Georgie pressed herself back farther, rubbing her clit on him and impaling herself on him. She moaned, already close.

She rocked forward, dragging herself nearly all the way off him before she started sliding back.

Something new nudged her.

When she looked back, Xan had his hand near her ass.

When she rocked back onto him, he was going to slide his finger inside her there, too.

His massage had left her so open, so relaxed, and the sensations had multiplied so much that she pushed with her arms, slowly sliding.

His finger was slick from her cream, and just the tip pressed her, pushing against the tight ring of muscle.

His leg under her sent ripples from her clit.

His cock was half inside her, and she wanted him so much that she slid back farther.

His cock and his finger filled her so much more than anything before. He pressed lightly down as she took him in, pressing his cock toward the top of her, and when she ground on his leg with her clit, everything pulsed inside her.

The shivers began, her body already trembling on the cusp of orgasm.

She rubbed back and forth, her clit dragging over his leg, his cock and his finger filling her completely. The pressure in her ass deepened his strokes inside her.

Her body pulsed, first a burst of pleasure from her clit, and then a deep storm that rolled through her.

The world dissolved, everything except Alexandre's hard body and the all-encompassing oblivion that rushed through her for long hours.

When the darkness had trickled away, Alexandre was lying on the bed behind her, his body curled around hers, holding her as she trembled.

He kissed her shoulder.

"Who are you?" she whispered.

"Alexandre," he said, stroking her arm. "Just Alexandre."

"You seemed like Xan. You haven't," she didn't

know what to say, but the clinical terms seemed wrong, "broken apart again, have you?"

"Non," he said. He rolled her onto her back, parted her legs with his knee, and slid inside her again.

Her swollen folds were still wet inside, but she gasped.

Alexandre held just enough of his weight off of her so that she could breathe, but he stroked her cheek with his thumb. He said, "I haven't, and I won't. I'm Alexandre. Xan Valentine is a character that I can play, but it's *me* on the stage. Alex is how I behave around the people I grew up with. There are no walls. There are no fault lines. I'm not going to break apart again."

Georgie wrapped her arms around his neck, the scars coarse on his shoulders under her palm. "I don't want you to hurt anymore."

"I'm not. I'm with you."

She lifted her head, pressing her cheek against his. "I love you."

"Je t'aime."

"Does it feel different?" she asked, her body beginning to respond to him *again.* She wasn't even thinking about it, but she lifted her hips, pushing at him.

He hesitated, a moment of contemplation and reserve that she associated with Alexandre, and his slight nod waved his hair falling around his face.

His body moved in hers with a gentleness that was all Alexandre.

"How?" she asked, her voice catching in her throat.

"Everything is more clear," he said. "Everything is brighter. Everything I feel is sharper because I'm feeling everything. Xan and Alex filtered everything I saw, everything I felt. Everything is just *more.*"

He dropped his mouth to hers and kissed her, and his body moved in hers until she was gasping again, and then he held her in his strong arms while she floated gently back to Earth.

Chapter Fifty-Eight

CALL OUT THE MEN IN GRAY

Alexandre Grimaldi

Alexandre brought his cell phone up to his ear and said, "I have a favor to ask."

He was standing on the sunny balcony of his house, the lowest one that overlooked the sunlit valley and little church down below. The early golden sunlight chimed low chords if he looked at the rays too long.

Georgie was lying on a towel at the far end of the deck. Christine had loaned her a bathing suit. When she had seemed reticent to take the top off, he had made up stories of paparazzi drones that had been seen in the area. The police were helpless to stop them, short of shooting them out of the sky, and Monaco was too tightly populated for gunfire. Georgie was lying on her back, watching the sky suspiciously, but she had kept her top on.

The strings on the top were placed differently than her other tan lines. Alexandre wondered just how long a woman had to sunbathe before she developed those delicious, pale lines.

There were no drones, of course. The police probably would have shot them down.

His sister lay on her stomach, baring those three terrible scars to the sky. Ten years had done nothing to dull the guilt and horror of seeing them drawn on her back, but the shock had faded.

Alexandre held the cell phone to his ear, and his uncle asked in suspicious red tones, "What did Pierre lose to you now?"

"Nothing, nothing. It's an actual favor. I was wondering if I could get married."

A sound like a badly tuned motorcycle sputtered from his phone, causing a taste like black pepper on his tongue, and Alexandre glanced at the phone before he held it back up to his head.

From the other end, loud coughing and sniffing lasted for a few more seconds. Finally, his uncle demanded, "Who put you up to this? Pierre? Or Maxence?"

"Neither. I want to get married."

"Don't fuck around with me, Alexandre."

He turned away from the girls and lowered his voice. "I need your permission to marry."

"Only if you're going to make a dynastic marriage. Are you serious?"

"Absolutely."

"Who is this stupid girl?"

"Her name is Georgiana Johnson, but her passport says something else right now. She's from Connecticut."

"She's an *American?*"

"Don't sputter, Uncle. Grimaldis have married Americans before."

"But that was *Grace Kelly,* not some Yankee from the Northeast. Does she have one of those horrid Boston accents?"

"She thinks she doesn't, and she very carefully pronounces her R's. But yeah. And it's cute as hell."

"Tell me that she's Catholic."

"She's Catholic."

"Truly? You're not just telling me that?"

"She is truly Catholic."

"Does she know about you?"

Alexandre walked to the other side of the balcony that overlooked the sea sparkling in the morning sun. "Everything."

"And she still wants to marry you?"

"She did last night."

"Has she sobered up yet?"

Alexandre brought one hand down on the railing. "Can I marry the girl or not?"

"Sure. Go ahead."

"Thank you." Sarcasm laced Alexandre's voice because, while he preferred to keep his estates and this house in particular, he would have married Georgie anyway. "How about this afternoon?"

"What!"

"Would you mind terribly tasking some of your efficient men in gray to procure a license for a small wedding this afternoon?"

"Do you have a church? Saturdays are booked for weddings months in advance."

"I was wondering if we could use the throne room.

We're just going to have a small ceremony. I'm thinking four o'clock."

"Are you serious?" he railed. "What would possess you to do such a thing? Is she pregnant?"

"No." He glanced at where Georgie and his sister were soaking in the early morning sun. *Not yet.*

His uncle sounded even more disgruntled. "You know that I just lost ten thousand Euros, right?"

"Only if she goes through with it."

"How consoling."

"What was the bet?"

"That you would end up not asking permission, accidentally marry a woman of ill repute in Amsterdam while drunk, and be kicked out of the line."

The line of succession.

"Oh, come on," Alexandre said. "We both know that it takes more than that to lose one's place in line for the throne."

"Let's not bring my youthful indiscretions into it. Thank God it was only a civil marriage to annul, and I hadn't managed to find a priest that night. A divorce would have meant that Pierre would actually be the prince right now, since his father died a number of years ago."

"God forbid. Hold on. Georgie," he called across the balcony, her soft name buzzing in his French accent. "Do we want a priest?"

Georgie rolled over, the white triangles of the bathing suit brilliant against her tanned skin. "Yeah, right? It resonates."

He smiled at her. "Yes, it resonates." He put the phone up to his ear. "Speaking of which, we should have a priest."

A strangled cry from the other end of the phone. "I thought you would have a religious wedding later."

"We want a priest. Call out the men in gray to get us a priest."

"You must go through counseling. You must be prepared for the sacrament. There must be banns published."

"We don't want to. Call your buddy *Il Papa* and get us a priest for this afternoon." His uncle Rainier and His Holiness the Pope had several charitable interests in common and often coordinated their efforts. Being one of the few Catholic monarchs left in the world had its perks.

"You might have made a good prince, Alexandre."

"I would have abdicated immediately because no one would have stood for a murderer on the throne."

"Yes, *that.* Good thing Pierre and Maxence are ahead of you, then."

They hung up, and Alexandre set his phone on the railing. It was a long way down to the lush ferns and palms below.

"So, are we getting married today?" Georgie called over to him, her voice a gentle blue rain that turned silver on his skin.

"Of course," Alexandre said. "Once the men in gray are on the job, everything will go off as planned. Luckily, my uncle likes me. I am a diversion from my cousin, whose escapades actually matter."

Georgie rolled over and grabbed her phone. "What time?"

"Four o'clock."

"I have to call a few people," Georgie said, "or else they'll send the German Foreign Legion after me or something."

She must mean Wulfram von Hannover, famous for his paramilitary security force.

Christine leaned over and poked Georgie's arm. "Do you have a dress?"

"Do I need a dress?" Georgie asked.

Christine's strangled scream echoed over the small valley, drawing the attention of the retired Formula One race car driver who lived two doors down, and Christine seized Georgie's arm and towed her inside the house.

Georgie protested, "Seriously, I need to call these people!"

Alexandre laughed. Having a little sister was fantastic sometimes.

Chapter Fifty-Nine

THE BLUE ROOM

Georgie

Georgie peeked inside the throne room.

Wedding guests packed the red-walled room between rows of chairs, while more people waited in the next room in the gallery. When the Prince's men in gray, as Alexandre called the staff, had heard about the probable number of guests arriving with only a few hours' notice, they had hustled and arranged not only seating but also a supper afterward.

Georgie retreated to the far end of the next room, a receiving room, away from the throne room, and waited with Rae, Lizzy, and a few others. Rae and Lizzy were holding their bouquets and hers, too. All were pale gold and yellow flowers plucked from the late summer palace gardens and greenhouses by someone retained by the men in gray.

The room the girls were standing in was a grand receiving room where ministers met foreign dignitaries before they proceeded into the even grander throne room to be presented to the Prince. This room was unimaginatively called the Blue Room, which didn't do justice to the silvery violet silk brocade on the walls and upholstering the gilded furniture. Enormous gold-framed portraits of illustrious members of the Grimaldi family, far larger than life-size, hung on the walls from above the couches and stretched far upward. The ceilings were a complicated coved structure painted in pale blue and gold. The chandeliers hanging from the ceiling were delicate gold filigree swaddled with ropes of crystal. Dozens of white candlesticks topped with tiny electric bulbs grew through the sparkling, shining bases. They looked like cloud cities at sunset, the candlestick skyscrapers flying on golden bases that glittered with steampunk magic.

The Blue Room was designed to humble visitors and prepare them to be further intimidated by the throne room.

It sure worked on Georgie. She felt like a flat ant scurrying around the bottom of the enormous room.

Alexandre had walked through the Blue Room with nary a glance up, but the people in the portraits were his ancestors. He had practically grown up here.

Mumbling rumbled from the throne room and mixed with the conversation in the Blue Room, dark male voices and higher women's voices floating on top. Rae watched the crowd, looking more amused than anything. She had gotten over her awe of royal stuff very quickly.

When Georgie had called Rae that morning, Rae

had laughed out loud at Georgie's announcement of her wedding, saying, "We will talk about this later. Don't think we won't," and then told her husband to "load up the wagons and hitch up the horses." After some rumbling, Rae had told him, more gently, "We've done everything we can here. You've sent everyone you can after her. She could have walked out of Switzerland by now. Maybe we should look for her in Monaco. Pierre is there."

Georgie let the phone drift away from her ear. Maybe she should "accidentally" get disconnected so she wouldn't overhear this private conversation.

Rae's voice dropped a half an octave and sharpened. "You are *not* taking it. If I see it on the plane, I will open the door and throw it out. Besides, Monaco is so overpopulated that you'd never get a clear shot with a clean backstop."

More rumbling over the line.

Rae told Georgie, "We'll be there around three o'clock."

Their plane had indeed landed at Nice soon after. A dozen large helicopters had ferried people who had been at the von Hannover wedding in Switzerland to the Monaco heliport like a swarm of bumblebees landing on the long strips that jutted over the sea far below.

Now, Rae stood beside Georgie in the hallway, and she reached over and smoothed Georgie's hair back into the complicated updo-bun-thing on the back of her head. Rae's auburn hair swung loose and curling just past her shoulders, and she wore her silvery reception dress again, which she had deemed thrifty and sensible.

Georgie handed her phone to Rae. "Like we planned?"

"I'm on it." Rae tapped some icons and started swiping her thumb across the screen, typing something into Georgie's phone and giggling as she did so.

Lizzy skittered up beside Rae, a tiny sprite of a girl with her blond pixie-cut hair waving from her constant hopping. She wore the same white dress that she had worn last week to be Rae's bridesmaid.

Lizzy said, "You look beautiful. How did you get a dress so quickly?"

Georgie glanced down at the long ecru dress she wore, a slim, silk sheath beaded with crystals so tiny that they weren't quite visible except as a glimmer in the light from the enormous chandeliers hanging far above them. "Alexandre's sister knows where to shop. We walked into a boutique. Another friend of mine, Boris, met us there. A consultant was waiting for us at the door and had already pulled four dozen dresses into a large dressing room. They discussed what would look good on me, current fashion, timeless fashion, designers who would be a statement if they were chosen, and *then* they asked what I wanted. Note the order of events. We narrowed it down to five. I tried them on. This one was perfect. They tailored it while Christine, Boris, and I had lunch. Those two get along too well. They discussed fashion like my professors discuss contract law. It was freaky."

Rae laughed and said, "Flicka does that," but then she pulled in her lips and glanced over at her husband, Wulfram von Hannover, who stood a few feet from them.

He was staring over at the end of the room, his

eyes narrowed. He wore a black suit and a sky blue tie many shades lighter than his dark blue eyes, and the light from the huge chandeliers above glinted on his gold-blond hair.

Over by the other set of doors that led to the throne room, Flicka's husband, Pierre, stood and fidgeted. The light reflecting from the white and dark powder blue walls tinged his skin, making his face seem very pale, even sickly. Maybe the light was just contrasting with his black hair or slanting too harshly over his strong cheekbones and square jaw. Georgie couldn't tell exactly what made his color look so unhealthy, other than he looked cold.

Alexandre was talking to Pierre, who stared out the doorway while Alexandre leaned toward him, gesturing with an upturned palm. Both of them frowned, their eyebrows tightening above their eyes. Alexandre seemed to be asking something, but Pierre shrugged, his crossed arms rising with his shoulders.

Alexandre stepped closer and grabbed Pierre's elbow with his healthy hand.

Georgie started over to them, pardoning and pushing her way through the hundred or so wedding guests who lingered in the hallway.

Beside Georgie, Rae's husband Wulfram also pushed through the crowd of dark-suited men and women wearing cocktail dresses as if Alexandre's move had compelled him, too. Rae had her hand on his arm, whispering fast, "Wulf, now is not the time. We can do this later, after the ceremony, somewhere more private."

Alexandre's uncle, who was also Pierre's uncle, strolled over to Pierre and Alexandre, said something, and guided Pierre away by the elbow to a corner. He looked different than when Alexandre had introduced him to Georgie as merely his uncle, Rainier Grimaldi. Georgie had looked him up on her phone months ago, figuring out that he was Prince Rainier the Fourth.

Four men in black suits were drawn with Prince Rainier and Pierre from where they had been blending into the crowd, but now they encircled them. Pierre stood among them, though they didn't talk to him. They were too busy scanning the crowd, listening to someone through their earbuds, and adjusting the odd bulks under each of their left armpits.

Alexandre walked off in the other direction, toward the throne room.

Wulfram stopped where he stood in the crowd, still watching Pierre, his blue eyes trained on him like a hunting hawk. Friedhelm, the security guy who had been loaned to Georgie for the wedding, and several other tall guys stood with Wulfram, all of them watching Pierre and his security.

Someone inside the throne room called out in French.

Rae told Georgie, "He's telling everyone to sit down. Do you want me to translate?"

"Yeah." Georgie reached over and took Rae's hand. "This feels weird, getting married and not being able to understand anything. Don't let me say 'obey,' okay?"

Rae laughed. "Of course not."

The rest of the crowd pushed into the room. Pierre's security guys ringed him, opening a path well away from the von Hannovers and leading him in. Wulfram's security staff spread out, watching the other team. Georgie had the impression that they were looking for a flaw in Pierre's security and were going to try to breach his defensive line to let Wulfram get to him. His hands were clenched into fists as they walked into the throne room and separated, Wulfram going to the left for the bride's side and Pierre to the right.

Rae turned to Georgie. "I am sorry in advance if anything happens between those two bull elephants. I will do my best to drag Wulf off, but his sister is missing and her husband won't talk to us."

Georgie shrugged. "If Wulfram gets some information out of him about Flicka, then it's worth it, huh?"

Rae hugged her. "I was worried that you wouldn't forgive me if I ruined your wedding."

"Well, I've been planning the wedding for six whole hours now, so you can see how much blood, sweat, and tears I have invested in the ceremony. And I stormed into your wedding and then caused a scene at the reception. Let me know if you need help holding him down while Wulfram punches him."

"If Wulf makes it past palace security, I'll whistle you up."

As the rest of the wedding guests were herded in through the doors to the throne room by men wearing gray suits, the doors at the end of the hallway slammed open. Running feet thundered toward them.

Georgie spun, dreading what might be coming at them. Her ankle bobbled on her high heel. Lizzy caught her arm and pushed her upright.

A group of about fifteen people were sprinting down the hallway, most of them very tall men.

Butorins? Had Sofiya Butorin changed her mind?

Georgie tottered backward in her heels, readying herself to kick off her shoes and make a run for it.

Except that she recognized those guys and especially the way that they ran.

She had seen them run through countless hallways, sprinting for the SUVs to get out ahead of the drunken traffic jam of the fleeing audience.

Killer Valentine had arrived.

Tryp was in the lead, sprinting down the hallway on his long, long legs, towing his tiny elf of a wife, whose quick legs were a blur. The other guys behind them ran flat out, too.

Jonas and Rhiannon brought up the rear, running just as hard. They had probably been last out of the cars.

Tryp yelled, "Are we too late?"

"You're fine," Georgie yelled back. "We haven't started yet. Take it easy!"

The group of them slowed to a jog and still made good time through the Blue Room.

Within a minute, they staggered to a stop in front of her, breathing hard. All the guys wore ties and suit jackets. Most of them leaned on their knees, panting.

Tryp wore leather pants, and the rest wore jeans. His black tie hung askew, half undone, and he braced his hands on his knees while he fought for breath.

He sputtered, "There were no helicopters in France. Some huge party that got here ahead of us rented all the helicopters. And then when we finally got helicopters, there were no taxis at the heliport, and the cars that Alexandre had sent for us couldn't get through the traffic jam. There's a traffic jam from here all the way to the heliport. It was worse than that time at Compton Terrace when we got stuck at the venue for nine hours before the traffic cleared. The heliport is, like, a mile away. We took two wrong turns. And this place is on a fucking *mountain.* And then the fucking staircase out there to get up to these rooms. And then so many fucking *rooms.* And these floors are *slippery.* Have you ever tried to sprint a mile, uphill, then stairs, across *glass,* in *leather pants?"*

Georgie was cracking up by the end of Tryp's rant, even though she was trying not to so she could hear what he was saying.

"They *creaked!* I sound like a haunted house! And my shoes are soggy with sweat!"

She told them, "We haven't started yet. Go on in."

"Okay. Okay." Tryp was still sucking wind. Elfie pounded him on the back, her long, blond braid swaying over her shoulder. He said, "I'm okay."

Georgie said, "Hey, Elfie, there's someone I want to introduce you to, here. Lizzy!" Lizzy turned around and came over. "Elfie, this is Lizzy. Lizzy, this is Elfie." She stood back to watch them realize that they were identical twins, separated at birth.

"Hey," Lizzy said and stuck out her hand. Her head bobbed like a New Jersey mob boss. "How're *you* doin'?"

"Howdy," Elfie said. "Pleased to meet 'cha."

They both looked up at Georgie.

She frowned. They hadn't gotten it. Georgie said, "So, you guys might like each other."

They both shrugged and said, "Sure," and smiled at each other.

"So, what do you do?" Elfie asked Lizzy.

"I manage a business with over a hundred employees and go to college. I'm going to get an MBA in a couple years. Whadda *you* do?" Lizzy's New Jersey accent had gotten stronger.

Elfie said, her accent full-blown Texan drawl, "Ah blow things up."

"That's cool."

They looked up at Georgie again, four blue eyes surrounded by blond hair and very close to the ground.

Georgie looked back and forth between them. "Oh, never mind. Go on inside, Elfie. Lizzy, stay a sec?"

The rest of the band congratulated her as they walked past her to the throne room: Tryp and Elfie, Jonas and Rhiannon, Cadell, and a group of roadies who wore jackets and ties in all the wrong sizes over their black carpenter's pants. Cadell wore his guitar case on his back and had his thumbs hooked through the backpack straps on the front.

Everyone filed into the throne room, whooping when they saw Xan standing up at the front.

All except Peyton.

Peyton was left standing in the middle of the state room, wearing a full suit, not jeans, that was fit like it was tailored. Of course the classical pianist had brought a suit on tour, just in case. The Federal blue on the walls and frescos made his eyes turn even more glowing green.

He said, "Hi."

"Hi," Georgie said. "I wasn't sure you'd come." Surely he wouldn't make a scene when they asked if anyone objected or try to change her mind or something. She steeled herself with arguments or just to tell him to get the fuck out.

She fidgeted, uncomfortable. Worse scenarios rose in her mind, very bad ones, ones where stupid, sexist assholes blamed her afterward because she had broken

Peyton's heart and men couldn't bear that. If she had only gone back to Peyton, then he would never have committed such a desperate act.

She glanced at Rae and Lizzy, who had turned to face Peyton, too, and they stepped forward to stand by Georgie's sides.

Georgie smiled. Her girls had her back.

"You're my oldest friend," Peyton said. He walked over to Georgie, his hands in his pockets. "I tried my best, but you decided on someone else, and now you're marrying him. I respect that, so this is the end of what came before and where our friendship begins again." He stuck his hand out to shake. "We were friends long before we were anything else, and we're bandmates now. I would like it if we can be friends again."

She took his hand and shook it. "I'd like that."

He dropped her hand at the appropriate point, and Georgie relaxed at the non-creepiness of it.

He said, "We have that non-fraternization clause, anyway."

She laughed. "Yeah. Those contracts, huh?"

"Who's walking you down the aisle?"

"I hadn't thought about it," Georgie said. Tears squeezed into her eyes, and she missed her father, that swindling, lying thief who had taken her to so many concerts and seen so many of her recitals.

Peyton shrugged. "I'm your oldest friend here. It could symbolize the transition in our relationship. I could give you away."

It was logical, but Georgie bit her lip. Alexandre wouldn't like seeing her with him, she was pretty darn sure, even if he did get to symbolically take her away from Peyton once and for all, and she didn't want

Peyton giving her to another man, either. “I don’t know.”

Lizzy and Rae crowded close to Georgie and linked their arms with hers.

Rae looked right in Peyton’s eyes, which she could because she was wearing high heels and that made her over six feet tall. She said, “Lizzy and I will walk Georgie down the aisle.”

Chapter Sixty

ANOTHER WEDDING

Georgie

And they did.

Rae and Lizzy held Georgie's elbows in their arms and were warm and comforting presences, surrounding her and encompassing her, as Georgie made her way down the short aisle to Alexandre. She managed to hold her pale gold bouquet, even with the girls' arms pulling hers. They entered from the side of the room, as all the receiving rooms were laid out in a row, a gallery of rooms.

Guitar music drifted through the air. Cadell sat on a chair, holding his guitar, and he played that song that used to be "Scrambled Eggs," which Xan called, "I Believe In Love."

The throne room was a study in scarlet, a room even larger than the Blue Room and designed to impress. The chandeliers were gold and green enamel filigreed hoops that sprouted brilliant light bulbs. Strings of crystals webbed the golden arcs and drooped below. A burnished crown connected each of them to long, red silk-covered chains that led to the ceiling far, far, far above, where beams separated the dark frescoes painted up there that depicted the surrender of Alexander the Great and the signs of the zodiac. Dark red brocade covered the walls below the immense paintings. Midnight red, silk velvet curtains swooped from an enormous royal crown, which was probably ten feet across and bolted twenty feet up the wall like a teester above a canopied bed. An Empire-style royal throne, very Louis the Fourteenth, stood below the crown.

Yeah, a *throne,* because they were in a *throne* room so it must have a *throne* because a Prince has to sit on a *throne.*

Georgie might be a little nervous about all this. She swallowed hard and held onto Rae's and Lizzy's arms.

The Grimaldi coat of arms and motto *Deo Juvante,* With God's Help, was hung above the *throne.*

A man who looked to be in his fifties with a full head of dark hair was sitting on the *throne.* He wore a suit and leaned back easily, his legs crossed at the knee. Georgie thought she might melt through the floor, but the shining white and gray-blue Carrera marble under her feet would probably be impervious to melting musicians.

At the front of the room, opposite the throne, Alexandre smiled at her, his leg jiggling just a little. Beside him, his sister Christine stood wearing a slim, dark blue dress that came down to her toes and wrists, a subtle suggestion of a suit. The high collar around her neck plunged to a deep neckline but covered her back.

Beside Christine stood Tryp, wearing his creaky leather pants and a boxy suit jacket. His tie had been reknotted, but his black curls were still windblown.

When they reached the front of the altar, Rae and Lizzy hugged her and then settled into their places as bridesmaids. Georgie took a strong grip on her bouquet. She didn't want to look stupid and drop it.

A priest dressed in white robes stood behind a few items on a table draped with a white cloth. A man in a black suit stood beside them, holding a few papers in his hand. He glanced at Alexandre and said something in French.

Georgie whispered, "What's going on?"

"This is the *maire,*" Alexandre told her, low and quiet. "He says that we can do the civil ceremony while the priest is preparing. Just say *oui* to whatever he asks. It's just to say that you're not married to anyone else and want to marry me, assuming that you still do."

She bobbled her head, equivocating. "Well, you know. Your uncle said that if I chickened out, he'd split the ten thousand Euros with me that he was about to lose—"

Alexandre grabbed her hand with his good hand. "Now you can't get away. *Monsieur?*"

The civil wedding was quick. Georgie said *oui* five times and signed the form, and then the priest was ready for the Rite of Matrimony.

Now this was a *wedding.* Snap, snap. Chop, chop. Efficient. *Awesome.*

The priest held his hands over the altar as if checking to make sure everything was in the right place. He asked Georgie, "Do you speak French?"

"I'm afraid I don't," she said.

"It is just a short ceremony, since we are doing just the rite. Do you want me to repeat in English, so that you may understand?"

"I would really appreciate that," she said, trying to put just how much in her eyes.

He smiled, pursing his lips. "I am glad. I will do." He said something in French, and everyone in the room stood up, and then he said something else for a minute or two. He whispered to Georgie, "I announced that Christ abundantly blesses this love of two people who wish to join in matrimony. He has already consecrated you in baptism and now he enriches and strengthens you by a special sacrament so that you may assume the duties of marriage in mutual and lasting fidelity. And so, in the presence of the Church, I ask you to state your intentions. Okay?"

She nodded.

He said something else in French, and then, "Alexandre and Georgiana, have you come here freely and without reservation to give yourselves to each other in marriage?"

Chapter Sixty-One

THE GAP IN THE FRONT ROW

Alexandre Grimaldi

Alexandre stood at the front of the throne room, holding Georgie's hands and listening to the priest.

Paul and Guillaume stood in the front row over on his side, a man-sized empty space between them. When someone had tried to stand in that spot, Paul had moved them aside. When someone told Guillaume to budge up, Guillaume had told him to sod off.

Alexandre's eyes kept stealing back to the missing man.

Georgie stood beside him, and though he loved her with every fiber of his soul, every single stitched-up fragment of himself, Alexandre still missed Adrien.

He had always thought that Adrien would be there when he married, but he had been a week too late.

Chapter Sixty-Two

OUI. YES

Georgie

The priest folded his hands over his stomach and asked, "Alexandre and Georgiana, have you come here freely and without reservation to give yourselves to each other in marriage?"

Several hundred people, sitting upright in chairs, were silent behind them.

Georgie held her breath. She was so used to people walking away when she needed them most.

Alexandre smiled and said, "*Oui.* Yes."

Because Alexandre was always there for her.

She blinked and glanced up, because Ice Princesses didn't cry. The frescoes on the ceiling far above depicted a bloody battle in the distance. She said, "Yes."

Behind Georgie, Lizzy started sniffling.

The priest went on for a few minutes, speaking

French and then translating quickly, until he said, "Since it is your intention to enter into marriage, join your right hands, and declare your consent before God and his Church."

They turned toward each other and held hands, Alexandre's fingers warm in hers. Georgie had a hysterical thought that it was a good thing that he hadn't broken his right hand because then the marriage magic wouldn't have worked or something.

As soon as she looked up at him and saw his smile, the tremors quieted.

Alexandre said something in French, his dark eyes shining. Then he blinked, so slowly, and said, "I, Alexandre, take you, Georgiana, to be my wife. I promise to be true to you in good times and in bad, in sickness and in health. I will love you and honor you all the days of my life."

Georgie blinked back the watery stuff that was in her eyes, grinned, and held her bouquet back over her shoulder with her left hand.

Rae grabbed the flowers and slapped Georgie's phone into her hand, screen glowing.

Because he told her that he loved her in French, because that was the language of his heart.

Georgie held the phone up to her eye level and tried to look at Alexandre as much as she could while she read on the tiny screen, *"Moi, Georgiana, je te reçois, Alexandre—"*

Alexandre smiled more as she spoke, and he blinked hard and stared at the ceiling frescoes for a few seconds, shifting his weight.

"—come époux, et je te promets de rester fidèle dans le bonheur et dans les épreuves, dans la santé et dans la maladie, —"

He touched the gauze bandages wrapping his left hand to the sides of his eyes.

"—pour t'aimer tous les jours de ma vie."

Alexandre stumbled forward and wrapped his arms around her, laying his left cheek against her hair. Georgie dropped her phone over her shoulder, hoping that Rae could catch it, and slid her arms around his waist.

The priest asked something in French, and Christine's slim hand stretched from behind Alexandre to drop the rings in the priest's outstretched palm.

Alexandre's arms cinched tight around her as the priest mumbled something over the rings. Georgie held onto his waist, holding his strong body against herself, unwilling to push him away for even a moment, even for propriety's sake. He trailed his right hand between her shoulderblades, and his left arm was a bar across her lower back.

This emotion was too much for Alexandre or Alex, but it wasn't the wildness of Xan, either.

It was too much for the Ice Princess, too. Her eyes burned and then overflowed, dropping hot lines down her cheeks.

Everyone around them said, "Amen."

The priest leaned over the table at them. "I hate to interrupt, but it is time for the rings."

Alexandre leaned back and dabbed at the corners of his eyes with the gauze on his hand again, and then he laughed and wiped hers. His bandage came away with a black mascara streak.

He backed up half a step and pinched the smaller gold ring from the priest's palm. "Georgiana, take this ring as a sign of my love and fidelity. In the name of the Father, and of the Son, and of the Holy Spirit."

He slipped the ring on her finger. She had worn the engagement ring on her other hand to give him a clean shot at it.

She did the same with the larger ring, but she slid it onto his ring finger on his right hand instead of his left. "Alexandre, take this ring as a sign of my love and fidelity. In the name of the Father, and of the Son, and of the Holy Spirit."

Yeah, it resonated. This was what she had always imagined when she had thought about getting married.

He drew her into his arms again, holding her tightly. Georgie leaned her face against his strong chest.

The priest sang a prayer over them, and Cadell plucked a harmony line from his guitar. People said, "Amen," and Alexandre's voice rumbled against Georgie's cheek when he repeated it, too.

Alexandre whispered, "I love you," and Georgie whispered back, *"Je t'aime."*

Chapter Sixty-Three

OVERHEARD AT THE RECEPTION

The reception was held in the tiled courtyard outside. Round tables set with white china and crystal glassware caught the light from the floodlights around them, the stars above the palace, and the silver candelabra in the centers of the tables. Dancing was at the far end, where a piano and space for a string quartet were carved out.

"So, there was a priest," Theo said, holding Lizzy in his arms and swaying to the waltz that the black-haired groomsman was playing on the piano. His honey-colored eyes were tilted with teasing, but his voice sounded a little too serious. "I could have dragged you up there for a double ceremony."

"Hah, you wish," Lizzy retorted, fluffing her short blond hair with her fingers. "We're having a Russian Orthodox ceremony. There's no way that we're having a wedding with one of your liberal, breakaway Roman

Catholic priests. You guys don't do it right. You change things all the time, and it's weird."

Theo bent, wrapping his arms more tightly around her, and whispered, "When?"

They had had this discussion too many times. It was time to put an end to it. "This spring," Lizzy said. "March. The second Saturday. In town. Before it gets too hot. We could have the reception at home."

"Or we could rent out the country club," he said. "I've been offered membership."

"Really?" Lizzy said, impressed. The country club was even larger than Theo's party house. "Well, okay, then."

Alexandre was standing by the bar when Jonas found him and asked, quietly, "Xan?"

He almost didn't turn around, not because he didn't answer to the name—he felt the harsh, dark sounds almost as keenly as his own name—but because if Jonas was going to cause a scene, Alexandre didn't want it to be at his wedding.

But he did turn, clenching his champagne glass in his hand. "Yes, Jonas?"

Jonas looked at his shoes. "Look, about what happened—"

"It's all right," Alexandre said. "You tried to get us a contract. The terms were not acceptable, so the deal fell through. It's business."

"I can't come back and work for Killer Valentine, not if you're not going to take a contract, any contract. All of them have those clauses. Those are non-negotiable for the recording companies."

"I know, and we thank you for these years of help. I'll buy out your contract, and best of luck with Rhiannon."

"Yeah. Thanks."

Alexandre handed Jonas a fresh glass of champagne. "I don't like the way this ended."

He drank and wiped his mouth with the side of his hand. "Me, either."

"So let's not let it end this way. We're forming a recording and distribution company to market Killer Valentine's music. In a few years, after you work with Rhiannon, we would probably be in the market for a head of Artists and Repertoire."

Instead of working with one band or artist at a time, Jonas could manage dozens.

Jonas raised his eyebrows, and he smiled. "That would be a very interesting proposition."

Alexandre held up his glass of champagne, and they toasted to the future.

Wulf was watching over Rae's head as they danced. She could feel the tension in his neck as they waltzed, and he wasn't looking at her.

When they turned, Rae checked out the corner where Wulf had been staring, and of course, Pierre was sitting at a table with his security arrayed around him.

"Why doesn't he just leave?" she asked.

"He's probably thinking the same about us," Wulf said, his voice steely. "This is his country and his cousin's wedding."

"Maybe we should leave."

"She might show up. She and Alexandre were friends at school before the incident, and she knew Georgie from Tanglewood. She might try to sneak in."

"If she is 'walking the Earth,' then she won't. If she's not, then she really won't."

"Then I won't go until I've exhausted every opportunity to talk to Pierre."

"You mean to grab him by the throat and throw him up against the wall."

"Semantics." He looked down at her, his blue eyes sharp. "How are you feeling?"

"So far, so good, just like the last six times you've asked today. And to answer your next question, I'll lay down in a little while. Not just yet. I'm having too much fun here."

And Rae was hoping that she might spot Flicka, too, and end this insanity.

"All right." Wulf turned her so that he could watch Pierre over her head again.

"You can go look for Flicka, you know," Rae said. "I'll be okay."

"And I'll answer that the same way as the last hundred times you have offered it: no, of course not, not even if you had not had the placenta previa problem. I'm not going anywhere."

"And yet, I have to offer it." Rae turned back to take a look at Pierre. "No, seriously. Why hasn't he left?"

"Pierre is Alexandre's cousin. It would look odd if he left early."

"It looks odd with him sitting in the corner, alone, surrounded by men with guns and not talking to anybody. Did Alexandre ever hang out with you and Pierre when you were in school?"

"No. I only met Alexandre a few times. He played cards with us occasionally, but he was ten when we were seventeen. He was a serious child and never laughed, just practiced the violin for hours on end as if his life depended on it. The only reason that Flicka knew Pierre was because Pierre was my roommate when she was sneaking into my dorm room at night, and then he came over to my house often when we lived off campus. I had no reason to know Alexandre."

"But they're cousins."

"They weren't close. I would have known."

"Yeah," Rae said, glancing back at Pierre. "So why hasn't he left?"

Back in the corner, Pierre sat with his back against the wall, sipping from a highball glass. He didn't look drunk at all. He scanned the room, his dark eyes roving the floor, peering at some people, and he glanced sharply at the doorways whenever someone new came in.

He had been doing that for hours, obsessively.

Just like Wulf.

Rae said, "He's watching for her, in case she shows up at Alexandre's wedding. He doesn't know where she is, either, and he certainly doesn't think she's dead."

"So," Georgie said, her hands clasped behind Alexandre's neck, his arms around her waist, and they swayed in each other's arms, "I made Xan Valentine cry at his wedding."

"I did not," he insisted, looking over the top of the crowd. "You were crying."

"I was not," she said. "The Ice Princess never cries."

Alexandre smiled down at her and cocked his head to the side. A lock of his blond hair had slipped out of his ponytail and hung near his cheekbone. "You're not an Ice Princess. You're always so warm in my arms."

She leaned against him a little more, smiling. She had smiled so much that night that her cheeks hurt. "Yeah, I guess you're right."

Chapter Sixty-Four

NOTHING ELSE MATTERS

Georgie

A Month Later

"So what's the secret?" Georgie asked Alexandre as they closed the door to the hotel room.

The band had been staying in New Jersey for a couple weeks while they recorded the new album, recording and re-recording and laying down tracks one at a time and together. This hotel room was getting to be too familiar, and she almost wanted to move on soon, to tour, to feel the audience reaching out, to share the new music.

Almost.

Okay, not almost. She itched to get out there and do the shows.

Alexandre smiled at her from where he sat on the

bed, the beige coverlet reflecting the light from the nightstand lamps. Behind him, a long window overlooked the dark skyscrapers of nighttime Manhattan, their lights glittering in the river.

He asked, "Help me take the bandage off my hand, would you?"

"Okay, sure." They had rewrapped it after he had showered before the recording session today, but she could humor him. The healed wound didn't need to be bandaged anymore, but he kept asking her to wind the gauze over it. He had mentioned that he was thinking of getting a tattoo down his hand to cover it, maybe a two-tailed dragon with the tails trailing down his fingers and the head resting on his wrist.

She unwound the gauze from around his hand and fingers, and she was careful not to flinch when saw the thick, pink scars running through his palm. His ring finger twisted near where one of the joints should have been, and he was still wearing his wedding ring on his right hand.

He flexed his fingers gingerly, and all of them bent at least a little. With physical therapy, he might get better.

Maybe.

His deep guitar case lay beside him on the bed, open. He reached inside, laid aside the guitar, and sprung the clasps hidden behind it.

Georgie held her breath. Surely he couldn't play it.

Alexandre tucked the violin under his chin and played scales.

She concentrated on watching which fingers moved.

Mostly, he played with his first two fingers, maybe ninety percent of the notes, but his ring finger and pinky moved, and he placed them carefully on the strings.

It was his timbre, she thought. As nifty as it was that he had played quicksilver-fast and so decisively, his bowing so strong that he could have been heard over an entire orchestra even without a mic, the voice that emerged from the violin was what set him apart from other classical violinists. The way that the violin sang in his hands was different than anyone else, the sweet, mellow tones in the low notes, and the treble notes never became shrill.

"One last time," he said.

Georgie nodded. "One last time."

Nothing Else Matters
by Metallica

Chapter Sixty-Five

THE PRICE OF LUNCH WITH TAMAR BEN HAIM

Georgie

Georgie and Alexandre stood on the sidewalk in front of Lincoln Center, the morning sunlight glaring off the mirrored glass. Georgie held a thick file folder in her hands, the sharp edges creasing her fingers.

The crowd flowed around them on the sidewalk, and they earned some squints from people for just standing, unmoving, in the middle of the pedestrians. The late-summer sunlight warmed the tops of her shoulders.

Alexandre hooked his thumbs in the backpack straps over his shoulders. A slim, rectangular case made of titanium, foam, and silk rested snugly against his back.

His left hand was wrapped in gauze, and he had wanted the splint on it that morning, which he hadn't worn for weeks. Maybe playing last night had been too much, too soon, and maybe he was sore. He would never say so, wince, or take a painkiller, though. Or maybe he just didn't want to have to answer anybody telling him that the twisted, puckered, knotted scars didn't look that bad.

Georgie asked him, "You sure you want to go through with this?"

He nodded. "I already told them I would."

"We can turn around and walk away. I'll field the calls for you."

"I should have done it years ago."

"You might get more of your dexterity back. You could play just for me."

"It's not fair to the violin. Stradivari are meant to be in the hands of great violinists, not dabblers who secretly play at midnight, locked away on a tour bus. They belong to the world and the ages, not to one person."

Yes, that was what he was telling himself, but his hands were clenched around the backpack straps. His knuckles had turned white during the cab ride over as he had held onto it.

Georgie stood with him another few minutes as he regarded the building, his breathing deep and measured, until he started walking forward.

She followed.

In the hallways upstairs, Tamar Ben Haim met them just coming out of her office. The sunlight glowed on her poof of silver hair. "Oh! Xan! You're early. Nice to see you again, Georgiana."

Tamar Ben Haim held out her slim hand to Georgie.

"Ni-nice to see you again, too." Georgie shook

Tamar Ben Haim's hand and hoped that Tamar Ben Haim wouldn't feel her hand trembling.

Tamar Ben Haim gestured to the case on Alexandre's back. "Is this it? Shall we step into my office?"

"Yes, on both counts," he said.

She led the way into her office and closed the door behind them.

Georgie handed the paperwork over to Tamar Ben Haim and took a seat, crossing her legs. Bookcases filled with sheet music and music theory books spanned from the floor to the ceiling. Color-coded tabs stuck out of the tightly packed paper, labeled with terms like *Romantic Era, Mannheim School,* and *Carnatic.* Georgie breathed in the scents of toasting paper and dusty ink. Anywhere else, she would have felt like she had found her tribe.

But *Tamar Ben Haim* was standing on the other side of the desk, so Georgie sat up straight and tried not to make a fucking fool of herself.

Alexandre shrugged the case off of his back carefully, not even jostling it, and laid it on her desk. The case had been delivered a few weeks ago, but he hadn't transferred the violin into it until after he had played for her last night. He opened the latches and dropped the key into Tamar Ben Haim's palm. "The provenance and the papers are in the folder. I've had them draw up a permanent, revokable loan."

"That's understandable," Ben Haim said, touching the side of the case.

Alexandre's right hand twitched, Georgie saw, like he had almost slapped Tamar Ben Haim's hand away.

Ben Haim asked, "It's the Lady Ley, right?"

He nodded. "It's dated to 1713, Stradivarius's golden period. There are perhaps nine other violins in the world that are its equal. It's incredibly expressive."

She said, "It's been your baby for a long time."

"I've had it for fourteen years, since I was eleven. I don't really remember playing anything else, but it's not my baby. I was only its caretaker for a few years of its life. The violin is more important than I ever was because it will endure and continue to make music for centuries. I borrowed it from the world."

Tamar Ben Haim cocked her head at him. "I never noticed that you have a French accent, Xan."

"It's been a rough couple of weeks. I'm lazy, right now. I learned English with a British accent, so I usually sound like I'm from London."

"Oh." Tamar Ben Haim reached, and her fingertips brushed the edge. "Juilliard appreciates your sacrifice. Young musicians need great instruments to play to develop their expressivity. You're doing the right thing."

Alexandre stared at the violin, impassive, and blinked slowly. Sunlight streaming in the window picked out the red in the violin's varnish until the wood grain glowed scarlet. He reached out and stroked the violin, brushing his fingers over the wood and the strings and touching the pegs as if to tune it. He had told Georgie, late at night, whispering in the dark, that once someone else performed with the Lady Ley, all the conductors would hear about it and know that he was gone for good. Once the Strad was out of his hands, they would leave him alone.

Georgie uncrossed her legs, ready to stand.

Tamar Ben Haim laid her hand on his shoulder. "I'm so sorry."

He shrugged. "I should have done this years ago.

Stradivari are meant to be in the hands of great musicians, not washed-up violinists who secretly play at midnight. They belong to the world and the ages, not to one person."

Okay, so he had composed and memorized that. Georgie's heart squeezed harder.

Georgie stood up and went over to him. He grabbed her around the waist and clutched her to his side, still staring at the violin. "It's the right thing to do."

"I know," he said. "I know it is."

Tamar Ben Haim asked, "Should I close the case now?"

Alexandre gripped Georgie more tightly and nodded.

She did, and she stowed the case in a tall vault tucked between two bookcases.

Inside the safe, sheet music was stacked on an upper shelf, and another instrument case leaned against the side.

Alexandre asked, "Do you have someone in mind for it?"

"Yes," Ben Haim said. "She's a junior and technically brilliant. She is playing what can only be called a piece-of-shit violin because that's all her family can afford. It's been holding her back. The Lady Ley will change her life."

Georgie felt Alexandre's body deflate as if the fight had gone out of him.

"All right!" Tamar Ben Haim said, dusting off her hands. "I made reservations for lunch. Shall we go?"

"Lunch?" Georgie asked, trembling starting again in her gut.

Ben Haim said, "That was the price that Xan

extracted for giving us his Strad: lunch with me. I am vastly amused that he thinks a lunch date with me is worth one of the most valuable violins in the world."

A smile lifted the side of Alexandre's mouth. "I thought it would be nice to sit and talk about music for a while. You two pianists will doubtlessly have more to talk about than I will."

Tamar Ben Haim smiled at her. "Xan has spoken so highly of you. I'm sorry that you didn't get a chance to come here, but maybe you can play for me sometime. I'd love to hear you in person. I've been watching your videos online, and you've got lovely sensibility."

The small office tipped sideways, and Georgie held onto Alexandre's waist to keep from falling. No one else seemed to notice the way that the building had almost fallen over.

"That would be great," Georgie stammered. "I'd love to, sometime, if it wouldn't be too much trouble. It probably would. I imagine that you're very busy. You don't have to if you don't have time. It's fine."

Tamar Ben Haim laughed and wagged her finger at Alexandre. "You'll have to do something about that confidence problem. If she had come here, we would have fixed that. Now come on, you two. Let's go have lunch."

Chapter Sixty-Six

RECORDING SESSION IN NEW JERSEY

Georgie

Georgie sat down at her keyboards and adjusted the height of the piano bench under her butt, scrolling it down a few inches.

The recording studio in New Jersey was larger than the one they had rented for the demo tracks in Prague, so everyone had a little more room to stretch out. Black egg carton soundproofing crawled over all the walls and ceiling, deadening the room by absorbing any spare wave of sound.

The only break in the velvety darkness was the window to the control booth, where the audio engineer sat. She was a skinny girl and wore enormous headphones over her short, dark hair, much larger than the ones that Georgie was wearing in the booth. She was frowning at the computer and at the band through the window, clicking the mouse and touching the screen as she listened to them messing around on the instruments.

Alexandre's microphone was set up in the center of the room, and he hung onto the mic stand, leaning it away from him while he studied the sheet music one last time before they recorded. He would sing along with the instruments, but he would lay down the lead vocals and backup tracks later in a vocal booth.

Tryp and his drums were back in another isolation booth off the back of the room, and Georgie could hear him noodling around back there over the earphones that covered her ears. If someone had walked into the live room while they were recording, they would hear the soft clacking of her keys hitting the base of the keyboard, the guitarists' strings popping and buzzing, and Xan Valentine singing his heart out to music that no one else could hear.

Peyton was strumming the bass guitar, working through the bass lines. Over the last month, he had been cordial to Georgie at first, then warmed up. She didn't flinch when she saw him anymore, and he smiled when he saw her, and in the right way. Shockingly, they weren't going to tear the band apart. Indeed, they had managed to work together, alone, several times, and they'd both ended up laughing and had a beer together afterward.

They were, after all, old friends.

Cadell hadn't shown up yet, and they still hadn't found a new backup singer for when they started touring again in a few weeks.

Georgie ran through arpeggios, working to get the tempo right.

The monitors above the window buzzed, and the

audio engineer demanded, "When is your guitarist going to fucking show up?"

Alexandre looked up from his sheet music and sipped burnt, black coffee from a styrofoam cup. "Has anyone called Cadell?"

Peyton said, "Yeah. He's not answering."

"Soon," Georgie called back. "Peys, could you call him again?"

"Sure." Peyton wrenched off his earphones and turned on his cell phone, holding it while it booted up.

A clatter, and light from the hallway outside shone into the control booth.

The audio engineer muttered, "Finally," and rolled her large eyes.

Cadell slammed open and shut the door to the live room. He trotted across the rubber-deadened floor, clutching his guitar case and saying, "Sorry. Sorry, everyone. Minor malfunction. Everything's fine."

Over the monitors, Tryp's voice said, "About fucking time, man."

"Yeah, yeah." Cadell unzipped his case and pulled out his bronze-burnished electric guitar. He grabbed the cord. The silver end flipped dangerously in the air as he pulled the cord through his fist and shoved the pin in the body of his guitar. "Just let me tune this thing."

Another woman was standing in the control booth with the audio engineer. She had amber skin, and her ebony hair framed her face with big, silky curls down to her shoulders. Her large, dark eyes shot sharp darts at Cadell through the window. She leaned over, her voluptuous curves and cleavage on display.

She grabbed the microphone and jerked it toward

her. Over the monitors, she said, "Cadell, get your butt out here now."

Georgie and Alexandre looked at each other, startled, and then back at the woman in the booth.

"I can't right now," Cadell said. "It'll have to wait."

"It can't wait," she said, her teeth grinding. "It's important."

Cadell glanced around and noticed everyone staring at him. "Um, yeah. Folks, this is, um, Andy," he looked back through the window at the woman, "my girlfriend."

Georgie tried not to let her jaw drop.

Alexandre said, *"What?"*

Andy rolled her eyes, her thick, black lashes standing out against her chocolate cream skin. "Yeah, whatever. You need to make a decision about this *now.* They said that we have ten minutes to accept or refuse it."

She spun around and stalked out of the sound booth.

Cadell lifted his guitar and unslung the strap from around his neck. "Guys, this'll just take a few minutes."

He trotted out of the booth after her.

The door swung open behind him, and the audio engineer sighed heavily and got up to close it again. When she sat down in the seat again, her expression had soured further. "So how long are we going to wait for him?"

"He said that he'll be just a minute," Alexandre said, "and so we'll rehearse once while we wait. Ready?"

Georgie nodded, and the rest of them said something.

They had run halfway through the piece when

Cadell walked back in with his head hanging and his eyes red. He snapped his earphones over his head, picked up his guitar, and joined in.

At the end of the song, Alexandre asked him, "So did you accept it or refuse it?"

"Refused it," Cadell said, "and I don't want to talk about it any more at all." His knuckles around the neck of his guitar were red.

"All right," Alexandre said, checking in with Georgie.

She nodded to him. *Yes, let it go. Yes, she was ready to play the song.*

Alexandre leaned forward to his microphone. "This one's a take. Everybody ready?"

Nods and affirmatives. Everyone was ready.

The audio engineer said, "Speed. On your mark."

Everyone was silent for two heartbeats.

Xan Valentine shouted into the microphone, "One, two, *one-two-three-four—*"

Georgie slammed her hands down on the keyboards with Tryp's downbeat.

Chapter Sixty-Seven

ONE LAST THING

Georgie

Late that night, in their hotel room, Alexandre held Georgie in his arms. The room was dark except for a pale glow from the alarm clock. Their bodies were sweaty, sated, and they both panted to get their breath.

Georgie curled against him and laid her cheek against his chest.

He was stroking her hair, curling it around his hands like he had been for the past hour.

She kissed his chest, tasting a hint of salt, and let her finger trail down his rounded pecs. "The recording session went well today," she said. "I thought 'I Can Breathe Again' sounded exceptional."

He said, "Stop taking the pills."

"What?" Georgie sat up, her long hair unwinding from his hands.

"Stop taking the pills." The blue glow from the bedside clock glinted in his dark eyes.

Georgie tilted her head. "But, you know what could happen."

She could just see him nod. "Yeah."

"But, we're going to be touring soon. This isn't the time."

"We might be touring for years. Or decades. Or forever."

"Do you want a kid?" she asked, her heart fluttering.

He rolled over to face her and took her hand. "Children."

"How many?"

He shrugged. "A couple. A few. This is a decision we can make one at a time. I don't think we have to set a number and hit a goal."

"Okay." That seemed logical. "Not like, ten, or anything, right?"

"No," he said. "Not like ten."

"Well, okay, because ten would be a lot. I don't think I could do ten. Or really, anything close to ten."

"Ten is indeed a lot. We shouldn't do ten."

"Okay, then. Less than ten."

"I don't even know if this is going to work," she said. "I run a lot. When I'm not on the pill, I'm not very regular."

"We'll take it as it comes," he said. "If we need to do something medical, we'll decide then."

"And, you know, we can't until the next cycle, anyway." She was blathering. Blathering like a blithering idiot. Blimey, she was a blathering, blithering bl-idiot. "Because, hormones. I told you that, right? Hormones?"

"I know. Hormones." He gathered her close to him and kissed her.

"And I don't know how to handle that," Georgie said. "What if I'm sick? What if I can't go on stage? Rae had to do bed rest. What if I had to do bed rest?"

He shrugged. "We'll figure something out. Gwen Stefani toured with her kids, and she has three. We'll make it work. We have figured out how to get the Butorins to leave you alone, pay off all your father's victims, and give you a life of music, and we figured out how to get me away from the violin before it killed me. We can figure this out, too. No matter what, I'll protect you, and I'll make everything all right."

Maybe Alexandre should have been the lawyer.

"Okay," she said. "Okay."

He kissed her, a long, slow, deep kiss, and whispered, *"Je t'aime, Georgie."*

She smoothed his hair back and whispered, "I love you, too."

WHAT COMES NEXT?

"Dream On" and "Keep Dreaming"
Get these special epilogues FREE from Blair Babylon.
Type this link into your browser:
https://blairbabylon.com/dream-on

Alexandre and Georgie Grimaldi, the Duke and Duchess of Valentinois and rock stars, attend the wedding of Theophile Valencia and Lizzy Pajari, but the hectic wedding schedule prevents them from doing a very important, time-sensitive *thing.*

To be read after the Xan/Georgie series, but before the Runaway Princess series.

WANT TO JUST KEEP READING THE BOOKS?

NEXT: *Once Upon A Time*

When a modern princess falls in love with her bodyguard, a royal fairy tale turns dangerous.

ONCE UPON A TIME, there was a beautiful princess. Flicka von Hannover lived an enchanted life. She jetted around Europe staging charity events with friends, had married a handsome prince in the most spectacular royal wedding of the 21st century, and should have lived happily ever after.

But then she found the handsome prince in bed with a duchess. And then a coffee shop barista. *And then her own goddamn secretary.*

Finally, the prince did the unthinkable, and the beautiful princess ran away.

The prince didn't want to let her go. He couldn't take his throne without her and sent henchmen to take her back to the castle. Her worried royal brother sent people to look for her, too.

The prince threatened her. He said that if the princess contacted her brother or any of her friends for help, he would kill her brother and her brother's new, pregnant wife.

So the princess ran to the only person she could trust, a man who was frankly not a handsome prince.

Dieter Schwarz had been Flicka's bodyguard for years. He had protected her from assassins, kidnappers, and high school dates who got too handsy after a few drinks. He was a sharp-witted, sharp-jawed, hard-muscled former Swiss Special Forces operator who had started his own private security firm, Rogue Security, and had no past that he spoke of.

No one knew that he had been her first lover and broken her heart, but he's the only one she can trust now.

Get Once Upon A Time at:

https://blairbabylon.com/books/once-upon-a-time/

A NOTE FROM BLAIR

Dear Reader,

If you're new to my books, the ***BID: Georgie*** series is part of the overall ***Billionaires in Disguise Universe (BID)***.

Each individual mini-series stands by itself, so look for the "Book #1" in each series. Some are collected in boxed sets, so keep an eye out for those collections. I've written over 40 books in the greater BID universe and have no intention of stopping anytime soon, so you have lots of books to fall in love with!

Here's a list of the first books in each mini-series.

Working Stiff ~ *Working Stiff* Audiobook - *Casimir van Amsberg, attorney to the stars with a little royal secret.*

Stiff Drink ~ *Stiff Drink* Audiobook - *Arthur Finch-Hatten, Casimir's English buddy who is not just an idle, rich nobleman.*

Every Breath You Take - Rock Star Xan Valentine is hiding more than you'd think.

Once Upon A Time ~ Once Upon A Time Audiobook - Flicka von Hannover's story. Bodyguard romance.

Billionaires in Disguise (Wulf and Rae) - The first BID book I wrote, kind of the lynchpin in the middle.

Falling Hard Do you like your romance a little . . . darker? This one is painted in the darkest shades of grey.

What A Girl Wants - The first of the Rock Stars in Disguise (RSID) series, but there's a point where the RSID plotline intersects with the BID plotline. You'll see.

Twisted Billionaires - A mysterious organized crime boss blackmails four budding billionaires into joining her organization, but they plan to destroy her evil empire.

Dragons & Magic - Do you link your romance heroes hot? Like, really HOT? Like, really-really-okay these guys can actually breathe fire. PNR.

The chronological reading list is here at my website, https://blairbabylon.com/reading-order/ . Really, each of the mini-series can be read by themselves, so you don't have to worry about doing it perfectly. But if you want the best, total experience, check out that reading order and start with *Working Stiff* ~ *Working Stiff* Audiobook .

If you want to know when I publish a new book or have a sale, sign up for my newsletter at https://blairbabylon.com/emailbx .

I also have a Facebook reader group, Blair's Babes' VIP Room, where we have fun and talk about books. I hang around in there and answer questions. A couple of times per year, we have an "ABA," or Ask Blair Anything, but I reserve the right to waffle if there are spoilers involved. I also do giveaways. My reader group gets the best prize boxes. We talk about a lot of books in there, and other authors drop in for their giveaways. It's a fun and positive place.

Make sure you're signed up for my **NEWSLETTER** (https://blairbabylon.com/emailbx) so you'll know when I have a new book out! Mailing list subscribers get FREE access to special epilogues and books that there's no other way to get.

Thank you again for reading.

Love,

Blair Babylon

ABOUT BLAIR BABYLON

What order should I read Blair's Books in?
https://blairbabylon.com/reading-order/
for ALL of Blair Babylon's Books.

Blair's Website: Lots of Fun News, Extras, Reading Order, List of Blair's Books, and More!
www.BlairBabylon.com

ABOUT BLAIR BABYLON

Blair Babylon is an award-winning author who used to publish literary fiction. Because reviews of her mainstream fiction usually included the caveat that there was too much deviant sex in her novels, she decided to abandon all literary pretensions, let her freak flag fly, and write hot, sexy romance novels. She's having much more fun now.

Made in the USA
Columbia, SC
01 June 2024

36473823R00317